I0680236

City of Peace

Book One:
The Red-Headed First-Born

DAVID PRASHKER

THE ARGAMAN PRESS

BY THE SAME AUTHOR

Welcome To My World (Selected Poems 1973-2013)

The Captive Bride (Short Stories)

Tall Tales & Short Stories

A Pilgrimage To Bayreuth

The Book Of The Ring

A Myrtle Among Reeds

The Day Of Atonement

Copyright © 2014 David Prashker

All rights reserved.

The Argaman Press

ISBN: 0692301755
ISBN-13: 978-0692301753

ACKNOWLEDGMENTS

I have read, studied with, and consulted literally hundreds of scholars over the past forty years, far too many to list here. My thanks to all of them for the work they have undertaken, and for enabling me to synthesise their work into the creation of this book.

Preface

Modern archaeology contests the existence of a Hebrew king named David, finding no physical evidence of a man of that name having lived or reigned. That contention is virtually irrefutable: so many are the layers of the tel that is Jerusalem, the deposits of three millennia ago lie too deep now to be excavated; too deep beneath the topsoil of earth and the shallows of succeeding civilisations; deeper and more impregnable still beneath the holiness of the site, which prohibits digging.

Modern Bible Study - from the 19th century school of Bible Criticism to the Minimalists of the late 20th century - cannot be so certain nor so cavalier as the archaeologists, for like it or not the texts are there, bearing his name and what is represented as his biography: the two Books of Samuel, the two Books of the Chronicler, the First Book of the Kings, especially the Anthology of the Psalms. But a text is not necessarily a history. A text may be many things: a work of pure fiction is unlikely, but the amount of fiction that creeps into any work of fact is beyond our power to measure. Thus, it might be, as Stefan Heym suggested with his tongue pressed firmly to his cheek ("The King David Report", 1972), a mere propaganda exercise, perpetrated by David himself to further his reputation with posterity, or reworked or invented by Solomon, to reduce or expand the legend of his father; and taking Heym's suggestion further still, we could suggest a work of mythic heroism in the tradition of the epics, designed to establish a national hero myth like that of Hercules or Arthur or Gilgamesh.

Whether David existed or not, whoever wrote the texts and for whatever purposes – we must assume the plural - what remains for the modern world is twofold: the text itself, and the popular traditions about David, picked from the text in the way a brambler might select a handful of the choicest blackberries, but leave the bush essentially unharvested; and quite oblivious to the fact that what seems to be one bush is actually a labyrinth of interwoven, mutually choking stems, each one fighting for space, each one threatening to undermine the others by the very roots.

What follows in this account, though rooted in the Bible stories, is far from the conventional picture of King David. My starting-point has been the text itself, but I have treated the popular traditions with the same iconoclastic scepticism that I have treated every phrase and phase and fable. As Yahweh Elohim created the world by order of the word, leaving Man to unravel and inhabit it, so does Man *in imitatio* create a text to define the borders of his world; and this too we learn in the unravelling. I have borrowed from the Talmudic Rabbis and the contemporary theologians their various techniques of exegesis, to unravel the text etymologically word by word; which is to say, seeking to recover how the words were likely to have been used and understood at that epoch. I have borrowed from the comparative mythologists, from the archaeologists, from the anthropologists; borrowing, but with no intention whatsoever of giving back, so call it stealing if you wish. I have borrowed from the great unravellers of the ancient world in much the same way, from Fraser and de Vaux and Robert Graves and Joseph Campbell and many others; all of them now dead, and since one cannot ask to borrow from the dead, call it tomb-plundering if you wish. My point being, that this is not a piece of dilettante speculation, seeking to "vondaniken" a private theory; rather it is a compendium of scholarly research that has taken two centuries to compile (would that I had had that long myself!), from which I have endeavoured to sift out the most plausible.

My goal in writing this has been to reconstruct the Hebrew world of circa 1000 BCE, at that moment when the alphabet was being invented, when iron was replacing bronze, when the Philistines were trying to colonise the Levant, when the Phoenician civilisation was emerging, and when the ancient pantheon of ruling gods, having been replaced by a new Trinity - Sun-Father, Moon-Mother and their Divine Beloved Son - was now taking the first steps in the final transition towards monotheism. After many years of studying and writing, and then re-questioning the outcome of my work and entering the forge again, I have become convinced that the stories of King David were always intended to be mythological, that they reflected the movements of the Heavenly Bodies, which ancient men explained anthropomorphically by turning them into god-myths and hero-legends. At a period of history when kings were always priest-kings, who ruled in seven-year cycles and were then replaced, there may well have been a dynasty which, like the Henrys and Edwards of England, like the Piuses and Johns of Rome, took a dynastic title, and this title may well have been Yedid-Yah, the Beloved of the Moon Goddess, whose diminutive form was Dodi, Daoud or David; and that Solomon – Shlomo, "Peacemaker", was his nickname, not his name; as we might say King Rupert the Wise or King Edward the Confessor - was the last to bear the sobriquet, because after him there was civil war and an end of dynasty. The priest-king being understood as the avatar of the presiding deity, stories of the deity would inevitably have become attached to the human king, and his own biography caught up. What is certain is that the Psalms, which tell the life of David mythologically, formed the central liturgy of the Second Temple (436 BCE-70 CE); that David was worshipped in precisely the same form as Jesus, which is to say messianically, as the anointed son of Yah and Yahweh, their right-hand-man, ruler of the world from his throne in Jerusalem, bringer of peace, harmony and justice, the overcomer of barbarianism and the bringer of civilised society.

Without any doubt, the text reveals again and again that the ancient

Hebrew world was really no different in its beliefs and practices from any of its neighbours; its only significant difference, the consequence of its adoption of monotheism, does not really take place until the 6th century BCE, when every other people was transmogrifying too: the extraordinary era of Confucius, Pythagoras, Aeschylus, Buddha, the triumph of Zoroaster; the age, in short, when the infant human brain emerged into adolescence by learning to think abstractly for the first time. But David's age is still the age of Homer, and it is comparable at every level. In David's story we can hear the echoes of Tammuz, Attis and Osiris, all of them local dialect versions of the same universal myth, where the Beloved Son is known by the sobriquet Adonis, or Adonai - My Lord.

No other myth is paralleled so closely in the tales of David as that of Orpheus; and there is evidence that the ancient Hebrews understood this: in the "Psalms Scroll" of the Essenes, the authors and practitioners of the Dead Sea Scrolls, the role of King David is given a status that explicitly makes his history echo mythologically the tale of Orpheus.

It is almost certain that Orpheus was itself a variation on the name Ephroneus (both names mean "born of the river bank", which definition implicates Moses and Osiris too) - the brother of the moon-goddess Yah, the "Ephron the Hittite" from whom Abraham purchased the Cave of Machpelah and whose city, Hebron, was David's royal city before the conquest of Jerusalem. In Greek mythology he was the greatest poet and musician who ever lived, presented with a lyre by Apollo and so gifted in playing it that mountains moved and trees and rocks changed places when he strummed. Like David in his travails with Saul - the Hebrew word for Saul and the Hebrew word for the Underworld are indistinguishable - Orpheus harrowed Hell, in his case searching for his beloved Eurydice, but like David employing his musical gifts to soothe the king of the underworld and thereby ensure safe passage. It is Orpheus who, in the Greek liturgy (I mean the Homeric epic and the other early writings which approximate to liturgy though formally there was none), taught the sacred mysteries, was the object of address in hymn and psalm, and who preached the evil of sacrificial murder; the final chapter of this novel echoes Orpheus even more than it does Biblical David. Orpheus preached the predominance of the sun-god Helius, who he knew by the name Apollo, just as David in my version preaches the predominance of Yahweh. The death of Orpheus binds him with the other Beloved Sons and thus completes the analogy; Dionysus, in envy at the apotheosis of his rival Apollo, sent his Maenads to murder him, and tore him limb from limb exactly as Tammuz and Osiris were torn to pieces in the myths of Babylon and Egypt. His head, by curious coincidence, was thrown into a river known as Hebrus. It was washed up eventually at Lesbos, where it was revered and used for oracles; his lyre was placed by the Muses in the heavens as a constellation. The

Hebrews to this day know that constellation as Oreph, and of course the name appears explicitly in the David story: the brides of Mahlon and Chilion were Ruth and Orpah; when Ruth returned to Bethlehem with Naomi, to marry Bo'az and begin the family of David, her sister-in-law remained in Mo-Av.

All this explanation is really unnecessary; the novel should explain itself, or fail to. I have set this much down here, only to engender an ambience before the reader starts to read, to put off those who are anticipating yet another pot-boiled fairy-tale romance. "City of Peace" is not of that genre known as "historical fiction". It is a modern novel, using the techniques of the modern novel, written in the wake of Freud and Jung, written post-Darwin and post-Einstein, written in full consciousness of the scholarship of Wellhausen and Vermes and Gesenius and William Drummond; but written by a modern David who learned to write by singing to the accompaniment of a steel guitar that was incapable of moving rock or mountain, and who could not harmonise the quixotic myth of Goliath, the agapé of Jonathan, the troubadour romance of the Psalms, and all the other seeming fairy-tales, with the dark and brooding barbarism of the head of Agag, the repeated go'el of the fifth rib, the drug-induced prophesyings of the stone-henge of Gil-Gal, and the dantesque journey through the netherworld. I know there will be many who will refute my arguments, some because ingrained dogma pre-requires them, others because the brambles are too prickly. I do not claim that my version is either accurate or authentic; only that it can be fully justified by scholarship; only that it is sincere.

Throughout the book I have used what are likely to have been the original pronunciations of names of people and places; conscious that my reader is likely to be accustomed to the modern pronunciation of these, a list of characters and places is provided at the end of each volume of this novel, designed to identify the modern with the ancient, as well as providing a reference.

David Prashker
Shavu'ot 2000

PART ONE: THE FINAL DAYS

ONE

Ah but the girl was beautiful - desperately, desperately beautiful. What did they call their goddesses in Shunem - Inannot? Skin the texture and colour of ebony. Long, slender legs, firm thighs, a narrow waist, tiny breasts that were like the upturned bellies of the doves of Asherah - no doubt most men would have thought her boyish and made facile, fatuous remarks about her buttocks. Whereas his own longing to touch her was so potent, it could have driven him to tears. The absolute *must have her*, like a ripe fig or a bunch of Genasseret grapes, or one of those marzipan cakes the Bene Yevus traded in the shouk. *Must have her* - so intense, his very bones were quivering. Desire such as he hadn't felt since, since Michal, since Avi-Gayil, since Chagit - since rather too many too painfully beautiful women whom he had loved and then abandoned if the truth be told.

But this was different. This was in the class of a Bat Sheva. This was longing far too painful to endure. And it wasn't even longing - not really. Not even desire. Not even the ritual coupling of divine surrogates. This was a form of lust so primal it was quite debilitating. Thighs, buttocks, belly, breasts: the very naming of her parts intoxicated him. His jaw was trembling. The lust to possess her, in body and in time, by being the first, and through being the only.

Only he couldn't. The spirit was willing, but the flesh was no longer competent. Saliva on his lips; sores on his back from lying unturned for several hours; the loss of circulation in arthritic limbs. And worse, his hands were literally pinioned at his sides, like Shimshon's in the temple at Aza - these hands that had once been famous, equally for caressing lyres and swords and flesh, these hands that had shaken hands with Yahweh Himself, these hands whose veins had literally throbbed at times, so vigorous were the reverberating echoes of the beating pulse. But the pulse was stilled now, the fingers flaccid - even with the occasional moments of remission to encourage hope, it was apparent he had hours, or days at most, to live.

The trouble was, the girl had gone from mopping his brow to putting ointment on his thighs, massaging the scalded flesh where hot compresses had been applied. Though numb in flesh, the very proximity of her nursing fingers to the source of lust still activated desire. His eyes were pleading with her. Until eventually it became necessary, though it spoiled everything, to reduce the divine to the crude banality of words.

"Touch me properly."

"Sire?"

"Try to make me hard."

He might as well have asked her to make him twenty-five again, or tall as Gol-Yat.

Still, she kissed him, though his lips just went on drooling, unresponsive. She touched him, as timid as a virgin - yet even were she to have caressed him with the versatility of a temple hierodule, still it would have made no difference. He had developed, in Ben-Ayah's army vulgarity, a prostrate prostate. His body remained cold, incapable of gratitude to her, let alone response. All day, all night, she could lie beside him, sleeping or caressing – "ministering to him" as that damned fool physician of king Hu-Ram's put it - sponging his sweating brow, feeding him warmth through the flesh, touching his impotence, trying to do her duty by the king. But it would do no good.

"Sire, I..."

"Keep trying."

"I am, sire, but..."

No doubt she was terrified that her failure to arouse the royal manhood would eventually be counted as a capital offence. Or was the persistent ardour of her ministrations born only of the hope - forlorn, surely, at this stage of the king's deterioration? - of her family's advancement; a royal marriage, after all, would make a sheikhdom of the sheep-breeders and camel-stealers of Shunem, and raise her from a tribal chieftain's daughter to a royal lady? But it really didn't matter why, since she was doing it entirely in vain. In truth she was no more use to him than a heated log wrapped up in linen. Less use even, for the log would have given him as much heat, but without kindling in the spirit what the flesh was far too weak to gratify.

Perhaps then he should send her away, replace this novice of Inanna with some more practiced acolyte of She'ol, transmute the maiden-goddess into the toothless hag, and let her begin the laborious process of weaving the royal shroud? Had he not heard the voices in the night, the voices of the Lilim, practicing their keening?

"Yea, though I walk into the valley of the shadow of death..."

"Sire?"

The king's eyes were empty, his voice hushed. Yet the corners of his mouth were surely smiling.

"You spoke sire. I..."

The silence in his eyes invoking her to silence. And to sensuality.

"I was quoting myself." Now he did laugh. "Speaking to myself seems to be the only intelligent conversation I have left."

"Daoud's wisdom is..."

"Hush," he said. He had always hated sycophancy.

The girl's arm, retreating from him for a moment, glistered goldly in the light through the inner window. Mitsrayim gold, triple-thonged and decorated in the colours of Isis; the primary colours: red, yellow, blue. The centre of the band showed a scarab-beetle so darkly life-like, the Lord of the Underworld might already have been hiding in its eyes.

"If it is conversation that my lord requires, I..."

"Use your tongue."

"Sire!"

"Use it, or keep it silent."

"My lord promised he would not make me do that."

Hair the colour of Nile mud. In which, for the chance to wallow, he would gladly have risked drowning.

"Shall I undress?"

He shook his head. Her nudity would have made his desperation worse, not better. For its inviolability. And because all women are less beautiful naked. The mystery is everything.

And besides, the silk of her tunic was far gentler and far kinder than the cruel silkiness of flesh.

"No," he said. "Just lie beside me."

When really he should have sent the girl away. There was deep cruelty in making this child come to him, with her half-formed breasts and her still almost hairless crotch. To touch her, willing though she was, would have been a form of rape; and for all his many sins - oh yes, no one else would dare to say as much, not even Natan, but he wasn't ashamed to admit to each and every one of them. Melech Daoud, Mashi'ach Elohim, King Yedid-Yah, the Anointed of Yahweh, the greatest leader of the Bene Yisra-El since Abou Mousa, the greatest poet in the Habiru language, the greatest soldier since Yehoshua ben Nun; Melech Daoud was also a mispar echad - a numero uno - a prize-winning, deconstipated shit, particularly when it came to worshipping that forbidden idol, the goddess Ishah - Woman. Yet for all his many sins he had never counted himself amongst the paedophiles. Not even with boys.

Not that he was actually capable of touching her; but would have done so, if only he could have moved his hands. He would have pulled down the very pillars on their heads if he had been able. Only the skin had wrinkled on the bones. Arthritis had knotted up the joints. The truth was that he needed her to hold his penis, not for priapic pleasure, but for simple accuracy in passing water.

Though he was scarcely aware that she was doing precisely that, precisely then.

"You should be in school," he said.

The girl was mopping his belly with one hand, while holding the chamber pot with the other - one of those gaudy enamelled pots that Sargon had sent from Warak, glazed with lion-shaped keruvim and crenelated like some Akkadian tower with images of Marduk as the Celestial Dragon; so that he could hardly resist making the same joke about pissing on idols every time he used it. He could smell the powerful odour of urine and knew without needing to ask that it would be a deep, dark yellow, the colour of extreme dehydration.

"Get me a drink."

The girl's dark skin was lit up by a smile as she went about her duties. There was a maturity, a grace about her, that marked her as a natural consort for the surrogate of Ba'al. In fifteen years, perhaps she would inherit Michal's shrine at Chevron and herself become incarnate as Queen Chava, Queen of Heaven, and wear the mantle of the sacred priestess, and deliver oracles through the skull of Adam or the jawbones of the Anakim. If his successor let her live.

"You are from Mitsrayim?"

"No, sire. I am from Shunem."

Of course. He had only just this minute been thinking about that.

And laughed, not the sad, the old man's laugh she had grown used to, but the fierce, ironic laugh of the young king, a laugh that dared to speak irreverence, to mock the gods whom men feared even more than they were scared of him.

"In Kena'an all men are foreigners," he said. "Especially the

Habiru." Laughing at some private, esoteric joke. "The Bene Yisra-El." The girl clearly had no notion why he was telling her all this. But listened, patiently, dutifully, as she had been trained to do. It was, at the very least, preferable to certain other duties. "I, for example, am from Mo-Av, on my great-grandmother's side." Another laugh. "'Wherever you go I will go. Your people will be my people, your gods my gods.' Beautiful as poetry, yes, but is it really sufficient for a person to acquire new citizenship, to be initiated into the cult?" Until she recognised that he wasn't talking to her at all, but musing in his own mind on something that troubled him, and needed the listening ear. "You must never mention this fact to anyone, especially Natan. My lineage is intended to father the Anointed Son of Yahweh, the reborn Adonis himself, King in Heaven and on Earth; it really wouldn't be helpful if word got out that the Mashi'ach wasn't halachically a Bene Yisra-El at all."

Apparently this was the funniest joke ever, though she could make no sense of it. Laughter was causing the king's jaw to palpitate, his teeth to chatter. Grunts issuing from his throat could have been enough to throttle him. Saliva was frothing on his lips and dribbling down his chin. But emptying his bladder had clearly been beneficial to his other humours too. The choler had lifted. Though whether present laughter would turn to bile or phlegm or blood remained to be discovered. Blood probably. The king had coughed a lot of blood lately.

But for the moment it was mostly bile.

"Bad enough we stole our history from the Bene Edom and our gods from the Bene Chet," he was spluttering. "But what do we do with them then? We abandon them for lesser tribal gods and goddesses, that's what we do. We worship at the shrines of idols."

If the girl did not understand the actual words, she knew that anger would be even worse for him than laughter. As he coughed, and spluttered, and moaned, and groaned. The blue line on the hour-candle by his bed showed three o'clock.

"So much for my great-grandmother, eh! 'Your gods will be my gods.' If she had known those gods would turn out to be Utu and Ninhursag disguised as Ba'al and Anat, she could have saved us all a lot of grief and stayed in Mo-Av."

It was quite extraordinary to witness laughter turning into wrath and back again so quickly. Terrifying, too. The famous temper, and the equally famous capacity to forgive. Her father had warned her not to be alone with the king when death arrived. Lest anyone accuse her of inviting him.

"You should be in school," he said again, when the fit was over. "In Shunem."

The affectionate tone was quite sincere.

"We have no school in Shunem, sire."

"Nor we in Kena'an. Not for girls. Not yet."

Another jest, she realised. And mopped the saliva from his chin.

"My lord should sleep."

As she leaned over to straighten his pillow, her tunic billowed forward and the tiny buds that were her breasts made shadows on his face. But his tongue resisted the terrible temptation to reach out for a nipple. And as to sleep? With half of his life's work still undone?

"It was Shmu-El's dream to establish places where young men could come to study the Tablets of Abou Mousa. And my glory to realise it. But my wife - Avi-Gayil - has long berated me for establishing these schools, and then restricting them to boys."

Even the smell of her armpits was intoxicating - alabaster oil and myrrh, if he wasn't mistaken. He was talking, saying anything, just to keep her hovering.

"She's right too. Traditions acquire the status of law within a generation. Not having done it at the outset, posterity will insist it wasn't intended. We were much better off when we were a matriarchy."

The girl smiled, to humour him. She would have liked to sleep, but sleep was not one of her duties. So she smiled, and lay down beside him to keep him warm, and made out that she was listening, though in truth she was thinking of a brooch inlaid with agate which the merchant from Botsrah had shown her that morning, and which she wanted to purchase as a birthday present for her mother. Lying with the royal manhood flaccid in her hand, herself to all intents and purposes stark naked, it might have occurred to her the brooch was a hetaerae's salary. But to serve the king was to serve the gods, whatever names the people threw at her. So she was contented.

While the king spoke of politics and famous men and salivated like a baby. All his banter, of course, was just an old man's madness that no one expected her to heed or to take seriously. Not even the king perhaps. A child could not understand the complexities of the adult world. And yet, was not intelligence an inherent part of beauty, discernible in the eyes especially, but also in the carriage, and the features? Comeliness, he had always believed, was measurable proportionately to mind, increasable didactically. If only his body were still as alert and active as his mind.

"You should be in school," he said it for the third time. A formula, really, for describing the conundrum. One part of him, tediously pompous, the righteous king, the inordinately hypocritical moralist, recognised that this child ought to be sent home and raised in quietude and innocence in the bosom of her family, never until marriage to know the touch of a man or the disappointments of love - except that marriage among the Bedouin of Shunem came at twelve, and deflowering by whoever took a fancy came a good deal before that. But alongside the cynic and the moralist, there also resided in him that insatiable beast which could not have resisted deflowering her himself, orifice by orifice, if only it still had the means.

So that he heard himself reciting, even as he was inventing it, what might have become the last psalm in a long life of psalms. Only there was nobody to write it down.

"Lord, I cry unto you, hear my supplication. I have ruined this child's life - (as I have ruined so, so many lives," it did occur to him to add; "and might have achieved still more if I had ruined more, or less). No man now can marry her, nor even sleep with her, for she has been the concubine of the Mashi'ach. And yet not. No temple will receive her as a priestess, for to declare her virginity would imply a slander against the king. Yet she is virgin. Adonai, one final prayer, for her sake, not for mine. Give me the strength to wallow in flesh just one more time. Pour me out like water till my bones are out of joint and my heart is wax. Bring me out of this prison of unrequiteable lust, lest this child live and die a virgin, and none believe it; lest this child live and die a virgin, and thereby breach your first commandment, to go forth and multiply. For her sake, Lord, not for mine - lest her life be turned to ash and bitterness. Lord, give me the strength to know a woman, just one more time before I die."

But it was as much as he could do to look into her eyes, those deep, dark pools of still-unsullied innocence, and weep for what he could no longer do, either to keep them fresh, or himself to sully them.

TWO

"Eli-Phaz!"

"Sire?"

"Bring me the Urim and Tumim."

Rather than Eli-Phaz, it was the house-boy who came running, wearing his tunic and not much else, a boy scarcely older than Avi-Shag, carrying a lighted taper and a blush on his cheeks pinkly sufficient to explain his state of half-undress. What did it say in the Scroll of the Priests? "You shall not lie with mankind as with womankind. To-eyvah hu - it is an abomination." The boy must have been the same age that he was, when Sha'ul invited him to join the royal choir, and laughed at his pious protests.

"I am not intending to lie with you as with womankind, my little one. You don't have the right bits. This is the precise reverse of soldiering, Daoud. Men at the back, women at the front."

Laughing that howling, grotesque laugh that could have engendered nightmares, were he not already engendering other, deeper, blacker nightmares still.

It had been painful, but he had endured it. Because ambition and loyalty required endurance. Because Sha'ul was king, and kings could not be contradicted. Whereas this boy looked as though he had garnered as much pleasure as Eli-Phaz, even from the sordidness of doing it in secret in the royal wardrobe, and despite having to leave off interrupted.

"The Urim and Tumim, Eli-Phaz."

Perhaps it was no bad thing that the servant was in his sixth year of service, and would have to be set free upon his jubilee next year.

Guards had taken up positions on either side of the door, their iron spears denoting both their power and their nationality - the men of Yisra-El remained in awe of iron weapons and still could barely be persuaded to adopt them. The guard was really only a ceremonial presence, since there was nothing to protect the king from now, unless midges and mosquitoes, and even iron spears could not keep these out. The king called them his mezuzot, bolted upright against the doorposts, stiff and solemn as the word of Yahweh. And wondered why no one laughed at his irreverence. Shuffling footsteps indicated that others - courtiers, ministers, sycophants, sons - were

8

dressing in their scarlet robes as hastily as Eli-Phaz, making ready to attend the royal call. Or more probably his death, awaited imminently since the Passover. The girl had made herself scarce. Susurrating whispers down the long corridors of the palace were easily deducible: "The king is calling for the oracular dice. He is going to announce the succession. He has reached a decision about Giv-Yah." Happy is the man who does not abandon hope.

"Sire, it is still two hours before dawn. The Urim and Tumim are locked in the Tabernacle. The guard-priest is sleeping."

"Which priest?"

"Tsadok, sire."

The High Priest himself! Then his death must be even closer than he realised. And that preposterous physician of king Hu-Ram's kept on insisting he would recover.

"Make the king a broth of herbs. Here, I've written down which herbs. Boil these in stock from the shoulder of a three-week lamb. Use no other oil but olive oil. Sprinkle marjoram and bay leaf. Remember it's the forty-third day of the Omer. Mix the oil with two parts flour, and pour the first drops on the ground for a libation. Don't forget to pronounce the proper blessing: ha michyah ve ha kalkalah..."

Recover! All this mumbo-jumbo would as likely drive a sick old man into his grave.

"Go and tell Tsadok, Eli-Phaz - Yahweh never sleeps. Then have him bring me the Urim and Tumim."

Rejecting, he was perfectly aware, one form of mumbo-jumbo for another.

Except that superstition you believe in is Yahweh's truth, while all the rest is flummery and heresy and idol-worship. Such are the ways of faith.

And as to sleep - were they completely mad? When a king is dying, he doesn't have time for sleep. And besides, sleep had long been impossible. Affairs of state occupied his mind, but they were not the reason. This faith of Yah and Yahweh that he had tried to impose as an official trinity to replace the hundreds of wayside tels and shrines, the groves and caves and hill-top megaliths and bamot, the anarchy of local oracles and sorcerers and quacks and witches and Ba'alim and Ashterot; this faith of Yah and Yahweh, in its inadequacy, did not admit the existence of ghosts, but he was haunted nonetheless.

Ur-Yah the Bene Chet in particular kept coming to him from behind closed eyes, a mess of mangled flesh and blood and bone rather, which could have been any one of several hundred thousand soldiers he had killed or sent to their deaths from Gol-Yat to - to that bastard Sheva ben Bichri, may the lice of a thousand camels lay their eggs upon his head. Or his own son Adoni-Yah for that matter. Another traitor, though he hadn't acted yet. But would, that much was certain. Adoni-Yah who lusts after my Avi-Shag as wantonly as I do myself. Yedid-Yah, my son and heir, read my thoughts. The girl is mine, only mine. No man shall marry her. No man shall share her bed. On pain of death, Shlomo, I charge you.

Because the writing of psalms had become so much a habit, perhaps also because no one else was listening to him any longer, he had taken to composing out loud, whether on religious or non-religious themes, talking to Yahweh in the language of prayer, densifying language to exalt the trivial. Natan was scandalised. Gad and Tsadok furious. Yet how else should a king discourse?

"Lord, we have come a long way together, you and I - and I fear that neither of us has served our people very well, despite our good intentions. Hypocrisy, megalomania, indifference to the common man and human suffering - these are the shared vices of gods and kings. But I have loved you - almost as much as I have sometimes hated you, and twice as much as I have loved both men and women. Let the people praise us, Lord; let the nation be glad and sing for joy; for we have judged the people righteously, and governed the nations of the Earth. Blasphemy? No, not at all. I have written more than a hundred songs for you, a monologue addressed to you in the only language that befits you - or perhaps, their being now published in Asaph's little anthology, perhaps I should call it a soliloquy? But all prayer, all song, is in truth an inner monologue. Always I have addressed the god in me through you..."

The inner monologue interrupted by the arrival of Tsadok in all his pomp and dignity. On his head the mitre with its blue band and its gold plate; on his shoulders the ribbons bearing in onyx stones the names of the twelve tribes; the tole of the ephod on his heart, and the full breastplate with its blue band and the twelve jewels of the twelve tribes; the plaited skirt-of-many-colours adorned by the band of the ephod, and with the bells of gold and the girdle and the pomegranates made of dyed wool and linen on the hem. So rarely did he see his old friend in anything but his casual robe and sandals, all white but for the common priest's girdle round his waist, it came almost like an apparition. So many shades of crushed murex: lilac, purple, scarlet, mauve. It was a sight truly most wonderful to behold.

And the white crystal of the Urim, and the amber of the Tumim, lit up as if by magic on his waist.

"Have you come to give me the blessing before I die?"

Tsadok looked embarrassed.

"No, Daoud. We are in the last days of the Omer. In seven days we celebrate the feast of Shavu'ot. I was dressing for the morning sacrifice when I was sent for. I'm sorry if I startled you."

A lie, of course. But you couldn't fault the integrity of the man, even in the way he lied. A wonderful conundrum!

"Give me the dice."

The white crystal cold, the softer amber warm in his hands, where Tsadok had sat to place them, prising open the king's fingers which were simply too stiff to take the jewels themselves. And yet, he thought, as always when he held the power of oracle in his hands, the word Urim signified light, and light was warmth. And Tuma implied the coldness of integrity, even to one like Daoud whose motive for throwing lots was sometimes not that scrupulous. The voice of superstition could have been trying to warn him off. And the eyes of Tsadok, which had always been suspicious of the king's ambivalence in matters of religion - now mockingly sceptical, now pious as a Nazirite.

"Let's ask a simple question."

The very intonation gave him away, even without the curling of the corners of his mouth.

Tsadok's face, on the other hand, betrayed impatience. But the hour-candle at the bedside showed that it was barely half-past three. The watchmen would not yet be seeking Sirius in the night sky, let alone preparing the shofar to announce the dawn. There was time aplenty for the sacrifices.

"Daoud knows better than any man living that there are no simple questions. And that asking questions leads, not to answers, but only to the misphrasing of further questions."

The king smiled. At last, at last, a man with whom he could converse at his own level. Why didn't Tsadok come to visit him more often?

"I'm going to die, Tsadok."

"We are all going to die, Daoud. The Lord gives and the Lord takes away. Blessed be the name of the Lord."

It might have sounded pompous, platitudinous, but the wry smile on the High Priest's face was an amalgam of affection and deep sorrow.

"I need more time. I need to know when it will be. There are sins to expiate. The plans for the land I bought from Ornah must be drawn up. Adoni-Yah's plotting. This new Pharaoh - Shishak - he must be..."

"Daoud, if it's for this that you've called for the oracle, then you're foolish. You know the oracle. 'The king's heart is in the hands of the Lord, he turns it whichever way he will.'"

The king's fingers were squeezing the Urim and Tumim, a barely perceptible movement though it cost an immense effort in every fibre of his body. He longed to ask, to know; but now, suddenly, he lacked the courage to let the dice fall from his fingers and his future to be read. What would it tell him, after all? That he had three days. Perhaps four. At the rate that he was dehydrating, he couldn't possibly last beyond that. So it was too late anyway, however many more the hours he had. Yet he must remain lucid for as long as possible. Even a dying king can still change history.

"The Temple, and the Confederation, Tsadok. Who can I trust to build the Temple, as Shmu-El, as Abou Mousa ordained it should be built? Who can I trust to build it, and still hold the Confederation together?"

"That is no choice, Daoud, to make on the throw of the dice. Not even these dice."

Not that the king ever did throw the dice. Just to hold them in his hand, until he knew which way he wanted them to fall. That was enough.

"Yedid-Yah will follow my instructions to the letter. But wherever the letters are even slightly ambiguous, he will allow the maximum scope for interpretation. So his wives will get their idols. So the worshippers of Tammuz will congregate - where, at the north gate? So the annual cycle of pilgrimage will give him the excuse to tolerate every wayside shrine and grove. So Yahweh will be defeated by his own victory. So the reborn Adonis will be martyred yet again. I know. I know."

"And Adoni-Yah, Daoud?"

"With Yo-Av's help, he would hold the Confederation. But he would take the capital back to Chevron, and surrender Yahweh to the gods of Kena'an."

"And Yedid-Yah with Hu-Ram's help would also hold the Confederation - if this Shishak can be reckoned with - and he would surrender Yahweh to the goddess of the Bene Chet. You can't control history."

"Truly? The people will love the land for ever, with or without the Confederation, even under foreign rule, because it's their land, by birth even before Covenant. But if the Temple is never built, who will yearn for it after its destruction, who will dream of rebuilding it and restoring Yahweh?"

From the roof of the palace, the long wailing sound of the ram's horn broke in upon their deliberations. Tsadok stood up to leave, but the king clenched the stones between his fingers.

"Perhaps it never will be destroyed."

No need even to respond to that. The Lord gives and the Lord takes away. Only History itself is ultimately indestructible.

"I must go, Daoud. The sacrifice."

"The Temple, Tsadok. The Temple."

The sad smile on the High Priest's face afforded no other interpretation than a last farewell. Until, that is, he would return to make the formal blessing. Yevarechecha adonai ve yishmerecha. May the Lord bless you and keep you. Ya-er adonai panav eleycha vi chunecha. May the Lord make his face shine on you. Yisa adonai panav eleycha ve yasem lecha shalom. May the Lord turn his face to you and give you peace. The blessing of the High Priest. In the name of a god who was the Sun. For a king who had spent his whole life, whether praying or barking at the moon.

THREE

With Tsadok's departure, the halls and corridors emptied again, too late now to return to bed, too early even for the devoted to put on the leather thongs. A familiar chillness lay upon Tsi'on - there had been snowfall the previous winter, and even now, on the eve of the new moon of Sivan and summer announced more than a month before, the mornings woke up cold and moist, especially in the frost hollows of the foothills beside Gihon. Only Eli-Phaz and the houseboy had stayed to make him comfortable. But comfortable, like coldness, was a relative term. In mid-winter you would yearn to be as warm as this; and four hours from now, a similar yearning to be just this cool. But comfortable? From his toes to his ears, there was not a cubit of his body free from pain.

So he lay, a man of almost seventy, a king for forty years. History which forgets so much would not ignore him; and for all his bad deeds, the good would be remembered first. What more could any king ask? But there was more. He had built the Confederacy, united - more or less - the twelve tribes as a single entity, centralised upon Tsi'on; he had established Yeshurun as the spiritual, Yiru-Sala'am as the political realm; and he had given it peace, security, national identity - a present, linked to the past. But the future - what of the future? As kings die, so also kingdoms. As human bodies, so also buildings. He knew that. But memory, which is the nub of History, can be eternalised, especially in buildings. Yet Natan had forbidden him to build the Temple - a tradition of the Bene Yisra-El that, to deny their ultimate achievement to their heroes, lest they be mistaken or mistake themselves for gods. Hubris, king Hu-Ram called it. Had Abou Mousa not been denied entry into Kena'an for a sin as petty as the one lodged against him - the mere drawing of water from a rock? No Temple then. No chance to erect what would have been his final monument - his cenotaph - his means of transcending death into immortality.

Not that death frightened him any longer - death, in all honesty, had held no terrors since that absurd morning in Sochoh fifty years before when he practically did become a god, writing it in stone on the forehead of Gol-Yat; still less since he went through Gat in search of foreskins to pay Michal's bride-price, and discovered that slaughtering a hundred human beings was little different from, say, squashing a hundred mosquitoes, smack between the palms of your hands, while lounging on the palace balcony with a concubine on each thigh, a glass of lebne on the table before you, and the sun of Yehudah warming your spirit so that you knew that Life and Yahweh were both One and wonderful, despite the mosquitoes. And could be rendered perfect, without them. Or as perfect as there could be. After all, even the Garden of Edinu must have swarmed with flies.

If not as many as were hatching, in the first rays of sunlight, on the glass and marble and porphyry that were the royal bedroom. Sixty years ago, these blue-flies, at this time of year, would have had him hunting in the sheep for maggots. He would happily have splattered a good few now. But called the houseboy. Even this pleasure only remained to him by proxy.

Splat! - breaking against the wall with all the wrath and twice the accuracy of Sha'ul's javelin.

How could a man be frightened of death, when he had thrice evaded that javelin, not to mention feigning madness in Gat, and fighting Chanun and Chadar-Ezer all the way from Eilam to Rabbah? And Av-Sala'am. Av-Sala'am! Merely to pronounce the word death was to invoke Av-Sala'am. He could have wept.

But for his own death there was no fear, for he had begun the process of his own immortality, in spite of Natan's injunctions. The land had been purchased for the building of the House of Yahweh, right there on the threshing floor of Ornah where the corn-god was born and sacrificed each year, right there on the hilltop of Mor-Yah where Abou Raham had sacrificed a ram in lieu of Abou Yitschak, right there where for centuries the Bene Yevus had thrown their first-born children down into the Valley of Hinnom, dashing them upon the Rocks of Moloch - purchased for an official six hundred shekels of gold, though in reality it had been legally confiscated with a mere fifty shekels of silver for compensation; but he didn't want to sound a cheapskate in the annals, did he? And he had laid down the plans, out of the ancient clay tablets of Abou Mousa that Shmu-El had rediscovered (it had never occurred to him, until he saw them, that Abou Mousa knew nothing of the Habiru language, that he wrote his instructions in the hieroglyphs of Mitsrayim): all of it, the dimensions, the materials, the ornamentation on the curtain of the Devir, the role of the Bene Levi, the allocation of tasks among the tribes; all of it, from the angles of the blood-gutters to the distribution of patronage as befitted a dying king. But there was still so much more to do, if the land were not to become divided again after his death, if the old pagan ways were not to come creeping back in, as they had done when Shmu-El first retired.

"Shavsha!"

It was Sera-Yah in fact, the scribe Gad had trained but who was not a patch on the secretary Hu-Ram had sent him, who came in. Evidently he had been waiting, wax and stylus ready, for the royal call. Scarcely younger than the king he served, his sandals scraped annoyingly as crickets on the marble floor.

"Where is?" the king began.

But remembered. Away, in Giv-On, working on the final draft of the treaty that was still unsigned after nearly four years of negotiation. The second secretary would have to do.

"Read it to me."

"The spirit of the Lord spoke through me, and his words were on my tongue. The god of Yisra-El said, the rock of Yisra-El spoke to me: 'He who rules over men must be just, ruling in fear of the gods...'"

"It's ungrammatical, for pity's sake. Why can't you write plain Habiru? Why always these awkward, convoluted...It's horrible. Rewrite it."

"So he shall be as the light of dawn, when the sun rises, a morning without cloud; he shall be as the tender grass springing out of the earth by clear shining after rain."

The king's brow was furrowing in dismay with every phrase he heard. What were they writing - a love poem or his obituary? Even this, even this you couldn't trust to others. In the name of Yahweh, did he have to do everything himself?

"Although my house is not so with the gods, still the Lord has made with me an everlasting covenant, ordered in all things, and sure; for this is the sum of my salvation, and of my desire, though he increases it no further."

Apparently they all thought his mind was as far gone as his body. Well it wasn't. By the blood of Adonis, it wasn't!

"Not so with the gods? Not so what with the gods? It doesn't mean anything, man."

As though Sera-Yah were employed to write, and not just to write down.

"But the sons of Bli-El - those who follow sin and false idols because they worship no living god at all - they shall all of them be cast aside like thorns, because no hand can grasp them. But whosoever shall touch them must be fenced with iron and the staff of a spear, and they shall be utterly burned with fire in the same place."

He stared so long and hard and so irascibly at the scribe that in the end he dropped the tablet on the floor and the clay broke. Either one of them could have been responsible for what was truly an almighty scream.

"Eli-Phaz!"

The chamberlain came running, suspecting no doubt another stroke, or heart attack. But it was much worse.

"Get Natan in here. And some fresh wax."

Eli-Phaz was biting his lip. And pulling at the strands of his beard. His own heart was pumping rather too quickly. But at least the king wasn't taking it out on Sera-Yah, who had already threatened to retire to Ramah twice this week.

"Sire, it has already gone to press. The vendors have permission to sell parchment copies of it at the gate this morning."

"By whose orders? Am I dead then? Cancel the permission. Stop the presses."

"But Prince Adoni-Yah, sire."

Adoni-Yah? Oh the cunning, devious little toad! Any trick to grab my throne. You bastard, Adoni-Yah.

The very name could have caused a blood vessel to burst. Yet it was the old servant who was looking thoroughly discomfited. While the king lowered his tone, and asked, almost confidentially, as if to an old and trusted friend, as if beseeching reassurance:

"Have you read it?"

"Yes, sire."

"And is it not piffle? Eli-Phaz? It's not even properly in my style. 'Fenced with iron and the staff of a spear.' Who wrote it? Asaph?"

"Asaph, sire? Asaph has been dead these fifteen years."

"Who then? That impostor Kohelet?"

"No, sire."

But he seemed reluctant to go further.

"Natan?"

"Oh, no, sire."

"No, I suppose not. Political polemic's more his forte. Some blasted apprentice of the Guild, I'll bet."

"No, sire. It was Prince Yedid-Yah, sire."

Until Daoud was laughing so much, it could very easily have been the death of him.

"Yedid-Yah? Poetry? You have to be joking!"

"He, I mean king Hu-Ram sire, says it is kingly to write poetry, as a, a balance to making war."

"A counterpoint, Eli-Phaz, not a balance. King Hu-Ram learned that from me. And it may not have escaped your notice that Prince Yedid-Yah has never been to war. Clean hands, he has. Clean hands."

"Yes, sire."

"These are my official last words, Eli-Phaz. Do you understand how significant a king's official last words are?"

"I do, sire."

"And do you think it appropriate that the people should believe that the king died a gibbering idiot who couldn't put three coherent sentences together and mouthed vacuities in third-rate poetic cliché? Do you?"

"Sire, your people know..."

"My people know precisely nothing. My people are whiners and moaners and worshippers of any idol that promises a plethora of sex and wealth. Which is why my people..." it was all beginning to have a most terrible effect on him: the veins swelling in his neck, his lower lip trembling, his breath coming dangerously faster in his chest. "Which is why my people need my last words to instruct them. Tell Prince Yedid-Yah I want to see him - now!"

"Yes, sire."

While Sera-Yah continued picking up the shards of shattered clay, and hoped the king wouldn't notice him creeping out of the room on all fours.

But there was no evading that beady eye. Or that wicked grin.

"Backwards, Sera-Yah. Crawl out backwards. You are departing from the presence of the king."

The scribe blushed and rose to his feet, scraping those blasted sandals on the marble floor.

"Sire, I was only gathering up the...Sire," he collected himself, "if I may be pardoned for asking, but is it your intention to issue two sets of official last words. Might that not be dangerous, sire, given that even one set of last words may be open to multiple interpretation, ambivalence, ambiguity, and thence confusion. Would not two?"

"They were not my last words, Sera-Yah. As you will yourself be able to report when you leave the palace, I am still very much alive, and speaking."

"Yes, sire, but nevertheless, they have been published. And two sets..."

"There won't be two sets."

"I am relieved to hear that, sire."

"There will be three."

"Sire!"

For some reason Sera-Yah had never previously noticed, but did now, the most delicate porphyry carving on the pillar behind the royal bed, of Osher he supposed, though it could have been Abou Mousa, being received from the waters of the Nile in his reed basket. Sera-Yah's eyes were riveted.

"One for the politicians, one for the clergy, and one for the people."

"Sire, that could be extremely dangerous. It could lead to factions. Who will be able to say precisely what the late king?"

But the answer to that unfinished question was already approaching the royal bed. Tall, handsome, distinguished, radiating authority, clad in his princely robes. If, perhaps - there was no use hiding from the fact - a touch, effete. The Prince Yedid-Yah. And not at all pleased to have been summoned from his bed at crack of dawn.

FOUR

Waking the Lady Bat Sheva in what, for her, was still the middle of the night, was almost as dangerous as disturbing the mountain lions of Ein Gedi. The greater the beauty, the more sleep required to nurture and sustain it; and Bat Sheva had been a very great beauty once, albeit twenty years ago. Natan was quite prepared to take his chance. The Elder of the Guild of Prophets, after all, was Yahweh's representative on Earth, closer even than the king, higher even than the High Priest. Yahweh was everywhere, at all times, in all things. Who then would bar his representative? Indeed, it was the thought of entering the harem itself that caused him consternation, rather than of any particular woman who resided there. The principal man of Yahweh may not have been a Nazirite, but he had dedicated himself to resisting the temptations of the flesh. Or so men said of him, and it was true up to a point. For were not asceticism and fasting and self-abnegation themselves the most irresistible of all temptations?

"What do you want?"

Less a face than a white mask, emerging from white linen.

"A brief word."

"You've had three too many already."

The woman had been viciously sharp-tongued for as long as he had known her. Nor had she ever shown a moment's sincere remorse for the death of her first husband. Ambitiousness was her hallmark. No one would ever accuse her of deliberately enticing the king, yet nor would they claim she had sold her virtue dearly. No one, except Natan. The word harlot had been reported back to her. An oracle that compared her with Tamar the daughter-in-law of Abou Yehudah was attributed. Yet was he not also her most vigorous public defender? Had he not denied Daoud the right to build the Temple, precisely because of his sin in the affair of Ur-Yah?

So that their relationship was strained, and complex.

So that he spoke the words he had prepared with salivating jowls.

"Have you not heard that Adoni-Yah ben Chagit is now king, and our lord Daoud does not yet know it?"

A man of spite might have said it just that way, deliberately to evince just that reaction. But spite wasn't in the man's nature.

Though her face was a picture.

"A coup?" she pronounced the word that would have spelled the end of everything, her own life in particular, if it were true. "Go behind the screen while I dress and tell me everything I need to know."

In one of his more pedantic moods - for he was, and knew it, a very considerable pedant - Natan might well have refused to go behind a screen, and not because graven images were depicted on it, but because a Prophet of Yahweh takes precedence in protocol over a mere Lady, and has, therefore, the right to look. On the other hand, he did prefer the screen. It hid him as much as it hid her.

Not that there was much to see, or to be modest about. Like most women, she slept in the same linen under-tunic that she wore by day, Galilee flax dyed a pale sapphire blue (made from the outer sheath of the flax and retted by laying it on the roof where dew could make it decompose - Bat Sheva wore only the best). Delicate embroidery at the yoke of the neck diverted from what might have been several double-chins. Ankle-length, so you couldn't see the varicose veins, one of which, it was said, had literally popped some months ago, so that there was her royal majesty lying howling on the floor like any badly slaughtered heifer, while a nine-inch fountain of red blood spurted from her ankle.

"The protagonists are Prince Adoni-Yah ben Chagit, the fourth and eldest of king Yedid-Yah's surviving sons, and therefore rightful as well as would-be heir; with him are Avi-Atar ben Achi-Melech the High Priest and" - a lengthy pause, to ensure she appreciated the full importance of this name – "Yo-Av ben Tseru-Yah, the commander of the king's army."

In truth the Lady Bat Sheva seemed more disturbed by the choice between a mohair gown and, because it was cold, a camel-hair cloak, one strip of light brown, one of dark, stitched together, coarse but warm.

"Natan," she said, "you are speaking to me, not addressing a seminar of Prophets. What actually has happened?"

Natan laughed. Power is a very beautiful commodity, and should be enjoyed to its last drop, on those rare occasions when Prophets of Yahweh find themselves in possession of the smallest phial of it. It was a great joy watching Bat Sheva squirm.

"Essentially Adoni-Yah has seized the kingdom." He could practically see the flesh in her throat warble as she swallowed. "And with Yo-Av behind him, that means a military, not just a political take-over."

"Is it too late?"

"No. Not yet. But we have very little time. If we can persuade the king to act, it can still be stopped. We have perhaps twenty-four hours. Perhaps less. But you cannot go to see the king like that."

Though she had dressed in her finery - the mohair gown, a lapis pendant with matching lapis nose and ear-rings, an ivory comb tucked into her braided hair; and for her head a square of crimson silk, folded diagonally, with a circlet of plaited wool to fix each fold upon her neck against the morning sun - all that remained of her nail polish was a blotch of crushed henna-leaf. And as to her face. Natan clapped his hands to summon a chambermaid, who was already waiting behind the door, armed with a full tray of maquillage.

"She must be radiant, Achi-No'am. As she was when he first saw her."

But remembered how that had been. And added, wryly:

"A clothed version."

The Lady Bat Sheva was fidgeting. How appalling to be beholden now in gratitude to anyone, but especially to this dirty, smelly man with his hair uncut for decades probably, and hoards of manna in his beard, and lice, no doubt, festering in his groin. Now that she came to notice it, he had brought in with him a most obnoxious smell, of damp, and dirt, and wilderness. What did he know of clothes and courts and fashion? Indeed, if this was the model of Man in the image of Yahweh, then she was very glad she had retained her faith in Asherah.

"Give me details, Natan. Everything."

While Achi-No'am worked fresh henna into her toe and finger-nails, galena and kohl into her face, with a tiny wooden spatula.

"When the Prince left Tsi'on last week, he took chariots and horsemen and fifty men to run beside him. Only Yo-Av and Avi-Atar were informed, but not Tsadok the High Priest, nor Ben-Ayah ben Yahu-Yada, the commander of the garrison, nor I, Natan the Elder of the Guild of Prophets, nor Shim'i nor Re'i, the king's chief ministers. Word, however, reached me."

"And you said nothing?"

"It is not for me to interfere in politics."

Bat Sheva laughed.

22

"Then what are you doing here now?"

"Prince Adoni-Yah," Natan ignored her, "went to Zochelet, which is near Ein-Rogel. Last night he slew sheep and cattle and oxen on the stone, and called to him all the king's sons except Prince Yedid-Yah, and all the tribe of the Bene Yehudah. But not Tsadok the Priest, nor Ben-Ayah ben Yahu-Yada, the commander of the garrison, nor I, Natan the Elder of the Guild of Prophets, nor Shim'i nor Re'i, the king's chief ministers. And, of course, not the Lady Bat Sheva."

"Who anointed him?"

"Not I."

"Then Avi-Atar."

"Quite possibly. But it is beyond his authority to have done so, without the agreement of Tsadok, who was not present. It will lack validity in law."

"Not in popular support though."

"If necessary, I shall publicly negate it."

"If necessary, Adoni-Yah will cut your head off to prevent you."

The possibility had clearly occurred to him already. Yet his calmness was awesome.

"None of my reports suggest that he has been anointed."

Bat Sheva was musing.

"No, he'll want that to happen in Chevron first, and then in Tsi'on, to mirror Daoud. How good are your spies?"

"Lady, I am a Prophet of Yahweh. I do not have spies."

Bat Sheva smiled. For a tiny moment, catching her own reflection in the polished-metal mirror, she knew she didn't need all these layers of make-up, the high collar, the black dye in her hair. For a tiny moment she was twenty-five again, devastatingly beautiful, a woman who had come from nowhere to seduce and marry one of the Royal Bodyguard, a woman who had sun-bathed naked in her courtyard beneath the palace, every morning for a month, until at last the king took note of her, a woman of supreme power in Yisra-El.

But it was a truly tiny moment.

"No," she said. "I know you don't. But you have Guild apprentices in every town and village from Dan to Ber Sheva, who know everyone, and part of whose religious duty it is to keep you informed of the spiritual state of the nation. How good are your spies?"

"You can be certain of them."

"I have to be. If I'm going to deal with Daoud, my facts must be unimpeachable."

"Can facts be unimpeachable? Irrefutable I think is the word."

"Achi-No'am!" she exploded. And banged the mirror down so hard upon the table that it left an indentation. Her eyes, blacker than her hair with kohl, were scowling at Natan while seeking to apologise to Achi-No'am. If only Achi-Tophel her grandfather were here to advise her.

"Then no one has yet anointed Adoni-Yah," she was muttering.

"Is that a question or a statement?"

"You're an irritating old pedant, Natan. This is vital. Has anyone anointed him?"

"In Erets Yisra-El a king may only be anointed by Yahweh. I am not aware that Yahweh has done so."

"What about Gad, he might have done it?"

"Gad is a Seer, not a Prophet. There is only one High Prophet in the land of the Bene Yisra-El. And I have not been near Zochelet since Succot three years ago. They used palm leaves for the roof of the Tabernacle as I recall. A brilliant innovation."

He could have been doing it on purpose, of course, just to irritate Bat Sheva, or to make some pointless theological point about there being no need to rush or panic, since everything was predetermined by Yahweh, and he, Natan, knew from the oracle what the outcome would be. But wouldn't tell, of course, so that he could claim, and who would gainsay him, to have been right, whichever way it went. Whereas for Bat Sheva this was literally life and death.

"Get on with it!" she moaned, not at Natan, but irritated by the slowness of her chambermaid in applying the perfumed rose-oil to her ankles. And to the Prophet:

"Will you back me for Shlomo?"

Using the name he would take when he was king, the name his father had given him, when Av-Sala'am was no longer fit to bear it. Man of Peace.

Though a man of war first, it seemed. If he were to achieve the throne ahead of Adoni-Yah.

"Why in the name of Yahweh do you think I am here, at crack of dawn, in a woman's bedroom, in the royal harem?"

The maid chuckled. The very idea of that old celibate Natan making a ribald joke!

"Let me give you some good counsel, Bat Sheva, if you want to save your life, and Yedid-Yah's."

And help me to save mine, he might have added. But it was evident from his face.

"On your knees, in front of the king, in these precise words: 'Did you not, my Lord, O king, swear unto your handmaid saying, Assuredly Yedid-Yah your son shall reign after me, and he shall sit upon my throne? Why then does Adoni-Yah reign?' At which exact moment I shall come in and confirm what you are telling him."

"Why do you want Shlomo?" Bat Sheva interrupted him, suddenly suspicious. "You more than anyone opposed my marriage to Daoud. You cursed the child, and offered blessings when it died. Why are you so keen on Shlomo now?"

"What does it matter?"

But it mattered everything. Bat Sheva's expression could have cut a man in half.

"Because Shlomo will build the Temple." His use of the king-name quite deliberate. "Adoni-Yah will revive the Ba'alim and Ashterot and we shall revert to the paganism of Sha'ul's day. I have spent twenty years inculcating in Daoud a wish to see the Temple built, and an acceptance that he cannot be its builder. It must be Shlomo."

Bat Sheva nodded, dismissing the maid with a gesture of her hand. If nothing else, Natan's honesty in matters of religion was not to be doubted. His objective may not have been her objective - indeed, it was evident that he was using her, reluctantly, as a pawn in some much bigger game - but their goal was precisely compatible: it must be Shlomo. And time was short.

"I'm ready to go."

Looking down at her hands, at the fire-red garnet she had astutely chosen for her index-finger, the tribal jewel of the Bene Yehudah.

"But please, Bat Sheva," Natan was still rehearsing her, "I know Daoud." As though she hadn't been married to him for twenty years. "Speak the words I have counselled; and then he will eat his anger out of our hands. But his promise first, before you kindle his anger, because otherwise he will not hear you?"

And the Lady Bat Sheva quivered. It was hard to tell what she was thinking, though the words on her lips regretted favouring the mohair gown over the camel-coat.

FIVE

The knock on the royal door could not have come at a more inopportune moment, what with the Shunemite upside-down beneath the sheets, persuaded at last to play on him what they called in the Galil "the Pipe of Asherah".

It was almost working too.

Though the girl kept gagging, and having to come up for breath.

When Eli-Phaz announced:

"The Lady Bat Sheva, sire."

Was that a snigger he detected on the chamberlain's mouth?

Or a memory sniggering in his own mind, of the virtuosity with which Bat Sheva had once played the pipe for him?

If it hadn't been such a pleasurable memory, if she hadn't looked so stunningly ready to perform for him again, he might have screamed at her for disturbing him just now.

But was in fact tempted to invite her to take over.

"Bat Sheva!"

So much beauty, and already on its knees. If only he were younger!

"What do you want?"

The Lady remained still, and silent, not from embarrassment, but because suddenly she was uncertain what to say or do. The king hadn't summoned her for months, not since the return of the Lady Michal and the arrival of the Shunemite, so all she knew of him was palace rumour and harem gossip. She hadn't expected to find him quite so ill, so very close to death. His hair had turned completely white, and patches of baldness were apparent. His skin was as blotched and desiccated as a rock-adder. But worst of all was the smell, which his servants had made every effort to conceal, transforming the royal bedchamber into a veritable conservatory. The room stunk of flowers: red mountain tulips, white narcissi, wild blue hyacinths that men called lily of the valley, the madonna lily whose bulb the king so loved to eat. Alabaster jars of spikenard imported from the land of Hodu. Trays of gall, educed from the seeds of the purple poppy. Vases of anemone, crocus, yellow chrysanthemum. She had never seen so many flowers since the last time the king took himself a bride. Or was it that he was preparing even now to marry Death?

For the smell of his decrepitude lingered beyond that of the flowers, so that you had to feel sorry for the poor girl sent to lick his flesh.

And flies. Flies everywhere. Embassies of Ba'al Zvuv, the Lord of the Underworld, father-in-law of the bridegroom of Death.

"My lord, you made an oath in the name of Yahweh to your handmaid, saying, 'Assuredly Yedid-Yah your son shall reign after me, and he shall sit upon my throne.'"

Pause. Wait. Let him wonder where this is leading. Then:

"And now Adoni-Yah reigns, and my lord does not even know it."

Dead eyes, blocked veins, reviving. Fingers that could not grip or touch suddenly beginning to tremble. A deep, frog-like grumbling in his throat, that would produce a froth of saliva before it could produce words. He seemed to be choking. But she didn't stop, because there was only now to say it, before the king's protectors made her stop.

"And you, my Lord, o King, the eyes of all Yisra-El are upon you, that you should tell them who shall sit on the throne of my lord the king after him. Otherwise it shall come to pass when my lord the king shall sleep with his fathers, that I and my son Yedid-Yah shall be counted as offenders."

Avi-Shag had taken her cloak and vanished. Eli-Phaz and the house-boy waited by the door, all but one hand of the former inside the room, while his left hand was engaged beyond the door in what could have been a complex set of coded messages with various of the king's ministers, who had been alerted, and come running, for the second time this morning. But it was Natan who demanded admission, hot-foot, or so it seemed, from making the discovery of the calumnious coup. Old age made it unnecessary to fake breathlessness.

Though bowing, though going completely prostrate on the floor, would have been beyond him, for reasons of pride as well as infirmity. Not that it was expected, of course. Not of the Elder of the Guild of Prophets.

Whereas the Lady Bat Sheva was conscious of several vertebrae, whose discs might at any moment slip.

"Is it true?"

"They eat and drink before him, and say 'May the gods save king Adoni-Yah'."

"The gods! Not even Yahweh? Just 'the gods'?"

With remarkable alacrity the Royal Bodyguard - foreign mercenaries every one, soldiers of the Bene Pelet and the Bene Cheret whose loyalty was as absolute as gold - had been summoned, and Ben-Ayah ben Yahu-Yada himself stood in the doorway now, whether to await orders or simply to reassure the king that what had happened at the time of the revolt of Av-Sala'am, what had happened at the time of the revolt of Sheva ben Bichri, would not happen again now. Yet where was Yo-Av? Surely, surely, his nephew could not have betrayed him too?

King Yedid-Yah's self-control was quite marvellous to behold. Clenching his fingers until the knuckles had blenched white. Taking breath after deep breath like an actor preparing for the New Year rites. Dragging himself upright. Swaying back and forth, back and forth, in rhythmic rocking motion, slow as prayer. Teeth grinding till it made a chill run down your spine. But no explosion. Or only that slow, controlled explosion such as kings of forty years let out when they are so completely boiling with rage that fury has reanimated them until they cannot even feel the pain, when they know that they, and only they, can chart the course of impending national crisis. His nostrils had flared up.

"Shlomo!"

"I'm here, father."

Waiting, with wax and stylus he had grabbed from Eli-Phaz's hands. Trying, but failing, to drag Bat Sheva upright to his side. With apprehension, tearing at his gut like ulcers.

As the king rubbed his hands together, slowly, finger by deliberate, arthritic finger.

"Where are my chief ministers?"

"We are here, sire."

A dozen obsequious, sycophantic voices, fawning in chorus. How he despised them all. Why did Bat Sheva know, and Natan, but not they? He despised them with a contempt beyond expression. But smiled, majestically, because they were all he had.

"Take down these words."

The king who had been dithering for months and months, had in a split second now made up his mind. Or had it made up for him. But which way? Which way? Would he acknowledge the rightful heir whom he was now powerless to reject? Or would he find some way to defeat Adoni-Yah, as he had defeated Av-Sala'am? Which way? Which way?

"Let everybody here now witness them, and take an oath to witness them again before Adoni-Yah."

So he had rejected Shlomo - what else could this mean? For expediency. For pragmatism. Because he was too old and too infirm to fight another war. Yet did he seriously expect Yedid-Yah to surrender without fighting? Didn't it occur to him that Yedid-Yah too could seize the throne, right now if necessary? With Ben-Ayah and the Thirty of the Bodyguard to back him - but would they back him? - the king held hostage, the harem his to plunder, and Natan at hand to anoint his head with oil. How could Daoud not recognise his plight?

"When Av-Ram our forefather came to this city, to Sala'am of the Bene Yevus, at the time of the captivity of Lot in Sedom, Melchi-Tsedek the High Priest of El Elyon brought him wine and bread, and made this blessing. 'Baruch Av-Ram le El Elyon, koneh shamayim va arets. U varuch El Elyon asher migen tsareycha be yadecha. Blessed be Av-Ram of the most high god, possessor of Heaven and of Earth. And blessed be the most high god, who has delivered your enemies into your hands.' These are the words by which each of you shall vow, to accept the decision of my judgement."

Voices willing or unwilling, obeying the command of a king who was still king, despite the alleged coup. Faces solemn and lugubrious in the mantra of incantation. Eyes seeking to avoid other eyes, yet conscious, intensely conscious, of the hundred eyes of Ben-Ayah ben Yahu-Yada and the Bodyguard.

"Let Tsadok lead the blessing."

"Baruch Av-Ram le El Elyon, koneh shamayim va arets."

A veritable choir in responsa, more harmonious than the Royal Choir itself.

But what, what were they swearing to? For he had inferred Adoni-Yah, though he hadn't yet named him. And if he were to name Yedid-Yah now, could he be sure...of anything?

"U varuch El Elyon asher migen tsareycha be yadecha."

"Be shem Adonai. In the name of Yahweh."

Tsadok adding this, without needing the king to prompt him. For this, this was everything. Yahweh meant Shlomo.

And the voices echoed back:

"Amen."

I will have faith.

Propped against its pillows, the body of the king was trembling with exhaustion. And his voice, cracked but sovereign. His eyes, fixed upon Bat Sheva, calling her to take his hand.

"Even as I swore to you by the Lord god of Yisra-El, that Shlomo shall reign after me, and he shall sit upon my throne in my stead. What I swore, I will do. Today."

From being so long prostrate on the floor, her maquillage absorbing dust, her face suggested whiteness whiter even than the fear of death.

"Let my lord king Yedid-Yah live for ever," she was muttering.

And yet, now that at last he had made the proclamation, hoping against hope that he would not do so.

"Call Ben-Ayah in here. We must move quickly. We cannot defeat Adoni-Yah, but we may pre-empt him. We must secure the city. Where is Yo-Av?"

The silence that failed to answer this question was more eloquent than any cowardly minister turning his back, recognising the imperative nature of certain duties elsewhere in the palace, wondering quite how solicitous it would be wise to be before Bat Sheva, who was suddenly no longer the forsaken former mistress of the king, but now the all-powerful gevirah, the king's mother.

Though she looked more like a temple prostitute who had been thrown out on the streets and beaten.

SIX

Tsi'on had never looked so beautiful as on that early morning. The late spring sun reflecting on the stones sent shimmers of lime-tinted light across the hillsides, pouring them like streams of honeyed water into the valleys of Kidron and Hinnom. Rumour of Prince Adoni-Yah's coup had not yet reached the city, but the royal heralds had got word among the people that the king had announced the succession that very dawn, that Prince Yedid-Yah was to be anointed in his king-name Shlomo and crowned that very morning, and even as the day came up over the Salt Sea and the hills of Aravah, crowds had already begun to gather along the road to Gihon, hoping to catch sight of the young prince in his royal robes. Even the Bene Yevus had swallowed their pride and taken to the streets, setting up market-stalls of crushed almond cakes or pitta bread and chumus wherever Ben-Ayah's police allowed them - though Ben-Ayah had made one of his more astute decisions, allowing local soldiers to patrol the streets that morning, confining to barracks the Bene Pelet and the Bene Cheret. Foreign mercenaries would not have gone down well on this of all mornings, particularly ones with whom Daoud himself had fought at Tsiklag!

The occasion had all the aura, not just of the celebration of the new moon of Sivan, the month of rejoicing after the long spring abstinence of the Sephirah, the Counting of the Omer; but the great feast of Shavu'ot which was less than a week away and for which the sacrificial feasts had been prepared. Statuettes of the risen Adonis had been hurried into gowns of turquoise blue to symbolise Shlomo and Yehudah. Effigies of the dead Adonis had been mummified in bandages of onyx green to symbolise Daoud and the Bene Yishai; and then concealed behind the Shlomo statuettes, because Daoud was not yet dead but only, at most, defunct; certainly was not yet ready to be cast into the waters and left to float away into the land of no returning. It was almost embarrassing to be anointing a new king, when the old king was still seated - or at least recumbent - on the throne.

Figurines and teraphim seemed to be on sale or display everywhere, in every imaginable material from corn-dolly to marzipan-cake, from alabaster to porphyry; innumerable clay doves and partridges and

31

tortoises that were the ancient emblems of the city; statues of Adonis with the face of the boy Daoud, carved in malachite, the royal stone. Oranges in immense abundance hung from willow baskets, or were set in jars in doorways and on garden walls, alongside quince and pomegranate, the fruit of Asherah. In every doorway, on every market-stall, a single, pious sheaf of barley, and a minuscule clay tablet bearing in a child's scrawl the letters mem-dalet, denoting that this sheaf was the offering for the forty-fourth day of the Omer. And where immense crowds were already beginning to line the streets, row upon row of them all the way from Tsi'on Palace to the Pool of Gihon, orange blossom confetti was being sold, as though a wedding not a coronation were taking place.

Yet was Prince Yedid-Yah not about to be married to the Queen of Heaven, and become her Earthly Consort? What else was the anointing of a king if not a rite of Asherah, the marriage of the Celestial Bride to her beloved Adonis Adonai, the wedding of Yah and Yahweh?

So the royal party made its slow procession from the palace on Mount Tsi'on to the Pool of Gihon, Tsadok and his cortège of priests and Bene Levi at the head, Gad and Natan walking on their staffs, the Prince seated - uncomfortably it must be said - on Daoud's mule, a grumpy, cantankerous old beast just like his master. The king was too sick, of course, to join the procession, and rather a lot of wives and brothers were missing too - the brothers because they had been foolish enough to misjudge the king's determination and had gone with Adoni-Yah to Zochelet; the wives out of simple pragmatism, bearing in mind the absence of their sons. Yet several had remained loyal, and several others had been fortunate enough to hear the news of the impending hasty coronation and had fled back to Tsi'on just in time. So that Ben-Ayah was able to note, as the Prince had asked him to make a point of noting, that Shammu'ah, Eli-Yada, Ivhar, Eli-Shu'a, Yaphi'a and Eli-Phalet were missing, but that Shephat-Yah ben Avi-Tal and Yitram ben Eglah, the last surviving sons besides Adoni-Yah of those born to Daoud in Chevron, were present, as were Shova, Natan, Eli-Shama and Nepheg of those born to Daoud in Tsi'on. Each of the names entabulated as if with a sharp knife.

So they came to the Pool of Gihon, the second of the four sacred streams that encircle Paradise, the second of the four umbilical cords that attach the Earth to the Kingdom of Heaven. And there, at the very edge of the navel of the cosmos, right there where the pulse of god was audible and tangible, the Prince Co-Regent Yedid-Yah ben Yedid-Yah of the House of Yishai the Bene-Yehudah of Beit Lechem Ephratah in Yehudah, to be known from now on and forever after by his sacred royal name as Shlomo, Man of Peace, removed all his garments save only the linen girdle round his loins - for man is dust and there is no king but Yahweh - and knelt on the blood-red soil of Yehudah from whose dust Yahweh moulded the first man, and washed his hands and face and body in the spring, till he was purified. Then Shlomo spoke the words that he had written, somewhat in haste, for the occasion:

"Adonis Adonai, you have shown great mercy to your servant Yedid-Yah, my father, who walked before you in truth, in righteousness, and in sincerity of heart. And you sustained him for this one great act of kindness, that you have given him a son to sit upon his throne, as it is this day. And now, Yah, Adonai, El Elyon, Melech Ha Shamayim, Melech Ha Olam, El Shaddai, El Elohim, Pachad Yitschak, Yahweh, you have made your servant Shlomo king instead of Yedid-Yah my father, though I am still young and lack the knowledge or experience of age. Lord, your servant stands in the midst of the people you yourself have chosen, a great people, a people so great they are beyond the power of a king to count."

As he had anticipated, there was immense cheering - each one as if a mutual vow of loyalty - from different sections of the crowd when he carefully pronounced all the appropriate names of Yahweh, including all the names connected to the city shrine. Yet who would have expected him to make reference, and in so critical a manner, to the census that had caused so much concern in Yisra-El and was probably the real reason why Yo-Av and Avi-Atar had defected to Adoni-Yah. Yet when he did so, the cheering doubled, and re-doubled, like a census of his own supporters. And Shlomo smiled inwardly at the success of his first kingly stratagem.

"Give, therefore, your servant an understanding heart to judge your people."

Yes, to judge them, before ruling them as king. His father had learned that lesson from Shmu-El and passed it on.

"Teach me to discern good from bad. For what man is capable of judging" - his voice rising to a crescendo as he finished with — "so great a people as this?"

There hadn't been such cheering, so many cries of Hallelu-Yah, since Daoud brought the Ark of the Covenant from Giv-On all those years and years ago. The joy was palpable - a joy mingled with relief too, that at last the long stalemate was over, that the always delicate Confederacy of the Bene Yisra-El had passed safely through the period of interregnum, that a new king had been given by Yahweh Adonai, to complete at last the building of the Temple, to establish at last and forever the Law of Abou Mousa and the reign of Yahweh in the City of Eternal Peace.

Provided, of course, that Adoni-Yah wasn't so foolish as his elder brother, who had insisted on making civil war over his disinheritance.

But the astutely-timed arrival of Chagit, dressed in a dove-white gown and carrying a garland of corn and poppies which she presented like a bouquet to the Lady Bat Sheva, had already set aside fears of such a civil war. Adoni-Yah had sent his mother, to attend but also, presumably, to negotiate, on his behalf. Yet what was there left to negotiate? No one in all Yiru-Sala'am could have mistaken this for anything but what it was - surrender.

Surrender made physical, indeed. Or would have been, had Shlomo not turned around in time to prevent his aunt from ruining her dress in prostration on the sandy floor. The gesture was enormous - after all, he would hardly save her dress and then demand her life. As he held out a naked arm before his almost naked body, the certainty of kingship clothed him with unchallengeable strength. His face was glowing with majesty and nobility. The look in his eyes was awe-inspiring. And Chagit bowed her head, as though the beauty of her garments were a humiliation, and kissed the fire-red garnet of the royal ring of Yehudah which Daoud himself had placed upon his finger as the final act before departure from the palace.

"Oseh shalom bimromav, hu ya-aseh shalom, aleynu ve al kol Yisra-El, ve-imru amen. May He who makes peace in the high places bestow that peace upon us and upon all Yisra-El. Amen."

Shlomo smiled, outwardly this time, releasing Chagit's hand. Shlomo, Man of Peace. These first omens were most auspicious.

In the absence of the First High Priest, Achi-Melech ben Avi-Atar, it fell to the Elder of the Bene Levi, the Second High Priest Tsadok ben Achi-Tuv, to take up the horn of oil which had been brought out of the Tabernacle, and to anoint Prince Yedid-Yah as Shlomo, king

34

in Yiru-Sala'am, Nasi of all the Clans and Tribes who comprised the Bene Yisra-El, king of the Bene Ephrayim and the Bene Yehudah, Lord of Chevron and Yiru-Sala'am, pouring the oil upon his head like shampoo on a baby, reciting with anachronistic solemnity the words of Abou Mousa from the Tablets of the Law:

"When you come into the land which I shall give you, and shall possess it, and shall dwell therein, and shall say, I will set a king over me like every nation round about, then you shall set him up as king only if the Lord your god has chosen him. One from among your numbers shall you set up as king; you may not set a stranger over you, who is not your brother. But he shall not multiply horses to himself, nor cause the people to return to slavery, neither shall he multiply wives to himself, lest his heart turn away, neither shall he greatly multiply silver and gold to himself. And it shall be, when he is seated on the throne of his kingdom, that he shall write a copy of this Law upon a scroll of parchment, and place it in the hands of the Bene Levi. And it shall remain with him, and he shall study it every day of his life, that he may learn to fear the Lord his god, to keep all the words of this Law and these statutes, and obey them. That his heart be not lifted up above his brethren, and that he turn not aside from the commandments to the right hand or the left. To the end that he may prolong his days in the kingdom, he and his children, in the midst of Yisra-El."

A man naked save only his loincloth, reduced to washing in a muddy pool, consecrated to a life of piety, asceticism and study, denied wealth, warned against tyranny, a mere first amongst equals. Such was the Mashi'ach of the Habiru, though they cried out in their thousands "The Lord Yahweh Save King Shlomo", till their adulation reached the gates of Heaven, and the sanctuary of Zochelet as well.

Servants were covering the shame and poverty of a mere man's nakedness in the most gloriously iridescent crimson, purple and scarlet of his royal robes.

And in the royal palace on Mount Tsi'on, the weary, sickly Daoud sat up in bed, grinning as the silver trumpets announced the molad, the new month, and the ram's horn proclaimed the culmination of the ceremony in one elongated tekiya that had the crowd holding its collective breath in disbelief at the length of time the shofar could prolong the note. More than a full minute till his breath gave out, and the sound of the ram's horn was transformed into one last whoop of exultation from the assembly. As one voice the Bene Yisra-El cried out yet again: "The Lord Yahweh save King Shlomo", and the king who was no longer king pronounced the amen in his heart. And grinned again, for all that had been done, or left undone.

Not that much had been left undone. The covenant of Abou Raham was now complete. His promise to Shmu-El was fulfilled. He had started out with a vision such as no man could possibly have believed achievable: the vision of a unified people, possessing the land that was promised to Av-Ram the refugee from Bav-El of the Bene Kessed long before he became Abou Raham of the Habiru, worshipping every one of them the same, single, all-encompassing, universal Omnideity, obeying the Laws He had given to his chosen people through the mouth of Abou Mousa, making their sacrifices on the very hill of Mor-Yah where Abou Raham came to sacrifice a ram in place of Abou Yitschak and bring an end to human sacrifice for ever. All that immense vision had been carried to the verge of realisation. And now he could hear the people of the twin city, the ancient city of the Bene Yevus and the new city he had built on Tsi'on, the twin cities he had reinvented as the One City, Yiru-Sala'am, coming up after their Anointed King to lead him to his palace, the Palace of the Anointed King on the Hill of Tsi'on, overlooking the Hill of Mor-Yah where the Palace of the Law, the Ark, the Tabernacle - the Omnideity - would soon be built.

Outside his window they were playing his own psalms on pipe and harp and timbrel – "blessed is the man who does not walk in the counsel of the ungodly, nor stand in the way of sinners, nor sit in the seat of the scornful" - and dancing, and cheering, and throwing still more orange blossom confetti, and drinking wine without diluting it in water, so that - as the Chronicler would express it – "the very earth was rent with the sound of them". Good. Good. Let them be happy. Let them rejoice in their good fortune. Let them remember Daoud in this way, and let their remembering found a dynasty, to rule Yisra-El until the end of days. Soon, he knew, they would begin calling for him to come out on the balcony and receive their acclamation. But he would not do so. Even were he physically capable, he would not do so. He hadn't spent thirty years preparing the ground for his successor, only to spoil Shlomo's glory by stealing the day back for himself. And besides, he was much too frail. Enough to lie back, and be grateful to that bastard Adoni-Yah for forcing his hand, for compelling him to do what he had most wanted to do, yet feared the consequences of doing. Enough to lie back, and enjoy the ministrations of his beloved Avi-Shag.

While thirty miles away, at Zochelet, Shlomo's half-brother, Adoni-Yah, went down into the refuge-city of Ein-Rogel, and grasped the horns of the sanctuary-altar, and prayed to the Lord god of the Bene Yisra-El that his mother's embassy should be successful, and that the fate of his brothers Amnon and Av-Sala'am and Chil-Av would not be his fate.

For it was well known in Erets Yisra-El that the fourth lamb still waited to be redeemed.

SEVEN

"Eli-Phaz!"

"Sire."

"Bring me the tablet."

"Which one, sire? There are now some" - flapping to count them — "seventeen versions."

The king was grinning. Were there really as many as seventeen? It would serve the meddling historians of posterity right - and himself even righter! The art of writing, he had learned a long time ago, lay in keeping control of all the ambiguities. Like palaces in the midst of summer, stray drafts were useful.

Ah, but he was on excellent form this afternoon. The puns were flowing.

"The one Shavsha brought this morning. The one Shlomo hasn't seen yet."

"The wax is not dry, sire."

"Well bring it anyway."

Strangely, given all the stresses and strains of the last few days, he hadn't felt as well as this in months. Perhaps because it was - officially at least - his birthday, and all his sons, even envoys of Adoni-Yah bearing honeyed messages of coy fake penitence, had come to bring him presents. Perhaps because they had counted the last sheaf of the Omer, so all Yeshurun was pronounced cleansed of its contaminations and impurities: religion was a marvellous prophylactic. Perhaps because it was that most burdensome of festivals, the Feast of Weeks, and for the first time in half a lifetime he was not the one who had to officiate at all those tiresome sacrifices. Poor Shlomo looked exhausted.

"I hear the bullock slipped its leash," he laughed.

"Fortunately one of the priests caught it by the horns before it could get free. We had a terrible time through the proclamations though. Whenever Tsadok tried to announce the holy convocation, one or other of the yearling lambs began bleating. It was terribly difficult not to laugh."

Thank Yahweh he didn't have some po-faced pompous son for a successor!

"Read to me, Shlomo. My eyes are hurting."

But Shlomo would not take the tablet, from whose edges hot wax was literally dripping. His father hadn't even noticed that two great bubbles of wax were solidifying on his arm. Had he lost feeling to that extent?

"The text can wait, father. I need to give an answer to the Bene Giv-On. We still haven't signed the treaty. Did you agree to their reclaiming Giv-Yah as the tribal capital?"

"Is it written down?"

"No."

"Then I did not."

"But you wrote nothing down, father. You never did."

Except his own history, of course, whole volumes of which lay piled up at his bedside, awaiting completion. Anything written down became an established, an irrefutable fact, whether it was actually true or not, because historians treated all documented evidence as authentic, and used it against you. So if it applied to your own history, write it down, and even if it wasn't true, history would validate it. Why else had he employed a personal scribe for twenty years, and spent a part of every evening going over the written account, changing it and changing it, eking out the contradictions, until he could be sure at every phrase that history suited the interests of the moment?

On the other hand, if it applied to politically convenient alliances which you intended to break as soon as they ceased to be politically convenient, then write nothing down, so there was nothing to commit you to.

But you had to have been a king fully forty years, and not a mere few days like Shlomo, to be aware of that.

"I wrote my poems down."

"Yes, father. But they don't count in the same way. What about Giv-Yah?"

"What does Shim'i say?"

The Joint Head of the Royal Council beamed with pleasure at this rare acknowledgment of his presence.

Though he also understood that his advice was only being sought as a method of evasion.

"Sire, the Bene Sha'ul are already angry enough about the seven who were handed over and hanged. If Giv-Yah is ceded as well, they will think the king has abandoned the royal family for foreigners. It will be poorly received throughout Yisra-El. Remember your promise to Yah-Natan."

"And you, Re'i. Can you find a way of disagreeing with that?"

The wiry Shim'i and the portly Re'i could have been a comedy duo if they had been born in some more light-hearted era. Never apart physically, they could not have stood further apart intellectually. Whatever the one advised, the other automatically rebutted - and each invariably had a text of Abou Mousa in substantiation. It had become proverbial. And to Daoud extremely useful, which was why he employed them in tandem. Though it was quite unfair of him to make a joke of it.

"As it happens, I do disagree, sire. Giv-On is accepted as the most important shrine in Yeshurun. After Chevron, of course. And will remain so until the House of Yahweh is established here in Yiru-Sala'am. A great debt is owed for the years in which the Ark was kept there. It is essential that this religious centrality be given political weight. The House of Sha'ul has that already, and can afford to yield. Think only of your promise to Yah-Natan."

Daoud wasn't even listening. His eyes had dropped shut. His head was turned sideways on the pillow. Mention of Chevron had induced a wave of nostalgic memories in which he was uncertain that he really wanted to indulge. But lay there, watching them. A blow-fly was quietly investigating the drops of candle-wax on his left arm, as though wondering if this were a suitable place to lay its maggot-eggs. Eli-Phaz brushed it away.

But the old king was oblivious.

"Father?"

He could have been faking sleep, of course. But in fact, on this occasion as so often recently, he had genuinely dozed off.

So that he was quite unaware of the appearance in the royal doorway of Avi-Atar ben Achi-Melech, erstwhile High Priest in Yevus, once his best friend, who had come from making the sin and peace offerings at the shrine of Ein Rogel, and wished to offer a handful of the wave-bread, a portion of the shoulder of the ram, as his own personal sin and peace offering to his king. So he had stood for more than three hours already, contrite in his plain white tunic, awaiting the signal that he might come forward and beg forgiveness, conscious that he would neither receive it, nor himself be received.

"My will, Shlomo," the voice croaked, upon awakening. "It must be included in the Second Scroll of Shmu-El, because he anointed me, and therefore in the Second Scroll of the Kings as well."

A tendency to fall asleep. A tendency to forget. They must have had this conversation at least three times today already.

"Your will relates to me, father, and therefore it must go in the Third Scroll of the Kings."

"Are their majesties aware that in Ephrayim the Chroniclers are compiling their own version of the life of Daoud?"

"Of course we're aware of it, you fool! I am writing an extremely detailed rigmarole about the Temple for it, to ensure the Bene Ephrayim are able to accept a central Temple for all of Yisra-El that's located in Yehudah. Kingship, you see, Shlomo," he added, in the most pointed of asides. "Forty years, Shlomo. Seven in Chevron and now thirty-three here in Tsi'on."

"I know the story father. What are we deciding about Giv-Yah?"

His son's impatience needed a lesson too. And besides, what better excuse for a good digression than the need to avoid precisely that decision?

"You know the story, yes, but not the history. Stories are nothing. Most of my official biography, for example, is pure myth - fiction, not fabrication – didn't you know that? Especially the parts that are true."

He must have made that joke a thousand times as well. In the days when people laughed because he was king. Whereas now the silence was frankly embarrassing.

"We are talking about history, father. A decision about Giv-Yah could determine..."

"History. History is quite another matter. History is something into which a man must fit like a link in an iron chain - fit, or be discarded by the blacksmith. Who would remember Barak were it not for Devorah? Or, or?"

He couldn't for the moment actually recall any more examples - though Shlomo was expecting the customary reference to Bo'az and his great-grandmother, especially as today was Shavu'ot. But his eyes were glittering. The very skin on his face had come back to life. For such a terribly frail body, his mind still had moments of quite extraordinary lucidity.

"Do you know why we study History in school? Not just to avoid having to reinvent the wheel. Not just to learn from the errors of our predecessors - which we fail to do anyway. We study History so that we can know in what shape to forge our own mettle, to know it and to understand it, and to extend the chain. Take my advice, whenever you have a hard decision to make, don't ask yourself what the people will think of it, or your ministers, or your wives. Not even Yahweh. Ask yourself how History will see it, and then decide. And even studying History isn't enough. You must know it, you must understand it. Because we are the perpetrators of a divine mission, Shlomo, inaugurated by Abou Raham, consolidated by Abou Mousa, anointed upon our heads by Shmu-El and Natan. A man achieves nothing who has no past upon which to build his future. How can he augment it if he doesn't know what exists and what is missing? How can he add if he doesn't know the sum?"

The boy - the boy? a grown man rather, long turned twenty and several times a father; but the figure in his mind was still always a child of six or seven, learning Habiru and Torah on his father's knee - the boy was tired of his father's tedious philosophising, his trite and banal platitudes. Stick to poetry and war, father, the two things you do best. Leave the philosophising to me.

"Giv-Yah, father." In the name of Yahweh he was nothing if not resilient. "If necessary I shall make and announce my own decision. But it would be better if it came from you."

The look in his father's eyes drew his own down to the old man's hand, which was trying to open. So he put his fingers inside his father's fingers, and understood that this was the blessing of the Ben Yamin, the favoured son, the son who was his father's right hand. How often had his father spoken to him of Abou Yah-Akov, who cheated his elder brother of this very blessing, and who gave his own blessing, not to his sons but to his grandsons, and not to the eldest but the youngest.

"Shlomo," his father whispered, the explosion of energy burned out in him, "you are too anxious to have me dead and no one else but your hands on the throne."

"Not true father."

"It is entirely true. I know you, boy. I know you will ignore my will. I know you will not bury me, but rather burn my corpse and have my skull taken to the Hill of Yevus to corroborate your edicts through the mouth of the oracle of Mor-Yah. I know you, boy."

"I wish to see our people governed, as they deserve to be governed, that is all."

"As they deserve to be governed? Then do it with spit and excrement, and twice daily beatings with a whip of thorns. Govern them as they need, Shlomo, and you will make them a great nation. As Adonai Yahweh governs - with an iron hand and arbitrary compassion. But wait till I'm dead."

An aroma that could have been patchouli wafted across the room. Servants come to replace one bowl of flowers with another, to add new flavours to the ambience of putrefaction that Shlomo, like Eli-Phaz, had almost ceased to notice. Fallen petals bloodied the marble floor like corpses, skin thick. The dank, fetid smell of the dead lilies could have been more pungent than any living flesh.

"Father you cannot give a man responsibility, and then deny him authority. There are factions gathering. Around Adoni-Yah in particular. Yo-Av has already declared which way he'll set his hand. Religious differences will drive us to civil war if they're not resolved. What kind of a bequest would that be to posterity, father - the ultimate war of the gods: El versus Yahweh, thunderbolt against thunderbolt in the valleys of Yiru-Sala'am? The people need a ruler, not a dying legend. This co-regency can't hold."

But paused. Such desperate frustration in his voice. Such desperate clinging on to life by clinging on to power, palpable in his father's eyes. Such pity and such compassion, squeezed through a son's fingers that now clenched those of his father. It was this that couldn't hold: this unprecedented closeness, this butterfly life. And Avi-Atar, still waiting in the door. Of all people, Avi-Atar. Surely the king would let him in. Surely the king would grant forgiveness. But he couldn't ask.

"The people are waiting, father."

"I know. I know. You don't have to tell me. Everything's suspended, frozen - a perpetual Sabbath day. I know. And in the meanwhile discontent increases, enemies plot, armies are gathered together, Adoni-Yah sits at Ein Rogel biding his time, safe until he leaves the sanctuary. I know all this. And do you think it will change if you have one of those silly crowns they wear in Pharat put on your head as well as the vial of oil poured over it? Kingship isn't about title or ceremony or official garments; kingship is about the way you rule, according to given circumstances at any given moment of time."

There was simply no replying to this. But the king was not done.

"How are you going to deal with Adoni-Yah, my son? That is the question that troubles me. He will resist your kingship, once I'm dead. Will you dare to drag a man by force out of the sanctuary? Are you capable of having your own brother put to death?"

"You must leave me to know that, father. Your task is to give me the opportunity to fail. And if I do fail, which I won't, it won't be your fault. But you must give me the opportunity, father. Now."

"I can't."

"Was it all a sham then, father? A pantomime anointing, not to make me king, but to prevent Adoni-Yah from making himself one?"

"It worked, didn't it?"

"For this week. But next week?"

"Have patience, my son. I am trying to die as quickly as possible."

EIGHT

In the lassitude of the sweltering afternoon, Daoud the old king dozed with his fingers still clenched in those of his son. Two guards, one of the Bene Pelet, one of the Bene Cheret, kept watch at the door, where Avi-Atar ben Achi-Melech waited with ever decreasing hope. The king's infant grandsons, Rechav-Am ben Shlomo and Yarav-Am ben Yedid-Yah (the patronymic one of many causes of strife between the boys), came to receive their blessings; but were sent quietly away, for fear of disturbing the king's sleep. Three times Avi-Shag came and left, dismissed by a harsh glare from the co-regent. Three times the king's physician came to attend his majesty, and looked, and nodded his head sagely, and departed. Sleep is a prelude to death, and in this majestic room where two kings sat, it was sleep who ruled. Yet even sleep was only an interregnum. The smell of death was more potent even than the lilies and the patchouli.

Because a decision about Giv-Yah clearly was not going to be made, Shlomo took up the wax tablet that had now dried, and began to read - a lesser poet than his father, but perhaps a greater orator. But stopped after just the opening phrase.

"'Yedid-Yah, my beloved son and heir...'"

Even now, so close to death, the wordsmith in his father was unsilenceable. "Yedid-Yah yedidi", he had written, exquisitely poetic: "beloved of Yah, my beloved", and his own name, Daoud, from the selfsame root; but the prosaic Shavsha had scored it out, superimposing the kingname Shlomo that protocol required.

Not that Daoud wasn't capable of descending to the most prosaic realms himself. An earlier version of this had read, "Shlomo, my adopted son and heir", an attempt to pretend that Shlomo was the son of one of his Yevusi concubines, and not Bat Sheva's child at all; she having been cursed barren by Natan after the terrible complications of that first still-birth, which mashed up her insides something rotten. All her children were to be declared adoptive, all six of them, fathered by him on his concubines but brought up "on her knees", as Yishma-El had been fathered upon Chagar by Abou Raham, and half the tribes by Abou Yah-Akov upon Tsilpah and Bilhah. That lie had been perpetrated when Shlomo took Yo-Av's side over the census, and his father threatened to disinherit him.

45

Threatened, but then retracted, and ordered the wax tablet to be melted down. But even now that tablet lay safely stored where only Shlomo knew of its existence - just in case, one day, it might be necessary to repudiate his mother.

Again he took up the reading. Unlike his father, he still had not mastered the art of reading silently inside his head, so that each word came out in breathy susurrations, almost silent, yet loud enough to stir the king, who hung in the darkness of half-sleep upon every word:

"'...I go the way of all the earth; be strong therefore, and show yourself a man. Keep the charge of the Lord Yahweh who is your god, to walk in his ways, to keep his statutes, and his commandments, and his judgements, and his testimonies, as it is written in the Law of Abou Mousa, that you may prosper in all that you do, and wheresoever you may turn. That the Lord may continue his word which he spoke concerning me, saying: If your children take heed to their way, to walk before me in truth with all their heart and with all their soul, there shall not fail you (said he) a man on the throne of Yisra-El.'"

"This is awful."

The old king's guffaw by way of agreement brought him up with a start.

"Read on," he said. "There's more. And it gets even worse."

The two of them laughing together at the absurdity of all these anachronistic circumlocutions. Or was Daoud simply pretending laughter, to distract from the dark earnestness of what actually followed?

"'Furthermore, you are aware what Yo-Av ben Tseru-Yah did to me, and what he did to the two captains of the hosts of Yisra-El, to Av-Ner ben Ner, and to Amasa ben Yitro, who he slew, and shed the blood of war in peace, and put the blood of war on the girdle that was around his loins, and in the shoes that were on his feet.'"

"Father, this is" - the word resisted utterance; but eventually Shlomo could not withhold it — "this is cowardly. If you can't do it yourself, you have no right to make me do it on your behalf." His father's silence, his tightly clenched eyes, offered a wall of dull resistance through which he had no choice now but to continue blustering. "This is Yo-Av, father, your nephew, the commander of your armies. If these acts merited death, why didn't you have him

46

killed years ago? Why now?"

"Because he went with Adoni-Yah your brother to Zochelet. The other acts were merely disobedience. This was treason."

"True. But it was also an extremely wise political move in the circumstances. Even you can't deny that. You hadn't forgiven each other over the census. And besides, all the odds were in Adoni-Yah's favour. And as the eldest son..."

"He should have waited."

"Why? You never intended to make him king. He knew that. I knew that. Natan knew that. Everyone in Erets Yisra-El knew that - except my mother."

The mask of hostility broken by that parenthesis. The father smiling in delight at so much arrogance in one still so young. It was, sadly, a necessary attribute for any leader of note.

"Read on."

"'Do therefore according to your wisdom, and do not let his hoar head go down to the grave in peace.'"

"Will you do it?"

Now it was the son's turn to screw his face up, to clench his eyes, to hide behind a wall of silence. So that there was this in common too.

"Read on, Shlomo. There are other matters besides this one."

"'But show kindness to the sons of Bar-Tsillai of the Bene Gil-Yad, and let them be of those that eat with you at table; for so they came to me when I fled because of Av-Sala'am your brother.'"

"A good man, Bar-Tsillai," Daoud interrupted. "You will do well to keep his eldest boy at court. What was his name?"

"Chimcham," Shlomo remembered, after a moment's thought.

"Chimcham, yes. Funny name. We seem to be acquiring a fashion for unlikely names. I came upon another like it just the other day. Mishmash. Do you know it actually means 'apricot stew'. He came with me from Gil-Gal. Chimcham, I mean."

He was conscious that he was rambling. And becoming sentimental. And stiffened.

"Read what I've written about your friend Shim'i ben Gera."

Shlomo found the passage.

"'...the Bene Yamin from Bachurim. He came down to meet me at the river Yarden, and I swore to him by the Lord saying: I will not put you to death with the sword.'"

"I remember, father. You were in one of your more generous moods. Av-Yishai wanted his head."

"I was too generous. Av-Yishai was right, in principle. But at the time it was the pragmatic decision. Shim'i had a thousand men and could guarantee support among the Bene Yamin. But that was then, and now we have no more need to uphold the principle. Read it."

"...'now therefore hold him not guiltless, for you are a wise man and know what you need to do to him.'"

Shlomo swallowed. He did not wish to begin his reign by spilling blood, especially not a friend's blood; most especially not one who his father had already pardoned; and even more especially not one whose death was likely to spark further friction between himself and Adoni-Yah. Unless he spilled Adoni-Yah's blood as well. And Yo-Av's. And how many others more? Father, is this what is meant by a royal legacy?

"He's an old man now, father. Let him die in peace."

But the ex-king was absolutely determined.

"No!" he would have pounded the bed-sheets with his fist had he been able. "That bastard swore at me that day in Bachurim, language such as I have never heard, to anyone, least of all a king. Av-Yishai was right."

His rising anger was alarming Eli-Phaz, who was gesturing with his hands to Shlomo to change the subject. Daoud's left eye had begun to twitch.

"You're right, father. He must be punished for his offence."

But Daoud would not let the matter drop.

"Agree now to humour me, and then rescind later. Your tone of voice gives you away, Shlomo. Let it be written down."

"It isn't necessary, father. I have agreed it will be done."

"No! It shall be written in my will along with all the rest. Shavsha, do you hear me? Write it down. These words exactly, Shavsha, so there can be no rescension." He paused, struggling to catch his breath. The blow-fly was making further efforts to settle on the drips of wax. "Call Shim'i and Re'i to witness this. Now write: 'Shim'i ben Gera of the Bene Yamin of Bachurim, who cursed me most grievously on the day I went to Bachurim. His hoar head bring you down to the grave with blood.' You can spell it w-h-o-r-e if you prefer."

The whole left side of his mouth twitching now, with what was trying to become laughter. Only the sounds came out half-chewed.

Shlomo took his father's hand. But his father was unaware of it.

"Forty years of glorious kingship," he was thinking out loud. "Any other people but ours would remember you as King Yedid-Yah the Great and put up statues in your honour. But in the end this is what it all comes down to. Petty vengeances. A mania for control. Saliva in your beard. And getting me to do your dirty work for you. It isn't much, is it, father?"

But his father could not hear him any longer. He had pronounced his final curse, his final vengeance, his final act of blood. The eyes had closed again, not clenched this time but simply closed, and the greyness of the lids told clearly that they would not reopen. The knuckles of his hands, normally so stiff with arthritis, had loosened. His breathing had stopped.

"The king is dead, sire," Re'i whispered.

Shlomo nodded.

"There are words, majesty."

"You speak them."

Quite unconscious that it was Avi-Atar who had addressed him.

"Adonai melech, adonai malach, adonai yimloch le-olam va-ed. The Lord is our king, now, and before, and for all the days to come."

And I, Shlomo wondered, what then am I, if not also king?

"I shall go and make the announcement," Shim'i was grateful for the excuse to make his departure from the royal bed-chamber. With Re'i, inevitably, at his side.

Soon enough all the women of the harem would rush in to begin the keening, an intolerable feline howl that would stir up all the women of the city to a caterwauling, until it came to sound like jackals baying at the Judean moon. But for the moment Shlomo was left alone, save only for the praying, weeping Avi-Atar and the silent, invisible Eli-Phaz, who was already transferring his loyalty to the new king, carrying out the task appointed to him weeks before, to gather up the reams and reams of royal manuscript and deposit them in his successor's study "for safe-keeping".

In theory, the presence of the discredited High Priest was a terrible affront, yet Shlomo removed his head-dress and his shoes and knelt as Avi-Atar instructed him, at the edge of the bed, to recite the Vidu'i and the Shema on his father's behalf, to tear the left lapel of his tunic, to stare into the eyes of the dead king his father, to consider his inheritance. How typical that Daoud had died raging and jesting in the same breath. It was how he had lived, after all, juxtaposing seemingly irreconcilable opposites, living out paradoxes – a beautiful beast, as Michal bat Sha'ul once called him. The tongue burning, yet still pressed to the cheek. And how typical that his very last words, spoken though they were in the coldest and angriest of flat prose, should reverberate from the parchment like the lyric of a psalm. They would be chanting them in the streets from Dan to Ber-Sheva once it became known that these were the very last to leave his lips. "His hoar head bring you down to the grave with blood." And they would remember him for the poetry, not the killing. And they would fail even to notice the verbal jest.

But for Shlomo, holding in his hands not just the last words that would be written in the Scroll of the Second King of Yisra-El, but the entire history, the reams and reams of parchment which now he was helping Eli-Phaz to gather up from the dead king's bedside and which he would take away with him to read, to study, and finally, most judiciously, to expurgate, all those hundreds of thousands of written and rewritten words became as if the living flesh of his inheritance, and he understood that now it was his turn to transform them into acts.

PART TWO: ORPHEUS IN THE UNDERWORLD

Parchment One

"To the Keeper of the Royal Annals, El-Chanun ben Machli, an account of the Confederation of the Bene Yisra-El, written for the instruction of the heir to the throne by Yedid-Yah, king in Yiru-Sala'am, Nasi of all the Clans and Tribes who comprise the Confederation of the Bene Yisra-El, king of the Bene Ephrayim and the Bene Yehudah, Lord of Chevron and Yiru-Sala'am, conqueror of Mo-Av and Ammon, king of Tsiklag, unifier of the Twelve Tribes of the Covenant of Yahweh, founder of Yeshurun, who was born to the house of Yishai ben Oved of the Bene Yehudah in the town of Beit Lechem Ephratah of Yehudah, the House of the corn-god of the river Euphrates whom men call Tammuz, in the tribe of Yehudah ben Abou Yah-Akov, on the sixth day of Sivan, the month of the Rejoicing of Asherah, in the tenth year following the battle of Even-Ezer, when the Ark of the Covenant lodged in the house of Avi-Nadav in Kiryat-Ye'arim of Giv-On, and El-Ezar his son was priest and guardian."

Don't you just hate all that ghastly official jargon? The vanity of the Pharaohs of Mitsrayim and the Satraps of Bav-El of the Bene Kessed, writ considerably larger than their actual lives, on hieroglyphic stelae, on monumental cairn stones, on pyramids and ziggurats. The arrogant self-identification of mere man with Almighty Yahweh. Still, it's expected - and at least my rendition is genuinely life-sized, quilled on parchment, and with a rather nice poetic flourish don't you think? You too will have to learn to write like this, Shlomo, though it's precious and pretentious, not to say convoluted in the extreme, and practically as unintelligible as the language lawyers use to confound their clients and extend the time their cases spend in court. You will have to learn to write like this, for the royal annals, for the Chronicler, for the documents of state. Do not, however, expect too much of that sort of flowery purple - purple? hah! an insult to the royal purple! - from me. I am not interested in flowers - or not the linguistic sort anyway. This is not a psalm. I have composed far too many psalms for one lifetime, practically all of them gloomy and supplicatory; nor will I write what arthritis prevents me playing. No, I write this to impart to you a vision that has occupied my life, ever since the day the Prophet Shmu-El came to my father's house in Beit Lechem Ephratah of Yehudah to seek a minyan for the sacrifice of a red heifer. I write this to teach you the necessary vices and the occasional virtues of kingship, because although it can never be made public or official until the day itself, it is you who I have chosen for my heir. And believe me, when you come to inherit, you will need this manual, even though your initial reaction will be to discard it. Be not hasty, my son, for lo, yea, verily and behold it is a proverb in Yisra-El that through wisdom is a house built, and by understanding is it established, and by knowledge shall its rooms be filled with all manner of pleasant and precious jewels. As my scroll shall be, Shlomo; as my scroll shall be. Though it is also a proverb in Yisra-El that a whore is a deep ditch and a foreign woman a narrow pit - and believe me there will be many a deep ditch and many a narrow pit in these pages too, literal as well as metaphorical. For if nothing else, I intend to tell you my version of the truth - emerods and all.

First, your kingdom, your territory, your domain.

"Then Av-Ram took Sarai his wife" – I have often wondered if that shouldn't be Sarah-Yah, or even Asherah-Yah, but save that for another time – "and Lot his brother's son" - the Bene Kessed call him al-Lat did you know and regard him as her, as female? – "and all the substance they had gathered, and the souls they had acquired in Charan, and they came into the land of the Bene Kena'an. And Av-Ram passed through the land as far as Shechem, and settled in the Plain of Moreh. And the Bene Kena'an ruled the land. And the Lord appeared to Av-Ram and said: 'To your descendants will I give this land'. And there he built an altar to the Lord who had appeared to him."

And there you have it, the beginning of everything. And one day, if we succeed, the end as well. Though I challenge anyone to go to court with such a text and argue for specific boundaries. The whole land of the Bene Kena'an, from Tsidon to the Red Sea? Or simply, narrowly, the town of Shechem and the Plain of Moreh? It's vague, Shlomo, terribly, unhelpfully vague. Yet there, precisely there, is where we must begin, for in those lines lie our covenant, and through that covenant our justification. Are you aware, for example, that your mother's tribe the Bene Yamin actually came from north-west Aram, under a king who bore the root of both our names - Yadad, "beloved" - came many generations after Abou Yah-Akov left "his Uncle Lavan's house" (the shrine of the white moon-god Lavan, that is to say, whom he served as sacred king for two moon cycles, each of seven years) in Padan-Aram, and only joined the tribes of Yisra-El by treaty? By Yahweh, that was another convoluted sentence! That the one we think of as Bin-Yamin was really called Ben Oni, because he was born in the city of the sun-god, in On in Lower Mitsrayim of the Bene Chem? Oh yes, indeed – I have spent a lifetime studying these histories in infinitesimal detail. There is no genealogical connection, you see - unless perhaps through Lavan himself, which would be marvellously ironic don't you think? - any more than with Ephrayim or Menasheh. Neither of the sons of Rach-El are truthfully sons of Abou Yah-Akov. Actually, none of the sons of Le'ah, Tsilpah or Bilhah either, if the absolute truth be told. But we are all brothers by treaty and alliance; all sons of Yisra-El – that's what matters now. We have all bound ourselves to that original covenant, through the rite of circumcision, through the cult of Yahweh, through the act of confederation. We are all Bene Abou Raham, Bene Yitschak, Bene Yah-Akov - and as such, because that is what they chose to call the original confederation that Abou Mousa assembled in the desert, we are all Bene Yisra-El. It's quite simple really.

But it strikes me that you don't really need me to give you a history or a geography lesson, do you? I mean, this isn't what you want to read, is it? My life story - yes? The royal childhood.

I was born, as is now well-known, in Beit Lechem Ephratah, a Yah-forsaken town if ever one deserved the epithet. The House of the corn god of the Euphrates. Who could fail to grow up a poet, coming from a place that bears so glorious a name - however squalid the reality? Every town and village has its resident deity, its local cult, though few can claim such longevity as our cult of the eternally dying eternally reborn lord of the underworld and the vegetation, born on the straw of the threshing-floor at the midwinter, cut down in his prime and nailed to the wooden winnowing-board in the spring. Mind you, I never really could see any difference between our Tammuz, and Dagon of the Bene Pelet, or Adonis of the Bene Aram, or Osher of the Bene Mitsrayim, or Asher of the Bene Chet - or any of the other dozen versions of what is surely the same, single corn-god. Our friend Hu-Ram tells me there is one named Attis, and another named Utu, and that on some brutish western island of hyperborea which the Bene Dan explored before they settled in La'ish, they call him Bran, and Balder and even, laughably, John Barleycorn - but I have no doubt there are a thousand of these gods, dying and reborning wherever men and women ask themselves where life began and how the miracle of nature consequences. Tammuz, anyway, was Tammuz of the Bene Akkad of Bav-El originally, the son of Ishtar whom we call Yah and Asherah; though why his devotees travelled to the Chevron Valley from that of the Pharat I have never understood - perhaps the same reason why their neighbour Av-Ram of Ur made the same journey. Ur and Charan and Yareyacho were, after all, the three principal moon cities of the ancient world.

Our family had officiated at the shrine for generations, and of course there is the May-King May-Queen pageant of my great-grandmother Ruth and my great-grandfather Bo'az meeting and falling in love at the time of the gleaning in the corn-field, which like my brothers I first heard in the crib, with all the Tammuz tales, and which I am told the children still act out in mime-play as part of the carnival of the Feast of Weeks. A pestilential dump, you see, a fly-infested, odoriferous, dilapidated hovel, may also be a most auspicious place to start one's life. Actually, Beit Lechem wasn't all that bad.

✡

I grew up on the hills and on the roof - a far cry from your privileged childhood, Shlomo, amidst the opulence and splendour of a royal palace. Beit Lechem was less a town than a few dozen adobe houses and a market in the fortified gateway, all of it owing its existence to the existence of the shrine, and to the good fortune of a trading road for which we provided a caravanserai. There were no streets, just cramped spaces between houses - narrow alleys at best, without paving, barely large enough for two donkeys to pass abreast. People fed their waste into open channels down the centre of those alleys, till the edges blocked up with debris: broken pots, garbage, old mud-bricks, pieces of rag. In the winter it became a swamp, and what ran down the alleyways was either disease or scavenging dogs. The smell was dreadful. In the spring you were grateful to escape to the hills, to spend eight months living with the flocks.

Our home in that fetid town was neither very rich nor entirely poor, despite what it may say in the royal annals. The family had occupied the same plot of land for generations, building one house, restoring or extending or replacing it, as wealth permitted or dereliction decreed. Originally, when our forefather Pharets ben Yehudah - Pharets whom Yehudah fathered incestuously on his daughter-in-law Tamar; Pharets the twin-brother of Zerach of the scarlet cord - when he established the clan in the time of Abou Yah-Akov, it must have been a very ordinary, two-roomed, mud-brick hovel, cold and damp and over-crowded and forever smelling of smoke from the unchimneyed fire. Chetsron his son, and Ram his grandson, and Ami-Nadav and Nachshon and Salmah his descendants, must have rebuilt it over and over again, replacing worn out mud-bricks, plastering layers of mud where rain had washed it out - but it remained essentially the same house for, what, three hundred years? The sort of house we put up on the hillside as a shelter for the men who watch the flock.

But our house was much grander - a house as befitted what was always, in truth, the royal line of Yehudah. Great-grandfather Bo'az built a whole extra room, on a right angle to the house, as a bride-gift for Ruth, and closed the other two sides in with storerooms. Grandfather Oved laid out the inner courtyard with shrubs and palms and paving slabs, and added an upper room to the extension. Father in his turn repointed most of the house, taking out the daub-and-wattle and plastering in a limestone mortar, which meant we didn't leak in winter like most houses. So we had four rooms, two of them subdivided by pillars, all with tiny, lattice-shuttered windows, high up on the walls, almost at the eaves, and painted blue to ward off malarial mosquitoes and the djinns and keruvim in which practically everyone but me believed. Putting the windows quite that high meant no light could enter, but on the other hand the heat rose to the ceiling in the summer, and then seeped out through the window, so you stayed cool; and in the winter, my mother put up great thick woollen curtains to keep out the cold - I can assure you that the hills of Beit Lechem can be freezing cold in winter, cold enough for snow. After years of living in a house like that, you can imagine the pleasure of inhabiting a sandstone and basalt palace.

My parents had their own bedroom; and not just a raised platform with straw mats, but a real wooden high-bed, and a table, and two chairs with covers of linen stuffed with goat hair, and a couch made of carved wood and inlaid with bone and ivory - symbols of serious affluence. They even had pillows for their beds, and fine woollen blankets, and extra clothes and bedding which they stored in chests. The eight of us brothers and our three sisters inhabited the other two bedrooms by haphazard, sleeping in whatever order we lay down, with the last room used for animals and guests and storage, and for any farmworker or goatherd or house-servant who might need a place to lay his head.

The floor was made of stone chippings worked into the earth. All we had was a raised platform at one end of each room, while the rest of the space was kept for storage jars and cooking pots and clothes and bedding. We had to share the rooms like No'ach's ark with animals throughout the winter, housing them for warmth in the area nearest the door while we occupied the area furthest from it. The underneath of the platform was used to store more jars, my father's work tools, and the very smallest animals. We had mats on the floor for seating, but no tables, unless you count a straw mat laid out on the raised platform. Some homes had low stools to sit on, but not ours. Bed was a thin woollen mattress, spread out in the evening on the raised platform; everyone slept together under goat's hair quilts which were stashed away in the morning, fleas and all.

"Daoud, will you stop scratching!"

And if not Daoud, then Mey-Zahav, or Nachshon, Tamar or Avi-Nadav. I never did understand why our scratching irritated my mother so much - perhaps she thought you procreated fleas by scratching them. She was perpetually swatting away flies herself, in the summer especially, when the house swarmed with insects. She possessed a beautiful ivory comb, with teeth as thin as needles and bone-sharp, and she was forever dragging it through our hair, pulling off nits or fleas or lice, catching them in the palm of her hand and squeezing the blood out of them before they could jump away. She could spend hours delousing her eleven children one by one.

"Now go and wash your hands and face. And make sure you clean under your fingernails."

As though there were any facilities for bathing, or water that was any cleaner than your hands. As though, living in a mud house, on mud floors, with animals in the straw and animals below the bed-platform, and only a dug hole and a palm leaf for the performing of your ablutions, there was any hope of ever being clean. As though, by the time she had finished work on child eleven, it wasn't time to start again on child one.

But she battled on, undaunted.

In winter it wasn't just the dirt she had to fight, but the smoke as well. The family hearth was really just a hole in the earth floor, lined with flints, into which we threw pieces of charcoal or thorns or dried animal dung - there was never any shortage of that about the place - and set them alight. No fireplace. No chimney either - and you had to be considerably wealthier than we were to afford a brazier. The smoke filtered up towards the high windows, but the woollen curtain blocked its egress, so it lingered for ever after in the ceiling joists. Mother had a convex baking-sheet, which she put over the fire like a tent and hung food from to bake, and a cooking-pot which could stand in the fire did the rest. Nobody made vegetable stew quite like my mother's - probably because of all the herbs she used. Leeks, beans and lentils for the substance, and then, to season it, cumin, dill, thyme, mint nuts, always coriander, several different breeds of onion - everything home-grown - and wild garlic. I have never known anyone so profligate in their use of wild garlic. One year she planted some in a corner of the courtyard, "just to see", and it took root, spread everywhere. My father's efforts to get rid of it were as heroic and as unavailing as my mother's war against the nits.

Because it was always so dark, and crowded, so full of smoke and flies, because the animals made you feel you were born in a manger like Tammuz rather than in a house like a normal human being, we youngsters sought refuge on the roof, weather permitting. When grandfather Oved built the roof-room, he also laid a kind of lattice of sycamore beams - he couldn't afford cypress, let alone cedar - across the flat surface of the roof, with layers of brushwood and clay between them to make a floor that we used to keep smooth with a stone roller. Whenever it rained, grass sprouted in the roof. Grass meant free grazing.

"But father..."

There was no point arguing.

"There are three orphan lambs that are ready for weaning. I am not asking you to take any of the big animals up there. But it's fresh grass, and I will not see it wasted."

Penny-pincher that he was, he was also right. If the animals didn't eat it, it would only take root, and then we would have cracks in the roof where darnel and tares and other weeds went burrowing. So we would take some of the younger animals up there to graze. It didn't matter how wet it got, because we had gutters at every corner, and ran the water off into cisterns that were waterproofed with a special mortar made from ashes, lime and sand. Personalised stored water - now there was another symbol of our wealth! The poor were better off without it though. Because it was dirty water, coming off that roof. You couldn't wash in it, and you only drank it if it had been boiled. Mostly father used it for watering crops. For six months of the year the cisterns were model breeding-grounds for the mosquitoes!

Most people got up to their roof by ladder, but we had a flight of stairs built into the outer wall, straight up from the courtyard to the roof. My mother used to lay the flax out on the roof to catch the dew for retting, and we always dried fruit and grain up there in summer. My brothers and I put up a tent of branches across the roof each summer, and slept up there for space and coolness. You could see the world from up there on the roof (as your mother, as all Yisra-El knows only too well, you owe your existence to my enduring love of roof-tops!). My brothers and sisters and I spent long hours on that roof, watching the stars, playing ludo and mancala, playing draughts with a rather rudimentary set we had made out of stones, playing tee-to-tum with two or four-sided pyramid dice, playing music mostly. We could drive half of Beit Lechem to despair on any summer's night when enough of us were down from flocking in the hills, and mother could assemble the family orchestra on the roof. Tone-deaf and club-fingered herself, she had the determination of the incompetent to live vicariously through her children, all of whom she had bashing and tooting sooner even than we could walk.

She adored music. She would sing while she sewed or cooked, singing in the most raucous croak you ever heard, until you thought one of the milk-ewes had a mastitis in her udder or a billy-kid had caught its horns in hay-twine. Aware that she was a threat to human civilisation if allowed anywhere near a real musical instrument, she made herself mistress of the tof, and bashed away a percussion accompaniment to any tune we might be playing. But if we were in three time, you could guarantee she would be in seven. Nor could she sustain it. Somewhere along the way she would miss a beat, but insist on carrying on the same thumping unrhythm, despite its total lack of connection with the melody. Poor mother.

My father's was the musical side. He himself led and trained the choir for all the festivals, of Tammuz and of Yahweh. People said great-grandfather Bo'az played ugav and kinnor like Yuval who invented them, and sang in a deep baritone that was a joy to hear. Family legend has it that his party-piece was the "Hikavtsu" of Abou Yah-Akov, in which each of the tribes receives its blessing in the form of an oracle, and that when he got to the eighth verse, he would pause, and look at any members of the clan who happened to be present, and redouble his fortissimo as though he were admonishing them.

"Yehudah, you are he whom your brothers shall praise; your hand shall be on the neck of your enemies; your father's children shall bow down to you."

Just like Abou Yah-Suph, eh? The royal line, Shlomo, through Pharets who was born first, though it was Zerach who came out of the womb and received the scarlet thread. People say I was just some Bene Yishai shepherd off the hills who had no right to succeed Sha'ul. But Bo'az knew, as grandfather Oved knew from studying the stars. Ours is the royal line of Yehudah, and Yehudah was, not the first-born, but still the first amongst the sons of Abou Yah-Akov.

"Yehudah is a lion's whelp; from the prey, my son, you have gone up. He stooped down, he couched as a lion, and as an old lion. Who shall rouse him up? The staff shall not depart from Yehudah, nor the sceptre from between his feet, until peace comes and the obedience of the people be given to him. Binding his foal to the vine, and his ass's colt to the choice vine, he washed his garments in wine, and his clothes in the blood of grapes. His eyes are red with wine, and his teeth are white with milk."

What does it all mean? I didn't understand it then, and frankly I still don't understand it now, not in its entirety. But such is the nature of oracles. They are bound in metaphor, and need to be deciphered like Mitsrayim hieroglyphs. But that it had the beauty of fine poetry I never doubted. And how we sang, informing all of Beit Lechem that, though Yehudah might not have the first-born rights of Re'u-Ven, though Yehudah might be tainted by his marriages to women of the Bene Kena'an, though the scarlet thread may have been placed on Zerach and not Pharets, nevertheless we, we were the descendants of Tamar, we were the guardians of her holy date-palm, we were the vergers of the shrine of Tammuz, we were the inheritors of the ancient rights of ultimogeniture; and I, I the youngest son, I was endowed with gifts of destiny...enough said. On star-filled nights, when you could sit on the roof-top and watch the camel convoys in the gateway preparing to set off for Ashur or the Red Sea, when you could see the lights of Ophel and Yevus and Mount Tsi'on flickering, not unlike tiny stars themselves, way off in the northern distance, when the sound of Nachshon blowing the chatsotsra and my sister Tamar her hallil, when the thundering of Shammah on the meziltayim and Avi-Nadav on the mena'anim, filled the night with echoes and reverberations out of ancient history, you could imagine almost anything up there on the roof, even the dream of royalty, even the untenable fantasy of making Abou Yah-Akov's oracular blessing come true, in one's own life. Poetry, Shlomo. Poetry.

But, of course, what we mostly saw from that flat roof was the still flatter, the mundane banality, of daily life: sheep and goats being milked; lamp-wicks being prepared; women fetching fresh water from the well in head-held pots; mother and whichever of my sisters happened to be handy, working the grinding mill so that supper could be prepared. It was that confounded grinding wheel that ruined my sister Tamar's health. Nine times out of ten it was she who worked the quern, and every time you could see the impact on her tiny body. Father insisted it was something in her blood or bones, or just the filth and smoke in which we lived. Perhaps he was right, though I have always blamed the quern.

✡

It was made of two circular stones. The larger, lower stone, the metaté, was fixed in place, and had a spike which went through the centre of the mano, the smaller, upper stone, that was turned around on top of it. You poured the corn through the central hole, and two women together turned the top stone with a handle, until ground flour ran out at the edges. It was quite extraordinarily hard work, and a desperately slow process. It also produced a kind of grit that destroyed teeth.

But it wasn't just Tamar's teeth that were destroyed.

She was fourteen, and I must have been seven at the time. She was a pretty, dark-haired child, with no particular talents but no particular vices either. People have a false but sentimental notion that all children must be innocent simply because they are children, but in Tamar's case it was surely true. If there was work to do about the house or field, you never heard a murmur of protest from her - unlike Mey-Zahav, who was the most talented of all of us, but poured her energies into greed and selfishness and tantruming, into finding perfectly valid excuses for being unable to do anything for anyone. Tamar would be up preparing lamp-wicks before dawn, digging and lining the hole to bake the flat-bread or taking off the next day's leaven, volunteering to carry her small head-pot to the well to ensure we had fresh water first thing. If there was nothing else to do, she would make bead necklaces for the pleasure of it, or locust bean syrup to sweeten our drink, while the rest of us were up to mischief somewhere that we shouldn't be. And of course it was Tamar who, with mother, nursed Eli-Av and cured his leg, when he came back from his first experience of soldiering, dousing his leg wound in red wine mixed with olive oil. So she was bound to be chosen. Because the gods are cruel.

She began by coughing, all day and all night till the rest of us were being driven mad by it. Then the fever. Then she began spitting out her teeth. Mother fed her wine mixed with myrrh and gall to relieve the terrible pain that she was in, but it was no use. Tamar was visibly dying, right there in the smoke and darkness of the house. Until her bowels went liquid and we had to put her to sleep outside the house.

61

"Fetch the ba'alat-ov," was Eli-Av my eldest brother's constant refrain. He had a deep belief in every kind of superstition, but especially the women who were possessed by what are called "familiar spirits". There was one such, who inhabited a cave apparently, in the hills behind the Tomb of Rach-El, just outside Beit Lechem. Women who were unable to conceive went there to ask Rach-El to intervene on their behalf with Sarah (by whom, of course, they really mean Asherah), and help them to get pregnant; women in pregnancy went there to ask that parturition might not kill or cripple them, and that the child be both healthy and male; women took their new-born babies there to thank the goddess with a gift-offering of the navel string. But others visited the shrine as well, and not for Rach-El, but for the ba'alat ov. It was said her name was Devorah, and that she had power over the many snakes with whom she shared her cave - though I have always been a sceptic in this matter, Shlomo, for snakes do not have ears, so how can they hear the music of the hallil and be charmed by it? And besides, I lived for months with rock-snakes in the Cave of Adullam, and found them far more frightened of men than we ever were of them. Still, men believe, and women more so, what it suits them to believe, and there is little to be gained from reasoning. When the spirit possessed her, she became a soothsayer, whose predictions were neither oracular nor prophetic, though by all accounts exact. She sang all manner of mantras and incantations, in languages for the most part of her own invention. All manner of miracles were attributed to her. Eli-Av was firm in his conviction that she could heal the sick.

"I will not have such a woman in this house."

When father was adamant, he was seriously adamant.

"She doesn't need to come into the house. Tamar's outside."

Facetiousness was unlikely to change his opinion either.

"She will lie in bed for seven days. That is the law for the sick. Her sin will become known in that time, and we shall make sacrifice to expiate it."

Eli-Av shaking his head in consternation at this superstition, almost as firmly as father had just shaken his head at Eli-Av's.

"Your brothers and sisters can play gentle music to her, to refresh her spirit. She will abstain from water and improper foods."

Which form of ignorance was the better, which the worse? My sense of all physicians, even the most sophisticated, is that they feed you chemical compounds and cut off your parts, because that's all they know to do; and in the end you die of something anyway. And as to Tamar. She had grown intolerably thin and frail. Insects crawled on her flesh, but she simply lacked the strength to rid herself of them. Mosquitoes were the worst, because they added disease to disease. Her face was leprous with white lumps of mosquito bites. Her prettiness was ruined.

"Daoud, play for me."

Improvisations in a minor key. Anything else would have been inappropriate to the ambience of doom and gloom and sadness she pervaded. At times I could hardly hold the kinnor for weeping for her.

"Shall I bring you a new lamp."

"Thank you."

That too was fundamental to her innocence. That even in the worst of times she remained courteous, tender, mindful of others. With Tamar all moments were moments of civilised behaviour. All through my life I have yearned to repeat them. It is, surely, the most that we can really ask of life.

I brought her the lamp. Probably she had cut the wick herself, weeks ago, which added a certain poignancy. Do you know these peasant lamps, Shlomo? Simple pottery dishes with a lip at one side, small enough to carry in your hand if you need to. Because it was so dark inside the house we kept lamps permanently lit on stands and in niches in the walls. You poured olive oil or animal fat into the dish and laid a wick made of flax or rag from the lip. It could stay alight for up to three hours. Longer than Tamar. She had lit up our lives for fourteen years. But now she flamed for half or maybe a whole hour - and then died.

We buried her the way they buried the nephilim in times gone by, a simple inhumation, neither shroud nor box, just placed her body in a shallow hole, with a few clay jars of grain, one or two of the bead necklaces she had made, a cutting from her hair - gifts for Tammuz when she came to him in She'ol. When it came my turn to throw earth over her, I secretly planted a single wick of flax, vertically, the way you might plant a cutting from a flower to ensure it rooted. I had dipped the stalk in lamb's-tail fat, as if somehow this might preserve it, even make it fertile, so the wick would blossom into light that could illuminate her journey through the underworld. I had never cried so much in all my seven years.

☆

The roof-room was built by grandfather Oved as an observatory. The little shrine of Tammuz which gave Beit Lechem its name had come into the custodianship of our family in great-grandfather Bo'az's time. He it was who harvested considerable wealth from several years of the most copious corn crop, and in gratitude to the god he offered to replace the gnarled and chipped stone teraphim with new ones, to plant a new date-tree above the ancient mound amongst whose many skeletons the bones of Tammuz were said to lie entombed, and to cede, not just the corner of his field that was required by law to feed the poor, and the tenth part of his wealth for the Priests of Yahweh and the Bene Levi, but a corner of his own threshing-floor each year to serve the cult. The gift was gratefully accepted, and in its place Bo'az received the honour of being appointed priest, an honour that he didn't take seriously at all, other than in the exalted social status that it gave him. Great-grandfather loved only one thing better than wealth, and that was the trappings wealth could purchase. Why else was the tale of his marriage to Ruth set down in a pageant, to be retold, re-enacted, every year?

But when he came to inherit the mantle from his father, grandfather Oved accepted the burden of priesthood with a very different heart. His actual duties in relation to the shrine were negligible and entirely vague, amounting to little more than a scrupulous tending of the palm tree, a gathering in and distributing of its annual fruit, votive offerings on festive days to the stone teraphim, and ensuring that the threshing-floor was free of tares both before and after the winnowing - before lest any darnel get into the grain, after lest any animals should feed on it, for the tares were as poisonous as foxglove. But he had been ceremonially anointed as a priest of Tammuz, and he saw it as his personal responsibility to carry out the functions of a priest, whatever they might be. Hence the planetarium on the roof, and the detailed records of the movements of the stars and planets that he kept, so that he was able to inform us of the rising of the moon and second star that announced the Sabbath and the festivals even before we had seen the beacons on the hills. Hence the camel trains sent off to Pharat bearing anything that might be saleable, with explicit instructions to bring back, not gold, not jewels, not perishable commodities, but knowledge. Our forefather Av-Ram came from Ur on the Euphrates - bring me details of the city, its cult, its shrines, the clothes its priesthood wears, its rites, its customs. Our Law of Abou Mousa is said to bear resemblance to the Law of Hammurabi of Bav-El of the Bene Kessed - bring me a parchment copy if one is to be found, a clay tablet if it's affordable. Our Lord Tammuz is worshipped as the corn, but also as the sun - and in Habiru the word for sun is shemesh, which is remarkably similar to Tammuz; and Shimshon is the corn and sun-god amongst the Bene Dan; and Tammuz is the name we give to the month when the sun is at its zenith. This can't all be coincidence. Bring me word of the language they speak, and seek out especially other common terms. And what of the star-gazers of Bav-El? Do they keep records of their observations? Are they aware that we have passed out of the Age of the Bull, and entered the Age of the Ram? And did they witness the fiery comet that stood still in the sky for seven weeks last year? His enthusiasms were boundless. And not just for Bav-El. How much of the fortune he inherited was spent on seeking wisdom out of Ashur and Mitsrayim? I might have grown up rich in goods had it not been for grandfather Oved; but had I done so, I would have grown up poor indeed in knowledge.

"You've heard, Daoud, many times, the life of Tammuz. How he was born under a tamarisk-palm, exactly as the one the Bene Ashur and our own cousins the Bene Asher call Adonis, exactly as the one the Bene Mitsrayim call Osher and the Bene Cheret Osiris. How he died after being gored by a wild boar, who tore his body into fourteen parts, which the jackals scattered. I have spoken to priests of the Bene Mitsrayim, and I will tell you the tale of Osher, and you'll see that it's really the tale of Tammuz, and that all tales are really the same tale."

As all of grandfather Oved's tales ended with that verdict. But in the lamp-lit darkness of his roof-room, with the entire firmament of the heavens stretched out above my head, such intellectual rhetoric meant nothing. He was a master of the art of story-telling, his voice mesmeric, his intonations poetry. I would happily have listened to him giving details of the weather.

"Osher was the son of Geb - yes, the same Geb that we know from the shrines of Giv-Yah and Giv-On. To the Bene Mitsrayim, Geb was the earth-god, who fathered Osher upon Nut the sky-goddess whom the Bene Kena'an call Anat, along with his sister-wife Eshet, whom we call Ishah or Isis. Together these two children planted the first wheat and barley, were the first to gather ripe fruit from the trees, cultivated the first vines. But Osher's brother Shet - yes, the same Shet who we say was born to the earth-god Adam and the mother-of-all-living Chava as the son of their redemption - this Shet whose sister-wife was the goddess Nebethet, was jealous of his virtue and his fame, and sought his death. He made a box from water-reeds and willows, caulked it with bitumen so it could float, and threw a party in his brother's honour. Once Osher was drunk, Shet called for a game of hide-and-find, and persuaded Osher to conceal himself inside the box. Then he nailed up the box and threw it in the Nile, where it floated among the bulrushes and out to sea, until it was washed ashore on the northern coast of Kinnahu, near Bav-El of the Bene Chet, which we call Ugarit. Where the coffin came to rest, a tamarisk tree grew up, but King Melchart and Queen Ishtar smelled the sweet savour of the tree, and ordered it cut down to serve as a pillar in their palace.

"Eshet was overwhelmed with grief, cut off her hair, put on sackcloth of mourning, and sought her brother everywhere, until at last she came to Bav-El of the Bene Chet and heard of the tree. She sat down by a well in humble disguise, speaking to no one until the queen's handmaidens came by; and when they did she breathed her sacred fragrance upon them to entrance the queen, who summoned her to nurse the new-born child who had been found in the willow-basket by the date-tree - Osher magically reborn. So she suckled the child, not on her breast but on her finger, and placed him in a fire to burn away his mortal parts. Only Queen Ishtar caught her, and dragged the child away from her, denying it thus the gift of immortality that the fire would otherwise have bestowed."

It was a long, long tale, and there was much, much more to tell. But I had long stopped listening. Grandfather Oved wanted me to understand that this was really Tammuz in some odd disguise - and not only because Ishtar was indeed the name of Tammuz's mother - that in some obscure way the myths of Tammuz and Osher and Adonis were all one. But it was of none of these that I was thinking.

"Grandfather," I interrupted him, "didn't Abou Mousa also float on the Nile in a box made out of water-reeds and bulrushes and caulked with bitumen?"

"Indeed he did, Daoud."

"And wasn't Abou Mousa also wet-nursed by his sister at the queen's behest?"

"Indeed he was, Daoud."

"And wasn't he scalded by hot coals when he was young, and later on denied the gift of immortality."

"Indeed, Daoud. Indeed."

"What happened to Osher next, grandfather?"

"Nothing that you'll be able to compare with Abou Mousa, I'm afraid. But with our own Tammuz, that's another matter. Osher's boat was put out again to sea by the hand of Eshet, who accompanied it all the way back to the river Nile. One night of the full moon, while hunting boar, his brother Shet came upon him and, disguising himself as a boar, gored Osher in the thigh and tore him into fourteen pieces, which he scattered to the four winds. Eshet gathered all the gods to help her find her brother-spouse. First she asked his brother Hor" - I didn't interrupt to tell him he was wrong, but here already was another fragment of the tale of Abou Mousa, for what else was his brother's name but Aharon; and who held up Abou Mousa's arms against the Bene Amalek but a man of the Bene Hor? - but I didn't interrupt to tell him all of this, because of course he knew it well enough already.

"First she asked his brother Hor, whose head was a hawk and whose symbol was a golden bull-calf. Then she asked Anpu the son of Nebethet, whose head was a jackal. Then Zehuti the moon-god, whose head was sometimes an ibis, sometimes a baboon. Between them they found all the parts of Osher save only his sexual organ, which a fish had swallowed. They bound his body in bandages, and performed the rites that are now the rites of the dead kings, and Eshet fanned him with her wings until he revived. And to this day he sits in the Hall of the Twin Truths, in the land of the dead of which he is the overlord..."

All tales, grandfather Oved believed, had their echoes in other tales. The tales of the gods as much as those of men. And later, several years later, was it perhaps from this foundation that I found it so easy to accept the teachings of Shmu-El my master, when he asked me to believe that all gods were really the same god, parts or attributes of the same One god, the Omnideity? I think my grandfather Oved had already intuited the same understanding.

"Can you count, Daoud?"

He never asked simple questions, so I had to presume this one was cryptic.

"In letters and in numbers," I replied, meaning only to show off that I was equal to his tricks.

"It was in letters and in numbers that I meant. How do you spell fifteen?"

"With the numbers ten and five, which are the letters Yud and Heh."

"And what do Yud and Heh spell, that we don't use them to spell fifteen, but use nine and six, Tet and Vav, instead?"

"The name of our god."

"Which name, Daoud? Which god? Not Tammuz, clearly."

"Yah, grandfather."

"Yah, the goddess of the full moon, grandfather. As in Abou Yah-Akov our ancestor, and in Hallelu-Yah may Yah be praised that my grandson Yedid-Yah has learned his lessons. What day of the month is the full moon, Daoud?"

"The fifteenth, grandfather."

"Indeed it is. Indeed indeed it is. And did you also know that, in the legends of the Bene Chet who brought the worship of Yah to Kena'an, her husband is none other than the sun-god Ephron. Where have you heard that name before?"

I thought and thought. Eventually I placed it.

"When Emet Sarah died, Abou Raham bought a burial place for her, by the terebinth oaks of Mamre, in the double cave of Machpelah, by Kiryat Ye'arim outside Chevron. He bought the land from Ephron of the Bene Chet."

"Very good, Daoud. Very good. Sarah, of course, is Asherah of the Bene Aram - the difference is simply one of dialect, but both names mean 'princess'. I have heard from men who have travelled beyond the Land of the Two Rivers, to the land of Hodu where the spices you love so much are grown" - I was chewing, as ever, on dried patchouli seeds, even as he said it – "They too have their stories of the gods. They too have their three patriarchs, who were grandfather, father and son. Their first father, like ours, is named the Great Father, and their language is remarkably close to ours. Do you know how they say Great Father among the Hodu, Daoud?"

"Av-Ram, grandfather?"

"Very nearly, Daoud. Very nearly. They say Brahma."

And as always, at the termination of these intellectual voyages that were officially known as "telling my favourite grandson a goodnight story", as always he smiled with devastating humility, and wondered out loud, "perhaps I am making connections where there are really no connections to be made. But we must ask, Daoud. Because it is better than fighting wars and ploughing barren fields. Now sleep. And dream of Tammuz reborn. And may he give you dates in great abundance."

He meant, "may he give you wealth in whatever form you cherish." It was the one and only piece of liturgy that grandfather Oved contributed to the shrine.

The Valley of Chevron is the most fertile valley in all the southern regions, but, other than the underground sources, there is very little by way of water to feed it, and so irrigation is strictly limited; there are simply no rivers and few springs to draw from. For our vineyards and orchards close to the town we were able to tap spring water; where it rose close to the surface we could conduct it into stone-built holding tanks and plaster-lined channels. But elsewhere you were in the lap of the gods, and the annual prayers for rain - mashiv ha ru'ach u-morid ha gashem - were pronounced with a solemnity bred of the most desperate hope.

All the arable and pasture land around Beit Lechem was owned in common by the village, shared out on annual basis by the village elders to ensure that nobody could become excessively rich or poor, and not because anyone minded wealth as such - quite the contrary, it is the one dream that unites all human beings - but because wealth does terrible things to people, because wealth bestows arbitrary power, because wealth creates castes. In great-grandfather Bo'az's time they still gave out land according to the jubilee, which is why he was able to enjoy his seven years of plenty and became so very rich. But, as if by way of compensation, first he after his seven years ended and the distribution in the meanwhile had become annual, and then grandfather Oved when he inherited after Bo'az's sudden and untimely death, found themselves repeatedly allocated some of the very poorest land. Had Bo'az not used a good part of his wealth to establish orchards and vineyards - needing generations to cultivate a viable crop, these were exempt from the annual distribution - we might have struggled to make any sort of living for ourselves at all.

People given land among the foothills subsisted by dry-farming, dependent on natural rainfall. Those who received their portion in the highlands, which had once been forest but were now goat-tramped into little more than barren moorland, carved stone terraces filled with soil out of the hills and strip-farmed whatever was amenable to cultivation. Hill farming was hard work, and far more labour intensive than in the plains.

But hardest of all was the desert floor. For several years of my earliest childhood, we were given land in the foothills, and being lucky with the rainfall, flourished. But in three of those years we had little more than strips of gorse and bracken, acreages of stones in which even the scorpions and rock-snakes found it hard to feed and drink, a wilderness of red clay so far dried out and crumbled it might just as well have been sand. Down there in the wadis there was nothing else to do but flood-farm. We - we? my father, my elder brothers - dug out wells of natural water that sand-storms and mud-flows had filled in; probably the same wells that Abou Yitschak spent a lifetime endlessly digging and redigging to feed his flocks. Or we made artificial wells, digging immense cisterns down into the rocky undersoil, lining them with mortar of ash and lime, and catching as much water as we could when the flash floods of winter brought the wadis briefly back to life. And then spent the rest of the year eking out the water drop by frugal drop, hoping it wouldn't evaporate in the summer heat or simply turn stagnant and be rendered useless. Those three years did more to prepare me for kingship, Shlomo, than any other lessons I have ever learned.

But those three years were also an exception, and even though they were hard, we never in our family experienced the real poverty that comes with drought and famine, when people sit down on the rocks around their home, stare out into the dust of dried out corn and barley, the black beads of grapes and olives that have withered on the stalk, the empty udders of the milk-ewes, and seeing the ribs in their children's abdomens visibly grey beneath translucent skin, simply give up living for the sheer despondency of knowing that there's nothing they can do. I have seen that, Shlomo, I have witnessed that - too often, far too often. But mercifully, in our family, we were never reduced that low ourselves.

✡

For very different reasons, both great-grandfather Bo'az and grandfather Oved loved to trade, and would have abandoned farming for some easier and more profitable occupation if they had been able. But my father, Yishai, was a born farmer, who loved nothing better than to be up with the dawn, and still up when the sun set, undertaking however many tiny jobs his neighbours hired labourers or sent their children to do for them. He rode his slow ass round the perimeters of his "estate" for hour after hour, checking wells or dry-stone hedges, supervising the loading of the market-carts, digging his hawthorn-staff into the soil to test its water, leaning on a gate to moan about the price of mutton, forever taking off and putting back his white bernous after shaking out of it the grit of dust and sand.

That bernous that always framed his head, also frames the picture of him in my mind's eye. White linen speckled grey like one of Abou Yah-Akov's sheep, he wore it wrapped like a scarf under his chin in the Bedou fashion, the woollen circlet that fixed it to his scalp hidden under a fold of cloth where it was draped over his forehead and down his back. All you could see was the great triangle of his nose, jutting out above the shadow of his black moustache. The moustache was so thick it hid his mouth, as the nose and the fringe of the bernous hid his eyes, so it seemed half of his features must have fallen victim to some leprosy - or that he was about to take up banditry. He was by no means ugly - though I don't imagine mother would have chosen him for his looks, had it been a matter of her choosing. Gnarled, I think is the word. Tall and gangling and very thin, he talked in a deep, guttural voice, croaking his consonants like a man spitting out catarrh. Or actually spitting. Where I chew patchouli, he always chewed sunflower seeds. If father stayed still in one place for very long, a circle of husks from the sunflower seeds would rise around him, the way dust gathers on old ruins and weeds around an olive tree.

Father tried his hand at everything - well, almost everything. We were too far from the sea to catch the murex snails for producing dyes; too far from marsh-water to collect sedge and rushes for

71

papyrus; too poor to own a train of camels, though we had donkeys in abundance; and the region was too hot and dry to farm fish or make textiles. We did experiment with pistachios one year, and with sycamore figs, and we always got a good crop of dates and pomegranates from the wild palms and bushes in addition to our cultivated trees, but mostly it was staple diet farming: grain, olives and grapes, fruit and vegetables, bee-honey, almonds, livestock. And of these, though you counted your wealth in livestock, you earned it in barley and corn.

The grain was planted by broadcasting on ploughed soil, a great ceremony that occupied most of the village for a week at least, half of us rushing around throwing corn into the wind or each other's faces, the other half looking as if they were making spurious experiments in human flight, though what they were actually seeking was to drive the real birds into the air. You could spend a day broadcasting a field of corn, and turn your back for half an hour, by which time the jays and crows and ravens would have stripped it bare.

Ah, Shlomo, we all look back with terrible nostalgia on our childhoods, we all yearn for the pleasures of the pastoral life as a counterpoint to urban living, and the truth is we are mostly filling our hearts and souls and minds with self-delusions. People speak of the dangers of the city, but I would far rather leave my children untended in the market than the garden. Snakes, scorpion, dirty water; farm implements like scythes and mattocks sharp enough to sever a limb; wild boar with tusks like spears; mountain-lion; a witch's cauldron of poisonous herbs and shrubs and plants that look so pretty yet kill so fast. Foxes and jackals. There is nothing more certain to take your life eventually than Mother Nature, not even the cruellest of men. So I acknowledge all the delusions - yet still I say, that I would give up tomorrow all the cares of state and all the opulence of this royal palace, for the chance to spend a summer farming in the Chevron Valley, or flocking in the hills above Beit Lechem. So you must forgive a touch of mawkish sentiment, and indulge me in my self-indulgence.

Once the seed was safely in the ground, it was a matter of hoeing for tares, of mattocking out any heavy stones that might threaten the roots of the growing sheaves. I have always loved to watch things grow: poems, plants, human souls. To sit and measure in my mind's eye how much change has taken place since the last time I looked, seeing new sprouts, seeing the male and female stalks appear, watching the first ears form on the skulls of the vegetation. When it came to harvest time the whole community took part, every farmer helping every other farmer by rotation. We harvested with sickles, hour after hour till your shoulder wept. The grain was gathered up by hand and taken to a threshing-floor, a flat open space of beaten earth, where the sheaves could be spread out. An ox pulled a heavy wooden sledge, studded underneath with jagged flints, in circles over the grain, cutting the straw and crunching the husks that were then placed in a broad, flat winnowing basket and tossed in the wind to shed the lighter chaff. We used that lighter chaff in brickmaking and pottery. From the corn-stalks we made brooms. But of course the grain was what Beit Lechem Ephratah was really all about - the corn-god, Tammuz. Every spring, on the feast of Ishtar, we cooked eggs and painted their shells to represent the resurrection of the world, and His conception. Every mid-winter's morning we gathered in the mangers with the new-born lambs, to witness His miraculous rebirth among the straw. Every harvest time we came like murderers, intent upon His sacrifice, armed with scythes to cut Him down. And at the festival of Pesach, Shlomo, the festival of the limping-god, we took the jars in which we stored the grain from the threshing-floor of Beit Lechem Ephratah to that of Ornah of the Bene Yevus, and made the corn-bread without leaven, as Abou Mousa taught us, and recalled how He was gored in the thigh by the tusk of a wild boar, betrayed by His brother Shet. And the women sat up through the nights, weeping and wailing at the doorway of his tomb. On Mount Mor-Yah, Shlomo. On Mount Mor-Yah. Three nights, between the last sight of the waning moon and the first sight of the new moon, the time of his sojourn in the underworld, and of his ascent into the heavens. Hallelu-Yah.

Did I ever show you the very first song I wrote - or carved, to be exact? In the days before song, for me at least, became entirely a matter of composing liturgy, I used to tackle all manner of subjects, inspired by whatever took my fancy. Fleeting friendships. Old stone ruins left behind by past invaders, whether Ach-Mousa or the five kings of Shinar. The starry firmament. Wind among the hollows of the hills - usually ending with some idiot baa-lamb gambolling once too exuberantly and falling straight over a cliff-edge like Azaz-El. Poetry. Poetry. Some of it set to music. And then this, not made up and forgotten like the other juvenilia, but cut with a chisel into some vast slab of granite, black as the mood that summons poetry. I must have fancied myself like Abou Mousa, carving his Law in stone that it might endure forever, imagining my poem of the same order, but lacking for the purpose only the divine sapphire. It took me days. No doubt, somewhere up there in the hills of Rephayim, you could probably still find it if you were of a mind to look.

I had been learning my letters. Such formal schooling as I did not receive from grandfather Oved, I got like most boys from my mother, but it was grandfather's advanced lessons that had inspired me. Mother taught me the names of the letters, how to use them as numbers, how to draw them with a stylus on wax. My brother Shammah had learned how to carve them in clay, and he passed that skill on to me as well. But grandfather Oved taught me the meanings of the letters, and that - though I had no idea at the time - is an esoteric magic known to very few.

Poetry is like wisdom is like wine - you lay down a small quantity of what seems ordinary enough, and some time later you remember it, by when it has matured from mere fermented grape juice into serious nectar. So I learned my letters, and had no use for them whatever since the only use intended was the study of the Law, and how many boys of seven eight nine ten are bothered to study what they have absolutely no intention of obeying? But up in the hills, among the ruined forts and abandoned sheep-folds, on dolmen and megalithic rocks, on tree-trunks even, on scraps of parchment stuffed in clay jars and concealed by someone who presumably intended to return but never did - up there, amid my thoughts and songs, amid interminable silences, I learned at last the awesome power, and not just of the letters, but of words.

Just north of the Valley of Rephayim I had found a cave, where I used regularly to take the sheep when it was lambing time and the weather had closed in. Today I can't mention the damned place without the whole world crying out in recognition, as though it were the pilgrim site to end all pilgrim sites which everyone claims to have visited though practically no one has. Adullam, I mean - the cave of my bandit years. But then it wasn't "the cave where Daoud trained his army and led his revolt against Sha'ul", or whatever it is that people say about it. It was just a cave. Damp, dark, dirty, smelly - a home from home indeed! - but full of bats and snakes and especially spiders, a cave longer and deeper than anyone in their right mind dared explore, full of the most tumultuous echoes. When sheep inevitably strayed, I took a tallow candle and went, somewhat tentatively, in search of them. But they were as timid as I was about penetrating what could have been the abode of Tohu and Bohu, the primordial beasts of darkest nothingness. It was very scary. But exhilarating too. I had found old bones, of sheep mostly, but also bear, hyena, other bones I couldn't recognise but some of which I would swear were human. And on the walls, though you could hardly make them out for age and darkness, paintings of nephilim - ancient troglodytic men who must have lived in the cave a thousand years before. Black marks on the walls suggested fire. Circular arrangements of stones, too wide apart for fires, made me think of the great stone circle at Gil-Gal where I had gone with father once to hear the annual reading of the Law. A sacred cave, no doubt about it; a place of oracles and the burial ground of ancient kings. Eerie shivers tingled up and down your spine. A boy of eight or nine, as I was, could easily succumb to fantasies of one day being holed up in a cave like this with fellow bandits!

How much did I understand then; how much have I added to my understanding in the years since, when I spent so many very different hours and days and weeks inside that cave? I don't know. But even as a child I had the sense of something strangely magical inside that cave, the smell of death on all those bones, yet something living and enduring too, in shards of pottery you accidentally kicked out of the dust, in dreams at night in which the shades of nephilim came back to haunt you. I used to see the paintings on the cave-walls, come to life inside my dreams: the great hunts, the stories I thought of as grandfather Oved's stories, acted out before me, rendered in blood. The killing of the boar especially, the sacred aleph, the boar who gored Adonis in the thigh, the boar who was finally caught and butchered, thrown on the sacrificial fire, the boar we eat as holy eucharist on the festival of Ishtar in the spring, and whose flesh is tabu on any other day. The god-boar, the murderer of Tammuz resurrected.

But what has all of this to do with learning my aleph-bet or writing down my poems? In that cave, on those hills, witnessing the sunrise or the sunset, turning inwards upon myself in all that solitude and beauty and aloneness, inspired by tree-shape or landscape, by flying bird or creeping snake...for me, Shlomo, what men call "religious experience" is not a matter of "belief in Yah and Yahweh", but of the inner self. The same intensity of inwardness may be achieved in prayer, by incantation, in love, by the bank of a river, in watching a falling star, by playing the kinnor - a thousand forms of inspiration that engender the mood we call poetry, by any one of several thousand names. So I flocked, and thought, and dreamed, and played - and wrote poems in my head from morn till night. And one day, happening into the Cave of Adullam at a time of year when normally I flocked much further south, the angle of the sunlight focused on a patch of the cave wall that had always previously been in darkness. It was covered, over a space no more than half a cubit wide or long, in the tiniest of picture-words, wonderfully carved: the telling of a lover's tale no doubt, or the misery of some concealed outcast. But not in any aleph-bet I knew. These were the letters of the priests and Pharaohs of the Bene Mitsrayim, though I didn't know it until I got home and could draw a few from memory for my grandfather.

"This is the goddess Hat-Hor receiving an offering."

Sha'ul's secret police never undertook detective work with quite the pleasure this was bringing him.

"I can't read the next bit. This says 'maryanu' which means 'noblemen'..."

I was convinced that he was making up his explanations as he went along. All I could see was a picture of a woman with the horns of a cow, a group of men with triangular heads, a bird sitting on a line, some pillars, all of it interspersed with various notches, scores, marks, embellishments and imprints. Imprints - they could have been footprints, made by some nesting bird before the rock set! But no, grandfather was adamant, this was writing, writing of a most serious and important kind indeed, and not for what it said, but for the fact that it existed, ancient archaeology committed into his hands. He made me promise to draw the whole inscription when I next went back, but I never did, and mercifully he forgot.

"Of course our letters have meanings too," he added, dare I say conspiratorially.

He had the look of someone who had just betrayed a secret. Or was about to do so.

"Each letter stands for a number, but also for an object."

And he told me all of them, and I learned them by heart, and over the next few weeks I put them all together in a riddling poem, and over quite a few weeks more I carved it on that block of granite in the hills of Rephayim. Years later I wrote it on wax as well, and have given it to many people to see if they could decipher it. Only one person ever worked the secret out. Shmu-El. And now it's yours, if you want it. It goes like this:

My first is the antelope-ox, but also the sacred boar
My second two houses, your's and Yah's
My third is three camels, each with two legs
My fourth four doors, but only one key

My fifth is the lattices of five open windows
My sixth six hooks, held by two nails
My seventh is weaponry, a cock, seven spears
My eighth two squares of fencing and hedge
My ninth is the serpent of the ninefold goddess
My tenth the ten fingers that make a hand

My next is a palm, the wings of a bird, twentyfold
My next an ox-goad, wielded thirtyfold
My next is the water, full forty waves
My next enough fish to fathom a quinquereme
My next is a prop to sustain two full months
My next the eye of the seventy gods
My next speaks the number of eighty closed mouths
My next wields the handles of ninety blunt scythes
My next is the hole in the hundredfold axe
My next is the source of two hundred heads

Then three hundred teeth last three hundred moons
And four hundred crosses are the branding of an ass

My eldest brothers were away at one of those shambolic military travesties that Sha'ul called his wars - I forget which one, but Aphek probably, where Avi-Nadav lost his ring-finger to an iron sword and then his silly wife accused him of seeking in this way to divorce her - when Avi-Gayil, my eldest sister, was married to a farmer of the Bene Yishma-El of Rechovot, and went to join his tribe. Interesting lot, the Bene Yishma-El, Bedou really, in the strictest sense, men of the desert, intrepid solitaries. Has it ever struck you how a man's inner life reflects his outer geography, and how often people are unhappy simply because they live in the wrong place? Abou Yeter belonged in the wilderness, alone with his wife, his camels, his gourd of water and the god whose worship occupied the long hours of his silences. Never was a man quite so content with his lot. When we went to visit them for the ceremonies of the first-born, I watched him squatting on his haunches for the best part of two days, whittling a piece of cane, never moving except occasionally to brush away a fly or check the fire in the hollow of the clay-oven. Avi-Gayil was straining and screaming, screaming and straining, but he just squatted there, confident that it would be a boy, and healthy, and that his woman would survive this and a dozen future parturitions. Was it not written in the destiny of a woman to give birth in agony? Had we not split a pomegranate on the threshold of the bridal-tent to ensure fruition? Could I not find patience and be sure the bread would cook in its own time?

"It is time to place the stones."

When the Bedou women give birth, their men place two stones slightly apart for them to sit on, so they can remain upright during the procedure. Then they leave. Abou Yeter had sat for two long days waiting for this moment, but when it came he simply stood up, placed the stones, commended my mother to the gods for her midwifery, and wandered off, no doubt to tend his flock at some far end of the wadi. I watched him disappear into the distance, black against the sunlight on the desert, leading a camel and carrying nothing but his gourd and knife. He stayed away for three whole days - time enough to wash the new-born baby, rub its flesh in salt, wrap it in swaddling-clothes, name it for its great-grandfather, Amasa, and circumcise it. Time enough to bury its mother, who had not survived.

✡

Parchment Two

This, then, was the small world in which I grew up. But there was also the big world, Shlomo, and since Beit Lechem was a pilgrim-town at corn time and at the winter solstice, since it lay at the side of one of the great trade roads and served as a caravanserai for travellers and merchants, we were never long out of touch with the bigger world...

So. I began to talk to you about your kingdom. I quoted the words of Abou Mousa. Let me repeat them:

"Then Av-Ram took Sarai his wife, and Lot his brother's son, and all the substance they had gathered, and the souls they had acquired in Charan, and they came into the land of the Bene Kena'an. And Av-Ram passed through the land as far as Shechem, and settled in the Plain of Moreh. And the Bene Kena'an ruled the land. And the Lord appeared to Av-Ram and said: 'To your descendants will I give this land'. And there he built an altar to the Lord who had appeared to him."

The beginning, as I think I said, of everything. And also the goal that we must pursue unto the very bitter end as well - oh yes, all ends are bitter, Shlomo; it is the will of Yah and Yahweh who together made the world, that all creation ends in uncreation. But the land, my prince. The land. Signed and sealed in legal covenant, witnessed by rainbow and burning bush, carved with a quill of sapphire, so they say, whetted with the knife of circumcision. Ours to inhabit until eternity is reduced to manageable numbers. Or until our neighbours challenge our right to do so, with force of arms.

But I issued a challenge of my own - and you have had the time of reading several columns of parchment to discern an answer to it. What - have you failed to find one? As I predicted! Boundaries, Shlomo; boundaries and borders. Defined for the most part by oath-stones and cairns of witness; which is judicially absurd, because any wandering vagabond can pick up an oath-stone lying on the ground, unaware of the significance of its existence, and move it for convenience a hundred paces east or west; any man with a house to build and a need for a solid buttress can lasso a dolmen to an ox and drag it homewards; any man with a burning cinder in his hand can have an accident with a carefully drawn map. Borders are not defined in court, Shlomo, any more than they are in fence or hedge. Borders are defined in garrisons.

So, with judicious use of the census information that has caused everyone but me such consternation, let me define for you some very specific boundaries.

The land which we Bene Yisra-El inhabit has always been a land of the most disparate peoples, and so the first lesson you must learn is this: do not govern in the name of the Bene Yisra-El alone, but be a king to all the people. All? But how many is all? I hear you ask - and rightly so, which is why I demanded that we take the census. So many, and so very disparate, and each with his own infinitude of gods and goddesses, that in truth we are pressing at the very borders of language and the boundaries of credibility when we try to impose a common name. Why, the descendants of Abou Kena'an alone include the Bene Tsidon, Bene Chet, Bene Yevus, Bene Girgash, Bene Arvad, Bene Chamat, Bene Tsemar - have I missed a dozen? And what about the Chivim, the Arkim, the Sinim of Mount Lavan? What about the Amorim of the eastern mountains, the Chorim of the central hills - I ask, Shlomo, because you must ask: did any of these choose us to be their king? What about the Bedou? What about the Bene Mitsrayim and the Bene Ashur, who came to conquer, and remained behind after their garrisons were taken? And what about the Bene Pelet - now there, there really is a question? What about the Bene Pelet? Yisra-El indeed! One representative of each group would fill the marble hall of the Palace of Tsi'on more full than all the ambassadors of all the foreign nations put together.

Grandfather Oved was the expert on all this, of course. Between pointing at the stars and telling me the myths, it was history history history all the way. Did you know, for example, that this land was called Kinnahu in the language of the Bene Chor, long before Adam and Chava begat Shet who begat Enosh who begat Abou Kena'an who supposedly bequeathed his name? Or that the Bene Chem of Mitsrayim also claim Kena'an as their own? Or that Kinnahu means purple - ask our friend Hu-Ram about that, because he calls his land "purple" too, and for the same reason; I am not good at pronouncing the tongue of the Bene Chet, though their aleph-bet is identical to ours: Phoinikia, have I got it right? And did you know that the Bene Chet, in the days when their empire stretched from the Bull

Mountains to Mitsrayim, called Kena'an Retenu, a name whose meaning even grandfather Oved was never able to discover?

So, Shlomo, a name. Your task for homework. A plausible and convincing name. An improvement if you can on Yisra-El. But please, not Ephrayim - it took me thirty years to persuade the northern tribes that they couldn't have two confederations, that in joining Yisra-El they had to discard Ephrayim. That name is dust now.

Then what shall it be? You could always try Arets ha-Habiru, as Abou Mousa did - one of the very few interesting things Natan has ever said to me, was to note that in all the tales that Abou Mousa wrote down, on all five of his great tablets, he himself never used the name Habiru, though he put it frequently into the mouths of other people. Should we then discard it, as being theirs, not ours? Grandfather Oved said it was the name coined by the Bene Mitsrayim for the Bene Chet. But it's a name that I refuse to use. Do you know its meaning? The Bene Mitsrayim of today will tell you it means "beyond the river", from "avar" meaning "to cross". But which river? Abou Yah-Suph ruled in Goshen - which is several hundred miles east of the Nile, and if you can find me any other river between the Nile and the Yavok, I shall be pleased to go and bathe in it and hope to cure myself of incredulity. No, Shmu-El discovered the answer - the calumny, I should say. When the Bene Chet conquered Mitsrayim, they ruled from Goshen, and they called their capital Avar, which the Bene Mitsrayim pronounced Habar. But because the Bene Mitsrayim hated being ruled by foreigners and dreamed of overthrowing them, Habiru became a term of abuse; by Abou Mousa's time it denoted anyone who came from "over there" - in other words, the foreigners, by then the slaves, the outcasts, the lepers, the generally ostracised, and most especially the Bene Chet. It is one of the tragic ironies of our history, that because Abou Yah-Suph rose to greatness under a Pharaoh of the Bene Chet, we the Bene Yisra-El are ostracised as Habiru and doomed for ever to bear the insult of that name.

What do you mean, Shlomo - does all this matter? Of course it matters. You cannot be a king without a realm, and realms are not nebulous geographic regions with disputed names. Of course it matters. You cannot unify and cohere and galvanise a people who are unsure if their neighbours are their best friends or their enemies, and who don't even know what to call the central focus of their lives. Land, capital city, law and god. The four cornerstones, Shlomo, that define a nation. Why do you think I planned so painstakingly the formal announcements of Yeshurun and Yiru-Sala'am?

Anyway, it's Erets Yisra-El now - by royal decree! And its borders? Ah, Shlomo, when the legal wording is vague, the decision rests not with the judge who sits in court, but with the king who has placed him there and who commands the army that will keep him there. Yours is the authority and the power now. It's up to you to define your own borders for your own kingdom - as I have done, and will continue doing - until they are sufficient. Or until you no longer have the power.

And where does power come from? Natan will tell you it comes directly from El Elyon, the god of gods, whom we call Yahweh - or indirectly actually, via Natan himself, but let's not digress into theological controversy. Remember how Sha'ul lost his power? Because he defied Shmu-El and disobeyed Yahweh, refusing to cut off the head of king Agag. So runs the dogma anyway. And yet Sha'ul did not cease reigning, just because Shmu-El withdrew smicha. No, he kept his throne right up until his death. But power, real, meaningful power, the power to command souls, and not just bodies - that he lost.

Think about it, Shlomo. The Bene Amalek controlled the whole of Chavila as far south as Shur on the borders of Mitsrayim, and were bound by treaty to the Bene Kayin of the central Negev. Shmu-El ordered him, on the basis of a blood-feud from the time of Abou Mousa, to lop off the head of Agag. But kill the king without subsuming his people into your own - which Sha'ul rightly had no wish to do - and what chance is there of an alliance with his son the next king? And without an alliance, what happens to the trade routes? Yes, Shlomo, the trade routes. Now listen to me very carefully, even if you never listen to me again. For I am about to explain to you the real source of power for the king of Yisra-El, and through him - yes, indeed, this way around - the power of the god of Yisra-El. Some facts. Some history and geography.

For generations, Shlomo, this land has been the key trading centre for the whole of the Levant. I do not use the scarlet dye for writing very often, but these words merit it. You have travelled through Sharon and seen them; you have visited the caravanserai. Every year thousands of donkeys and camels, trading in grain, in wine and olive oil, in perfumes and spices, in livestock, in dyes and textiles, follow the two major trade routes. That is our strength. It is quite simply impossible to move between the empires of Yavan and the Nile and the Pharat without crossing Erets Yisra-El. We are the world's gatekeepers, the guardians of the toll-booths. You've travelled the roads. The Derech Ha Yam, the Highway of the Sea, which comes up from Lower Mitsrayim through the lands of the Bene Pelet; along the coast via Aza, Ashkelon, Ashdod, Yafo and then inland through Aphek and along the Plain of Sharon, where it bifurcates; one route along the Valley of Yazar-El, and over the River Yarden into Ammon, and then on to Damasek and the great empire of Bav-El of the Bene Kessed beyond; the second fork continuing northwards through the Plain of Carm-El into the kingdoms of Tsur and Tsidon, into Aram and Ashur. Some of the most beautiful countryside in all the kingdom; some of the finest oases anywhere in the world. And the Derech Ha Melech, the King's Highway, less beautiful but just as important, over the highlands of Gil-Yad, Ammon and Mo-Av, through the tribal lands of Menasheh and Gad and Re'u-Ven, all the way from Damasek in the north to Aqaba in the south by way of Ramot Gil-Yad, Gerasa, Rabat-Ammon, Dibbon, Sela (and yes, I know you know all this, but to pronounce the Word is the act of a divinity, and what greater pleasure is there than to pronounce, one by one, the principal quarters of one's kingdom. Recite them, Shlomo, as you recite the beads and thongs and prayers, until you are rendered incapable of ever giving them up.)

Natan will tell you that your power and our strength comes from Yahweh, and I don't say it's untrue. But Yahweh is a theology, not an economic strategy. Yahweh is a god, not a currency of exchange. Yahweh is an abstraction, not a commodity tradable in the market place. Yahweh is only our strength if the king commands his borders. Do not squander that strength in over-hasty treaties. Do not set one god above another when all gods are the same god, and may be married in convenient alliance. Do not lop off the heads of kings whose thrones sit at the junction of three continents. Not even when the Elder of the Guild of Prophets orders you to do so in the name of Yahweh.

Your kingdom then. Your kingdom and your people. Whether or not they are confederate in the alliance of the tribes, whether or not they are Brit Milah, they are all Bene Shem and Beney Ha Shem just like ourselves, distant cousins according to the royal lists, but each and every one of them can trace their lines back either to Yishma-El or Abou Yitschak. The Bene Kayin spent many generations, Shlomo, wandering in the Land of Nod, before they established their home on Mount Se'ir. The Bene Edom claim descent from Kayin, and from Essav, the brother of Abou Yah-Akov, and from Yishma-El, the brother of Abou Yitschak, whose daughters intermarried with the Bene Kayin. Do not establish favourites. Do not cause division between the tribes who are not Bene Yisra-El. Do not mistake their gods for foreign gods, simply because they have foreign names. Do not forget that our ancestors were foreigners too, and that the line of those who were here before us is not cut off. We are all one nation, descendants of Av-Ram even if not of Abou Raham. We have only One god, the Great Multiple Plural as Shmu-El liked to call him, the Omnideity who is all gods simultaneously, first and last, whatever name he goes by, whatever rites and ceremonies are performed in his honour, in whatever form we worship him, and regardless of whether we name him He or She. And only two people are our enemies, though we have all-too-often fought against what should be our friends: the Bli-El, those who acknowledge no gods at all; and the Bene Pelet, whom we must resist at any cost, because they would conquer and destroy us.

So, enough polemic. Let me now describe to you the kingdom I inherited from Sha'ul, after the Battle of Mount Gil-Bo'a. Let me, I mean, start to tell you about being king, rather than kingship, which in the end you will have to learn by trial and error for yourself, in practice not through theory.

The south-western coast and the Negev desert bordering Mitsrayim were held by the Bene Pelet, a domain stoutly enough defended that the whole tribe of the Bene Dan had upped tents and moved to the slopes of Mount Lavan, where their new royal city was growing in splendour. The north-western coast, and all the western plain from Carm-El to Chermon, was a coalition of city-states inhabited by the Bene Chet but dominated by the Bene Cheret of Tsur and Tsidon. The Galil was in the hands of Aram - including the palm-kingdom of

Damasek and its tributary city-states. Except for Yavesh, the Heights of Gil-Yad belonged to Ammon, whose chief city Rabat-Ammon controlled the springs of Banyas at the source of one of the main tributaries of the River Yavok, and whose kings were in perpetual territorial dispute with both the Bene Ephrayim and the Bene Yehudah over the exact boundaries of Gil-Yad to the north of Menasheh, and of Midyan to the east of Naphtali. South of the River Arnon was Mo-Av, where my great-grandmother had been born; but more inclined to follow the example of Orpah than of Ruth. And from the Salt Sea southwards, on both sides of the Aravah, our half-brother Edom, whose chief city Botsrah was heavily fortified, and whose anthem then as now appeared to be the warning: remember that Yah-Akov stole Abou Essav's blessing, and not once but twice; we seek revenge.

Not much, was it, to call a kingdom? Less twelve tribes than twelve tributaries. Abou Mousa envisioned unity and national sovereignty as the pre-requisites for kingship. But where were they? Oh, there were kingdoms, but most of them weren't ours. There were coalitions of city-states, but most of them weren't our cities, let alone our coalitions. There were nations, plethoras of nations - but ours could scarcely be listed among them. True, there were tribal domains, unofficial enclaves bound within the greater kingdoms, landlocked in the interior so to speak, but that was no more than Abou Raham himself achieved. There were tribes interconnected by loose alliance too, but it meant little more than an arranged marriage and shared rights to a well. The northern tribes liked to flatter their vanity by denoting themselves the Bene Ephrayim, but it amounted only to a number of nomadic sheikhs who possessed sufficient sheep and cattle that they could fix the price of grain at certain markets. No kingdom there, though Sha'ul ruled it, and I was its inheritor.

And as to the south, the lands of the Bene Yehudah. So destitute had it become, so far had the economic desert come out to meet the actual desert half-way like a diplomatic negotiator, the Bene Yehudah had all but absorbed the Bene Shimon, whose numbers were so far depleted and whose stock was so fatally inbred, they were scarcely even clans any longer. And as to having a capital city – why, Chevron was in the hands of the Bene Chalev. That's right, the descendants of that Chalev ben Kelba or whatever his probably several fathers were called, who had once been glorified among us as one of Abou

Mousa's spies and second-in-command to Yehoshua ben Nun, but who then showed his real colours by driving the Bene Anak out of Chevron - Chevron, Shlomo! - and keeping it for himself.

Some kingdom! Some inheritance! A world divided between the sophisticated, modern city-dwellers and the nomadic farmers and shepherds of the hills and plains who still inhabited the world of Abou Yitschak - an utterly inconsequential life, as far as anyone can tell from reading Abou Mousa, a life of nil achievement, a life dedicated to digging out his father's blocked-up wells, a life that would have gone entirely unremembered had he been the son of any other father, the father of any other sons. It goes without saying that the city-dwellers were almost never Bene Yisra-El. But the rest - the rest were: rustic not rural, pastoral to their idylls, nomadic goat-boys and sheep-flockers, cattle breeders, hill dwellers. In short - peasants. For whom Abou Raham's vision, let alone Abou Mousa's, had become a fairy story to lullaby themselves to sleep on childless nights. Organise a kingdom? - these people could barely organise a minyan. And where was Yahweh in all this? Where were the covenants? Ruled by narrow-minded judges, who could see no further than the Tablets of the Law, and who had made virtually a new cult out of it to supplant the proper worshipping of Yahweh - prostrate on the ground before the smoke of sacrifice please, not sedentary at a desk, before the pallid face of some unfathomable schoolmaster. That is the truth of it, Shlomo. Which is more important, the Law of Yahweh or the god himself? The Ark that carries his Law about, tented in its Tabernacle, or the life that it's intended to fence around? You cannot have both. And our judges, until Shmu-El at any rate, all that concerned them was to uphold and interpret the Law, to parade the Law, to kiss the fringes of the Law - to worship it, as though it were itself a god. Idolatry! And idolatry is one of the principal sins the Law itself abominates. And as to the covenant - forgotten, a distraction, irrelevant. Worse, an inconvenience. Because two-thirds of the Tablets of Abou Mousa are concerned with the building of a single, central Temple, with the initiation of a Temple Priesthood, with the regulations for the Temple rites of sacrifice - and to realise all of that, you first have to conquer and acquire the holy site. "When you have occupied the land." So Abou Mousa told us. And occupation of the land means all the land, not just the pleasant coombs and dusty screes a hundred miles from nowhere. Occupation means every inch of it, from Dan to Ber Sheva, from Shechem to Shiloh, and particularly from the shrine of the father to the shrine of the mother, from Chevron of Ephron the Bene Chet to Mor-Yah on the summit of Mount Yevus. A king, then a Temple – "when you have occupied the land." Yet Sha'ul didn't even think it worthy of the attempt.

So, Shlomo, we were speaking of borders and boundaries, of oath-stones and garrisons, of coastal plains and city-states. Of Ammon and Mo-Av and the Bene Chalev. It wasn't much, but a kingdom I was given, and I swore on that day that nothing less than a real kingdom would I leave to my successor. So it was written, and done. Now every inch belongs to us - to you. Even Edom, which for centuries had barred the routes to the Red Sea and denied trade access to our ancestors of the Bene Mo-Av as much as to ourselves. Edom the great rival, Kayin's land, Essav's land, Yishma-El's land; the land of the other Habiru, the outcast, the red-headed elder brother; the red land of the red Adam who engendered us. But we, the descendants of the younger brother, we have followed his example and seized the birthright! The Bene Yishai of Yehudah! Your kingdom and your inheritance, Shlomo. I have given you the land, right down to the architect's scale model for the holy site. Now build our Temple.

But of course, I haven't given you all the land, have I? Along the coastal plain to the south and west, in the Plain of Aza and the Wadi Gat, right there where the Negev meets the Sinai and the two deserts meet the sea, there is still that coalition of city-states - Ashdod, Ashkelon, Ekron, Aza, Gat - who give their allegiance to the Bene Pelet. Oh yes, I am well aware of that. How could I not be, I who ruled, for my shame, at Tsiklag?

Since we seem to be having a lesson in etymology as well as history and geography, their name - guess what? - means foreigners, or wanderers, or strangers, or even, just the same as Habiru, outcasts - which is precisely what you must ensure that they remain. Make an ally as well as a friend of Hu-Ram, for he too is their enemy, though he was once their brother. All the years that they have been threatening us, they have made their raids the whole length of the Great Sea coast, from Avar on the Nile Delta to Bav-El of the Bene

Chet on the west coast of Aram, trying to gain footholds, to establish colonies on the Levant. They have attacked Tsur and Tsidon repeatedly. Why? I learned from Hu-Ram why.

They come from an island in the Great Sea of Yavan which they call Creteen or Cheret, and they are known amongst themselves as the Bene Minosh from the name of their royal line. It was they who finally brought to an end the great empire of the Bene Chet that had ruled the whole world from the lands of the goddess Anat in the Bull Mountains. They worshiped a sun-god in the form of a bull, and kept a famous wild bull at the royal palace, whom young men and women were trained to leap and goad in contest; kept him at the centre of a maze, apparently: the Labyrinth they called it. But there were feuds on the island, across the whole archipelago of Yavan indeed; and the feuds led to fires, until the Royal Palace of Chnoss itself was razed and their kingdom ruined. Priests of great wisdom and knowledge had established the realm, but warriors of the aristocratic families had extended it by conquest and now sought the rewards of power, and they vied for the ears of the king until they had destroyed each other.

The priests fled in all directions, seeking refuge in the shrines of the sun-bull, at Pharos in Mitsrayim, in many places in Yavan, and in Tsur and Tsidon of the Bene Chet. The rest sailed off to try to make new homes anywhere they might be welcome: on the northern coasts of the Bene Chem, beyond Mitsrayim, throughout the islands of Yavan, even as far west as Sepharad - it was these who acquired the name Pelet which they now wear like a badge of honour, though it was given to them as an insult. But where priestly Cheret was a great civilisation, those who fled the feuds were evidently not the intellectuals. A race of giants they may be, warriors and aristocrats as well, but what now sits on our borders is pure brawn, and not a gerah of brain worth mentioning amongst them. I have lived among them, Shlomo. I have sojourned in the cultural wilderness of Tsiklag. And I know. They are ignorant people, who still bow down to the bull though we long ago entered the Age of the Ram. Do you know that in the whole of Tsiklag there were less than twenty who could read and write?

Hu-Ram's people, on the other hand, are quite remarkable, and you would do a lot worse than to nurture the friendship I have already developed with the king of Tsur. Go visit Ugarit, Bav-El, Tsidon,

Tsur itself. Look at their palaces - some of the finest architecture you could imagine; the designs I gave you for the Temple were commissioned from one of Hu-Ram's senior architects, a fascinating man who learned his craft, as I understand it, restoring the shrines to En-Lil all along the River Pharat. Did you know it was they who invented this new form of writing that I am using even now, this aleph-bet to replace the old picture-words? Mind you, after this long rigmarole, you will probably wish they hadn't, because I could not have written half so much if I were still compelled to hire a scribe to scratch out picture-words on tablets of wet stone. Ah, but I do love the feel of a fine goose-feather stylus in my hand, especially now that my fingers are too stiff to pluck a lyre. Whether writing in wax or on parchment, there is an inner peace that comes, simply from the act of concentration, simply from the physical process of drawing the hand across the page, of eking out the precise words from the deepest recesses of the brain, whether to create prose or poetry. Happy is the man, eh, Shlomo! Yes, but you try telling any of that to the illiterate barbarian ignoramuses of Pelet! They still haven't reached the stage of picture-words, let alone letters.

Mind you, it was fishermen of the Bene Asher who discovered that if you crush the shells of the murex-snails - you know the ones I mean? the sea-snails; they're practically endemic all along the Coast of Carm-El - you can educe a purple dye that is perfect for ink as well as ideal for colouring clothing. We taught Hu-Ram that.

But I am digressing - an old man's vice, I am afraid, like repeating myself; I re-read that first parchment when I couldn't sleep last night, and realised I had told you the real name of Emet Sarah three times over. You will have to make allowances I fear. However, the Bene Pelet - what was I saying? Yes, that the tribes of the Bene Ephrayim and the Bene Yehudah had for years been unable to drive them back, to prevent them from extending their colonies. Not that we ever lost a war to them. But they kept on returning, year after year, as soon as the winter was over and the sea traversable (derech agav, as they say, I talked to a Bene Pelet sailor once, when I was at Tsiklag, who told me that the sea beyond Sepharad actually disappears for hours at a time, every day; it dries up, or sinks below the sand, so you can walk on it like the Bene Yisra-El did at the Sea of Reeds. He really believed it too. "Sometimes you go down to the beach and there's no sea at all and the boats are high and dry. Then you come back a few hours later and it's there again. But a few hours more, and again it's disappeared." Tides, he called them. Picture the man's face, all wide-eyed credulity. I told him, by way of paying kind for kind, that I kept pig-tailed ostriches in my garden, and that the goddess Anat was my gardener. They don't understand sarcasm either, it appears.)

Where was I? Yes - so regular were their invasions, and so much in thrall the Five Cities, that people came to refer it as the Coast of Pelet, when it should have been called the Coast of Sharon, or possibly the Coast of Shimon - nobody even remembered that it had once been called the Coast of Dan. In the south, around the Five Cities, they had even begun to intermarry with the women of the various tribes, to mix their particular idol-worship with the various idolatries of the region. The threat was growing ever more serious, religiously as well as militarily. But what could be done, except continue to resist them? Resistance requires leadership however, and who now was there? The days of Devorah and Gid-Yon were past. The Guild of Prophets did not yet have the authority that Shmu-El gave it. Eli the High Priest at Shiloh carried more authority than any other, but he was an old man. Twelve tribal chieftains, each with their own internal problems, meant that any tribal gathering consisted of a hundred and forty four opinions. The answer lay in monarchy, in confederacy - only no one was yet ready to consider the option. But it was so startlingly obvious. How could a land fragmented into tribes conquer and defeat an alien intruder? It simply couldn't. And if it did, how could a coalition of tribes ruled by law-judges and religious clerics subdue a people it had brought into its hegemony? It simply couldn't. So there had to be a king. Only - which tribe could provide a king, without the other eleven refusing to bow down to him – even allowing for the oracle of Yehudah? And besides, coastal invasions were local matters. Why should men of Gad die to protect the Coast of Zvulun? Logically the problem of the Five Cities should have been left to the Bene Shimon, who were geographically the most vulnerable. But the Bene Shimon were desert people, goatherds and camel traders, oasis dwellers - they couldn't stop the Bene Pelet on their own.

You begin to see the whys and wherefores. We were naked,

divided, ripe for plucking. And then, then. We are leaving pre-history behind, Shlomo, and entering the modern world, our era. They came again, a new wave of invaders from across the Great Sea, and this time they attacked us further north, along the whole Plain of Sharon from the Brook of Kanah to the town of Dor. Their ships had duck-shaped prows and sterns, were driven by sail alone, without slaves to man the galleys. Their warriors brought weapons we had never seen before. Iron spears and javelins. Round shields. Long broadswords, also of iron. Their chiefs were truly giants - men a head taller than our tallest. They wore kilts embroidered with tassels, and corselets, feather head-dresses, horned helmets. They rode in ox-drawn chariots. The whole of the Shephelah lay at their feet, and how could we resist them?

The men of Zvulun and Yah-Shachur and Menasheh agreed at last to join with those of Ephrayim, under the leadership of the Bene Ephrayim. A League, they called it, the League of Ephrayim, and all the other northern tribes save only Gad and Bin-Yamin pledged their support. But confederation now was tantamount to locking the manger door after the fox had entered.

They came ashore, the Bene Pelet, virtually unchallenged, and they marched inland. The League had to gather its forces quickly, and to do them credit they achieved it. The Bene Pelet camped near Aphek, the Bene Ephrayim outside Even-Ezer. The Bene Pelet had the high ground above the Brook of Kanah, and they swooped on the Bene Ephrayim by surprise. Four thousand Bene Ephrayim were killed, and the leaguesmen fled in numbers. Naked, divided, and already half-plucked. And then, then - the most extraordinary, the most crassly, treacherously, stupidest decision anyone has ever taken through all the long years of our all-too-often foolish history. By unmerited chance the most momentous too, the watershed, the one that would come to change the course of history for ever. Though not one of those idiots could have known it at the time.

They brought the wounded back to camp and despaired of finding strength to bury all the dead. Aphek had been lost, but Aphek was a royal city only of the Bene Chor, and the Bene Chor had not participated in the League. But Aphek controlled the sources of the Brook of Kanah, which ran through Gat-Rimmon to Yafo and the sea; and with the Five Cities already lost, Yafo and Dor were the only sea-ports still remaining to the Bene Yisra-El. And from Aphek, the

Bene Pelet could march east across the Shephelah, to attack the shrines at Gezer, Ai and Beit-El. All Ephrayim to the very borders of Yehudah was threatened. So spoke the chiefs and elders in their tents that night. None dissented. The certainty that total defeat was now imminent blackened their mood darker even than the blood that had been spilled that day.

Whose voice was it that dared to offer the suggestion? A tribal elder? An aluph whose troop had been so decimated he could only believe the face of Yahweh must have been turned aside? A clansmen from amongst the Bene Kena'an who had joined the League but didn't understand the full import of what he was suggesting? I have tried, many times, to imagine how it could have taken place, but I have not succeeded. So much blood, torn flesh, the smell of cadavers already rotting in the summer heat, the noise of jackals and the squawks of preying birds, descending on the bones of those they had not yet found time or space to bury. All this must have added to the mood of doom and gloom and sheer despondency. The Bene Pelet worship a god they call Ba'al-Zvuv, the Lord of the Flies, and it must have seemed that he had come amongst the Bene Yisra-El, to torment the still-living in the severed limbs and mutilated members of the dead. The keening of the women throughout the camp as well, those who had found their own loved ones, professional mourners offering their services to those who had no womenfolk beside them to grieve for a lost brother, father, son. And perhaps, also, the distant sounds of jubilant celebration, heard or imagined from the ancient palace at Aphek, and the conviction that amongst the spoils of battle were the wives and daughters to whom they had pledged victory when they set out that very morning.

Naked, divided, plucked. In such circumstances, anything is imaginable, anything is possible. Even this.

And so it was agreed. To play the final trump, because no other card seemed strong enough.

"Send to Shiloh."

Momentous words indeed.

"Give orders that the Ark of the Covenant be brought here to assist us. Let Yahweh come into our midst, and be our chief."

Who could have dared to utter such an order? To command a god onto the battle-field! Any god, but especially Yahweh. I could never have issued such an order.

Eli resisted, of course. As High Priest at the shrine, what else could he have done? It was madness. Had men forgotten the punishment of Abou Mousa, for daring to strike the rock at Merivah without permission? The Ark was the focal-point of unity for the twelve tribes: the royal litter, the substance of the Tabernacle. A copy of the Law of Abou Mousa - the original copy of the original Law, the second set of tablets given to Abou Mousa by Yahweh on Mount Chor - was contained in it, and its lid was the Mercy Seat, the very symbol of the presence of Yahweh among the tribes. It had lived in Shiloh since the time of Yehoshua ben Nun, and it could not be moved, except of course for the annual pilgrim festivals when it was peregrinated from town to town, from shrine to shrine, that all the people might see it, and prostrate themselves in worship at its feet. But never otherwise. And now, now it was to be driven into battle like a chariot of the Bene Pelet, drawn by a tethered ox no doubt, and with spearheads, no doubt, poking from its sides.

The old warrior-judges like Devorah and Gid-Yon would never have allowed so blasphemous a travesty. Nor Shmu-El. But Eli was ninety-eight years old, and almost blind. And besides, though he was Chief Priest in name, it was his sons who officiated and they were of a new breed of judge, politicians rather than religious leaders, administrators of the Law rather than interpreters of Justice. Clerics, not teacher-prophets. Weak men too. Shmu-El in his great scroll called them "worthless men", and he of all people should have known, having spent his childhood almost as a younger brother to them. And they were utterly corrupt. Hophni abused his office by seducing women who visited the shrine; Pinchas took home the best part of the sacrificial meat. Eli was a good man, a noble man, an honest man, but how should he resist the orders of the chiefs and elders of the tribes, when his own sons not only approved them, but asked permission to accompany the Ark themselves? How should he prevent them in this matter, when he could not prevent their other sacrileges? Resist, yes, but not prevent. And besides, he wasn't the sort to refuse when threatened, as surely he was threatened, and not by bullying, but by the sight of so much grief and desperation.

So the Ark was transported out of Shiloh, exactly as Abou Mousa had transported it across the wilderness, the golden casket carried by four priests on four poles attached to golden rings at each of the four corners, transported in solemn procession across the land. Like pallbearers of Warak, carrying the coffin of the dead king of the Bene Kessed. Forgive my irony, Shlomo, but what in the name of Yahweh did they expect to happen? That the two keruvim would leap from the casket, their wings outstretched to guard and deliver Yisra-El? That thunderbolts from Heaven would rain down on the Bene Pelet and obliterate them? Yahweh is not a god who intervenes, but only, at most, inspires. And yes, the presence of the Ark might well inspire Yisra-El to take the battlefield once more against the Bene Pelet, but it couldn't inspire a sudden alteration in the numbers, in the quality of weaponry, on either side; it couldn't inspire a miraculous shifting of the strategic balance, so that the Bene Ephrayim now held the high ground, and it was the Bene Pelet who were trapped in a hollow underneath. And what if? What if? What if the Ark were captured, what if the god were beaten - who could ever believe in him again? And then what bond would remain to hold the tribes together, what chance could there be of staving off annihilation at the hands of the Bene Pelet? What desperate, desperate measures! What desperate risk!

It must have been magnificent though, to witness its arrival. That day we brought the Ark up to Yiru-Sala'am, when we sang the Hallel psalms for the first time - ah, you were too young, Shlomo, to remember it. But something of that order. To see the procession coming over the hills - thousands, thousands had joined at every village it passed through - the gold of the casket glistering in the morning sun. To be a mere foot-soldier, a nobody of the ranks, and yet allowed to gaze upon such splendour. To be amazed, as I was the first time I beheld it, by its sheer size - wider than a man's arm, and almost twice as long. To see the winged keruvim, wrought in gold by a craftsman of quite dazzling artistry. To smell the deep scent of acacia wood, the deeper perfume of the pot of manna. To stare upon the very rod that Aharon the First High Priest had carried, the almond rod he turned into a snake before the Pharaoh, the rod that blossomed overnight. To see, face to face, what only the High Priest at the Fast of Azaz-El should see. What privilege! What blasphemy! What inspiration!

Such was the joy at the Ark's arrival, such was the dancing and celebrating and crying - of Hallelu-Yahweh, I presume, rather than Hallelu-Yah - the noise must have terrified the Bene Pelet, who nearly fled. But it also distracted and exhausted the Bene Ephrayim, who danced all through the night on the entirely logical religious grounds that a man may not sleep in the presence of a king, that Yahweh is the Ultimate King, and that Yahweh never sleeps. Inspired to devotion, they squeezed every last drop of holy wine that could be poured in libation from the sacred goat-skin flagons, and drank the full dregs of benediction in the arms of those many hundreds of women who had joined the Ark's procession from Shiloh. Farce and insanity! What of the five thousand they had scarcely buried? What of the seven days of mourning? What of the Bene Pelet, recovered from their terror, now armouring themselves in Aphek, preparing to descend once more upon the fold?

It was truly terrible, Shlomo. The slaughter. The carnage. Men too drunk, too exhausted, too inspired to fight back. The iron weaponry. The sheer weight of numbers, strengthened from the Five Cities while the Bene Ephrayim were at their revels. The speed with which the chariots could descend. The horns of the oxen. The screaming, hysterical panic of the women. The rocks and trees at each end of the hollow, preventing flight. It was truly terrible. Thirty thousand footmen were slain. And the Ark, the Ark was captured.

The sons of Eli were killed too. Hophni was run through by the horns of an ox as he tried to defend the Tent of the Tabernacle in which the Ark was held. Pinchas died in the arms of a woman of the Bene Zvulun, speared while sleeping off his night's debaucheries. It was just punishment, men said, for their past sins and their present blasphemies. As though it had been their idea to summon the Ark. As though only they had perpetrated such a sacrilege. As though men can ever claim the right to say, it wasn't my fault, I was only obeying orders. All Yisra-El was guilty, Shlomo. Because they wanted the Ark there as an idol, as a talisman, as a teraph they could kneel before and worship like the Judges do the Law. Do you see? Do you? Shlomo, our god is neither wood nor stone. Go to the summit of Mount Mor-Yah, the very summit, to the black rock, the granite rock where Abou Raham went to sacrifice a ram in place of Abou Yitschak, the rock where Melchi-Tsedek and his people have been sacrificing their first-born for millennia. Go there and lie face down on the rock - but hold your nose, for the smell of stale blood is truly sickening. Put your ear to the rock. You will hear a sound, distant and at times so faint you will think you are playing tricks upon yourself, but rhythmic, a metronomic ticking, issuing out of the rock. I am told it's because of the high density of quartz within the granite. But I tell you, it is the pulse of the universe that you can hear ticking and beating - Lev-Yah not Mor-Yah: her heart, not her tears. Put your hand to your own pulse and feel it. It's the same, the exact same rhythm. Not wood, not stone, but the heart of the goddess of the Hill of Sacrifice, the voice of Yahweh speaking to you in the only voice he has. Tick. Tick. Tick. Pulsating through the rock and through your blood. And those fools thought a god was just a teraph in the Tabernacle of the Ark, some divine icon that would come magically to life in the form of "the invincible warrior", would materialise from behind the Veil and defeat the Bene Pelet single-handed! Some superhero like they made of me at Sochoh. The fools! The ignorant, idiotic, idol-worshipping fools!

Thirty thousand men, Shlomo, slain in a single day. And the Ark lost. It was as if someone had taken an axe to the black rock of Mor-Yah, and gouged out the ticking pulse. Thirty thousand men, and Yahweh taken captive. A soldier of the Bene Yamin - one of my brother Avi-Nadav's troop - brought the news to Shiloh. Eli was ninety-eight years old, the greatest judge in all the lands of Yisra-El. They say he took the news of Hophni and Pinchas quite serenely, as if it served them right. But the news of the Ark was too much for him. He fell off his chair and broke his neck, though I suspect his heart had broken long before he reached the floor. Pinchas' wife was close to term, and the news shocked her into labour. When the child was born, she refused even to look at him, and he was given to a wet-nurse of the Temple to bring up. She named the child I-Chavod – "dishonoured". Then she too died.

It might have been worse though if they had lived. Rabble of the Bene Pelet marched on to Shiloh in search of loot, and razed the town, and there is little doubt from the way they treated other village elders that Eli would have been singled out for special treatment, not simply the abomination of making an example of him in the public streets, but torturing him. They did enough though - rape, murder, pillage; the customary aftermath of victory. Such was their jubilation, they seemed ready to march on and seize all Yehudah next, and then Ephrayim, and on, northwards to Menasheh, Yah-Shachur, Zvulun.

But they too had failed to understand the nature of the god of

Yisra-El. You cannot seize a god like Yahweh, and think to make a prisoner of him.

They took the Ark to Ashdod, and set it up in the temple of Dagon, a place as dark and dreary as the inside of their own imaginations. Did they expect the Bene Ephrayim to send ransom? Did they think Yahweh who had chosen Yisra-El would change his mind, abrogate his covenant, and offer to serve instead as chief god to the Bene Pelet? Did they not remember what took place at Aza, not a generation previously, when last they took on Yahweh in a fight? Nor were there seven locks of his sun-gold hair to cut, nor eyes to blind, nor arms to rope around the pillars. This was no sun-priest of ruined strength, betrayed by the Witch of Darkness, calling on Yahweh to avenge him. This was the god himself.

In the morning, the priests found the statue of Dagon lying on the floor. Face-down too, which was an even worse omen. The priests put him back. But the next morning, there he was again, lying prostrate on the floor - seemingly in act of worshipping the golden casket of the Ark. But this time his head and hands had been cut off; only the stumps remained. The priests fled, never to return. Two days later, the city was devastated by an epidemic, some kind of bubonic plague carried by the fleas that lived on rats. Probably it came on boats of the Bene Pelet, a whole armada of which had docked in Ashdod bringing further reinforcements. But of course men blamed or credited Yahweh. The Ark was sent to Gat, but the plague followed, and in addition there was a terrible outbreak of haemorrhoids. To Ekron then, but the Bene Ekron refused to take it, believing that the Ark was itself the carrier. Which in a sense it was. For seven months the Bene Pelet dragged the Ark from town to town, but nobody was willing to receive it, and wherever they went disaster befell them. Until, at last, the priests of the Bene Pelet recommended that it be returned, and in addition, as a trespass offering - imagine the face of the craftsman receiving this commission! - five golden emerods and five gold mice, symbols of the two plagues! I have them even now, locked in the Treasury on Mount Tsi'on. Mazalim tovim, you might say - good luck charms!

Whatever the relative merits of their two armies, Dagon of the Bene Pelet had proven after all to be less powerful than Yahweh of the Bene Yisra-El. Because Dagon is indeed a mere icon, a stone teraph, while Yahweh is the invisible presence inside the empty

Tabernacle. Because Dagon is merely something men have carved on stone - just like the Law - while Yahweh is the very Creation of the Creation of the universe itself. Let the Lord arise. Let his enemies be scattered. Let them who hate him flee before him. As smoke is driven away, as wax melts before a fire, so let the wicked perish at the presence of Yahweh. But let the righteous be glad; let them rejoice before the Lord. Oh yes, let them rejoice exceedingly!

But they weren't glad, and they didn't rejoice. Messengers came from the Bene Pelet, asking the Bene Ephrayim to take back their talisman. But it was not that simple. For one thing, great impurities had been incurred through all these months, and men - being of simple disposition - were frightened of the wrath of Yahweh once he was reinstated on his throne. It had been deemed improper to make any of the sacrifices of purification as long as the Ark was missing. New moon feasts and even pilgrim festivals had passed unnoted, for there was no Ark of Pilgrimage, and who could be sure that the loss of the Ark did not infer an ending of the Covenant? But more than that, those who saw in the defeat at Even-Ezer a proof that Yahweh was not the powerful almighty god they had been told, had turned to worshipping the Ba'alim and Ashterot once more. At every standing stone or stone circle in Erets Yisra-El, they made obeisance to the gods of sky and earth, and planted trees, and sacrificed their first-born on the stones. In preparation for the spring rites, fir and willow trees were uprooted and stripped to their trunks, dug back into the ground as sacred dancing-poles of Asherah, and mock-kings and mock-queens were chosen to surrogate the Lord and Lady in orgiastic congress at her shrines. Not since the death of Yehoshua ben Nun had such things been seen. But Yahweh had failed his people, and a people requires leadership; and if no human leadership is given, then men will look to gods. So it would be for the next twenty years.

Then word reached Yisra-El of the two plagues. Yahweh had not forsaken his people after all. Quite the contrary. Some at least of his people now understood how far they had forsaken him. The blasphemy of summoning him to the battlefield, exacerbated by the sins of the Ba'alim and Ashterot. But the land was split. There were many, many indeed, who were openly delighted that the stern god and strict laws of Abou Mousa were no more, that an era of liberty had come again. Men could do as they saw fit in their own eyes. So it had been before the time of Abou Mousa. So it had been in the first days of the Judges, after the death of Yehoshua ben Nun. So it might be again now.

In the months since Eli's death a new oligarchy of priests and tribal elders had begun to judge in Yisra-El. When the Bene Pelet again sent messengers, by now pleading that the Ark be taken back, offering guarantees of peace and even tribute in exchange, the elders saw no alternative but to agree. But on condition. To demonstrate the hand of Yahweh once and for all, untrained oxen, milk cows newly calved, were harnessed to the cart on which the Ark was to be carried. But carried where, now that Shiloh was no more?

"Let the Ark be sent out of Pelet on the road towards the east," it was decreed. "But let no man lead or guide the cart, that it may find its own way. The Ark was taken captive in the temple of the sun. Let it then go by way of Beit-Shemesh in the direction of Shiloh, and it shall be seen that Yahweh seeks his home. Then we will welcome him. But if not, if the cart is turned in any other way, we shall recognise the hand of chance, and know that the Covenant is broken. Then must the Ark remain in Pelet."

It was much the same as the method Shmu-El recommended for proving witchcraft - of making the suspect float belly-down in water. If they floated they were witches - so you stoned them. If they drowned, they drowned.

You would expect the cows to have howled for their calves locked up at home, as is the way of nature, and to have turned back towards Pelet. But they pulled like trained oxen, and drew the cart towards Beit Shemesh, arriving in the field of Yehoshua ben somebody-or-other whose name was not recorded. So the righteous were now able to be glad, the pious to rejoice before the Lord. They offered purification sacrifices to celebrate the triumphant return. They received in formal ceremony the gifts of the kings of the Five Cities, and sent their emissaries home in peace. They read aloud before the congregation from the Tablets of Abou Mousa, and one by one the Elders of the tribes - those who had not fought at Even-Ezer as well as those who had - came forward to recite the Covenant of Abou Raham, to bind themselves by swearing on the Mercy Seat, and to receive once more the priestly blessing. Men need such rituals, Shlomo, to give meaning to the rites of passage - those of a nation just as much as those of the individual. The men of the Bene Kena'an and the Bene Chor and the Bene Shemesh who were present must have felt this too. More than a thousand of them offered themselves for circumcision, and they too were accepted into the Covenant.

The stone of Beit Shemesh is an ancient stone. From chisel-notches on its several faces, you can easily recognise the signs of sun-worship. The golden cow of Delilah, the Witch of Darkness, cloaked in black cloth; the tomb of the dead Shimshon; the map of the seven circuits of his tomb - all of it denoting the winter solstice. The sun itself, bull-horned, but scratched out because the sun no longer rose in the Bull but in the Ram. And at the dead centre of the stone circle, where the summer sun at its zenith touches the menhir at the mid-day, the face of the Awaited One, the Reborn, the Water Carrier, the Fisherman, in whose house the sun will begin to rise at the winter solstice in - what? - less than another thousand years.

On this altar they made the sacrifices, the guilt and sin offerings at the start of the ceremony, the burnt offerings at its end. For kindling they broke up the cart that had brought the Ark, and laid it on the altar stone. For fat to feed the fire, they slaughtered the milk cows who had drawn the cart. The tokens of the covenant taken from the men of the Bene Kena'an and the Bene Chor and the Bene Shemesh were likewise thrown onto the pyre. And Shmu-El, the young Shmu-El with his flowing locks, he who in his infancy had prophesied that Hophni and Pinchas would die on the same day, and that their deaths would bring to an end the line of Itamar ben Aharon, the youngest son of the First High Priest of Yisra-El; Shmu-El who had been raised by Eli as a Nazir consecrated to the shrine and who alone was left of all its heritage; Shmu-El was called up by the Elders, to recount the death of that greater Nazir Shimshon in the Temple of Aza - what other story should they tell that day? History ends where history begins. For the first time, a leader of the Guild of Prophets took his place at the forefront of our nation. Though it would be twenty years before it was repeated.

O happy day spoiled by the foolhardiness of the unbelievers! When it was all over, when the ceremony was done and the festivities had eaten up most of the night, when every sheep and goat for miles around had been sacrificed to feed the many thousands who were there, seventy men could not resist the temptation to lift the coverlet of the Ark and look inside, in the hope no doubt of finding some golden idol they could touch as a living god - or steal, more likely. But the god of the Bene Yisra-El - how many times do I have to say this? – is neither of cloth nor clay. And his face is not for men to look upon. All seventy were struck dead, and the rejoicing was mellowed. Even the official records, which invariably operate in rounded numbers, state that at the Battle of Even-Ezer the number of the dead amongst the Bene Yisra-El was thirty thousand and seventy. As if these last dead had been added on.

Nevertheless the Ark had been delivered safely to Beit Shemesh, and from there it was escorted in triumph to Giv-On - where else, with Shiloh gone? - to the woodland grove at Kiryat-Ye'arim, to the shrine whose priest was Avi-Nadav of the Bene Giv-On, where it would remain for thirty years. His son Eli-Azar was given personal charge.

And you, Shlomo, must now understand why the signing of this treaty is so important, whatever may be the wishes of the Bene Sha'ul. At Giv-On the sun stood still in the heavens for Yehoshua ben Nun, as the moon did over the Valley of Ayalon. Whatever deceits the Bene Giv-On may have worked to secure peace with Yehoshua, the Ark that was lost came into their safe keeping, and the one act cancels out the other. Let the House of Sha'ul build itself a new royal palace, elsewhere than Giv-Yah. Our duty is to build the greater house. The Ark of the Lord Yahweh, Shlomo, whose Temple I bequeath to you the honour and obligation to construct. History, Shlomo. It is only by understanding the past that you can plan the future in the present. And the doing of that is the sum total of kingship. Enough.

Parchment Three

Shmu-El. My second father. My godfather, you might say. Cometh the hour, cometh the man - though this particular man came, in the manner of the Elders of the Guild of Prophets, dressed almost comically like a shepherd or a fisherman: the thin, white, linen apron that scarcely reached his thighs, and over it one of those innumerable goat-hair coats he had, worn-out and far too small for him - his mother used to bring them as an annual gift when he was growing up at Shiloh. Hair like Shimshon. Beard uncut. Eyes dilated. But who cared what he looked like? Lunatic or vagabond he might well seem, but here, at last, was a Judge in Yisra-El who understood. There hadn't been such a one since Yiphtach died.

He was initially a circuit-judge, highly trained in matters of Law - an expert, as it happened, on the complexities of food hygiene and personal purification - who spent the first thirty years of his professional life in annual circuit around the major shrines: Beit-El, Gil-Gal, Mitspeh, Shechem, Ramah. He was a superb teacher, who could explain the complex moral ramifications of seething a goat-kid in its mother's milk or the reason why childbirth constituted a technical sin that required an offering to cleanse it - the answer, derech agav, lies in the blood - could explain it with quite breathtaking clarity, even to the uneducated. But the pernickettiness of some of the specific laws drove him to distraction, and he was forever finding himself having to adjudicate the most trivial of matters, such as whether some baker's leaven or some butcher's meat was still kosher, because a rabid dog had relieved itself against the bakery wall or a stray goat left its hairs on the altar-stone. His rages were proverbial, and always unexpected. He once closed down a training-camp for soldiers recruited from amongst the Bene Gil-Yad, screaming at the adjutant that: "I know it's a commandment to wipe out the seven nations of the Bene Kena'an, but it doesn't say when, and these are on our side. Nor are you expected to achieve it by breaking the laws requiring proper sanitation at a military camp." It was true, by all accounts, that the place was filthy - no proper latrines or cooking facilities, and the men were riddled with lice. He once found in favour of a usury case against a wealthy merchant of the Bene Yah-Shachur, on the grounds that, though it was legal to charge interest to a foreigner, it was illegal to take interest from the poor, and that this must also include the foreign poor. When the man protested and threatened to lodge an appeal, Shmu-El fined him a hundred shekels, for contempt of the laws of charity!

His fervour when he was young was likewise proverbial, but middle age had left him bilious and short-tempered. He gave the distinct impression that he hated people, but really it was just the frustrated passion of a true philanthropist, as though what he hated was not them, but the absurdity of trying to love them even with their flaws. People will tell you that I do not suffer fools gladly. Shmu-El quite simply refused to countenance them at all.

Yet at the same time he was a truly radical reformer. Unlike that fool Natan, who has wasted twenty years trying to reduce the entire Law to three hundred and fourteen commandments, one for each letter of the name of Abou Raham's god, Shmu-El had deduced that there were already six hundred and thirteen commandments - the six hundred and five denoted by the numerical value of the word Torah, plus the seven laws of No'ach, plus the original commandment, the one given first to the beasts and then to Adam and Eve, to go forth and multiply - and began the process of codification which would become the elder Gad's life's work. His teachings on the status of the Laws of No'ach in particular were as remarkable as they were significant.

"The Laws, Daoud, were made for the perfection of Man. But Man is not perfectible. Which should we do then? Force men to change to fit the Law, or adapt the Law to meet the needs of men?"

Dangerous question!

"The Law was given by Yahweh to Abou Mousa. How can we claim the right to change it?"

My answer was the one that anybody would have given - obvious, conventional and correct. But prophets aren't priests - they have the authority to state what isn't obvious, to challenge the conventional, to question the correct. What would be the point of them if they did not?

It was the word "given" that made him raise those massive, bushy eyebrows.

"Given?" he echoed me, his voice so heavy with irony the two tablets of stone could have cracked. "What if I were to say 'inspired'? Does Yahweh 'give' at the metaphorical level, or at the literal?"

This kind of intellectual questioning went so far above my head that I simply remained silent, waited for the explanation he was bound eventually to offer. Though it did occur to me that grandfather Oved would have been in his element.

"Daoud, it is the obligation of a judge to interpret the Law for common usage. At what point does interpretation end and transformation by precedent begin?"

Not an answer at all, just a different way of phrasing the same question. Yet he seemed to be throwing out his questions as though they were themselves answers. And in so doing, claiming for himself the right to initiate change. As a young man, I found that profoundly shocking.

"Do you know why it is forbidden to eat shellfish?"

"Because it says..."

"Not where. Why?"

"Because Yahweh..."

"Not who. Why?"

"I have no idea."

"Nor does anybody." He laughed. He had clearly played this game before. "The Law only tells us what we may or may not do. It never tells us why. And perhaps that's deliberate, to give us an involvement in the making of the Law. By forcing us to ask why. Do you think it is healthy to obey a Law just because it has been given, without first asking why?"

A perfectly fair question to ask a young apprentice to the Guild of Prophets. But was it a fair question to ask a choirboy of the king? Or the king himself, for that matter? Before their great falling-out over Agag and the sacrifices, Shmu-El used to spend long days and nights attempting to teach the Laws of Abou Mousa to what was, it must be said, a most reluctant king. What need for divine laws, after all, when a man sat on an earthly throne and dispensed justice with equanimity? Ha ha!

"Do you think it is healthy to obey a Law just because it has been given, without first asking why?"

On anybody else's lips but his, the Bodyguard would not even have waited for the royal signal, but would have moved to arrest what wasn't just insolence, but open dissention, even treason. To challenge the duty of obedience, in the very face of the king? Yet he was merely posing an intellectual question – wasn't he? He meant the Law of

Yahweh, didn't he? I found myself wondering which of several recent edicts had aroused his displeasure and induced this lengthy rigmarole. But it wasn't my place to speak, only to listen, to provide upon request a musical accompaniment to thought and silence. Mostly silence. But eventually Sha'ul said:

"Presumably you do have an explanation."

Shmu-El laughed, not that enormous belly-laugh that so belied his reputation for solemnity, but a slightly arrogant guffaw, the sort that teachers use when they've been leading you up to something with great stealth and patience, and at last you have arrived.

"I have many explanations, all of them plausible, none of them certain. What would you make of the hypothesis that Abou Mousa initiated the Law concerning shellfish when the Bene Yisra-El were camped at the Red Sea, and using the sea as a latrine for want of any better form of sewage?"

Now it was Sha'ul's turn to laugh.

"I certainly wouldn't want to eat any shellfish gathered in such water."

"Precisely. And would you say the same is true of shellfish farmed in the carp-pools of the Galil?"

"Technically, yes."

"The correct answer. I had a case, five years ago now, in Korazim."

At last, I thought, he was coming to his real point. Shmu-El never told stories for the love of stories. Shmu-El invented parables. Which edict, then? Which edict?

"One of the clans of the Bene Naphtali had taken to farming Genasseret shellfish, prawns mostly, and were selling them to the Bene Ammon, who have no tabu on eating them. The case was brought by a market trader who had had complaints about food poisoning after the sale of some carp reared in the same pond as the shellfish. He alleged the shellfish were responsible, that they had polluted the carp, not by bacteria, but as a punishment for breaching the Dietary Law. The truth was he never cleaned his knives properly and his shop was full of flies. How should I have ruled?"

"A conundrum," the king had recently learned this word and for several days was using it at every opportunity. But it wasn't an answer. It was a way of evading answering while still seeming to appear clever. Nor could I have done much better. For the life of me I still could not work out to what he was referring in this abstruse manner.

"Indeed it was a veritable conundrum. If I ruled for the shellfish farmers, I was apparently condoning the eating of shellfish; but if I ruled against them, I would unfairly deprive them of their livelihoods, because the Law only forbids eating them, not farming them. On the other hand, if I ruled for the fish-trader, I would be allowing his lack of hygiene to go unpunished. And of course, there was also the matter of the Bene Ammon. How does one judge in a dispute between those who are wrong but Bene Yisra-El, and those who have rights, but are goyim?"

The donkeys at Shechem - so it was that. The Bene Dan had petitioned against the reacceptance of donkeys at the shrine, arguing the ancient blood-feud from the time when Shechem ben Chamor raped their sister Dinah. It had always been a donkey-shrine, and the presence of the donkeys honoured Shet the son of Adam and Chava, who no longer had a shrine now that his temple at Avar had been smashed to pieces by the worshippers of Osher – they had even decreed it a crime to write his name. When Sha'ul agreed to let the donkeys back, he had anticipated a petition from the Bene Asher, since it was their tribal lord whom Shet had killed. Yet not a murmur. And as to the Bene Dan, Shimon and Levi had avenged the rape, and received their punishments. That blood-feud was settled. Nevertheless, Sha'ul revoked his original decree and ordered the removal of the donkeys, arguing that Shechem was now a shrine to Yahweh, not Chamor, but really because - well, Shmu-El had used the pejorative term, but also the correct one. Because they were goyim.

"What did you do?"

"I called for some fresh shellfish to be brought, and invited one of the Bene Ammon to eat them in the presence of the court, then to return after forty-eight hours under judicial supervision at his home. He came back in perfect health, and declared the shellfish absolutely delicious, which exonerated the farmers. I then delivered a sermon to the court of such fire and brimstone on the subject of the cleanliness of Yahweh being the holiness of Yahweh that the fish trader went straight home, cleaned his entire shop from roof to floor, set his knives in the fire for a day and a night, and then brought me a box of the most beautiful carp and invited me to choose as many as I deemed fit for a sacrifice. They too were absolutely delicious."

Sha'ul, on the other hand was furious, because of course he was himself a worshipper of Shet, albeit secretly. You could see the mechanical parts of his brain trudging slowly towards thought, but arriving no nearer than a febrid blinking of his eyelids. No doubt he would have liked to make some punning observation, about how cleverly Shmu-El had made donkeys of everyone, just to let him know his dart had hit its mark. But of course, with Shmu-El, there were so many darts, all being fired at once, that you would need to go over the entire conversation in your head before you could even count them all, let alone pick out the poisoned ones. Whereas Sha'ul just took the point and reinstituted his original decree. And marked it down as one more reason why he hated Shmu-El.

Ah, but I loved him, Shlomo. Loved him? I adored him, as I adored grandfather Oved - better than my own father. I imbibed his style with his wisdom. Can you recognise it? You would do yourself no harm to learn it too.

Of course, had he not been fired by so much evangelical fervour, had he not been entirely beyond reproach in his own life, all this might have brought down on him an accusation of irreverence. Yet he was a strange, mixed bag of contradictions. And such charisma. Such fire. Unlike any other of the judges, when Shmu-El was due, a town cleaned up its religious act in fear and trepidation. For fear of Shmu-El, not Yahweh! The Elders sat in the gate, at the entrance to the town, and judged men's acts, but Shmu-El sat in their consciences, at the entrance to their souls, and judged their lives. So it came as no surprise that he was the youngest ever to be elected to the Guild of Prophets, and then became an Elder within just three years. He was exactly the man all Yisra-El had been praying for.

He had the advantage, too, of being trans-tribal, and semi-patriarchal by descent. He also had that nearly mythical status that comes of being nisu'im pilgshi - the son of an apparently barren first wife who had given her maidservant to her husband and borne children, as they say, on her maid's knees, as Eshet Sarah did with Chagar, as Eshet Rach-El did with Bilhah and Eshet Le'ah with Zilpah. His father, El-Kanah ben Yero-Cham, could trace his ancestry back to the time when Av-Ram lived in Ur of the Bene Kessed, and Shmu-El took great pride in speaking of Tohu ben Tsuph as a man of Ephrat - indeed, I always suspected it was one of the reasons why he so loved Beit-Lechem, and railed against every form of idolatry except the worshipping of Tammuz.

He was born in the hill country of Ephrayim, in Ramatayim-Tsophim - named for their forebear, though it deserved the name anyway, for the region was famous for its honey, and through it ran any number of brooks and streams created by the winter rains, so that it was forever flooded. But he hardly knew the place, for no sooner was he weaned than Chanah, his mother, dedicated him as a nazir at the shrine of Shiloh, and he was brought up there, personally trained there, by Eli himself. The weight of such an upbringing was something no one in Yisra-El could deny, nor any other judge or prophet rival - especially when his infant prophecies came so spectacularly true. He was Eli's heir by simple, inexorable right of destiny - would have been, even if Hophni and Pinchas had lived. The hand of Yahweh marked him. And when you heard him preach on how the unity of Yisra-El depended on its common faith in Yahweh, and on the six hundred and thirteen laws which Yahweh gave - yes, gave - to Abou Mousa on Mount Chorev, well, there was nothing more to say.

"You shall have no other gods before me. Does that mean, you shall have no other gods? No, it does not. Worship your standing stones and your sacred pillars. Keep your teraphim in your vineyards and olive orchards. Make corn-dolls for your threshing-floors. Observe the movements of the stars and the waxing and waning of the goddess Moon. Celebrate the mid-winter festival. But first, first and foremost, before any other gods, fear Yahweh, for he is your king."

Stirring stuff!

But he was right, Shlomo. Nothing else united the tribes, now that Shiloh was destroyed. Not even the land, for though all the land belongs to all the Bene Yisra-El by covenant, it had also been shared out, as autonomous inheritances for all time, between the tribes. What happened at Even-Ezer proved it. The Bene Shimon will fight and die for the land of the Bene Shimon - but for the land of the Bene Dan, why should they lift a finger? A confederacy, then, for national unity. And Yahweh, for a national god. Where else do you think I learned it?

"But when you place your teraphim in the entrance to your orchard, when you gather up the chaff to make your corn-dollies, remember that we are also commanded not to bow down to idols, and ask yourself, if you have already placed your fears and hopes in Yahweh first and foremost, why do you need these other gods, why can Yahweh not serve you first and last?"

His subtleties seemed irrefutable. Men and women ate out of his hands - or would have done, though they were rarely clean enough. If he had been brought before himself in court to be judged for his personal hygiene, he would have had no choice but to sentence himself to several weeks of ritual bathing! All great men are hypocrites, eventually.

"What sort of people is it that prefers the practice of ritual prostitution under the sacred trees of Asherah to taking on the challenge, thrown down by the Almighty, to become a living light unto the nations? It is a people of quite massive ordinariness and mediocrity, that is what it is. Because sexual indulgence is so much easier than the abstinence required for moral leadership. Are we, then, to be just another ordinary and mediocre people, copulating in the trees until we are exhausted by our incapacity to find new forms of sensual delight? And what of our part of the bargain then, what of our commitment to the covenant? Do we turn from Yahweh only because his challenge is too difficult for us? If so, it is ourselves we fear, ourselves we are turning from, not him. Leaving the land of the Pharaohs would have been too much for such a people. We would all be slaves in Mitsrayim even now."

That was what he preached that day at Mitspeh. My father heard him. He went with Shammah and Nachshon. I was too young to go with them, but I grew up hearing my father forever quoting from that speech – "copulating in the trees" became practically a proverb in our house, whenever any of us strayed from the path. "And what have you been up to then, copulating in the trees?" It's hard now not to laugh at hearing it. It became my father's own, personal speech, his own, personal illumination. I didn't hear Shmu-El myself till many, many years later, by when he had already become the inspirational force behind my own convictions, as if by proxy through my father. What a phrase: "a living light unto the nations"! Would that there were another like him now in Yisra-El. But we shall not see his like again, Shlomo - not in the ranks of Gad and Natan anyway.

✡

Yes, Mitspeh. I must speak of Mitspeh. Of how Shmu-El gathered the tribes below the watchtower and demanded - literally demanded - a national revival. And got it - though not, it must be said, in quite the way he had envisaged. Because his vision was not yet their vision. Because twenty years had passed since Eli's death, and the sins of the parents do not have the effect they are supposed to on the children. Because the Ark may have been kept safe in Giv-On, but the Bene Ephrayim and the Bene Yehudah were still as willing as ever to take it with them onto the battlefield should the Bene Pelet launch another assault.

Twenty years may have passed, but Shmu-El's fits of ill-temper hadn't. If anything he had grown more irascible, year by year, as he travelled the land from tent to tent and town to town, from unholy tree to half-holy shrine, from refuge-city to refuge-city, following the Ark on its annual pilgrimage, passing judgement in legal cases, teaching, chastising the people with his rages that were as holy as they were unholy. People say he began raging on the day that Eli allowed the Ark to go to Even-Ezer - Shmu-El was one of the few apprentices who openly argued against it - had gone on raging as he watched it fall into the hands of the Bene Pelet and knew that the people had lost their faith in Yahweh. Even when rumours began circulating that the statue of Dagon had been decapitated, even when the Bene Pelet tried to rid themselves of the Ark and did finally persuade the Bene Ephrayim to take it back, still Shmu-El continued ranting and chastising and verbally flagellating the people. Because they had put Yahweh to the test, and Yahweh was not a god who allowed himself to be tested. No, indeed, he was a god who did the testing - and they had failed him. Why else had he let himself be captured, but to make the point? But the faith was undermined, and it would take something quite exceptional to restore it. It would take, indeed, a most extraordinary paradox - and Shmu-El's genius to appreciate that. Only by testing Yahweh once again, but this time making sure he was victorious, only thus could he begin to get his people back onto the proper path. But how? It was a monumental task, surely beyond the capacities of any ordinary man - except that Shmu-El wasn't any ordinary man. But still, how? For twenty years he had racked his brain, unable to find a way. Now, Yahweh himself provided it.

"If you will return to the Lord with all your hearts, then put away the foreign gods, put away the Ashterot, and make yourselves ready in your hearts, and serve him. Then he will deliver you out of the hand of the Bene Pelet."

He had carried that message for more than two years now, from Dan to Ber Sheva and back again. In each sacred grove, under every holy tree, by every cairn and masebah, at every covenant stone and memorial to the dead, in the temple towers at Chatsor, Shechem and Megiddo, by the twelve stone pillars that Abou Yah-Akov set up at Luz, in Arad, at the temple of the Bene Mitsrayim at Beit-She'an, by every ancient altar of mud-brick or quarried stone where people gathered to sacrifice and worship, Shmu-El had stood up and delivered what he liked to call his "sermon on the mount", berating the tribes of the League of Ephrayim - and when they allowed him into their domain, the Bene Yehudah too.

"Turn away from Ba'al and Asherah. Repent. Return to Yahweh."

Only he never put it quite like that, because nobody would have listened to him. He put it, rather, into poetry, and delivered it like a temple chorister at the new year festival, in the words of the ancient psalms.

"Blessed is the man who refuses the counsel of the ungodly, who does not stand in the way of sinners, nor sit among those who are scornful. His delight is the Law of the Lord, and on this Law he meditates both day and night."

Who could possibly resist such eloquence, such poetry?

"He shall be like a tree planted by the riverside, which brings forth fruit in its season. His leaf shall not wither. Whatever he does shall prosper."

Who could possibly resist such promises, such rewards?

"But not so the ungodly, not so the worshippers of Ashterot and Ba'alim, not so the children of Bli-El. They are like the chaff which the wind drives away. The ungodly shall not be called on Judgement Day, nor shall sinners stand in the congregation of the righteous. For the Lord knows the way of the righteous, but the ungodly shall perish."

No one was certain what the congregation of the righteous actually referred to. But no one wanted to be ostracised, no one wanted to receive the ordinance of the leper - especially not from a man so obviously nearer to god than they: his flaming eyes, the long strands of hair falling over his shoulders or wrapped around the bald patches on his skull, the clothing he hadn't taken off or washed in months, the skin cracked and callused from too much desert air - the whole, fake, theatrical costume of his Prophetcy, the hours of preparation that went into all that spontaneous hyperbole. Don't you believe me, Shlomo? No, you are right not to, because it isn't true. But there were many, very many, who lodged the accusation. Never openly, mind you. No one would have dared to say it to his face.

"Blessed is he whose sins have been forgiven. Blessed is he whom the Lord can not condemn for iniquity, because in his spirit there is no guile. Blessed is he who turns aside from idols and worships Yahweh with all his heart, for he shall be delivered from his enemies."

That last did indeed sound like something he had made up to fit the occasion. But no matter. Everyone wanted the means of delivery from their enemies. Especially as there were once more rumours of the Bene Pelet armouring themselves for war.

It had begun to work too, by sheer weight of repetition. Mount Tsaphon, Ba'al's holy mountain, had become decidedly hors de faveur of late - even those wealthy Bli-El who liked to take their winter holidays snow-walking had switched to the resorts on Mount Chermon, which had fewer religious associations. And just as good facilities, even if the snow was thinner. Megiddo, Chatsor, even Shechem had been practically abandoned. The annual play-festival at Beit-Reshef had been so seriously disrupted by the heckling of Shmu-El's disciples that it had been impossible to hear how Ba'al fought Yam the sea-god, and Reshef himself fought Mot the god of death, in order to save the land from flood and famine. Great story, great play, but pagan, and Shmu-El simply would not tolerate any form of paganism - foolishly, if you want my opinion. Much better to accept all forms of worship, and then subsume them within the greater concept of the Omnideity. People will more quickly abandon Ba'al for Yahweh if they genuinely understand that Ba'al is merely a minor attribute, a single aspect of the greater Yahweh. No one wants to worship a lesser god!

But this wasn't how Shmu-El saw it - in his book, anathemas had to be extinguished; and perhaps, at that time, he was right. His own work has made it less necessary now, for Yahweh is predominant thanks to him. And of course, through all his harangues, he studiously avoided mention of either Yah or Anat, abhorred the

Ashterot but never the Lady Asherah herself, and by constantly referring to Yahweh as "the Lord", he inferred a kind of tacit acceptance of both Tammuz and Adonis which was politic to say the least. It was really only the practices of the Bene Kena'an that he disapproved. The rest was merely rhetoric designed to whip up evangelical fervour for Yahweh.

And gradually he was winning the Bene Yisra-El back. That year of Mitspeh, indeed, the city-elders of Beit-Reshef cancelled their festival altogether, for fear of financial catastrophe - though publicly it was stated that the gods themselves had decreed a jubilee. Wonderful pragmatism! And at Yareyacho, in the temple of Inanna the grandmother of Asherah, the phallic teraphim were smashed one night in an orgy of iconoclasm and general destruction by a group calling itself "the Chassidim of Yahweh", "God's Faithful". They smashed windows and looted half the town, beat the old bo'ab at the shrine of Nevi Nimrod so badly he was left crippled; and on the temple altar, with their throats cut, they left a scorpion, a snake, a turtle-dove and a gazelle - the four principal animals of the goddess - sacrificed.

Shmu-El's influence lay behind all this fundamentalist sedition of course, though there was no evidence of his hand actually stirring the pot, and in public he condemned the outrage, if only because violence hurt his cause. No, while others acted to precipitate the final victory of Yahweh, he was happy to wait until the time was right, urging it in his sermons and court judgements, knowing it would come when Yahweh was ready, and not a moment sooner. Nor did he need hallucinatory drugs to help him predict the future, as so many of the charlatan priests and prophets did - and do, Shlomo; and still do. Yahweh's signal would be unmistakeable: the kindling of the forges of the Bene Pelet, the smelting of iron for the fashioning of weapons. And so it fell out.

They gathered in Ekron, before the shrine of the city-god Ba'al-Zvuv, and dedicated themselves in public ceremony to provide for the Lord of the Flies a festal sacrifice of corpses of the Bene Yisra-El. Of the frontier towns, not only Ekron but also Aphek had been reinforced, as had Gat. The coastal cities were emptied, and ships had been arriving daily from Cheret and Caprisin and the islands of Yavan. Whole tracts of the hill-country had been ransacked to provide stores in expectation of a long campaign. Men of the Bene Chor, and other tribesman of the Plain of Sharon, had been compelled against the lives of their wives and daughters to swell the ranks of foot-soldiers. It was the largest army the Bene Pelet had ever put into the field, both in numbers and the sheer physical size of some of their warriors. No one would think of it now, but some of the generals who commanded them that day must have been the same ones who would lead them at Sochoh: Gol-Yat of course, Shimshon, Saph who had six fingers on each hand - and six toes on each foot, as we found out years later, when Yah-Natan ben Shim-Yah my nephew killed him in the battle at Gat.

The presumption was that they were going to launch an attack on Kiryat-Ye'arim, and that their purpose was not the capture but this time the destruction of the Ark. A logical stratagem. But also a mistake, the common mistake of all our enemies, who fail time and again to understand the link between national and religious politics. Had they simply moved against Beit-Shemesh, or Zorah, or Sorek, or even Timna or Eshta'ol, extending the frontier a further dozen miles, conquering by gradual encroachment as they had been doing for so long, the Bene Ephrayim would have fought alone, perhaps assisted by the Bene Yamin but without the League. Rivalries would have precluded the Bene Yehudah from coming to their rescue. And without the support of the Bene Yehudah, there was no direct route for the Bene Shimon to help either. And as to the League. Memories of Even-Ezer haunted them. Why should northern tribes like the Bene Dan or the Bene Asher send men to die for the sake of southern towns like Zorah or Beit-Shemesh - the Bene Dan especially, who had once inhabited precisely that coastal region where the Bene Pelet were now ensconced, inhabited it for two hundred years until the invaders compelled them literally to up tents and seek a new tribal territory three hundred miles to the north - but I've mentioned that before, haven't I? My memory, Shlomo, is like my eyesight, excellent for long distances, but no good at all close up. Anyway. The threat was to a religious shrine, to Kiryat-Ye'arim, to Giv-On itself, to the very house of Avi-Nadav where the Ark was kept. After listening to Shmu-El's exhortations for the past two years, no one doubted any longer that every man in Yisra-El was implicated. The term had not been meaningful since Abou Mousa died. But now, again, it was. This was a national crisis.

So it was that Shmu-El summoned the tribes to the watchtower at Mitspeh, for a service of cleansing and repentance. Two days of libations and fasting; precisely the activities most conducive to the sort of fervour he was seeking.

"We have sinned against the Lord."

And Shmu-El judged them. And found them sorely wanting.

Thinking that they were unprepared, that a time of prayer and fasting was the perfect time to catch the Bene Yisra-El off guard and inflict the ultimate defeat, the Bene Pelet brought forward the date and changed the direction of their assault - two acts of foolishness, as any military man will tell you. Now they decided to attack the Bene Yisra-El right where they were praying, right there at Mitspeh. To attack the lion in its den - a further foolishness to compound the other two. Look at any map, Shlomo. Take a radius six miles around Yiru-Sala'am, and you will locate almost all the principal shrines of Yisra-El, shrines for which every clansman of the Bene Yisra-El would die rather than accept defeat. Imagine it like a sun-dial: Giv-On and Ramah and Giv-Yah between twelve and one, Beit Anatot at two, Yareyacho and Gil-Gal at four, Beit Lechem at seven, Kiryat-Ye'arim at nine, Mitspeh at eleven. Kiryat Ye'arim is the most westerly, and the hills are at their steepest there. To attack from Ekron, all they needed was to march due east across the Beit Shemesh ridge, avoiding all the garrisoned towns completely, and come down upon Kiryat-Ye'arim from the heights, just as they had come down on Even-Ezer twenty years before. Nor can I see how we could possibly have stopped them. But to reach Mitspeh required a more northerly route, flatter and more open and therefore more easily defended, passing through Chephira on the other side of the Beit Shemesh ridge, and more importantly having to take on the garrison at Giv-On, which Yo-Av will tell you from hard experience is a good challenge for anyone who takes an interest in military strategy.

So they came on, slowly, ponderously, resisted all the way, but with sufficient weight of numbers that obstacles were insufficient except to delay them. And meanwhile, there was Shmu-El - with hindsight it was arrogant to the point of being comic - aloft in the watchtower with half the army of Yisra-El prostrate beneath him while he berated them once again, summoning them back to Yahweh, congratulating those - and there were many - who had abandoned the Ba'alim and

115

Ashterot already, firing the rest with the sort of pious fervour they would need when the Bene Pelet finally got past Giv-On and appeared over the horizon, the dust of an entire army of Ba'alim and Ashterot, come to take on, not Shmu-El, not even Yisra-El, but El Yahweh himself, in what had now transcended the national, and become a holy war.

"The Lord is my light and my deliverance. Who should I fear? The Lord is the strength of my life. Of whom should I be afraid?"

His arm outstretched, his long, bony finger pointing westwards towards Ekron.

But the distant sound of hooves and iron echoed its own warning.

"When the wicked, when even my enemies and my foes come upon me to devour my flesh, they shall surely stumble and fall."

He was playing with the words, extemporising them, turning the past tense of the familiar song into the present tense of the familiar predicament, bringing the words to life as though by conjuration in the looming shadows of the approaching horde.

"Though an army sets itself against me, my heart will not fear. Though war should engulf me, in this I will have confidence, that the one thing I have desired of the Lord will be granted me, that I may dwell in his house all the days of my life, that I may look upon beauty, that I may enquire at his Temple."

His Temple, Shlomo. His Temple.

And how they sang! Thousands, thousands of voices joined in song, the harmony of Yisra-El, the unison of all the tribes. How my father must have been uplifted by this, as by nothing else in all his life - he for whom choir practices and festival performances were the reason he had been put on Earth. And what a choir! How I wish I had been there. And how ironic that of all his sons the two my father had brought with were Nachshon and Shammah, the noisiest of players and the least melodious of singers; Nachshon whose blowing of the chatsotsra might have routed the Bene Pelet single-handed; Shammah whose thundering on the meziltayim could have invoked the full infinitude of gods. But Shmu-El was already doing that. Just by stretching his arms out in the manner of the conductor of an orchestra, just by selecting with inspired precision the most apt verses from the most fitting psalms, he was generating an atmosphere amongst the crowds that was very close to mass hysteria. Too much libation wine upon entirely empty stomachs exacerbated it. With every pause the cries of Hallelu-Yah reverberated more and more insistently, until it became clear why, of all the gods and goddesses he had anathematised, she, Yah, goddess of the moon, sister-wife of Ephron the sun-lord of the Bene Chet, she whose shrine protects the Tomb of the Patriarchs, she who is the mother of all living and whose bitter tears gave their name to the hill of sacrifice in Yiru-Sala'am, she to whom you were dedicated, Yedid-Yah, as was your brother Adoni-Yah and my beloved, ever-mourned, never-forgotten Yah-Natan ben Sha'ul; she was too much in the hearts and souls of Yisra-El even for one as great as Shmu-El to remove her. Hallelu-Yah, they cried, over and over. Shmu-El could call for worship of one god, of Yahweh, all he liked. But she will never be erased from the hearts or from the songs of Yisra-El, for she too is eternal – the divine radiance, the holy spirit, the female principle, the mother of all the gods.

"Ve anachnu nevarech Yah, me-atah ve-ad olam. Hallelu-Yah. We will pour out our blessings towards Yah, now and forever. Hallelu-Yah."

I have heard of fanatics in the East, Shlomo, men of Bav-El and El-Am and the lands of Hodu far beyond, who in this state will flagellate their bodies till they bleed, or throw themselves alive upon a kindled fire. But this, this was no Ark, no Tabernacle, no icon, no divine warrior summoned up by magical incantation. This was the congregated host of Yisra-El, seeking the mystery of its own soul, recreating itself from within. Yahweh is not a god who intervenes, because he does not need to intervene. Yahweh inspires, and men themselves perform like gods. And what inspiration! This middle-aged, frail, ascetic man, physically short-sighted but o what vision, his bones visible through flesh rendered practically translucent by fasting. But the power. The power. You could almost hear the pulse racing.

"In times of trouble he will hide me in his pavilion. In the secret of his Tabernacle he will conceal me. Then he will set me up upon a rock."

As Abou Mousa had been set upon a rock when the Bene Amalek attacked, and as long as his arms were held outstretched, Yahweh was with his people, and they prevailed.

Even this, even this, Shmu-El had thought of and evoked.

While all around him men were preparing themselves for battle, moving into their tribal formations even as he continued singing out

117

the psalm.

"And now my head shall be lifted up above my enemies, though they gather round about me. And I will offer in his Tabernacle sacrifices of joy. And I will sing, yes, I will sing unto the Lord, for he has triumphed gloriously; the horse and his rider has he thrown into the sea."

It was the most inspired of all his inspirations. Of all the songs, there were just two he might have sung now, the Song of Devorah after she and Barak defeated Sis-Ra of the Bene Yavan, or this. But Devorah had defeated a tribe of the Bene Kena'an, and men of Kena'an were fighting with us this day. Whereas this, this was the song of the victory of Yahweh himself, against an enemy far greater and far crueller even than the Bene Pelet. This was the song of a god who could stop the seas from flowing, so that his people could cross over dry-shod. This was the song of a god who, in the very aftermath of this miracle, would confirm once more his covenant with his chosen people, by giving the Law to Abou Mousa. But more, Shlomo, more and more important, this was probably the one and only song that every man in Yisra-El was guaranteed to know, and which every man in Yisra-El truly loved to sing, even those who did not follow Yahweh. And they sang it now with gusto, even as they began to march. And the troops arriving from Kiryat Ye'arim to join them, they too heard the chanting, and joined in. A hundred thousand voices crying out:

"Ashira la-adonai ki-ga'oh ga'ah. The Lord is my strength and my song, and he will be my salvation. Your right hand, O Lord, has dashed the enemy to pieces. I will draw my sword. My hand shall destroy them."

And then, almost at the end, an amazing line, an error surely, sung by Abou Mousa at the Sea of Reeds, what, three hundred years before, and yet a line belonging to today, to now, as though he had foreseen precisely this:

"Shamu amim yirgazun chil achaz yoshvey pelashet. The people shall hear and be afraid; there will be trembling amongst the inhabitants of Pelet."

How could we lose? How could we lose, when the arms of Abou Mousa himself were raised on our behalf?

Shmu-El had descended from the watchtower by this time, had gone to the great altar on the hilltop, where a suckling lamb was

118

brought to him for sacrifice. And even as he brought the knife down to the young lamb's throat, he called on Yahweh to institute once more the special covenant with his chosen people.

And how better to institute it, than in a proper ceremony of sacrifice. Not the easy, symbolic baby-lamb, but the full-grown paschal beast. Yet where, where was the ram, bleating in the bracken? Ah, yes, there was the ram, its horns primed for the assault, marching eastwards from Ekron.

"Teach us your way, O Lord, and lead us along a straight path, because of our enemies. Deliver us not into the will of our enemies, for they are risen against us, even now they are breathing cruelty toward us."

Breathing? They were positively panting.

But no one was listening, unless possibly the ghost of Eli. Armed with sword and psalm, one hundred thousand men of Yisra-El - one hundred thousand men of Yahweh, more to the point - were champing like horses at the bit.

"Wait on the Lord. Be of good courage and he will strengthen your hearts. Wait, wait, I say. Wait upon the Lord."

But they could wait no longer.

For Yahweh had assented.

Shmu-El was vindicated.

The Bene Pelet were overwhelmed.

It was, truly, a most terrible rout.

Parchment Four

Sha'ul ben Kish, a Bene Yamin from Giv-Yah, went in search of his father's asses and came back king of Yisra-El. So does history come to chance - or is it chance to history? He tracked them north-eastwards through Mount Ephrayim - a steep and hazardous journey - and the land of Shalisha, then turned west to Shalim, and crossed Ben Yamin. Along which valleys, which hill-paths, stopping where for the night, eating where by day? The royal annals do not give details, and Sha'ul himself was remarkably reticent on the subject, given its significance in his life. He must have passed just to the east of Ophrah, because he turned south again somewhere between Beit-El and Mishmash - did I ever tell you my fascinating discovery, that mishmash means "apricot stew"; now there's a mystery that is probably not worth the delving into - before circling back towards his starting-point. But he didn't stop at Giv-Yah, because he still hadn't found them - here at least I can empathise, remembering how many sheep I lost to wolves when flocking; like every shepherd, the cost of them was deducted from my wages. On he went south, skirting Mitspeh, by-passing Ramah, to Givat-Elohim; but still he didn't find them. (Mind you, Sha'ul spent most of his life being hopelessly lost and a complete ass, so maybe this strange journey should be treated as allegorical!) So he came to Tsuph, where Shmu-El was visiting his family at the time of the annual sacrifices, and he went to ask the great man's advice. Only, instead of discovering the whereabouts of his asses, he found himself anointed Ephrayim's donkey. For what else is a king but a beast of burden, upon whom all the baggage of the land is loaded, until he falls over the cliff from simple weariness, and becomes Azaz-El?

So runs the story anyway - my interpolations apart. At least, so runs the story as recorded by the chroniclers at the royal behest. For myself, I have always found it deeply unsatisfactory - and I of all people should know; as you will, when you too have found good cause to instruct the scribes as to how exactly certain events might best be remembered to posterity. The royal privilege, Shlomo - to attempt to rule the future, as well as the present, by continually updating recorded memory of the past. Because in the end there are no living witnesses, but only words, and stones.

But most deeply unsatisfactory. For example, was this some twelve-year old ninny too scared to go home and say "daddy I've looked everywhere for those donkeys, I've been twenty miles north and south and I can't find them and I'm very sorry and it's not my fault"? Or was it a grown man of thirty-eight, who had just come home on leave after captaining a platoon at Mitspeh and spending three months afterwards leading the pursuit of the Bene Pelet all the way to Zorah, "and damn your blasted donkeys father, look for them yourself, but I'm off to be made king of Yisra-El"? Stories have to be plausible, after all, don't they, Shlomo? And for another example, has it ever occurred to anybody that the route he took was remarkably similar to the route of the Ark of Pilgrimage, from Kiryat Ye'arim to Giv-Yah and on in circuit round the very shrines Sha'ul apparently by-passed? Coincidence? Maybe. But then I have often wondered what happened to those donkeys he expelled from Shechem.

And then, consider this: did Sha'ul choose to go to see Shmu-El, or was he summoned? They say his father told him to go and seek advice. But for the whereabouts of some missing asses? Surely not? A minor seer perhaps, but not Shmu-El. What would he possibly have expected Shmu-El to do - cast a spell and summon up a familiar spirit who would catch a glimpse of hidden donkeys in the crystal pool and give him cryptic clues on how to find them? It was, too, an extraordinarily long journey to make, and even stray asses do not normally wander quite that far without someone finding them and tethering them. Not even human asses, though I have known a few who tried. But seriously, what kind of a man is it who makes pilgrimage to the most revered Judge in Yisra-El, just to ask him if he has had news of a stray mule? Then was it a parable, or a true event? (I find myself asking the same question of the birth of Abou Mousa. "Father, I've found a child, floating in a basket in some bulrushes. O please say I can keep him. Oh do, daddy, please. My stomach? Are you saying I look fat? Nine months since I last graced your presence? Now father, this is most unfair. What are you insinuating?" Well tell me, Shlomo, how do you read those so implausible events?)

But enough of asses and donkeys for the moment.

After the defeat at Mitspeh, the Bene Pelet retreated to Beit-Kar, and the tribes returned home. All, that is, except the Bene Ephrayim, who pursued the Bene Pelet coastwards towards Sorek, and then on south towards Zorah, driving them further and further back with each new assault, reclaiming their cities into Erets Yisra-El, one by one from Gat to Ekron. Until the crisis had been averted. And for a long time after this they made no more raids along the coast.

Though no one had any doubt that they would return soon enough.

Shmu-El, in the meanwhile, had retired to Ramah, a national hero, but old now, and very tired. Not old in years, but the effort to prepare the ground for Mitspeh had taken its toll on him. And after the great ceremony at Shen, when he set up the Stone of Even-Ezer as an altar of commemoration for the thirty thousand and seventy who had been slaughtered all those years and years ago, it seemed the right time to hand over authority to someone new. But who? Who could follow him - the eternal dilemma of every leader? (I know of one queen who, aware that the iron hand with which she had ruled her people had eventually made them hate her, rescued her reputation by abdicating in favour of a wretch so utterly grey, so totally incompetent, so completely incapable of leadership, that within two years the whole nation was pleading for her to return. Yes, but a dead king doesn't have that option.)

I'm sorry, Shlomo. Too much irreverence yesterday, too many digressions today. I am seventy-three years old, I think. Can you imagine how far Metu-Shelach's brain must have atrophied, living as he did to nine hundred and sixty-nine? I suspect they had a different way of counting in his day. Where was I? Sera-Yah, bring me some more patchouli - no don't write that down you fool! There, Shlomo, it's me again - you can tell by the wobbly handwriting. Half a page of dictation and already a parchment ruined. In the end one has to do everything oneself. Now where was I?

Who could lead the newly revived Yisra-El? For they were - we were - truly, revived, resuscitated as a nation. But who had the authority, let alone the audacity, to be a national rather than just a tribal leader? His own sons - Yo-El and Av-Yah (hard, isn't it, to imagine Shmu-El having sons!)? Everybody knew they were corrupt, that they took bribes, that they treated Ber Sheva as their personal fiefdom. As Eli suffered from the sins of Hophni and Pinchas, as I have suffered from what Amnon did to Tamar, and from the betrayal of my beloved Av-Sala'am, so did Shmu-El know he had brought up sons to disappoint him. And what of your sons, Shlomo - do you understand that it is the fate of leaders, that they may be expert in the matter of abstract humanity, but all too often fail when it comes to flesh and blood? What of your sons, Shlomo - will they be a disappointment to you? Take care of them.

A tribal chief, then. But which one? To choose any one tribe was to exalt it above all the others, feasible for the Bene Levi under Abou Mousa and Aharon, but to do so today would be to plough the ground in which the seeds of internecine squabbles would be sown. And besides, a national leader must have religious credentials, not just tribal and political. Then let Yahweh decide.

So the Elders of the Bene Yisra-El came to Shmu-El at Ramah and made their views unanimous - they wanted a king. Not a Judge, not a Prophet. A king. Preferably a King, with a capital and a palace. Had Abou Mousa not said that when they came into the land and were established, they might choose themselves a king? Well, they were established. They wanted him now.

"Then if you are so well established, and if you are the Elders of the Bene Yisra-El, appoint one from amongst yourselves."

Impossible. Such a choice simply could not be made. Shmu-El must proclaim a king. But Shmu-El did not want a king at all. Shmu-El wanted a successor Prophet. Stalemate.

Then Shmu-El came up with the most extraordinary suggestion.

"Appoint the Elders of the tribes by rotation."

The initial response was hardly more enthusiastic.

"In the Scroll of Abou Mousa, we are told which jewels should be placed on the breastplate of the High Priest, one jewel for each tribe."

The Elders nodded their assent. But wondering where all this might be leading.

"We are told, also, that when the Temple is built, each tribe should send a number of men to serve in it, the mishmarot, one month each by rotation. Is it not likely that Abou Mousa intended that the same be done for the kingship?"

Sly old fox that he was, he had found a piece of rope of just the right length for them all to hang themselves upon. It was the supreme compromise. Only they were no more ready to make it than he was to have a king at all. All of them longed for submission to a higher authority. For Shmu-El that meant Yahweh, and perhaps one day it would mean Yahweh to the tribal Elders too. But until Yahweh was truly established, an earthly authority would have to substitute.

Yet had Shmu-El not made the suggestion, the confederacy might never have become achievable later on. It was a typical piece of Shmu-El genius. Each of the tribal Elders yearned to be the one chosen for king, but all had already accepted the impossibility of such an elevation. Yet here, now, was another possibility, of ruling for one month every year. One month wasn't much - yet one month was also a great deal. A man could wield an awful lot of power in just one month. But which month for which tribe? After all, there were important feasts and festivals and national occasions in certain months, none at all in certain others. The tribe that ruled at the Pesach or the Fast of Azaz-El would gain enormous status. It wasn't going to be easy to work out a fair rotation. But there too Shmu-El's genius was at hand.

"Your stone, Abou Yah-Suph ben Elie-Ezer of the Bene Menasheh, is the achlamah, the amethyst, is it not?" The question was entirely rhetorical. "And all Yisra-El knows that the achlamah is a charm against drunkenness, and that it is worn in the autumn, when the vines are harvested."

Much laughter. Shmu-El discussing pagan superstitions! This was indeed a novelty.

"Then the kingship must go to the Bene Menasheh in the harvest month of Elul. Abou Pinchas ben Av-Raham of the Bene Dan, your name means Judgement, and the month of the scales of justice is Tishrey, so the Bene Dan will follow the Bene Menasheh."

No mention of any tribal jewel there. But the Elders had got the idea well enough. Shmu-El intended to concoct an arbitrary list, and give it the weight and authenticity of pseudo-scholarship. It might have worked too. The reluctant Elders would have to agree it between themselves, and realistically it would reduce sacred kingship to the mere chairmanship of a council of Elders, but in their ignorance of jewels and zodiacs, and with power visible just beyond their fingertips, they were happy to grasp at any crown of wisdom that the great Prophet might bestow upon them.

But what the Elders had not reckoned on was Shmu-El's young apprentice, Natan ben Yerachme-El. Every threshing-floor has its tare.

"Master, the order of the tribes in the list of the jewels is not the order of birth of the sons of Abou Yah-Akov."

This was true enough. But since Ephrayim and Menasheh had

taken their father Abou Yah-Suph's birthright, and with Levi becoming the priestly tribe, the order of birth could surely be discounted?

And if not the order of birth, then the tone of Shmu-El's voice, prevailing upon his apprentice to desist.

But Natan always was thick-skinned.

"Nor are either of these the same as the order in which Abou Yah-Akov gave his blessings."

Evidently Natan was even more opposed to kingship than his master. And determined to scotch any attempt to establish even one as negligible as this.

"And then again there is the order in which Yehoshua ben Nun divided the land."

Shmu-El by now was getting angry.

"Natan," he attempted to upbraid him gently. But it was obvious something sterner was required. "If we are to consider all the lists, should we not also consider the order in which Abou Mousa established the camp in the wilderness, for the protection of the Tabernacle in time of battle?"

The Elders of the tribes stared agog and in astonishment. To accuse his own apprentice of the sin of Even-Ezer! But Natan was so full of himself, so inured against any form of censure, he simply didn't take the point.

"Master, if you place the Bene Menasheh in Elul and the Bene Dan in Tishrey, according to the jewels you must place the Bene Yehudah in Nisan." Oh what a clever boy he was to have worked it all out so fast! "But the month of the lion is Tammuz, and in the Hikavtsu of Abou Yah-Akov we are told that Yehudah is a lion's whelp. He must have Tammuz."

Natan who just happened to be of the tribe of Yehudah. Tammuz which just happened to be the most important month.

By now the Elders were beginning to argue among themselves, and we have to imagine Shmu-El trying not to let his anger (or perhaps his laughter) get the better of him as he watched his little scheme collapse. The Bene Re'u-Ven were claiming the New Year month on the grounds that their stone was the odem, the beautiful rust-red sard, that odem came from the same root as Adam, the first man, that the one consistency in all the tribal lists was the first-born status of the Bene Re'u-Ven, and that therefore they must be given the first month. But this simply inflamed all the tribes, who had long ago accepted ultimogeniture, and the Bene Yah-Shachur in particular, ostensibly because they had been given the first month, but really because they suspected that the first edict of the first king would be to abolish the rotation altogether and set his tribe up as an eternal dynasty - no doubt the ploy each one of them was planning for themselves. The Bene Zvulun, in the meanwhile, demanded to know which New Year the Bene Re'u-Ven were deeming so important to their dignity, for the Tablets of Abou Mousa clearly denoted four new years, a new year of the corn in Nisan and a new year of the trees in Shvat, which was the Bene Zvulun's month, given them by Yahweh, before witnesses, through the mouth of his prophet Shmu-El...while the Bene Asher were furious that Shmu-El was proposing to give the Bene Re'u-Ven the mid-Winter month of Tevet, at which time was celebrated the birth of Adonis ben Asherah, and which must therefore be the month of their kingship by sacred right. Abou Eli-Natan ben Yah-Nadav of the Bene Levi had also realised that Iyar was the month of the twins, that the twins of course were Levi and Shimon, that Shimon had already been allocated Tammuz, and that just because the Bene Levi had been given refuge-cities in lieu of tribal territory, this was no reason to assume they had been given the priesthood as an alternative to kingship – on the contrary; what is a king after all, if not the Highest of all High Priests, Kohen Ha Kohanim? But Iyar had been allocated to the Bene Gad, despite the fact that the Bene Gad were the one tribe not to have a jewel in the priestly breastplate; which complaint, of course, they would not fail to interject as soon as suitable occasion offered...

Shlomo, you are wondering why I am putting all this comic farce down in so much detail - no, you are intelligent enough not to be wondering that at all. I imagine you sitting with your head in your hands, shaking it in dismay and consternation, wondering if you shouldn't just have left all this to Adoni-Yah and gone to live in Sheva with that lovely wife of yours; but still thinking ahead to the day when you will build the Temple, and must face again what Shmu-El previsaged that autumn afternoon in Ramah. How will you resolve it - by scholarship, or by imposition? I have thought long and hard about this over many years - every time I summon the Elders of the Confederacy to Privy Council, in truth, and end up wishing I could hang the bally lot of them, and only relent for fear their replacements will be even worse. Before he died, I consulted the oracle several times. Grandfather Oved, I mean. At Gil-Gal there are twelve stones that make up the sacred circle, and each of these stones marks the high point of the sun in each of the twelve months. Am I not right in saying that the twelve tribes take their places at the covenant festival each year, always by the same stone? No one knows why, but no one has ever questioned the tradition. Neither Shmu-El nor Natan thought of it. But grandfather Oved did. Perhaps you should as well.

So much, then, for a shared tribal kingship by rotation. Shmu-El had no doubt thought by this clever ruse to rid the Elders of their mad yearning for kingship altogether. But they remained adamant. And since choosing a king from the Elders of the tribes was demonstrably out of the question, the Elders looked again to Shmu-El, with the authority of Yahweh behind him, to do what they could not. Though what they really wanted, of course, was Shmu-El himself.

Officially he was still just an ordinary circuit judge, who sat quarterly in each of the four sanctuary towns - Beit-El, Gil-Gal, Mitspeh and Ramah. Officially he had retired, and was spending his last years in seclusion with his wife and one or two disciples, teaching and dictating his memoirs. Officially the hordes of tribal Elders, visionary priests, foreign ambassadors, advice-seekers, would-be students, merchant representatives of scholars from Bav-El and On and Ugarit, men and women who wished only to have touched his sleeve so they could believe it had cured them of piles or acne; or worse still the men and women who wished only to have touched his sleeve so they could dine out for years to come on their personal knowledge of the fact that Shmu-El was a fraud, a quack and a charlatan; they and all the other hundreds of people who turned up to disturb the peace of Ramah daily - officially they were not to be admitted, though of course they always were.

Because the reality bore little resemblance to the intention. Shmu-El was the great man of Yisra-El. Like Devorah and Gid-Yon before him, the judge had become a Judge, the prophet a Prophet. He was treated as Yahweh's appointed leader of the Bene Ephrayim and the Bene Yehudah and all the other sons and grandsons of Abou Yah-Akov - a king in all but name and trappings, a king in the most ancient of traditions, the priest of god who reigns.

127

But one who was as adamantly opposed to the kingship as the Elders were determined there should be a king.

"All Yisra-El waits for you to announce him."

He had taken up weaving - a rather silly gesture designed to show him as a man of the people. Whenever someone came to talk to him, but with whom he did not wish to talk, he would stand in front of the loom - he used a vertical one; he was too frail to use a horizontal loom, which would have required him to squat on the ground - dressed as ever in the humility of his linen apron and one of his mother's goat-skin coats repaired so often there was little of the original left in them, working three or four warps at any one time, muttering away about how inexpert he was, how determined he was to reach the point where he could work all six warps at once and make more complicated patterns.

It was all decidedly infuriating.

"Master, a name. You must declare a name."

Sheikhs of the Bene Yah-Shachur and the Bene Gad, who had travelled in full camel-train a hundred miles to visit him, with wives, sons, counsellors. And an old man in a linen ephod, muttering about seamless robes.

"If we could add another beam at the base, a rotating beam, it would be possible to make much longer rolls of cloth."

Had he become an inventor in his old age?

"A name, Shmu-El. Or at the very least a tribe. A clan."

"A tribe? But surely it is obvious which tribe. In Yisra-El, each son is supplanted by his younger brother. Kayin by Hevel. Yishma-El by Abou Yitschak. Essav by Abou Yah-Akov. Aharon by Abou Mousa. Zerach by Pharets. Menasheh by Ephrayim. Then what of Yisra-El himself?"

He left the thought unfinished. But it was understood. His disciples, Gad and Natan, would later argue that the kingship must be focused on the central shrines, and that all but four of the central shrines were located in the same tribal territory. But this was exegesis, not scripture. Shmu-El had pronounced his oracle. If there must be a king, he should come from the youngest clan of the youngest tribe. So it was said, so it would happen.

But still no name.

Yet still I have never understood, what I leave to you, Shlomo, to

128

interpret, to try to fathom. Why, if Shmu-El was so reluctant to appoint a king at all, why did he first appoint Sha'ul, and then me, to be bad kings, when he could have allowed Yahweh to anoint him as a very good king himself? Or perhaps he knew that Sha'ul would fail, as I have failed, as you will fail - as all rulers ultimately fail; and chose him for that very reason. Shlomo, I believe this may well be the truth of it. Shmu-El was opposed to kingship itself, because he believed it would bring an end to the era of the Judges and the Prophets, because it would concentrate temporal power in human hands, and in thus undermining the clergy would eventually undermine Yahweh too. Heed this warning, as I have tried to heed it. Shmu-El chose Sha'ul - I should underline these next words, but the quill might tear the parchment - in scarlet then, to emphasise it - precisely because he knew that Sha'ul would be a failure as a king.

But why him, of all possible candidates? After all, you don't have to look very far to find a man to fail – it's the potential successes who are so few and far between. Yah-Natan thought it was because he was so tall, which is as good a reason as any when you are at war with Saph and Lachmi and Gol-Yat! Mind you, his pedigree was immaculate. He was a Bene Yamin of the Matri clan; the son of Kish, son of Avi-El, son of Bechorat, son of Aph-Yah who was one of those whom Yehoshua ben Nun summoned to Shechem when he set up the Covenant Stone. His home was in the hills above Giv-Yah, and if you are going to exalt one clan above the rest by choosing a king from among them, then surely the Bene Giv-Yah were the one clan you could justify, because they were now the Guardians of the Ark. And yet, he wasn't a follower of Yahweh - the donkeys, Shlomo, remember the donkeys. He was a pantheist like most of his countrymen - exactly the sort of pagan Shmu-El most despised and railed against. His pantheism was apparent even from the names he gave his children, seeking to placate every one of the gods by dedicating a child to each: Yah-Natan for Yah and Yahweh, Ish-Ba'al - Ishu'i, as Av-Ner always called him, though everyone else preferred his nickname Ish-Boshet - whose god-link hardly needs stating; then Melchi-Shu'ah for Moloch, Avi-Nadav for the ancestor worshippers of Kena'an, Merav his elder daughter for the Lady, Michal for El. His wife was Kena'ani too, Achi-No'am bat Achi-Ma'ats. Yet the tribes accepted him.

And what about the opinion, commonplace at the time, that Sha'ul did not even want to be king, that initially he declined Shmu-El's invitation - if invitation is what it was? After all, it is politic to turn down a proffered crown - provided you are certain it will be proffered a second time - in order to pre-exonerate yourself, to pre-establish impunity, something you are bound to be glad of later on. Every ruler plays these tricks - like threatening to resign in order to force an issue in your favour. I know. I've done it many times. Though whether Sha'ul was clever enough...

Do you know, derech agav, Shmu-El's "Oracle of Kingship", his great vision that put even Abou Mousa's cynical warnings to shame: forced conscription, forced labour, taxation, complete loss of personal liberty! How did I, how will you, Shlomo, be reckoned on that tally? (Yes, and how much easier it is to be a commentator than a player!)

"He will take your sons and appoint them for himself, for his chariots, and to be his horsemen; and some shall run before his chariots. And he will appoint captains over thousands, and captains over fifties, and will set them to ear his ground, and to reap his harvest, and to make his instruments of war, and to be the instruments of his chariots. And he will take your daughters to be confectionaries" - (I do like that word, Shlomo, so perfectly apposite: 'confectionaries'. It ought to have been a euphemism, far sweeter than 'concubines'; but it wasn't. He really meant confectionaries) – "and to be cooks, and to be bakers. And he will take your fields and your vineyards and your olive orchards, even the best of them, and give them to his servants. And he will take the tenth of your seed, and of your grape, and give it to his officers, and to his servants. And he will take your menservants and your maidservants and your goodliest young men and your asses" - (those asses again; with Sha'ul you cannot avoid those asses) – "and he will put them to work. He will take the tenth of your sheep and you shall be his servants. And you will cry out on that day because of the king you will have chosen; and the Lord will not hear you in that day."

And this Pharaoh, this tyrannical despot of an autocratic megalomaniac, he will also take your disunited land, and establish an amphictyony of the tribes, and give it a solid foundation from which to develop into the mightiest power in the world: an infrastructure, a central government, an organised civil service, a modern army, and dignity, trade, an empire, schools, literature and music, new and better methods for the farmers, the aleph-bet, religious tolerance, freedom for all the people and not just the Bene Yisra-El, and a genuine forum through which all the people can take responsibility for their own lives and the life of the nation, and be heard. But don't think to mention any of that, Shmu-El. Don't bother to suggest that a great king might indeed make Yisra-El a light unto the nations, that the City of Peace will not be built without him. I'm sorry. I mustn't rant. I know.

And anyway, why am I telling you all this? Because in truth he was right; most kings are bad kings, and even great kings err; and however much good a king may do, there is always the problem of the succession. And because, Shlomo, if you are to be king of Yisra-El, you must understand the first law of kingship in Yisra-El, which is that you have no right to be a king at all. "And the Lord said to Shmu-El: 'Hearken to the voice of the people in all that they say to you, for they have not rejected you, but they have rejected me, that I should not reign over them.'" Never forget that. If Yahweh is our king, then we do not require and should not have a mortal king. To be anointed king is tantamount to usurpation of the throne of Heaven. Yet Abou Mousa inscribed it, and Shmu-El permitted it, however reluctantly, and even had the justification written in his scroll. There had never been a king in Yisra-El before, and despite what the Elders wanted to believe, the conditions set by Abou Mousa for the anointment of a king were far from met. To establish a monarchy presupposes the ending of the era of the Judges, and changes dramatically the nature of the Guild of Prophets and the authority of the tribes. It was the most radical step the nation had taken in two hundred years, and it lacked the authority of covenant.

And as to thee and me. Never become so arrogant as to think you are yourself a god, as so many kings allow themselves to do - just look at that young peacock Shishak in Mitsrayim if you want an illustration. You are Yahweh's anointed representative on Earth, whatever the ceremonies and prayers and blessings may infer. You are the king of men, appointed by men, anointed in the name of Yahweh, but you may not act without his blessing, and most definitely not without his sanction. Without covenant, there is no divine right. Do more than that, and you become his usurper, falsely occupying his throne. One day there will be a true Anointed King, as Abou Mousa prophesied, but only when the land is settled and the

Temple built. You are not the True Mashi'ach, only, perhaps, his forebear. You are not a god, as some kings like to call themselves. Remember the liturgy, Shlomo. Avinu Malkeynu - Our Father is our King. You, the earthly monarch, are a mere impostor, a temporal ruler with a job to do on behalf of an Almighty who does not require kings because he has given all men free will and responsibility in equal measures. Kingship is a species of responsibility (though it is not, I confess, without its pleasures and its satisfactions too); but it must be a form of service, or else it is nothing. Allow yourself to be seduced by your own power and you will become a despot, a tyrant. Do you know that I had Shmu-El's "Oracle of Kingship" inscribed on a sapphire stone and for years wore it on a necklace like a yoke. I shall make sure it's kept for you in my will.

But I must speak about Sha'ul, the first king of the Bene Yisra-El. In name, anyway. In reality, he was barely king of the Bene Ephrayim let alone the whole of Yisra-El, little more than a tribal sheikh with middling ambitions, and unlike myself - and forgive my immodesty, but modest men make modest achievements - none of the capabilities to fulfil even those middling ambitions. In the kingship leagues he comes nowhere - a Yitschak who would have been an Av-Ram. He was king over - what? the hill-country north of Giv-Yah where his clan was based, on the Ephrayimite borders. Yes, but Chivim and Arkim also inhabited the region, and they did not accept his rule. According to the official annals he fought two major battles early in his reign, to try to expand his kingdom - the first at Giv-Yah against the Bene Pelet, the second at Yavesh Gil-Yad against the Bene Ammon. But Bene Pelet at Giv-Yah? After the Battle of Mitspeh? Surely not? A raiding party possibly, but not an army. The annals state that the Bene Pelet camped at Mishmash, on the northern side of the valley, that the Bene Giv-Yah controlled the southern crossing, and that Sha'ul established his royal palace at Giv-Yah only after he had expelled the Bene Pelet. However...but no, I shall not defame the memory of a dead king, not even in private. Let us simply leave it to history to question the detail and prove the matter one way or the other. And as to the Battle of Yavesh Gil-Yad, I will have more to say about that little matter in a moment. Certainly it happened, and Sha'ul won, but the Bene Ammon never accepted his dominion, and becoming sacred-king of Yavesh Gil-Yad can hardly be described as establishing the frontiers of an empire. Yes, he fought other battles against the Bene Amalek, culminating in that silly monument he set up in Carm-El of Chevron. But even at the time of his death at the Battle of Gil-Bo'a, he controlled no more than the central hill country as far north as Yazar-El; and he fought that last battle only to try to wrest control of the whole valley. A whole valley! Nimrod ruled nothing but a valley either - only his was the Pharat, all two thousand miles of it. And Sha'ul never even held the whole valley, because he was killed trying to take it. His entire kingdom was really quite spectacularly small - Ephrayim, the pastures of the Bene Yamin, Gil-Yad. But even within that territory there were major cities which retained their independence - Sala'am, for example, and more significantly Chevron. Even when he was pursuing me, to Adullam, into the desert south-west of Yevus, or the wilderness south-east of Chevron, he never ventured far from home, and needed the permission of the tribal elders to enter "their" domains. His whole life was lived in the tiniest of geographical areas. And people call him king of Yisra-El! In all his life he never so much as visited the lands of Asher, Naphtali, Zvulun or Dan, and only went southwards into Mo-Av, Edom, the Negev and beyond to pursue wars that had no outcome, or to pursue me to the same effect. And when he entered Shimon or Re'u-Ven or Yehudah, it wasn't as a king touring his realm, but as a distant wanderer, hoping for a welcome in a foreign land.

But I sound embittered, and I don't mean to sound embittered. It is hard, Shlomo, sometimes it is very hard for me to be objective about Sha'ul. As king anointed by Shmu-El it was my duty to honour him, and to respect his person, which I can vow before Yahweh that I always did. As a person I found him nigh on impossible, as all men did; his insecurity was so profound, his moodiness so completely unpredictable, that one never really knew where one stood with him. He wouldn't take advice either, had no ministers as such, no Privy Council, appointed drones to do his donkey-work. When he did gather the Elders for a council, it was only so that he could shout at them - a device he used, having no other, to show how much power he had. In his throat, anyway. But he never listened to anybody. Sha'ul always knew best, so why did he need to listen? No, what

Sha'ul needed from the Elders was a head or two that he could chop off when things inevitably went wrong - and no one could outrival him in the skill of picking from a group of ruthlessly ambitious sons-of-bitches which one or two in particular no one would care less about if they were given their come-uppance. Yah-Natan used to say that he was so egocentric, he would have insisted on running a conspiracy single-handed. (Ah, Shlomo, you cannot imagine the pleasure of writing all this down, of venting my spleen in this way; as satisfying as the movement of a bowel after a long period of constipation!)

As my father-in-law he was a complete pig, who first refused to let Michal marry me, and then took her away from me, and then spent several years pursuing me in order to kill me, and finally drove me to the greatest sin of my whole life, the betrayal of my people, the choice imposed upon me by his paranoia: to stay in Yisra-El and die, or to flee for safety among our enemy the Bene Pelet. I shall never forgive him for doing that to me. And there are other matters, of which no man or woman in Yisra-El knows anything despite the gossip, and of which I am still undecided whether or not to speak, but for which I cannot forgive him either. You must deduce for yourself what I am inferring.

He was thirty-eight, tall, handsome, and with a reputation for bravery that he had won in the pursuit of the Bene Pelet into Sorek. He had married Achi-No'am in the years before Mitspeh, when men worshipped who they worshipped, and married who they married. At war's end he had two choices. As a junior officer with a reputation, he could make a career of soldiering; but if he did so, what of his wife and children? Or he could return to Giv-Yah, and farm, and take his place on the Council of Elders of the Bene Matri - a life of little consequence and few rewards. Being Sha'ul, he couldn't make a choice, but went home, in the hope that fate would make it for him. It did.

Then – you will understand, Shlomo, that I am telling you what actually happened, and not necessarily what is written - then word travelled amongst the clans that Shmu-El had relented, had agreed that a king might be appointed, and that he should come from the youngest clan of the youngest tribe. But who exactly did that mean? The Bene Yamin, obviously - you could tell from the smug looks on the faces of the market traders as the Elders gathered in every town

134

of the tribal territory to make their plans. But which clan - that was what required planning?

"We have consulted all the scriptures" - I imagine that much the same was said at every meeting; the local priests and seers and prophets having been given practically no time to undertake their research, their answer needed yesterday – "and there is nothing anywhere about Bin Yamin leaving sons."

Yet surely he must have done, or how else could the tribe exist today? There must be a hint, a clue, a cryptic reference, somewhere.

"In the hikavtsu of Abou Yah-Akov we are told that 'Bin Yamin is a ravenous wolf, in the morning devouring the prey, and at even dividing the spoil.'"

That must have gone down like a pig on an altar! Everywhere except in Beit Lechem anyway, where grandfather Oved was on hand to explain what, to be fair, was common knowledge among those who had made a study of the planets.

"The word is properly Jamin, not Yamin. To the priests of Bav-El of the Bene Kessed, and to the priests of Bav-El of the Bene Chet, he is the sign of the Twins which appears at its fullness in the House of the Wolf-Centaur, which rises in the morning in the sign of Anpu the Wolf-Dog who transports the souls of the dead, and which makes its circuit, sometimes in the morning, sometimes in the evening, around the planet of prophecy Nevo, which lies closest to the sun. This is the meaning of the blessing of Abou Yah-Akov."

All terribly fascinating, but of absolutely no use whatsoever in deciding which clan should have the honour of providing a king. Where else then?

"In the blessing of Abou Mousa we are told that 'Bin Yamin is the beloved of the Lord, he dwells in safety by him'" - quite clearly, with the benefit of hindsight, an ancient prophecy that the kingship was always intended for the Bene Yamin. But which clan?

Kish ben Avi-El, Sha'ul's father and chief of the Elders of Giv-Yah, had not lived his entire life on the very borders of Ephrayim, without learning that the tribes of the Northern League painted a very different picture of history from their brothers in Yehudah. The men of Ephrayim had always scorned the tales of Rach-El and Bilhah. Abou Yah-Akov, they insisted, was a Bene Aram who did not go to but actually came from Padan-Aram, whose only wives were Le'ah and Tsilpah, whose only sons were the eight they bore him, and of course one daughter, Dinah. To them, the Bene Dan had never inhabited the Coast of Sharon, but had always lived in the north around La'ish, alongside their brothers of the Bene Naphtali. (Ah, Shlomo, what a terribly complex realm we rule!) To them Bilhah the maidservant was really Bilhan the warrior. To them Rach-El was a name for the ancient mother-goddess, and no more a "wife" of Abou Yah-Akov than Sarai was to Av-Ram. To them Yah-Suph was a priest and vizier of the Bene Chet when they ruled Mitsrayim, and not a son of Abou Yah-Akov at all. And most importantly, to them, Ben Oni - as Rach-El called the boy - meant "man of On" not "son of sorrow", that he claimed Rach-El for a mother only because Yehoshua ben Nun gave him for a territory the land that happened to include Zelzah, where she is buried, but that he was really a tribe of the sun-city On of Upper Mitsrayim, the very city in which Yah-Suph had ruled.

And this too was all very interesting. But it happened also to provide a resolution. For in the Chronicles of the Bene Ephrayim it is written, that ibn Jamun was a son of Bilhan, and that ibn Jamun had not one but three sons, whose names were Bela, Becher and Yediya-El; and that Yediya-El, the youngest, had a son, who was named Bilhan for his great-grandfather. This Bilhan was a warrior, who established the kingdom of the Bene Jamun in the northern lands of the Black Sea where the Bene Chet had once ruled. Soldiers of the Bene Jamun came south, establishing themselves as Bene Dan and Bene Naphtali, and settling at last alongside the Bene On on that narrow strip of land across the Hills of Yehudah, from the Shephelah to the Yarden Valley at Yareyacho, which Yehoshua ben Nun had given to the tribe that now called itself the Bene Yamin.

"And we may not have a king who is not of the Bene Yisra-El. So it is written, by the hand of Abou Mousa."

You could almost hear the smacking of Kish ben Avi-El's lips as the information was imparted and the realisation slowly dawned. Yet there was still sweeter fruit to follow.

"So the Bene Matri, who alone can prove from scripture that they came out of Mitsrayim with Abou Mousa, and counted amongst the Bene Yisra-El even in Gershon of Mitsrayim, from them may a king be chosen. But from the other clans, from the Bene Jamun, who cannot prove such a descent..."

Unlike his son, Kish ben Avi-El was not a man to hesitate. He had sought an answer, and though it had taken time and money to procure it, and though the scholarship was convoluted, controversial and probably contentious, still it was the answer that he wanted.

✡

The Elders of the Bene Yisra-El had gathered once again, in Tsuph this time, to press Shmu-El for his answer, and just as Kish was now preparing to do, so every one of them who could had come with proof that his clan was the youngest of the youngest, and Bene Yisra-El to the grave-dust of its ancestors. And no doubt Shmu-El was delighted to have so many claims and counter-claims, because it gave him yet another pretext to delay what he would rather have postponed for ever.

But then something unexpected happened. A donkey-rider appeared in Tsuph, dust-slaked and breathless from a hurried journey. His message was a request to Shmu-El to come urgently to Zelzah, to the Tomb of Rach-El, where an oracle relating to the kingship would be prophesied.

Shmu-El went. At Zelzah three men were waiting for him, one dressed in the robes of a prince, the other two his servants. There was no sign of the ba'alat ov who inhabited the cave, and whom Shmu-El presumed to be the one who had summoned him.

"Why have I been called here? And what business has a prince of the Matri clan with familiar spirits?"

A question of some prophetic power, given what came later!

Sha'ul must have been impressed that his royal colours had been recognised - though it was an act of the utmost arrogance to wear them. Still, the whole occasion was an act - a carefully staged performance. His father had made him rehearse it all a dozen times. He was trembling with apprehension.

"My father has sent me on a pilgrimage, to learn the route of pilgrimage for the Ark of which the Bene Giv-Yah are the guardians."

Excellent opening gambit. Shmu-El may have come with reservations, but would now remain, intrigued. Yet is it not strange how even to mention one's father, to state that one acts at his behest, makes one seem a little boy of ten or twelve. Sha'ul certainly felt as such. Then it was necessary to assert himself.

"In Mitsrayim, the Bene Matri, like all those of the Bene Yamin who are Bene Yisra-El and not the warriors of Bilhan, in Mitsrayim we honoured Shet amongst the many gods, because we were outcasts from the land of Yisra-El, as Shet the red-haired was cast out from the company of the gods. And now that we are no longer outcasts, now that it is time for the anointing of a king, my father has sent me to ask if Shet too may return..."

"You travel by donkey?" Shmu-El interrupted. But he was thinking: your father sends you on pilgrimage, to ask the gods their blessing in the choice of you as king. A prince of the Bene Matri of Giv-Yah. Why not? Why not?

"Of course. The donkey is Shet's beast."

"And also the hippopotamus, the boar, the scorpion and the crocodile. A dangerous god is Shet." As though his mind were testing out the omens. But they seemed auspicious. "You have been to..."

"Shechem first, of course. Then Beit-El, Mitspeh..."

"Not all of these are shrines to Shet."

"No, Master. But they are all shrines of the Bene Yisra-El. And lastly I shall to go Givat Elohim, because it is the shrine of all the gods. If Shet is to return, he must be accepted without omission. It has been too long since the ass went wandering in the wilderness, and who knows if it is not lost. The gods must say."

Shmu-El's laughter reverberated across time as well as space. This was exegesis worthy of the pedantry of Natan.

"Prince of the Bene Matri, I can tell you precisely what the gods will say. That the lost ass has returned of its own accord, and that your father will be at home worrying about you, thinking that you are dead. But come with me first, and let us hear the oracle."

As if he had not already heard it, and understood it perfectly. And with that radiant smile, given it his approval.

"There is no oracle, Master. Forgive my father's deceit. We came to the Tomb of Rach-El only to pay our respects to her, as the mother of the true Bene Yamin, the beloved wife of Yisra-El." He was in grave danger of overstating it. But there was still one more vital thing to do. "My father requests that you officiate at the sacrifice. One of my companions is a priest. Will you give the blessing?"

There were those who said that Shmu-El should have anointed Kish ben Avi-El instead, the father being far more worthy than the son.

"Yes, Sha'ul ben Kish of the Bene Matri of Giv-Yah. Yes, I will give the blessing."

They climbed the hill above the cave until they came to the oak grove that guarded and enclosed the entrance to the Tomb. In honour of the goddess, all manner of sacred trees had been planted or had tried to seed themselves - palm and quince and pomegranate especially - but so little water was there in the soil, that now a veritable copse of dried-out roots and desiccated stumps waited to trip up the unwary. Only the oak trees could endure such arid, stony soil, and a number of slender kerm oaks stood like sentinels on either side of the path, while two enormous holly oaks, like temple pillars, rose on either side of the entrance to the sepulchre.

Five hundred years ago, when Eshet Rach-El died, Abou Yah-Akov planted a sapling by her grave, the mere stork's-leg of an infant tree. Now it was full-grown, the largest oak in Yisra-El they said, the panoply of its branches more expansive even than the terebinths of Mamre of the Bene Chevron, its shade as cool as autumn. They called it the Terebinth of Tavor, and it was sacred to the Bene Yamin as the tree of Yahweh. When we crowned the King of Spring at the festival of the Reborn Lord, we always anointed him beneath this tree, dressed in robes of scarlet of the colour of the kerm oaks, and with a crown of thorns made from the leaves of the holly oaks.

I very much doubt that Sha'ul knew of these practices, because although he was a Bene Yamin, he did not follow the mother-goddess nor her son - few town-dwellers do. Shmu-El knew though, and I cannot help wondering if it crossed his mind as they climbed between the oaks. How appropriate it would have been, to dress him as the King of Spring and anoint him underneath the terebinth. But they went on beyond it, to the mouth of the sepulchre, where not one but three priests of the Bene Giv-Yah were awaiting them. The day had been full of omens and surprises, but this, now, was the culmination, for who should he recognise but Eli-Azar ben Avi-Nadav, the son of the High Priest of Giv-Yah who had been given personal charge of the Ark and who had studied at the feet of Shmu-El for many years. Yes, yes - what other clan could he have chosen to provide a king, except that clan which Yahweh had already chosen, by placing the Ark in their abode, by making them, as a consequence of their deceit of Yehoshua, the water-carriers and wood-cutters of the Tabernacle? It should have been apparent from the outset. And of the Bene Giv-Yah, why not the Bene Matri? In time of drought, a drop of rain was what men needed - and here, especially, at the dried out sepulchre of the goddess of fertility. The auguries were most propitious. Eli-Azar's presence added gravitas as well as certainty, though he seemed a most unlikely figure in his solemn white tunic and his overgarments of the priestly sacrificer, while three kid goats gambolled on leashes at his feet.

The second priest was holding three loaves, the third a bottle of wine.

"How many kiddushim are you planning?" Shmu-El laughed.

"One here. The next at Givat Elohim."

"And the third?"

"We were hoping to return with you to Ramatayim-Tsophim, to make sacrifice there, to honour you with a meal."

Kish ben Avi-El was evidently the sort of man who knew that feint heart, so to speak, never won fair lady. But then, this was not an opportunity that would present itself a second time, and he could not have guessed success would come so quick.

"Not today, perhaps. But I will be pleased to welcome you in Tsuph another time. Is your family well, Eli-Azar?"

In any other circumstances Shmu-El would undoubtedly have embraced him, but had desisted, for it seemed to reduce to the banal what was, truly, a most solemn occasion. Yet how could he not ask the merest of polite questions?

"My family is well, Master," the priest bowed slightly from the waist. "Though my father has been much concerned of late that oxen will once more lead the Ark in pilgrimage, instead of men."

"Then let us sacrifice this goat of yours, Sha'ul ben Kish, and make the blessing on the wine, and you and I will at the very least break bread together."

Shmu-El did not leave them then, as no doubt they had expected that he would. Sending one of Sha'ul's servants on to Tsuph to let his plans be known to his disciples, he accompanied the pilgrims as they travelled on from Zelzah, across the Plain of Rephayim to Yevus, and then along the eastern route - it must have occurred to Sha'ul at some point to suggest going via Giv-Yah, a detour of only a few miles, in order that Shmu-El might be given hospitality in his father's house. Shmu-El, anyway, had made it clear he wished to visit Anatot, where he had some business to attend to.

So it was already evening when they came at last to Geva. Eli-Azar had sent one of the priests ahead, to warn of their arrival, and even as they came up the hill, so did a company of prophets come down it, a dancing procession coming from the shrine with psaltery, tabret, pipe and harp, as though it were their intention to bring the king into his palace. But recognising Shmu-El they stopped at once, grew solemn, embarrassed, apologetic; then turned back, escorting the Prophet and the company of pilgrims to the shrine.

It lay in ruins then, of course. In the year before he died, Yahni began the restoration work, and in his honour I completed it. It was he who found the entrance to the hill - not by searching for it, I should add; he was hiding from his father for the umpteenth time, and stumbled on it quite by chance, right at the very foot on the northern side, covered with broken rocks and shrubs and weeds. He often hid there, and for years it was a dare on all his friends, myself included; you couldn't join the company of the royal prince if you hadn't descended into the underworld and come out again the other side. It was truly terrifying. Until you go inside, you would swear it was a natural hill. But it was raised by men - who knows how long ago? Inside there were catacombs filled with the bones of the ancient dead, each one in its own comb. Dig out the bones, dig through the mud, and another set of bones appears, all the way upwards to the sky, so that they scaffolded the hill internally. And such terrible darkness - you entered through the mouth of She'ol, and he devoured you. Yet the priests say it is a place of life, not death. For the paths are the womb of the Great Mother. And the darkness breeds resurrection. I don't know. I don't know. I only know how terrified I was, and that it is not a journey I would ever wish to make again.

But above, on the hill itself, there is nothing but pure light. Arriving in the early evening as they did, the sun was setting over the Great Sea beyond the horizon, and the sky was crimson with its dying blood. Such are the minerals in the rocks of the gil-gal, they are always best seen at sunset - sandstone from the deserts of the Bene Edom and the Bene Re'u-Ven, rich with irons. When we cut the rock to make the twelve pillars for the gil-gal, we smelted all the surplus in the forge and wrought from it enough swords to equip a troop. But the pillars at this time were the ancient ones, darker, blacker, chipped and chiselled rocks - do you know how many were spoiled, simply by silly people carving their names or the names of their beloveds? - as gnarled as olive trees. It is a place of the most exquisite silence though - I don't know why this shrine should be more still than any other, but it is. An absence of birds, of grasshoppers, even of mosquitoes. But also a deeper silence. Perhaps it's because all the gods are present here, and rather than diminish the shrine with the noise of their perpetual rivalries and squabbles, they sulk, and leave us mortals to commune alone. Perhaps.

What happened that evening I know in every tiny detail. But I am sworn by my kingly oaths and priestly duties never to divulge it. You, Shlomo, will learn them soon enough, will come to know all the mysteries when you too are anointed king and play your part. Suffice it to say, as the annals do, that "the spirit of Yahweh came upon Sha'ul, and he began to prophesy, and became another man." What did he prophesy? What was the oracle he gave that day? Why, the oracle of Kish ben Avi-El, of course, who had bought it from the Bene Ephrayim, and which gave to the clan of the Bene Matri a stake above all others in the kingship of the Bene Yisra-El.

So they parted company, Shmu-El to return to Ramah for a week-long hearing, Sha'ul - at Shmu-El's instruction - to go and wait in Giv-Yah till he called him. For what exactly was he waiting though? For Shmu-El to become certain? For additional auguries and omens? For the voice of Yahweh in a thunderbolt? For other claimants to come forward with a better case? For what he had done at Givat Elohim to become known, so that the mockery could start even before his coronation and Shmu-El find out how well he could take it?

"Is Sha'ul too among the prophets?"

The answer was: he took it very badly. Like all people who love nothing better than to dole it out but can't take it themselves, he was liable to aim his javelin at anyone who teased him.

"Is Sha'ul too among the prophets?"

Yahni told me that the young boys in the village used to gather toadstools and hang them from the lintels of the house.

"Is Sha'ul too among the prophets?"

Relentlessly chanted, like a mantra, till the last days of his life.

But what was he waiting for? Kish ben Avi-El would have issued the proclamation himself, if he had not been wise enough to keep his counsel. Yet all Yisra-El knew that Shmu-El had made his mind up. Even if, in truth, he hadn't.

And yet, of course, he had - it wasn't about Sha'ul that he remained reluctant; it was the very fact of kingship, which his gut, his instinct, his deepest intuition told him was not right. If there had to be a king, then why not Sha'ul, he was personable enough, he was quite suitable. He admired, too, the determination of the Bene Matri. The fake oracle pleased his sense of humour and his sense of how things should be done. And what he had heard from Sha'ul - about Shet the red-haired being gathered in from exile - coincided with his own beliefs. And the involvement of the Guardians of the Ark implied Yahweh's approval. But did there really have to be a king at all? That was the dilemma.

Shmu-El sat in court in Ramah for a week, and mercifully it was a case requiring three judges to sit together, for not a word of it did he absorb, not a second's worth of attention did he give to either plaintiff or defendant; he could not even have told afterwards what the case had been about. He simply sat, and thought, until he was so tired of the whole process he simply wanted to have it done and over.

"Is Sha'ul too among the prophets?"

The phrase kept echoing and echoing inside his head, until he was convinced it meant something more than mere mockery. And then he understood. For was mockery not itself an aspect of the rite of coronation? When they anointed the King of Spring at the Terebinth of Tavor, along with the kerm-coat and the holly-crown, was there not also the mockery? The teasing question, "Are you the Reborn Lord? Are you the rightful king?" The sour wine to mock the wine of blessing? The sticks poked into his thigh to mock the goring by the boar's tusks? Was the holly-crown not itself a mockery? Because was the whole rite not a mockery - in the proper sense of mockery: a counterfeit, an imitation - of the actual birth and death and resurrection of the real Lord? Then perhaps the answer was yes, Sha'ul was indeed among the prophets, and the pilgrimage of the asses was at once a parable and an act of irony. Do you see, Shlomo? Whether Kish ben Avi-El intended it or not - and given that he was counselled by Avi-Nadav of Giv-Yah, you can be quite certain that every detail was quite intentional, even if Kish understood little if any of it himself - Shmu-El was a man who looked for signs and symbols everywhere, because that is the nature of the craft of prophecy, because that is how the gods speak through the mouths of men. Shmu-El was only prepared to accept a king in Yisra-El, if the chosen one agreed to wear the mantle of the sacred priest-king. Why else are we anointed, and not crowned? Ah, Shlomo, what a dreadful burden he has placed on all of us, on Sha'ul then, on me and thee since, and upon our heirs. Think of it like this: that Abou Mousa received not just the Torah on Mount Chorev but more importantly the smicha, the authority to interpret Torah in the name of daily judgement; and he handed it to Yehoshua ben Nun; Yehoshua gave it to the Tribal Elders, and the Tribal Elders to the Judges and the Prophets; and now the Prophets have handed it down to the Anointed Kings. Be deliberate in judgement, Shlomo. Find men who understand. Erect a fence around the Law. These rites of Shmu-El impose on you a mighty burden. To be Melech Yisra-El - the mightiest amongst those who strive with the gods. And to be Mashi'ach Yisra-El - his sacred king.

And as to the hapless Sha'ul, he simply lacked the wherewithal to corroborate this vision. It should have been obvious from the outset - that Shmu-El had either to transform Sha'ul, or discard him in favour of somebody who understood. But he left one terrible omission - he made Sha'ul perform the mysteries but, thinking their extraordinary impact would suffice, he never once explained them. Then was it Sha'ul's fault that he wanted to be a king like any other king, to rule a land, to command a people, to inhabit a palace, to enjoy the privileges of power, and did not know he had to be a pope as well? Was it his fault that he acted out a pantomime, and was now expected to live in it as reality? Was it his fault that no one, nobody at all outside the circle of priests and prophets who were his disciples, held a view of kingship that coincided with Shmu-El's one single jot?

And perhaps Shmu-El knew that as well.

The ceremony of anointment took place, appositely, in the turret of the watchtower at Mitspeh where Shmu-El had roused the people to throw back the Bene Pelet. Thousands came to witness what had never taken place before in all the long history of Yisra-El - not simply the anointing of a king, but the fulfilment of a prophecy of Abou Mousa. As it was written, so, now, it was done. And after it, could not the whole word of Yahweh be fulfilled?

Shmu-El in his memoirs recorded the events in detail - or one of his disciples did it by dictation, because Shmu-El wrote down none of his scrolls himself.

"Then I took a vial of oil and poured it over his head, and kissed him, and said: 'The Lord has anointed you to be captain over his inheritance.'"

Interesting word that - captain! Al nachalato le-nagid. Shmu-El prevaricated to the very end, until he simply could not sustain reluctance any longer, until he was quite alone, until even Gad and Natan were opposed to him. Yet he held out. Even at Mitspeh he anointed him only in the priestly role. He never actually named him Earthly King till after Bezek!

Parchment Five

Let me return to history, to the litany of glorious achievements of my redoubted father-in-law. It is surely one of the most illuminating tales of lunacy and incompetence that will ever be written down!

The king of the Bene Ammon had come up from his capital at Rabat Ammon, occupied the Heights of Gil-Yad almost as far as Golan, and one by one had crossed the rivers of Gil-Yad - the Zarqa, the Kufrinja - taking land and towns until he camped against Yavesh Gil-Yad itself, and laid siege to it. The Bene Yavesh sued for peace, were frankly ready to agree almost any terms, but what was asked was more than even they could give.

"On this condition will I make a treaty with you, that I gouge out all of your right eyes, and thus bring disgrace upon all Yisra-El."

Nice man, the king of Ammon. His name was Nachash, you know, and he liked to live up to it. People say he hissed even when he was playing mancala and ludo. His seal was in the shape of a cobra and his throne had gold mountings showing two pythons mating, a pair on either side. He was very partial to fat women, though I don't know what that has to do with snakes. None of the stories men tell about him would surprise me in the slightest. Except perhaps the favourable ones.

As you might expect, the Bene Yavesh declined - I like to imagine their ambassador being asked his answer, and simply, in total silence, giving a very firm wink, of the right eye obviously, and then departing. More plausibly he grovelled a terror-stricken "no" and was grateful to get back to Yavesh with his hands still attached to his arms. I jest not. Years later, when Nachash died and his son became an even more pitiless king than his father, I sent Yo-Av to besiege him with his Bene Ashur mercenaries at Yareyacho; the ambassador who went to call for the surrender was delivered back, strapped to a camel, with his penis in his mouth and his wedding finger up his anus, ring and all. We took much satisfaction from avenging him.

Sha'ul came to the defence of the Bene Yavesh with an action - I cannot gainsay it - quite as stunning as Shmu-El's at Mitspeh. Given that Yavesh Gil-Yad is on the far side of the Yarden, fifty miles and more north even of the borders of the Bene Gad, and that the Bene Gil-Yad were not even treaty-allies but only friendly neighbours, only two plausible reasons present themselves for Sha'ul agreeing to send help at all. Either he needed to prove himself in his new sovereignty. Or else he was genuinely worried that Nachash had his real sights, not on Gil-Yad at all, but on Yisra-El itself. Maybe both reasons together. But the Elders of the tribes could only see the vanity in the first reason, the misplaced anxiety of the second, and declined support. Declined? Had Yisra-El at last chosen a king so that he might be declined? Ah, Shlomo, you should have seen Sha'ul in full tantrum - from the far side of a keyhole in a spearproof door if you wanted the safe as well as the ringside view. His sulks were proverbial - a grown man in swaddling clothes, with his thumb sucked through his chin - but his tantrums could have stirred the envy of the gods. Stamping like a wounded bullock. Gritting his teeth so hard you could see the jawbone pressing through his cheek. The nostrils lifting outwards, quivering. The breath gathering, not in his lungs, but right there in his nostrils and between his gritted teeth. Slowly his right hand would clench into a fist, and start to beat time, pounding on whatever came to hand - his thigh, a table, the very air if nothing else would volunteer. Then the lungs would begin pumping, and you knew it was time to vacate his presence. Soon, very soon, he would look around for some means of emptying the full gut of his anger - a sword to hack with, a knife to stab, a spear to throw, a plate if there were nothing better. Then he would bellow.

"How dare they!"

Each word stretched out until it contained at least a dozen syllables.

"It is not a matter of requesting, is it? Did I not issue an explicit order?"

Howling at the moon. Who didn't answer either.

"I am not in the habit of prostrating myself before some mealy mouthed, po-faced, liver-rotted..."

His pejoratives invariably double-barrelled, presumably because the sound was so much more explosive.

"By the blood of Ba'al..."

You could learn which gods he really worshipped at these times. He never once swore by Yahweh in all the years and years I knew him. Ba'al was his favourite. Ba'al-Chadad in particular - Shet by another name, though I don't suppose he knew that. Strangely, he regularly swore by Nimrod too. Probably didn't know either that Nimrod was a king and not a god.

"I will have support from every tribe in Yisra-El, if I have to invoke the very gods and goddesses of the underworld to get it."

Invoking the gods and goddesses of the underworld was of course his speciality. Sha'ul, She'ol.

He did too. He got the support. Which gods he actually invoked I couldn't tell you, but gods were certainly invoked. He slaughtered and sacrificed a complete yoke of oxen, hacked them into pieces, and sent a joint to every town and coast of Yisra-El, with messengers calling them to come to Yavesh Gil-Yad – "for Sha'ul and for Shmu-El." Not that he needed to send messengers, because surely they had already heard his bellowing from the palace. And besides, the message of the oxen was plain enough. Come to Yavesh Gil-Yad, or else watch out for your own oxen! They came.

They gathered in Bezek, more than thirty thousand Bene Ephrayim and three thousand men of Yehudah. They crossed the tribal territory of Menasheh in a single afternoon, stopping at Chamat where the Elders of Menasheh had come out to meet them.

"Yavesh Gil-Yad is due east, and to reach it you must cross the Yarden at Avel Mecholah. But turn south-east, Sha'ul, and cross the Yarden at Tsaphon. It is only a short climb from there to Succot, where Abou Mousa gathered the Bene Yisra-El to hear the reading of the Law, and where he left them to climb Mount Nevo and depart. There we should gather, and make sacrifice, and prepare ourselves for battle."

Spiritually it made perfect sense. Religiously too. In terms of his kingly status, Shmu-El had he been there would undoubtedly have approved it. And from Succot it was but a short distance to the sources of the River Zarqa, to Machanayim and the shrine at Penu-El. Penu-El - where Abou Yah-Akov strove with god and won his name! Where better for a newly anointed king to make an offering, before the first great battle of his reign?

"And Sha'ul, though Yavesh is in the territory of the Bene Gil-Yad, it was part of the gift of Abou Mousa to the Bene Menasheh, and Nachash knows this. His threat was not only to the eyes of the Bene Gil-Yad, but also to the honour of Yisra-El."

Which clinched the matter, for Sha'ul anyway.

But not for Yah-Natan. And here, right here, began that terrible cordelia of love and hate that would...but no, there is no need to detail it. Not yet. Not yet.

"Father, we force-marched the men to Chamat so that we could reach the Heights by nightfall and attack at dawn. We don't have enough rations for a long campaign. If we keep to our plan, Nachash won't expect us. But if we go to Succot, his spies will report back, and we will have to take him in the open fields. It's madness."

To be countered by his own son, in the presence of his generals let alone the Elders of Menasheh, was more than Sha'ul could take. Had Sha'ul ever once crossed Kish ben Avi-El, his father? Was it not one of the supreme commandments, one of the ten, to honour your father - so supreme indeed, that it alone of all the commandments carried a reward, of long life on this Earth? Or did it need a reward, because unlike in his day, some sons had now acquired the fashion of thinking this commandment applied to everyone but them? How dare Yah-Natan question his decision? How dare he impute madness? How dare he put his own life in jeopardy, challenging the gods to shorten it, by showing disrespect?

Yahni should have known it - he more than anyone could read the signs. But thankfully, though all of this was in the king's eyes, and in his mind, it had not yet completed the invariably slow and arduous journey to his lips. The Elders of Menasheh stood waiting for their answer. And Sha'ul, who had not yet given official orders to change plans, looked into the eyes of his generals, and recognised that, though they would agree the change for duty's sake, in terms of strategic planning they were with Yah-Natan.

"What says Oved-Yah ben Gid-Yon?"

The man who had led the footmen of the Bene Ephrayim at Mitspeh understood that he had just been offered a promotion.

Yet what he said, he said for all of them.

"Sha'ul, to reach Yavesh Gil-Yad from Succot requires fording the Kufrinja, and we have thirty thousand men to take across. It will require several days, or a detour through the high passes. We cannot be certain how Nachash has garrisoned the Heights. We cannot be certain for how long the siege will hold."

They crossed as was originally intended, at Chamat, and to satisfy the Elders of the Bene Menasheh, they briefly sacrificed at Avel Mecholah, to stake the claim of the Bene Menasheh to the Heights of Gil-Yad east of the Yarden, and to render this no longer a war in support of friendly neighbours, but a holy war of Yahweh.

But when it came to dividing the host into battle formation, Sha'ul quite forgot his promise to his son, and denied his princely right to lead a troop.

The climb into the Heights of Gil-Yad was exhausting and the men were hungry. The night was mercifully dark. Clouds blacked out all but a few stars, and the moon was close to waning. Sha'ul moved his men in three companies, taking advantage of the hills to creep up unnoticed upon Yavesh. Sworn to total silence – they had brought only the barest minimum of animals with them to save noise - the men were given rest and water in an ambience of almost reverential tension. Not a sound. No fires were lit. The watch was kept close by the camp, and those sent out to reconnoitre went disguised as shepherds. The element of surprise was everything.

The camp of the Bene Ammon was even quieter. Guards manned the embers of cooking fires where they would have served better manning look-outs. Men slept in their tents or on the ground beneath goat-skins - in either case, without their weapons readily to hand. Oblivious to the Bene Yisra-El, those who were awake looked towards Yavesh, and dreamed of booty. They would raze the town, of course. Women were the property of the generals, but only if they were still worth having after the lower ranks had used them first. Gold and jewels were the real prize though. Men dream of power, status, fame and sex, but all of these are hard to acquire. Gold and jewels, on the other hand, can be looted from a burning city. And gold and jewels can buy all the power, status, fame and sex a man could possibly desire.

So they dreamed, in the pitch darkness that preceded dawn. And as the night-watch began to make the rounds, stirring those who would replace them for the morning-guard, exactly then the three companies attacked, separately from the north and south and west, and the men of Yavesh Gil-Yad heard the rout, and joined it. The battle was over in less time than it takes to count the dead and send men off to catch the cowards who deserted. By noon Sha'ul was lunching in Yavesh Gil-Yad, on black olives and pitta bread and chumus, on palm-dates one of Yahni's men had picked with his own hand in Damasek, and wondering if a ceremony of thanksgiving might not be appropriate. In Succot, say. Or even in Machanayim or Penu-El.

"What do you say, Yah-Natan?"

Yahni had a flesh-wound in his right arm, but was far too proud to show it.

"That the men are tired, father. They have marched long and fought hard."

"Then what better than a truly monumental sacrifice. Sheep this time, not oxen."

If he had had a paunch, he would have been rubbing it, such was the satisfaction he was feeling. A leg of mutton and the cheering adulation of thirty thousand Bene Yisra-El was just what he needed to round off the day.

While Yah-Natan was tugging at his elbow like a little boy with fleas. What in the name of Anat was the matter with him?

"It would be cruel to make them undergo another march."

Too honest, Yahni. Too quick to speak your mind, believing that your opinion was what he sought, when all he really wanted was your love in the form of your approval. Say yes, Yahni. Agree with him on every count. Why not? Agree with him and say you love him, and perhaps you might have lived to become king.

"They are soldiers, Yah-Natan. Marching is what they are good at. God knows they ought to be, they practice it enough."

He hadn't been in such good humour since - well probably ever.

"Then let them march back to Chamat, and be dismissed, with orders to march to Gil-Gal in a week, where we will give them a national celebration such as they haven't..."

He stopped. No, not because the look on Sha'ul's face had frightened him. Rather, it had made him turn around. Because there, in the doorway, stood Shmu-El. No formalities. No steward to announce him. He had simply tethered his donkey, and come in. A dozen generals, a prince, a king - yet it was as if their teacher had arrived to rebuke a class of naughty boys.

"You have done well, Sha'ul. I congratulate you."

However majestic the king, the presence of Shmu-El always made you feel that a veritable deity had come into the room. This, this was the form in which the angels appeared to Abou Raham at Mamre.

"I didn't expect to see you in Yavesh. Bring food and drink. Come, sit by me."

"There are urgent matters to attend to first. Has anyone been appointed to take care of the wounded? The dead must be buried before the sun comes up tomorrow."

He seemed suddenly to realise that these matters were no longer his concern. There was a king in Yisra-El. Kings took responsibility. Or failed to do so, as he had been so shocked to find. But this was not the time to issue reprimands.

"I shall take one of these," Shmu-El quickly and deliberately lightened his tone. A bowl of cactus fruit was being handed round, the hard shell split open so it looked like yellow custard. Someone joked that they had been picked in Rabat Ammon, in the garden of Nachash the Snake, and someone else replied that the snake had been evicted from the garden, belly-wise, crushed beneath the heel of Sha'ul. There was much laughing and slapping of thighs, a male atmosphere of comradeship and innuendo in which Sha'ul felt at home. Yah-Natan tore the sleeve around his wound, and his father found some wine and cloth to bathe it. So the disagreement seemed to be forgotten. So Sha'ul's good-humour prevailed. But then.

"Did someone speak about a national celebration at Gil-Gal?"

Sha'ul could not have turned more red if he had pricked his finger on a spike of cactus fruit.

"It was Yah-Natan, my son's suggestion. I, however..."

"At Gil-Gal?" Shmu-El was simply musing. He didn't mean to interrupt. But it was too late now. "Yes," he smiled, "yes, let us go to Gil-Gal, and renew the kingdom there."

Sha'ul bit his tongue, not understanding what Shmu-El intended, that he was offering him the rewards of victory, that he was acceding finally and completely to the kingship. But Shmu-El had not heard the previous disagreement. For the second time in as many days his son had caused the king to lose face before his men. His mood was utterly destroyed. When now they brought pitta bread and lebne for Shmu-El, he made them take his own away. And when the Elders of Yavesh came in, he was quite sourly discourteous.

"Sha'ul, many of the Bene Ammon who escaped have now been captured. What is your pleasure?"

His pleasure? The man was sulking, could they not see?

"What would you have me do with them?"

Stated less gruffly, it might have been a noble act of generosity, allowing the Bene Yavesh to decree their own revenge. But he said it so dismissively, so crossly, the Elders were not inclined to ask too much.

"Let them be brought before you, and put to death."

It was only as much as would have happened to themselves had the battle fallen out the other way. Sha'ul was looking to Shmu-El for support. But this too was a king's decision, not a Prophet's. And the king was in his swaddling-clothes.

"It seems that my son Yah-Natan always knows best what should be done. Speak, prince. Let us hear your words of wisdom."

The deeper his sulk, the sharper his sarcasm.

"Father, let them be put to death."

And deeper still, and sharper.

"'Father, let them be put to death.' There speaks a prince." He stood up, fists pounding his thighs, his jaw brittle, appearing to laugh, but it was a scathing, sneering, mocking laughter, intended only to demean. Then he lifted his head, high and proud, and he was, truly, quite majestic. "But now a king shall speak, and say what is, and what shall be. Let it be written. Not a man shall be put to death today, for this day is a day of salvation in Yisra-El. Let the men go to their homes."

And from the way he said it, it was clear he meant, not just the captured Bene Ammon, but the soldiers of the Bene Yisra-El as well.

They went up to Gil-Gal in their hundreds of thousands, to anoint Sha'ul publicly, to offer sacrifices for the victory over the Bene Ammon, and to "renew the kingdom" as Shmu-El put it, in a sermon I shall not waste space repeating, since Shmu-El recorded it in full in his great scroll and you can go and read it there if you are so minded. But what a sermon! Shmu-El's vision of the Sacred Kingship, detailed so finely there could never again be any doubting what it was that he expected. This was to be no earthly king, like Nachash of the Bene Ammon or Nimrod of the Bene Kessed. This was not a sheikhdom nor a principality, some private realm ruled autocratically by a demigod before whom men prostrated themselves. No ceremonial, no bodyguard, no walking backwards, no purple, no porphyry, no marble, no harem, no crown, no throne. This was to be a bishop of Yahweh, whose constitution was the Law of Abou Mousa, whose seneschal, whose mouthpiece - oh yes - was still Shmu-El himself. Because he could not relinquish his own power, he could not yield control. He, Shlomo, he, not Yahweh. I have rarely had cause to find fault in Shmu-El, but here, here I know he was in error. The people wanted an earthly king, but he wanted Yahweh to be their king, and that required his personal authority. Even now, even after Yavesh Gil-Yad, he still could not accept a compromise, but would force upon Yisra-El, by forcing upon Sha'ul, his own - yes, autocratic - vision. Even as he poured the oil on Sha'ul's head, inaugurating the kingship, he himself was laying down the lines of battle that would render it unworkable.

But the people had their king, and the vast majority of them never even heard the sermon, and those who did were probably not listening, and those who listened probably didn't understand. They had their king, and they would dress him in purple and prostrate themselves before him and bring their children out on rainy days to cheer his riding by and expect him to inhabit a marble palace and spend their evenings discussing which princess his son should marry and whether his elder or his younger daughter was the prettier, and all this would enrich their lives and give it meaning, because men are lost and subservient creatures who need gods to bow down to and receive orders from, but they cannot believe in abstract gods, they need to see them face to face, to touch their robes, to feel the glow of their approval, to be able in all humility to render service, and especially to be chastised by them. Give them the king they wanted, and they would do away with all the Ba'alim and the Ashterot for ever, useless lumps of stone and wood, surplus to requirements. Tell them this king was Yahweh incarnated, or even just Tammuz his Beloved Son, and the universe would be governed by One god.

But Shmu-El could not make that compromise. Kingship had to rest with Yahweh, uniquely, ultimately. So he anointed Sha'ul, but he also brought about the final apotheosis of Yahweh in a great storm of thunder and lightning that he called down on their heads - libation and anointing all in one - to wash away the sins of Ba'al-worship and Ashterot-worship for good. And they cried Hallelu-Yah, and Hallelu-Yahweh, and they cheered Shmu-El the Prophet of Yahweh standing side-by-side with Sha'ul the King of Yahweh, at Gil-Gal the most ancient of all the shrines of Yahweh; and they applauded themselves, their own best heroes, the Bene Yisra-El, the chosen people of Yahweh. The Bene Pelet and the Bene Ammon had been scattered, and the tribes stood side-by-side at Gil-Gal, united in their kingdom.

And surely, surely, the age of the Mashi'ach was at hand.

But the ploughing of the wind had also started. And the sowing of the seed that reaps the whirlwind.

Though not quite yet. For two years, indeed, the apprenticeship of the Mashi'ach seemed to be continuing apace and all the auguries were favourable. Shmu-El's approval especially - open support, not a word of public criticism. Not even when Sha'ul moved his family from their cattle-farm outside Giv-Yah into the town itself, fortifying the town and building a new home that was not exactly palatial, though you could see he had expansive plans. Not even when he established a permanent battalion of three thousand Bene Ephrayim, the first professional army we had ever had, keeping two thousand of them in Mishmash and Beit-El, and one thousand under Yah-Natan in Giv-Yah - yes, Yahni was a general now. All other soldiers were demobbed. There was one raid by the Bene Pelet, little more really than a testing of the fortifications at Geva of the Brook of Kanah, but Yahni routed them with ease - though Sha'ul, of course, claimed all the credit. But an era of peace seemed close at hand.

The whirlwind was building though, warm, humid air at one level, cool, dry air at another, waiting to collide - it takes two, after all, to dance the ogev! When it broke, to be fair to him, it wasn't all Sha'ul's doing. Shmu-El's home was at Ramah, little more than a mile north of Giv-Yah, but for convenience he was living almost entirely at Giv-Yah now, in a small house attached to the "palace". The two of them were working in what seemed like harmony, the one advising, the other issuing the edicts, conscious that each needed the other to achieve his goals. Nor were Shmu-El's goals made up entirely of visions and abstractions. Quite the contrary. War and Civilisation, Shlomo, are as much shatnes as wool and linen! It was as if the gods had been waiting for an era just such as this, to put into practice some quite extraordinary ideas.

The Law was the nexus, but the new aleph-bet which the Bene Cheret of Ugarit had invented was the catalyst. The Ten Commandments had been carved on stone tablets, using the only written form available, the picture-words of the Bene Mitsrayim. They were terribly simplistic - the hieroglyph against adultery is frankly crude - and anyway they were museumed out of the reach of common men behind the Veil of the Tabernacle. The first task was to make them available, in a form that could be written on wax with a stylus, and hung in the houses of the people, a talisman to replace the teraphim, a physical reminder of the words that every child for three hundred years had learned by rote, but few adults realised were meant for acting out.

But that was only the start of it. If the Ten Commandments could be set down in aleph-bet, why not the entire set of Tablets of Abou Mousa, why not the legends of the Patriarchs, the Judges, why not a written liturgy for the shrines, why not collect the teachings of the priests and prophets, the common wisdom of the people, the folk-songs, the play-scripts? What other purpose was there, in this new era of the kings, for a Guild of Prophets, if not to carry out such tasks? Shmu-El gave it to Natan, and knowing Natan I imagine he is working at it even now, in some dark study-chamber in the vaults of Heaven, crouched over his writing-table with a goose-feather quill and a bottle of blue dye and a strip of parchment, quite prepared to sit up through the night if necessary, but determined, utterly determined, to record the authentic words of Abou Mousa, and not some fireside story-teller's spiced-up version, editing the groundwork of several hundred acolytes. It will be a strange thing, when it's done, to speak of the Scroll of Abou Mousa, and to mean something actually written down.

Shmu-El dreamed, too, of opening a school in every town and tribe, so that priests and prophets could be properly trained, and common men receive their knowledge. He dreamed of universal literacy - for how could men obey the Law if they did not know the Law; and how could they know it if they could not read it for themselves; and how could they understand the Law, if wiser men than they did not explain it? It was too soon then - but I have done my share to make the dream reality. As you must, Shlomo. As you must too.

But even more than this, the greatest surely of all the undertakings he began, was the Codification of the Law, a task he likewise put into the hands of his disciples, under the leadership of Gad. It was a most extraordinarily complex enterprise, if only because the Laws are so spread out across the Tablets of Abou Mousa, and sometimes you will hear a fragment of a tale, and not realise it shapes a Law - such as the moment in the tale of Abou Yah-Akov at Penu-El, when the adversary puts his thigh out of joint, from which we learn that the sinew of the thigh is sacred. Like Natan with his written Law, so Gad's Codification remains unfinished, and will take many years yet to complete. Thus far he has deduced six hundred and five commandments given on Mount Chorev - a significant number, since that is what the letters Tav-Reysh-Hey, Torah, equate - plus seven others given to No'ach and one to Adam and Chava. You will find a parchment copy of both the Code and the Tablets of Abou Mousa - work in progress obviously - written in aleph-bet, amongst the papers I have given into Eli-Phaz's charge. Finish them, Shlomo. Finish them.

A kind of harmony, then - the secular and the clerical working hand in hand; the king raising taxes and fortifying towns, the Elder of the Guild of Prophets teaching and preaching and judging and guiding the spiritual and moral life of the nation. And even though his kingdom was in truth contained within the narrowest of geographical boundaries, even though each tribe retained its own identity and hierarchy and autonomy within the theoretical monarchy of Yisra-El, still people were beginning to discuss the possibility of confederacy, to debate its virtues. It might have happened. Even under Sha'ul it might have happened. But he was bull-headed, Shlomo, as that infamous statue showed. Such was the depth of his insecurity, he had to demonstrate that he could do it on his own. Without Shmu-El. Even if that meant doing it without Yahweh.

✡

And so the dawn proved false, and the hot air currents were pushed upwards by regular thunderstorms, where the colder, drier air arrested them, or pushed them back with a thunderstorm of their own. The whirlwind was inevitable.

Because it changed, Shlomo. I do not know why; I cannot even pin-point when; but it changed. Where there had been harmony, suddenly there was discord. Where Sha'ul had welcomed, even encouraged advice, now he was sulking about interference and asking sarcastically if Shmu-El would like to swap his staff for a sceptre. Shmu-El was forever going off to sit in court or officiate at some sacrifice or to advise the tribal Elders, but one time he went home to

Ramah instead of Giv-Yah, and he never came back again. Or not to stay. Then it was Gad's turn. He too was forever rushing off to seek the scholarship of priests and prophets at the shrines, and one day he sent a messenger to Sha'ul asking permission to remain in Beit-El rather than return to Giv-Yah. It changed. Sha'ul had been taking lessons in the aleph-bet, determined to be among the first to learn it; but one evening he sent the tutor away, saying he had a head-ache, and the tutor was never summoned back again. Just two years of the kingship, and already it had changed. So many instances like these. And rumours of disagreements, quarrels, arguments: thunderstorms. Suggestions of abuse of power. Gossip about certain predilections of the king that no one wished to name explicitly. The appearance on the hill above Giv-Yah of a certain statue, bull-horned and bearing a dragon-banner in its hand, which Sha'ul claimed was a representation of Abou Mousa with Nechushtan, placed there to demonstrate who ruled in Yisra-El. And so perhaps it was, but everyone could see from its chiselled features and its flame-red hair that at the very least it was inspired by the features of the king.

How, after Yavesh, could it go so badly wrong? How could it change so fast? Yet was it not, in truth, inevitable. Were not Shmu-El and Sha'ul too a kind of shatnes?

It was the sacrifices that caused the final breach. Towards the end of the second year of his reign, while Shmu-El was travelling through Asher and Naphtali to resolve a local dispute, Sha'ul took advantage of his protracted absence to summon the tribes once more to Gil-Gal. It wasn't a mo'ad, a festival season, so there was no religious ceremony as such. Yet not once in all these years had any national celebration taken place without him. And of course Sha'ul intended to make sacrifices, to offer prayers. But without Shmu-El. Gad was in Beit-El and could attend, standing in for Shmu-El; but this was not the same. His exclusion was an immeasurable slight. Sha'ul had announced the gathering as a Triumph for his victory over the Bene Pelet at Geva of the Brook of Kanah - his victory, note. A second triumphal gathering of the clans and the chance to show himself before his people as the mighty man of Yahweh. Surely, at his side, should have stood the greatest Prophet in the history of Yisra-El. But no Shmu-El. Did Sha'ul believe that he really was among the prophets?

It got worse though – Sha'ul's errors always managed to compound themselves. For months the Bene Pelet had been regrouping. The raid on Geva had been a mere sortie, to test Sha'ul's resolve and see his strength; a trial-run, it was presumed, before a raid on Shechem. Now they were planning a full-scale assault, and not on Shechem at all, but on Giv-Yah itself, an assault upon the king inside his fortress. An advance guard, not properly equipped to fight, crossed the Brook of Kanah at Tapu'ach, came south past the ruins of Shiloh, then skirted east, deliberately avoiding both Beit-El and Mitspeh, but camping before Mishmash, east of Beit-Aven, where Sha'ul had placed a thousand troops under Av-Ner. Never had the Bene Pelet dared to challenge this far east. The warning trumpets were sounded everywhere. From Shechem, the priests sent messengers to inform Sha'ul that a division of some thirty thousand chariots, with six thousand cavalry and huge numbers of foot-soldiers, were being made ready in Aphek to march southwards.

It was only the second battle of Sha'ul's reign, his first against the Bene Pelet. He had wanted to prove that he could rule alone. Now was his chance to do so.

Oved-Yah ben Gid-Yon had been sent to verify the information from the priests, and now returned. The old soldier had seen war more times than most, yet in his face there was a look deeper even than fear.

"It is understood at Aphek that the gathering at Gil-Gal is a muster. They expect an imminent attack. They are preparing to launch their own pre-emptive strike."

This was alarming, but not surprising - a mere pretext really. Sha'ul received the information coolly and dismissed him. It was Yah-Natan who took him to his tent and offered him refreshments.

"I feel like Abou Yah-Akov, when Essav came in from hunting, offering you a mess of potage," Yahni laughed, his easy way making momentary light of whatever was troubling Oved-Yah. "It's stew," he added. "Onions, leeks, beans and lentils. Not much goat-meat I'm afraid. They're saving that for the festivities. Now tell me what's got you so alarmed."

Oved-Yah tucked in, chewing his thoughts as hard as he had to chew the meat. Then, as though it were the name of a god, or some beast that had vanished in the Flood but now returned, he pronounced the word:

"Iron."

Yah-Natan said nothing, just waited till Oved-Yah was ready to continue. Clearly this was terribly important.

"The priests at Shechem told me they were making it, that they'd been foraging the hills along the Carm-El Ridge for months in search of certain kinds of rock. I took a small band into Aphek – yes, I know he told us not to. We went disguised as camel-traders."

He reached into his pocket and brought out a small ceramic pot, glazed with spirals and with birds on stork-like legs.

"Beautiful, isn't it? I bought it in Aphek, as a souvenir. They say it was made on an island called Caprisin."

The vision of distant isles and the beauty of the pot had lightened him, but only for a moment. There were matters of grave importance to impart.

"They've been quarrying everywhere along the coast. They break the rock up into shards to get out the minerals, then smelt them in these circular furnaces. I managed to get to see one, but not enough to tell you how to make our own. There's a sort of basin-shaped interior to catch the molten metal. They keep the fire going with ceramic bellows – don't ask me how."

Oved-Yah was thinking, not just of the weaponry the Bene Pelet must have spent long months forging, but of how the Bene Yisra-El might do the same themselves. It was beyond him.

"They've used iron before. But you should see these weapons, Yah-Natan. They've got javelins of iron, with points so sharp you could split a tree with them. Every chariot's now got iron-spiked wheels. Every charioteer and foot-soldier has an iron sword. Every one of them. We've never fought weaponry like this."

"We must inform the king."

"Yes."

"And Oved-Yah, not a word of this to anyone. Not even the other generals."

But the gloom and desperation was so far apparent in his face, it would take little time for everyone to know.

And only now, when it was probably too late, only now did Sha'ul send word to Shmu-El; official word that is; the chance of Shmu-El not knowing anyway were zero. For his Triumph, he had needed Shmu-El absent; but in crisis he was urging him to hasten to Gil-Gal as fast as possible. But all that came back were equally urgent messages, beseeching Sha'ul not to do anything until he arrived. It would take him seven days.

Seven days! Seven days for the Prophet to come to Gil-Gal and rescue his people in their darkest hour since the last darkest hour, by personally conducting the sacrifices as he had done at Mitspeh. Seven days for the advance guard at Mishmash to size up the strength of the Bene Yisra-El and send back information. Seven days for those thirty thousand chariots and six thousand cavalry to make their journey southwards and choose the best positions to set up their lines. Seven days before the Bene Pelet captured Giv-Yah, and in so doing seized the kingdom. Or so it must have seemed.

But seven days passed, and still no Shmu-El. At Gil-Gal, the Bene Yisra-El were waiting for a feast of celebration. While Sha'ul's footmen told him the Bene Pelet were almost ready to attack.

"How long?"

"They've been smelting iron for weaponry for weeks now. They can't surely need much more. But they're still bringing up foot-soldiers. There's another division just north of Mitspeh."

"How long?"

"Perhaps two days."

And perhaps only two hours.

And perhaps Shmu-El would not arrive in time.

And perhaps he should have placed more trust in Yahweh.

"Av-Ner, what's your view?"

Besides being his military commander, Av-Ner ben Ner was also his first cousin. I mention this merely for the historical interest.

"The king must decide."

And because there are two rules for selecting generals. The first is: never appoint a man to anything just because he happens to be your cousin. The second is: never choose a man who lacks the courage to offer considered advice, simply because he fears you may reject it.

Leaving Sha'ul to decide was like leaving the plagues to rule Mitsrayim. This was a man who could not open the curtains of the Tabernacle without unintentionally tearing the Veil.

"Bring burnt offerings and peace offerings. Prepare the altar."

161

It was impossible, inconceivable. No man, not even a king, would dare.

"Shall we send for Gad?"

"There is no need."

"He's only in Beit-El, sire. It'll take less than an hour."

"I said there is no need."

Confusion. Consternation. Would he then allow a lesser priest the unprecedented privilege? Or worse, did he intend to exalt the Bene Giv-Yah above all the tribes of Yisra-El, by giving the honour to the Guardians of the Ark? It was unthinkable.

Though not half so unthinkable as what he actually did.

The fields surrounding the shrine were swarming with Bene Yisra-El - so many, they would be sacrificing beasts for days on end if they were to feed them all. Around the circle of the twelve pillars, Sha'ul had permitted only the Elders of the tribes and the senior ranks of the army, though this was still sufficient to fill up the space. Inside the circle of pillars, only Sha'ul and the priests of the Bene Levi who were the guardians of the shrine, most of them supervising the sacrificial beasts, but four of them, including Avi-Shaddai ben Luz the High Priest of Beit-El, preparing now to wash the hands and feet of the king, before robing him in the white apron of the sacrificer.

If there had been any lingering doubts about the king's intentions, these were now removed, for after his ritual washing he appeared before the altar in the full and formal garments of the priestly sacrificer (imagine, Shlomo, the thousands upon thousands of badly-stifled gasps), the white linen breeches and the white apron, his feet unshod. So he reached down and gathered ashes from the edges of the fire, filled both his hands, spread the ashes on the altar, and then placed on them the clothes he had been wearing previously. Now, slowly, to the amazement of all Yisra-El, he lifted the bundle of ash and cloth and walked through the circle of stone pillars, two priests on either side of him to mark his way, a barefoot king, a king in priestly garments, a king in all humility descending a hillside through a gathered throng of worshippers, stepping out beyond the camp to deposit the bundle of impurity - the final act of ritual purification.

Back he came now, barefoot but majestic, king and prophet all in one, perpetrator of the most appalling blasphemy - or initiator of a new regime in Yisra-El. No one dared even to pose that question, though its answer was climbing back in all his glory to the shrine.

They had brought sheep and goats and cattle into the inner ring by random gathering of whatever roamed about, and the noise was truly deafening. Priests moved among the flocks, selecting out the females so they could be set aside for the peace offerings. Once this was done, they went among the males again, removing those with blemishes of any sort, the priests placing their hands one by one upon the foreheads of the beasts, to make the atonement on behalf of all the people.

The great fire beside the altar had been lit the night before, kindled with willow and other sacred wood. Now it was stoked with more wood, until the flames could be seen even at the farthest corners of the camp. Sha'ul stood at the south side of the altar, facing northwards, and one by one they brought the animals to him, holding the beast by the legs and neck to stop it struggling, and laying it on the altar. Quickly, Sha'ul cut its throat, severing the jugular. A tiny squawk, but no time for pain. To reach the jugular, the windpipe had to be cut first, and the beast was invariably dead from lack of oxygen before the knife had cut the vein. Sha'ul had not been raised a cattle farmer and a soldier without learning the proper way to kill.

So the holocaust began. Blood flowed everywhere - the smell of it inducing terror in the waiting beasts - spouting from cut throats or deliberately sprinkled around the altar as the Law required, until the king was wet and red with blood. Then the dead animal was butchered, the head laid on the fire, the fat gathered for the cooking. Jars of water at the side of the altar enabled the innards of the beast to be completely washed, the legs too, until not a single drop of blood remained. Then salt, to soak up even the invisible blood. So each of the joints was laid on the fire by the priests, and the offering was roasted. If the gods were angry with the Bene Yisra-El, the rich aroma of the gravy would rise in the smoke of the offering, and the sweet smell would placate them. That was all they required. The remainder of the joint was for the people. (And yes, I said gods, not God, or Yahweh.)

No sooner had Sha'ul finished than Shmu-El arrived, drawn, you might have said, by the odours of the roasting meat. Unlike the gods, however, the smell induced rather than propitiated anger. Sha'ul went down to meet him, clean now, dressed once more in kingly garb - but all he got for greeting was a torrent of insult and abuse.

163

"I told you I would be here in seven days. This is the seventh day, is it not?"

Was he hurting from the slight, or simply angered by the blasphemy? And had he forgotten who he was addressing? Yet Sha'ul, who could bully hard when he was minded to it, appeared to be cowering.

"There have been desertions reported. People came for a celebration, not a week of military exercises. They were restless, and scared."

None of this was getting anywhere. Shmu-El's eyes were set obstinately, fierce and offended. It wasn't excuses that he was looking for. But excuses were all he got.

"The Bene Pelet are in Mishmash, in Beit-Aven. They are threatening Giv-Yah. They are ready to attack."

But still nothing. Eyes that seemed to dismiss all this as trivia, ephemera. The greater scheme of Yahweh had been threatened too. The roles of priest and prophet were under attack.

"You didn't come."

He sounded like a jilted bridegroom. Hurting. Both of them were hurting.

"I did what I thought right. And necessary. How could we go into battle without first making proper supplication to the gods?"

Gods, you see? Gods plural? No doubt he had meant to say Yahweh. But it came out as gods.

"Someone had to take the authority. No one else could. So I did."

The eyes in the statue of Shmu-El appeared to shiver. His head was shaking, ever so slowly, side to side. But still no voice.

"In the name of Yahweh," he got it right this time; but too late, surely, "why else was I anointed king? Someone had to take responsibility."

But it was as if he had said: Yahweh was not with us, so I presumed to put on a mask and present myself as Yahweh.

"You are a fool, Sha'ul."

"What should I have done?"

Of all the parts of the human body, it is the voice, not the eye, that cries most tears.

"Waited. Obeyed the commandments. Had faith."

"You said seven days."

Shmu-El simply stood there, as only he could stand, a man who could fast for days on end and then set out to walk a hundred miles; a man who could sit vigil for the dying, night after night after night, yet never reach the end of his compassion; a man who could order the stoning of an adulteress, and stand and watch, and seem unaltered by it; Shmu-El of the infinite contradictions; Shmu-El the ultimately unknowable. Who could blame Sha'ul, for trying so hard to do right, but getting it all so badly wrong? What on earth was right, was wanted of him, anyway? The act of sacrifice had wearied his body and shattered his emotions - more than a thousand beasts, exposed to the knife. And now, here, stood Shmu-El, silently shaking his ancient head in disappointment. Disappointment? No, the word is neither wide nor deep enough.

"Where are you going?"

"I am returning to Giv-Yah. There is nothing for me to do here."

Such anger held under such extraordinary control. It could have been worse though. He could have said Ramah.

"You can't leave, Shmu-El. The Bene Pelet. You can't desert us."

Sha'ul was desperate. But Shmu-El simply shrugged his shoulders.

"It is not me who is the deserter here. The king has performed the sacrifices on his own. Then let the king conduct the battle on his own as well. Perhaps Yahweh will reward you with a victory. But the reward you had hoped for, of a throne for your son and for your grandson, the reward of a dynasty for the House of Sha'ul, this you have forfeited."

In the full hearing of the generals, in the king's own tent, so there could be no denying he had said it afterwards.

Yet why should the sins of the fathers be inflicted upon their sons?

It wasn't the departure of Shmu-El that cost Sha'ul the support of the army, though that was one more rotten grape to spoil the vintage. Rather, it was the rumour of the iron weaponry, which by now had spread throughout the camp in a form enormously exaggerated. For several days there had been a slow trickle of desertions, hardly noticeable in so vast a gathering. Then the troop-captains had begun complaining, about morale, about depletions, about soldiers who seemed close to mutiny. This was hyperbole too, and troop-captains always make precisely these complaints, as the best way to get noticed for promotion - but it was hard to be certain. With days and possibly days in which to wait for the sacrifices and the celebrations to begin, orders had been given to separate the men and women, to call each tribe to muster, and then to exercise, prepare for battle. But men who had come for a celebration did not wish to be separated from their wives, to be suddenly conscripted without warning. Lack of food, of skins for sleeping, of sanitation, of drinking-water, added to the unrest. Intense training exacerbated it still further. And then the rumours, that the Bene Pelet were not simply forging implements of iron, but an entirely new armoury of weapons - iron beasts mounted on chariots that men could sit safe inside while hurling stones and javelins; iron balls on iron chains with spikes like iron cactuses; all manner of machines, ballistics, arms. And they were coming in their hundreds of thousands, resolved to destroy the Bene Yisra-El entirely, to annihilate us, to drive us right into the sea. Powerful beast, rumour - more powerful than an imaginary beast of iron. Fear is even more powerful. Men took their wives and children, and slipped out by dead of night. Men hid in caves. Just a few at first, but then so many you could see the tracks their feet were pressing in the fields. It was becoming pandemonius.

Who could blame Sha'ul, in such circumstances, for doing as he did, for pressing on with the sacrifices? It worked too, in so far as it stopped the flood. Some, who had hidden nearby, even returned, attracted no doubt by the smell of a free meal. But then Shmu-El came and went. Now it was a matter of divided loyalties - the king versus the prophet on the one hand, the nation versus the Bene Pelet on the other. I am guessing, Shlomo, but this is how I read the decision of the Elders to withdraw - Shmu-El had rightly reprimanded Sha'ul for his arrogance and blasphemy, the Bene Pelet were threatening Sha'ul alone by pointing their attack upon Giv-Yah, and they, the Elders, were the ones responsible for making Shmu-El anoint a king in the first place. Now they could see their error. See it? They could smell it in the air, a holocaust of sheep and goats whose ash and charcoal had penetrated the very robes they wore. Clearly the Bene Pelet were the agents of Yahweh, sent to punish Sha'ul and put to rights their error. I am guessing, Shlomo. But the only other explanation I can offer is - sheer cowardice.

Whatever the reason, the tribal Elders gathered, each in their own tents, and announced their decision to withdraw. Entire camel trains dispersing northwards must have passed the bewildered Bene Pelet on the road. Within hours the troops were deserting en masse. They fled to Gad and Gil-Yad eastward, the hills of Ephrayim to the west, while Sha'ul remained in Gil-Gal, desperately trying to keep the Bene Ephrayim at the very least together. By the time the Bene Pelet finally launched their attack, he had only six hundred men left.

Three groups of Bene Pelet came out of Mishmash, one company heading for Ophrah in Shu'al, the second for Beit Horon, the third for the valley of Tsevoyim towards the wilderness. Giv-Yah had been a blind, and Sha'ul had fallen for it, concentrating all his forces on the defending of the town. Not that he had much to defend it with - neither men nor weaponry. There wasn't yet an ironsmith in Yisra-El to make swords or spears, but rather than armour his men with their familiar weaponry of bronze - take note of this Shlomo! – he had made an agreement with the Bene Pelet that their ironsmiths and blacksmiths would provide!
As you might imagine, the goods failed to materialise.
But not the Bene Pelet.

It rained that week, as I remember. Unseasonal rain. It came in bursts, the way it does in springtime. A brief shower, backed by cold, blustery winds, then clear, blue skies again, and sun warm enough to dry the ground so you would not even know it had been raining. Ophrah fell in less than two days - besieged, threatened with imaginary iron monsters, attacked repeatedly, its walls set alight, the town surrendered. If the Bene Pelet had fought with one eye cast behind them, expecting the Bene Yisra-El to ride to save the town, they needn't have bothered. No army of the Bene Yisra-El appeared.
Beit Horon fared little better - it lasted four days, and again it was the fires set against the city walls that brought the Elders to the gate. More tightly disciplined than any troops the Bene Pelet had ever sent against us, those who won the victories at Ophrah and Beit Horon did not turn to pillaging and making victory personal; they left behind a garrison and went to join their confreres in the Vale of Tsevoyim. But there was nothing to be done there either. As at Ophrah and Beit Horon, no army of the Bene Yisra-El confronted them. Just rain, and then more rain.
And then it stopped raining, and the wind changed direction. This

was more familiar, the chamsin blowing out of the Negev, strong, hot and dry, a wind of dust that slakes the throat and parches everything that grows. The skies began to rumble. Lightning tore branches from the trees, set bushes ablaze spontaneously, so that men began to think that these were portents, and to remind each other how Abou Mousa had seen Yahweh in just such a bush. Three companies of the Bene Pelet sat in the Vale of Tsevoyim, wondering why the weather was so strange, and what had happened to the army of the Bene Yisra-El. It was almost worrying.

Then the sound of thunder grew unlike the sound of thunder. It roared and bellowed; it rolled across the sky; but it wasn't thunder. The very shaking of the ground told you that it wasn't thunder. It was an earthquake, not a strong one, but it rattled the columns that hold up the world for several minutes, and left behind it furrows deep enough to trip and break an ankle in. At Yareyacho, the Elders looked with pride on walls too sturdy to be broken. At Ophrah, the garrison of the Bene Pelet laughed at so much devastation, and wondered why their generals had not waited for an extra week. At Migron of Giv-Yah, where Shmu-El was sitting under a pomegranate tree, the trembling was Yahweh's answer to the terrible questions posed at Gil-Gal. And at Gil-Gal itself, where Sha'ul was sulking in his tent, lamenting his lost kingdom and the new house he had barely finished decorating, there was at least a reason, after six days of sitting doing nothing, knowing there was nothing he could do, to do something now.

"Av-Ner. Go see if there is any damage. Check our numbers."

It was something. It was an excuse to go out to the water-cart, and wash his eyes. It was a space of time to look around himself, and appreciate the full extent of what he had lost.

"Well, cousin. Are we still six hundred?"

Sarcasm, always sarcasm, at his most despairing.

But Av-Ner's black looks were not a jest.

"No," he said. "We're missing two. One of them's Yah-Natan."

There was an earthquake, a fairly small one, but it seemed portentous, and at the practical level it gave Sha'ul a reason to check his numbers, and thereby make the discovery that Yah-Natan was missing. I have tried to convey it more poetically, but in prose that is the sum of it. So what did he do? Order a search? Presume Yah-

Natan was doing something militarily useful in his role as commander of the king's own battalion at Giv-Yah? Wait? No - he panicked. Some men have within themselves misfortunes waiting to take place; Sha'ul was three complete disasters, all of them already happening, all of his own misdoing, all at once. He assumed Yah-Natan had been captured, kidnapped, in a secret foray by the Bene Pelet. He feared, more than ever, the imminent humiliation of defeat. He ignored the lessons of history which Yisra-El had learned at Even-Ezer and, believing that his role as priestly-sacrificer authorised it, sanctioned it, summoned Achi-Yah ben Pinchas, the grandson of Eli the Priest of Shiloh, to his tent, and - yes - ordered him - I know it's hard to credit, but he did it Shlomo, almost as if in deliberate spite of Shmu-El - to fetch the Ark which had been brought down to Gil-Gal for the celebrations! Then he gathered what was left of the six hundred, mounted the Ark on his own chariot, pointed it in the direction of Tsevoyim - and hoped. Well, hope was the only decent weapon he had left.

Yahni, it must be said, was quite phenomenally lucky. But then, a man makes his own luck. Having grown up there and spent so much of his childhood exploring for places in which to hide from his father, there wasn't a square inch for a dozen miles around Giv-Yah that he didn't know as well as his own hand. Tired of waiting for his father, furious at the desertions, frustrated by the unwillingness of the other generals to act without orders, it was time to take the initiative himself. He wasn't planning any heroics, just reconnaissance. The Bene Yisra-El "thousand" under Oved-Yah had come down from Mishmash to Gil-Gal, leaving the city open for the Bene Pelet to march in. Mishmash was strategically essential; it controlled the hills that sloped due westwards down to Beit-El, south-westwards to Ramah and Giv-On, south-east to Gil-Gal and Yareyacho, not one of them more than ten miles distant. The entire territory of Bin Yamin and the religious heartland of Yisra-El lay vulnerable if they couldn't hold Mishmash. But likewise reconquerable by the Bene Yisra-El, if they could re-take it.

Accompanied by his armour-bearer, a young man of Ramah named Yiphtach ben-Chayil, Yah-Natan slipped out of the camp much as the first deserters had done, under cover of darkness and armed only with good shoes, a dagger and a sword. The rain had eased up and you could literally feel the wind changing direction on your face, as though two winds, one cold, one hot, were fighting out a battle. They reached Mishmash well before dawn, slipping in between two sharp rocks called Botsets and Seneh - the one as white as chalk, and very steep; the other spiked and craggy as a broken tooth - and made ready to enter the garrison in disguise. But Mishmash was as silent as Ophrah and Beit Horon. The army of the Bene Pelet was away in Tsevoyim. No more than twenty men were left to hold the guard. By the time the sun came up, that number was reduced to zero.

It was a small raid, not obviously significant in the context, but the three raiding-parties of the Bene Pelet had been sharpening their swords to ease the unrelenting boredom of the Vale of Tsevoyim - it contains some of the finest weeping oak trees in the world, and you can regularly find hyrax-badgers in the rocks, but try telling that to soldiers - ever since the fall of Beit Horon. Rain had dampened their enthusiasm. Earthquake had roused their fears. The expectation of an army of the Bene Yisra-El had turned to wondering. Why had they not attacked? What were they planning? That Sha'ul was cunning as a fox - think only how he had stolen up on Yavesh Gil-Yad by dead of night, and crushed the snake of Ammon. Then came the news - the garrison at Mishmash had been slaughtered. Now they understood. They had been drawn out into the Vale deliberately. Ophrah and Beit Horon had been sacrificed to lull the Bene Pelet into false security. As cunning as a fox that Sha'ul.
"Retreat to Mishmash," came the order.
But that was crazy. Mishmash was now in the hands of the Bene Yisra-El, and who knew how many of them were holding it? Thousands probably. They had been ambushed, they concluded. And there, right there, coming along the road towards them, bearing once more that Ark that had brought such plagues on Pelet, there was the advance guard of the massive army of the Bene Yisra-El, closing the ambush at last. Three battalions of the Bene Pelet panicked and broke ranks. Iron weaponry was abandoned as men fled in any direction that they could.
Ah but the ambush had been set with stunning care and forethought and precision! Crack troops of the Bene Yisra-El had been secreted away in caves, in the lofty boughs of trees, in the barns of peasant houses - even in the beds of peasant women I don't

doubt. From the north came the six hundred – sorry, five hundred and ninety-eight - charging valiantly into the shadow of their certain deaths; from east and west and south, deserters of the Bene Yisra-El now saw the pandemonium among the enemy, reckoned that it was greater even than their own pandemonium, saw their chance for plunder or redemption, and in what was by now the veritable apotheosis of farces (oh, Shlomo, we ought to be the laughing-stock of all the nations), soldiers who had previously turned tail now crept back out and swelled the numbers, picking up discarded iron weaponry along the way and claiming it for their own. By the time the battle passed over into Beit-Aven, Sha'ul had practically the whole army of Yisra-El behind him once again.

Only it wasn't an army of Yisra-El, not any more; at least, it was an army, and it was made up almost entirely of Bene Yisra-El, but the Elders were not there to lead them, and left to themselves they fought like mercenaries and killed like butchers, slaughtering the Bene Pelet and spoiling them for their last agora and buckle-belt and goat-skin, in a rout that extended all the way from Mishmash to Ayalon, looting flocks and herds they came upon, killing the beasts and cooking them on open fires without even draining off the blood, without salt, without first making proper sacrifice, eating blood and flesh together, in breach of the most basic Laws. When they ran out of women to rape, they started in on eight and nine year old girls. And when these were still too few to satisfy their lusts, boys too. It was carnage. Everything, everything that Shmu-El had taught at Mitspeh, everything was lost, abandoned. What started as a Triumph for Sha'ul was ending as a Triumph for the Bli-El, wallowing in the blood of victims animal and human.

Before they set out from Gil-Gal, Sha'ul had given orders that no one should eat anything until the battle was over. It was a stupid order; however holy it might render him, you cannot ask a man to fast and fight. Myself, I always insisted on no sex the night before, which was a good deal more sensible though just as impractical to police, since it channelled the men's aggressive energy where Sha'ul's edict merely sapped it. But after the disaster of the sacrifices, it was precisely the random looting and eating of improper meat that he most feared.

Yah-Natan and the men who had now rejoined him at Mishmash

were blissfully unaware of the order. In the silence of Mishmash, patrolling the hills behind the town at donkey pace to catch the last deserters from both sides, they found some honey in a tree, and ate it. That was all, the whole incident. Less than an hour later, the same soldiers were riding towards Gat, fighting at Sha'ul's side, urging their less fastidious companions not to forget the moral code of Abou Mousa. But the eating of the honey would return to haunt them.

Ah, Shlomo, what a catalogue of absurdities and comedies and sheer fiascos! Blood sins and honey sins. Panic and misunderstanding. The Ark used as a talisman. Orders to fight on empty stomachs. Orders given for which he would not be willing to punish the offenders. Desertions all around him. And then allowing the deserters back with neither punishment nor even a rebuke.

To give credit where it is due, when he heard about the blood sin, he did send orders for all livestock to be brought to him at Gil-Gal, so that it could be sacrificed properly before being eaten. Except that he himself again performed the sacrifices.

And perhaps because it was the only pragmatic way of bringing the soldiers back under any sort of military discipline, he compounded that by asking the soldiers if they wanted to pursue the fleeing Bene Pelet and "spoil them until dawn", and "leave not a man of them alive." More blood, as if there hadn't been enough already, human as well as animal. And then, on top even of this...

I have a strong impression, beneath all these events, of a man who had found it humiliating to be mocked to his face, and who was forever afterwards looking over his shoulder because he thought people were continuing to mock him behind his back. He had to prove himself a worthy and a serious king, over and over again. And standing there at the altar of Gil-Gal, with no Shmu-El to back him, and all but the shrine-priests departed rather than risk incurring Shmu-El's wrath, I see a tall, solid, square-shouldered, powerful man, his hair and beard the colour of the fire and the holocaust, yet one who seems to think that he is tiny, thin, loose-shouldered, weak, one who feels that the whole congregation of the twelve tribes have come here for the express purpose of watching him make a fool of himself.

Which he therefore proceeded to do.

"Shall we pursue the Bene Pelet tonight, and spoil them until dawn, and leave not a man of them?"

Shall we? Shall we? What kind of a king is it who asks his troops if they feel like making war?

"Do what you think is right."

Well, what answer did he anticipate?

The slaughter resumed, two days and nights that I refuse to visualise let alone set down in words. The men did everything their hearts and heads desired, until it had purged the better among them of the need ever to repeat it, lancing that boil and dispersing its pus; but in the worst it only bred a certain numbness and familiarity, so that even in the act of doing it, their minds and bodies already longed for repetition. Such is the nature of evil, Shlomo.

They came back to Gil-Gal exhausted. Mayhem, cowardice and confusion had made alliance with horror, and all men could see the consequences. Now that what had happened over the past weeks was becoming clear, there was a deep wish to cleanse themselves. But how? How? No Shmu-El, obviously. No Gad or Natan. Not even Avi-Nadav or Eli-Azar his son - the Guardians of the Ark had seen more than their eyes could bear, and retreated to Giv-On. But the Ark itself remained in Gil-Gal. And the priests of the shrine would not refuse. Especially if Sha'ul were to raise a brand new altar, an altar of his own.

"Ashamnu. Bagadnu. Gazalnu. Avinu."

Each soldier prostrate on the ground, his skull pointed towards the altar, his head covered in his bernous, then coming up to his knees and one hand beating his chest with the name of each sin he pronounced.

"Ve al kulam, eloha selichot, selach lanu, mechal lanu, kaper lanu."

The liturgy of the Fast of Azaz-El, borrowed for the purpose of redemption.

"I swear to bring an offering at the first opportunity to sacrifice upon the altar, as atonement for these sins I have committed."

What a terribly easy thing redemption is, Shlomo, when a man can do such dreadful, dreadful things, and just say sorry, put his hand in Yahweh's, and be forgiven. Yet the kinsfolk of the victims - their sorrow is not so easily redeemed.

"Salachti. Forgive me."

Beating their breasts in sorrow, perpetrator and mourner both.

Till every man of the ranks, and every officer, had come forward to

173

the altar, recited the vidu'i avonim, the prayer for forgiveness, pledged by his honour to honour his pledge, and received the king's pardon. The king's. Even Sha'ul was not so arrogant as to think he could bestow Yahweh's.

Until it was the turn of the generals.

"I have killed men in battle, and soldiers in defence of Yisra-El. No sin is on my head."

Yah-Natan's brave, heroic, handsome face lent dignity to an occasion steeped too much in blood and sin and self-indulgence. As he uttered his claim and his denial, a cheer went up from every soldier in the ranks, so loud, indeed, it would continue to reverberate inside his father's head till he had breathed his last.

"Sha'ul," they cried, "has slain his thousands, but Yah-Natan his tens of thousands."

When in fact he was claiming not a soul above forty.

Then something brought the men to silence - and it wasn't only the look on Sha'ul's face. It was a low muttering, spreading like a grievance, amongst a small group of those who had hidden in Mishmash, offering their service to the Bene Pelet in exchange for sanctuary. When the battle turned back the way of the Bene Yisra-El, they had turned back with it. And now that they had confessed their many sins in full, they could not see why the generals should claim impunity.

"What muttering is this?"

Sha'ul was torn between his own anger at the cheering and the insult being offered to his family.

"What muttering, I say? If there is a sin that has not been declared, let anyone come forward and declare it."

For a long while no one dared to move. Then, removing his bernous as a gesture of humility, a camel-rider of the Bene Gad came forward.

"Sire, forgive me if I speak. May the gods...Sire, you gave orders that no food be eaten. On pain of death. We were in Mishmash. The prince, sire, with his men...There was a tree, full of honey. The Prince laughs, sire, but it is so."

To say Sha'ul was shocked would be understatement indeed. Not at the sin, which in truth deserved Yah-Natan's derision. Not at the impudence of the man for coming forward to accuse a royal prince. No, he was trembling at the first touch of the whirlwind, which he himself had sown. Because he had uttered a foolish threat, and now, surely, he must execute it.

"Draw near, all the Elders of the people, and know and see wherein this sin has been this day. For as the Lord who saved Yisra-El lives, if it be in Yah-Natan my son, he shall surely die."

He was - quite seriously, quite genuinely - ready to follow the example of Yiphtach with his daughter, and sacrifice Yah-Natan, right there on the altar he had raised to cleanse the blood sins. To show that he was king. His own son, in a human sacrifice. And with his own hand - he couldn't shed the role of sacrificer just because this killing was personally painful. But what a terrible irony, this spilling of blood in order to expiate a blood sin. And not a ram bleating in the bracken for miles around! He would have done it too, if they had pressed him. No doubt he would have poured honey over the body before burning it, to make sure of the proper sweetness of the aroma of the incense, to soothe the nostrils of whichever god it was he was appeasing.

No one answered him, of course, not even the camel-rider of the Bene Gad. Yah-Natan was the hero of Geva of the Brook of Kanah; it was Yah-Natan whose breaching of the garrison at Mishmash had been primarily responsible for the winning of the day. And who was the king asking if the sin should be cleansed in this way, but the very troops whose fingers were still sticky with the unsacrificed blood of stolen lamb and looted veal!

So Sha'ul stood, before the altar of Gil-Gal, and it must have gone through everybody's mind that this was how Abou Raham stood, before the altar of Mor-Yah, wielding the knife above his son, willing and prepared to cut the jugular. And not a ram, not even a day-old fledgling or some ancient piece of mutton, not a ram could be heard bleating in the bracken for miles around! No, indeed. He himself had slaughtered all the rams a while ago.

And there I end this parchment, Shlomo, for lack of space and lack of wherewithal to deal with what came next. Though I know I must, and will, eventually - like Yahni's catacomb at Givat Elohim, you cannot join the company of the wise if you haven't descended into the underworld and come out again the other side. And for what other purpose than the search for wisdom, and the teaching of wisdom, would a man ever think to write? But for now, Shlomo, for tonight, just this. The image - made, we are told, in the likeness of the gods - the image of a man standing in the tatters of his soul, a portrait of Yisra-El's first king, his clothing splattered with blood and his soul drowning in it, kneeling now before an altar he had raised with his own hands because the Elder of the Guild of Prophets had turned his back on him, himself the Guardian of the Ark because no priest had stayed to guard it, himself the Sacrificer, himself the Elder because the Elders had withdrawn, himself the commander of the armies, himself, alone, the king. And yet no king, for his "crown" had been struck off in a fit of pique, his dynasty condemned to death by his own hand, and his head, his own head, breaking open, Shlomo. He had gone mad, quite mad. You could see it in his eyes, the way he stared into the emptiness before him. What was he seeing? Honey? Blood? Honey gushing from wounds and blood on the stings of bees, and then still more honeyed blood, and the very real probability that it would all end in the blood of Yah-Natan and his own hand plunging in the knife. Mad. Quite mad. His very bones were trembling.

Oh, Shlomo, Shmu-El was right to choose Sha'ul, if what he really wanted was a king to fail, and who in failing would discredit the very idea of monarchy in Yisra-El, once and for ever.

Yet no, the parchment may have run out, but the tale has not – I have had Shavsha sew two more strips on to the scroll so I can carry on with it. It is not a pretty tale, I know, though it is undoubtedly most edifying. The tale of a man who, frightened of looking stupid in the eyes of his people, frightened of being mocked, had made himself a figure of complete buffoonery. The tale of a proud man wounded by the most terrible humiliation. The tale, Shlomo, of a king who lost his reason. Believe me, I know. I witnessed it. Closer than any other person in the world, I witnessed it.

Shlomo, it is a very strange thing to kill another human being. Every man fantasises the act at some point in his life - most, I imagine, seeing their wives in their imaginations after twenty years too many - but the execution is never how you imagine it. Nor is there any difference if the killing is an act of self-defence or the most wanton aggression. I have seen startled men, taken by surprise in their sleep, half-murdered before their reactions were alert, simply use their natural brute strength to overcome a weaker opponent, and crush them the way one would a spider, strangling them like Shimshon in his dream strangled the snakes. I have seen men blithely, dispassionately, take the knife to this throat or that, and then pour a glass of wine into their own throat, put their arms around a woman - and weep like an infant on her breast. I have seen all manner of killings, from catapults to javelins, from mattocks to coulters, from the babies dashed on the rocks to the tripped horse - but I have never seen killings like the ones Sha'ul perpetrated after the fiasco at Gil-Gal. He became as if obsessed with the need to repeat the same act over and over again, as if in that way he might erase it, or make it credible. Or even redeem it. But none of these were any longer possible.

At Gil-Gal he lost the support of Shmu-El, and he would never get it back. At Gil-Gal he lost the support of Yahweh in the same manner. Perhaps that is what he thought he wanted - I don't know. He didn't lose Yah-Natan, but the breach was immense, and the gulf unfordable; what he certainly did lose was Yah-Natan's respect – "my father has upset the entire land" was all he said, and if it was diplomatic understatement, it was also true. Although in an odd and startling way. For after Gil-Gal the tribes, the people, accepted him as their sovereign lord almost without challenge or critique. Inspired by fear, not admiration. And as a king of men, not as the King of Yahweh.

Rejection, mocking humiliation, a measureless gravy of sacrificial blood - people said an evil spirit had possessed him, and I suppose it had. What else can one do with an evil spirit, except seek to exorcise it? I prefer to say of Sha'ul that he went mad with guilt and desolation, and could find no other way out of the darkness.

The massacre was relentless, and it went on for several years - indeed, it never really stopped until he died. Where there might have been an era of peace, with neighbours who could see the benefits of peace, Sha'ul provoked bad reasons for bad wars. Where enemies could be created, he created them. In Mo-Av. Amongst the Bene Ammon. Against Edom. With the kings of Tsovah. And of course the Bene Pelet. And he didn't simply fight them – "he vexed them".

But never again did he permit the looting or the sacrifice, let alone the eating, of the flocks or herds. Only the human foe. His men could do as they pleased with the human foe: tear their flesh with oxgoads, test out the potential of the three-pronged fork, the limitations of the circumcision razor, the double-headed axe. But not the animals, all of whom he now deemed sacred to the point of making them tabu. Had he simply killed so many he had reached the end of killing them, and wanted to see if there was a similar end to killing men? Perhaps. Was it sentimentality about the innocence of animals, which vice or virtue you could never honestly apply to men? Perhaps. Was it that you need hatred to really enjoy killing, and while even the most predatory and poisonous of animals remain essentially loveable nonetheless, every human being is capable of detestation if you really look for it. The person Sha'ul hated most, of course, was his own self.

Nor will it surprise you to learn that, when it came to killing people, he now favoured iron weaponry above all others. He paid the Bene Pelet huge sums for iron swords and spears - and then, of course, turned them back upon their makers. I watched him killing many times, stood at his side doing much the same myself. Yet it was not the same. As a professional soldier, you learn to do what is hateful, but necessary, and you find ways to accommodate it in your mind. I often wondered what was in Sha'ul's mind when he killed, who it was that he was seeing in his imagination when he ordered the slaughter of another town or village. The men he had let go at Yavesh Gil-Yad perhaps?

It went on, as I said, for several years. It wasn't a war of empire, for we gained no land by it. It wasn't a war of conquest either, for though we fought every one of our neighbours to their knees, though we razed their towns and sacked their farmsteads, though we destroyed their armies and their royal lines, we never tried to blot out their identities, and therein lies the goal of conquest. It was a war almost for the sake of war, the way a king might hunt mountain-lion, or wild boar - for the sheer brutal pleasure of the kill. When all this madness finally burned out, we had made no gains, unless you count a reputation for brutality and barbarism as a gain. But at least it did burn out.

Or, rather, Shmu-El retired from his long retirement, recognising at last the responsibility he had abrogated, and used his gifts of prophecy to bring the killings to an end. Symbols, Shlomo. Symbols, parables, mythologies - better teachers by far than dry facts. Shmu-El understood the human mind and heart and soul better than any man I have ever known - but he had no other language through which to express his knowledge except that of symbols. So he turned the tables on Sha'ul, by forcing him to see his own insanity, and to confront it. How? By launching the very opposite of Sha'ul's campaigns - a war of purpose, a "holy" war.

More than two hundred years earlier, when Abou Mousa led that band of slaves, refugees and outcasts known as the Habiru out of Goshen of the Bene Mitsrayim, when they crossed the Sea of Reeds dry-shod and set out in desperate hope across the wilderness towards Mount Chorev, they came thirsty and tired to a place called Rephidim. And there, at Merivah to be precise, Abou Mousa committed that sin of arrogance and impostoring for which he was denied the right to enter Erets Yisra-El - symbol number one in Shmu-El's parable - the striking of the rock to bring forth water, the taking upon himself of the right to perform the miracle, when he should have called on Yahweh to perform it, should have called him through the mouth of Aharon the Priest.

So Shmu-El preached in Ramah, and in Mitspeh, and on the day of the Fast of Azaz-El itself, of all days and of all places, at Gil-Gal.

It took little time for Sha'ul to learn the detail.

"So Abou Mousa committed the sin, and lost his legacy as punishment. But there is punishment now, and there is punishment later. For punishment now, Yahweh sent the Bene Amalek, a murderous, barbarous people, willing to attack even a gaggle of escaped slaves in flight across the desert, vicious enough to attack the women and the children first, to hack down the old and lame, too cowardly..."

Symbols and parables, Shlomo. Simplistic, you might well say. Trite, schoolboyish and short on subtlety. Very well. But anything more subtle, and all of Yisra-El, let alone Sha'ul, might well have missed the point.

"But the Bene Amalek too were punished," Shmu-El reached the crescendo of his peroration (lovely word that, Shlomo - peroration). "For it is written in the Tablets of Abou Mousa, that 'I will erase the memory of Amalek from underneath the heavens.' For Yahweh swore, that he would have war with Amalek, 'from generation unto generation'. Why then do we fight in Mo-Av and in Ammon? Why do we attack Tsovah and Botsrah? Why does this generation not fulfil its obligation? In what name do we fight - the name of Sha'ul alone? Let us make war in the name of Yahweh. Do we fight for blood, or to avenge blood? Let us go down to Rephidim, and find Amalek, and erase his memory from underneath the heavens."

Sha'ul hardly needed a second invitation. And with Shmu-El at his side to hold his arms aloft, as Aharon the Priest had done for Abou Mousa, all that was lacking was the man to take the role of Chur.

Two hundred thousand Bene Ephrayim and ten thousand men of Yehudah gathered in Telayim. I shan't bore you with the details, Shlomo – I have littered this parchment often enough with the debris of warfare. Suffice it to say that the Bene Kena'an who were in alliance with the Bene Amalek were advised by Sha'ul's ambassadors to move aside, to save themselves from massacre - advice they seized wholeheartedly. Av-Ner and Yah-Natan led the assault on camels - something no army of the Bene Yisra-El had ever done before. But this was desert warfare, and you cannot plod into battle on a donkey nor plough furrows with a cart-and-oxen, and expect to be victorious.

The Bene Amalek were routed from Chavilah to Shur; their king, Agag, was taken prisoner. Addressing the troops before they set out, Sha'ul had spoken words with which they were by now familiar. Only this time they were not his words. They were Shmu-El's.

"Go down to the desert, to the lands of the Bene Amalek, and destroy everything they have. Do not spare so much as a woman or a child, not even a baby suckling..."

In fact Shmu-El had added "not an ox or sheep, not a camel nor an ass", but this Sha'ul left out. Indeed, the contrary. Town upon town was attacked and seized. Followed the customary carnage. And with each victory Sha'ul gave the now-customary order:

"Raze the town. No prisoners. Do not touch the flocks or herds."

Do not touch the flocks or herds!

Shmu-El waited for news at Ramah, and daily they brought him the most gory particulars of the Amalekite demise. Then, one day, it ended.

"Master, Sha'ul is riding to Carm-El of Chevron. It is said he will raise a memorial to the victory."

How terribly ironic! Think of it, Shlomo. You start with the specific goal of wiping out a people, eradicating them, annihilating them, so that there will be no memory of them under Heaven. And then, to commemorate your triumph, you ensure their memory will live for ever, by raising a cenotaph to the battle. Shmu-El was furious. He didn't even set out for Carm-El, lest he be asked to give his blessing on the monument. Nor did he wait for news of Sha'ul's plans. Even madness has its patterns, its logic, its consistencies. He knew precisely what the king intended next. And went to Gil-Gal to meet him.

And there indeed he was, squatting like a Bedou in his newly-acquired black tent, dining luxuriously on roasted partridge and goat milk and sea crab that had been brought up specially from the Red Sea. Two beauties of the Bene Amalek served wine and grapes to numerous friends, family, officers. A young lutanist played quietly, accompanying one of the old priests of Carm-El whom Sha'ul had brought with him, a blind man with great white lumps of leprous tissue on his knees and elbows, who knelt before the company reciting the New Year marriage song of Earth and Sky, the one the Bene Kena'an call the "Song of Songs".

"I am the rose of Sharon and the lily of the valley. As the lily among thorns, so is my love amongst women. As the apple tree among the trees of the wood, so is my beloved amongst young men. I sat down with great delight, and his fruit was sweet to my taste. He brought me to his banqueting house, and his banner over me was 'Love'."

What Sha'ul had brought to his banqueting-house was Agag, king of the Bene Amalek, black-robed and white-bernoused. An enormous scimitar bound against his thigh showed him to be no captive, but an honoured guest.

"Shmu-El! Welcome. There's food...not this, this isn't kosher." He clapped his hands. "Bring food for Shmu-El."

So much for the return of his sanity, which Shmu-El had hoped to engineer. This, this banquet, this poetry, was an ever deeper form of madness into which he had now sunk.

But Shmu-El had not come here to give up hope of saving him. And in truth, was this not the perfect setting, not some private act that could be denied or abrogated later, but right here, before his family, his friends, his generals, right here at Gil-Gal where the sin had first been uttered? Now, now he began to wright his magic, preparing the shock-therapy that would bring Sha'ul back from madness. No, not *to* sanity, but *from* madness - as far as any man is able to return. King Hu-Ram calls it katharsis - cleaning. Yet who can but wonder what it did to Shmu-El himself?

"You have won great victories."

"I have done as you asked."

Kish ben Avi-El, his father, was particularly beaming. My son, the king.

"They tell me you left none alive."

"None that we could find." He laughed. "It isn't easy to find a hiding-place in all that desert."

"So you turned the red sand redder?"

So habituated to his own sarcasm, could he not hear the rising irony of anger in Shmu-El's voice? Others could hear it. One by one they were remembering orders that needed to be given, wives who had been promised, long journeys homeward. The tent was emptying.

But still enough remained to witness.

"Women? Children? Even babies at the breast?"

It was dawning, slowly dawning.

"We destroyed everything."

"Good. Yahweh will be pleased. The children, the suckling children. This especially will have pleased him. One young child, after all, could grow up and father a whole new generation. One child would have been sufficient for you to fail in your responsibility."

The pain on Agag's face was growing torturous as Shmu-El squeezed, and squeezed, and squeezed.

"Did you hack their limbs off, in case they were feigning death?"

Even Sha'ul could take no more of it. He who found the act so easy, found that he could not tolerate the words.

"I have done as you asked."

Looking from Shmu-El to Kish and back again. Like a little boy so keen to tell his mummy he has passed a school exam. And at the same time deeply embarrassed, about the food which he could not possibly invite Shmu-El to share, about the company he would be unwilling to share it with, about the two half-naked beauties of the Bene Amalek, about the erotic poem recited in a tent as black and comely as the tents of Kedar. All of this, feeding the growing realisation that he had failed - again. And would be made to pay for failure.

"What is that sound of bleating? I didn't know the king kept sheep and oxen for a pastime."

Sha'ul was having difficulty swallowing the last pieces of partridge.

"We brought them from Rephidim. Since Beit-Aven my men know that I will not permit the pointless waste of good flocks and herds. Some will be sacrificed, in the proper manner, to thank Yahweh for giving us this victory. The rest will be shared out as the spoils of war. The men have earned them."

You could, as the quaint saying puts it, have knocked Shmu-El over with a breath of stale wind.

Ah, but how marvellous he was when his fury was aroused!

"Sacrificed? And you, of course, will officiate. You who are renowned as the greatest slaughterer in Yisra-El? Who else should do it? Who else should strike the rock at Merivah, and bring forth water? Who else, Sha'ul? And were you not told to destroy everything. Everything. The oxen and sheep and camels and donkeys. Everyone and everything. In the name of Yahweh."

The king could take no more of this. What did they want of him! What did they want of him?

"Sit down, Sha'ul. When you were a little nobody in Giv-Yah, I made you head of the tribes of the Bene Yisra-El, and Yahweh anointed you King over Yisra-El. Is that not right?"

Sha'ul was nodding, but trying not to catch the eye of the embarrassed company - his sons, his father, his cousin who was also his chief-of-staff. This was humiliating.

"You are no longer Sha'ul ben Kish, who makes the decisions that Sha'ul ben Kish thinks right. When you became the public king, you forfeited the private man. Now you are nothing. But you are also the Nasi of the tribes of the Bene Yisra-El and the Anointed King of Yahweh, and at all times you must do as Yahweh orders. Is that not right?"

Nodding and nodding, like a little boy whose mummy isn't satisfied with a mere pass in the school exam, but expects her son to top the class.

But would she simply chastise him for coming second, or actually punish him, by taking away his favourite toy?

Shmu-El's voice was rising in tone towards crescendo.

"And through me Yahweh sent you on a historic mission, to go and utterly destroy the Bene Amalek. Utterly destroy, Sha'ul. Something you enjoy doing. Utterly destroy, better even than you did the Bene Mo-Av and the Bene Ammon and the kings of Tsovah.

Fight against them 'until they are consumed'. I recall the word exactly. Consumed, Sha'ul. Consumed. Like sacrificial lambs and oxen with the blood still in them! Why did you not obey the voice of Yahweh? Why have you sinned in this manner? Why did you strike the rock at Merivah?"

Mummy, I passed the exam. Mummy, please, all I want is a nice, reassuring cuddle and an almond biscuit and to be told I'm doing my best. I just want to be loved, mummy. Please.

"I have obeyed the voice of the Lord, Shmu-El. I was sent to conquer the Bene Amalek, and I have conquered them. I razed their towns. I wiped out whole populations. I avenged the House of Abou Mousa. I brought back the King as my prisoner. Do you see these hands? Do you know how much blood is on them? And even now we are preparing for more sacrifices than have ever been seen in Yisra-El. What more do you want?"

"Nothing more. But something less. Yahweh does not want your sacrifices. He wants your obedience."

For all the quality of Sha'ul's swordsmanship, it was Shmu-El who was the greater killer. Clinically - straight through the heart. And all it took was a single, precise, razor-sharp word.

"Obedience?"

"To disobey is tantamount to rebellion, and rebellion is a greater sin even than witchcraft. And you, you disobey with consummate stubbornness, and stubbornness is a worse sin even than idolatry. Because it announces that you reject the word of the Lord."

Sha'ul bowed his head. He could feel the blow descending.

"And he who rejects the Lord" - this was it – "asks to be rejected by him. You have already forfeited your dynasty; now you have forfeited your kingship."

Sha'ul was on his knees.

As I would have been, Shlomo. As I would have been.

But now he had to save himself. At the very edge of the precipice, what can a man turn to or else plunge into the abyss? Hope? Belief in miracles? Or - reason? The fullest power and capacity of his reason that he can muster - we possess no other implement - to think, to work it out, to make it make sense, all in an instant of combined knowledge, and instinct, and intuition. I must save myself - and this is how. And this is how desperately the grovelling Sha'ul was clawing his way back. Thinking his way through pitch darkness, black with coagulated blood. And there was Shmu-El, waiting on the cliff-edge, hands outstretched to haul him in. Back he came, fingernail by torn fingernail. Out of madness - reason.

Though even reason is not yet the same as sanity.

"I admit my error. I feared the people and listened to them instead of Yahweh. What must I do to gain forgiveness?"

Crying, like a suckling babe.

And if I am right, if Shmu-El chose him because he knew he would fail, if this was the moment Shmu-El had been building up to over five long years - then what cruelty, from a god and a prophet whose primary epithets were mercy and compassion, what terrible cruelty to do what he did next. But necessary. The final, healing act. But first.

"What must I do?"

"It is too late."

"No!"

Shmu-El had begun to depart.

"Please! Shmu-El. Don't turn away. Pardon me. Worship with me."

"You have rejected Yahweh, and therefore you have forfeited the right to rule."

Shmu-El stepped forward, intending to depart. But the grovelling Sha'ul grabbed at his cloak to try to hold him back - and the cloak tore.

It was as if he had rent the Devir itself, the Veil of the Holy Tabernacle.

"Now the oracle is written in your own hand. There is a companion of yours, one who is dear to you, one who sits close to you, one who you know well. The Lord will tear the kingdom from your hands exactly as you have torn my cloak, and he will give it to that man."

Prophetic words indeed! I have often wondered if that line came out spontaneously or not. And did you recognise the little lutanist, reyat ha-melech, the companion of the king, fourteen years old and clinging in terror to his music in the shadows of a black, black tent? Me, Shlomo. Me. The Prophet was looking at me.

But Sha'ul was simply staring at the ground.

"Please! One more chance!"

Racking his brain in all lucidity to find some means to stay the Prophet's hand.

But he was shattered. Shattered. Humiliated beyond humiliation, his very humanity stripped naked. Shmu-El had made him what, presumably, he wanted him to be - a mere creature, malleable in the hands of Yahweh, a puppet who would perform the words and deeds of Yahweh through the mouth and hands of Sha'ul. But with its strings pulled by Shmu-El.

And then Shmu-El turned back.

"Very well. One last chance."

The healing act. The ultimate barbarity, acted, perceived, understood. So the mind recovering its lucidity could know what it had done when mad. So it could know, and engrave the knowledge once and for good on the deepest receptacles of the soul. So it could never be repeated.

"What must I do?"

Shmu-El glanced about the tent, as though seeking some appropriate act of expiation, something to test Sha'ul's new-claimed faith in Yahweh to the limit. And beyond. But he didn't need to look. He had known from the outset what it would be. Symbol number three. He had spoken of the commandment of obedience. Then let it be fulfilled.

"Before the Elders of the people?"

"If you say so."

"Before the whole of Yisra-El?"

"If you say so."

"Let us then perform the sacrifice that was ordained. Let us destroy everyone and everything. Until their memory is blotted out from underneath the heavens."

The sheep. The oxen. The camels. The donkeys. Every last one of them that would have made a nice addition to the flocks and herds of every soldier in the ranks, and saved the king from paying them. But there were no complaints, no "stubborn disobedience" - except by one or two of the more obstinate rams.

But there was still more.

"The two serving girls. This black tent. The scarab ring I saw you taking from your finger. It is all plunder."

Sha'ul bowed his head, and yielded.

"There remains still one last sacrifice to make."

Now Sha'ul looked genuinely perplexed. And then, quietly, quite literally, incredulous.

"No, Shmu-El. No!"

"It is required. From the mouth of Yahweh through the lips of

Abou Mousa himself. There can be no turning aside from this."

"I cannot, Shmu-El."

No answer. Just four eyes in confrontation, the two like fire burning ever deeper into the empty cavities of the other two. Surely he could not fail now, having come this far. The silence was awesome. The space between them was nothing more than that - an empty space, filled up with nothingness, or gods. The world had been turned as black as ash.

"Bring up Agag, king of the Bene Amalek."

"No!"

They brought the king, his hands tied behind his back, a look of almost stoical resignation on his face as he approached Shmu-El and the altar where the last remnants of his tribe had been erased. The two exchanged looks for a long time, and you could sense that Agag felt as sorry for Shmu-El, for having to do this, as Shmu-El did for the victim; that he too understood that one more death could bring about the end of killing, and was ready to be martyred to such a worthy end.

"Surely the bitterness of death is past."

His dignity extraordinary at this last moment of his life.

"As your sword has made women childless, so shall your mother be childless among women."

They tied Agag to the altar-stone, something in the manner of a dead Pharaoh in his sarcophagus. Then Shmu-El held out to Sha'ul the scimitar the king had worn. It was his last chance. But Sha'ul simply shook his head.

"You had no trouble with the Bene Ammon. I am told you personally cut the throats of all the Elders of Beit-Chadad. It is a sacrifice, Sha'ul. A sacrifice to Yahweh. No different from sacrificing a ram. If I put honey in his mouth, would it become easier? Do it in the name of Yahweh."

But Sha'ul's head went on shaking. Blood from the altar had encrusted his hands. He was sobbing now, a little boy's tears. When he pulled his hands away from his face, you could barely see his features for the blood. His tongue was licking at it.

"Do it in the name of Yahweh, and let all your sins be pardoned."

On one side, the looming precipice, the hinterland of nothingness that may or may not after all be the kingdom of the gods. On the other side, a Prophet at least half as mad, but twice as visionary. That side, too, may or may not after all be the kingdom of the gods. Who could distinguish? Who could know? And the scimitar, held out to his grasp.

Who could know? Who, even marshalling the last grain of human reason, who could know?

Yet marshalling human reason to assert free will, a man could choose.

Sha'ul chose.

"I cannot do it."

"Because he was once a king?"

The head shaking and shaking. The eyes flooding tears. And Shmu-El pushing him, pushing him, right to the very edge of the abyss.

Yet never actually letting go.

"Now he is less even than a man. He is mere eucharist. Why can you not do it?"

"Because I am sick of blood."

It was the truthful answer, and both knew it. So it was done.

And yet, not yet.

Because if it was done, then what need any longer for this final sacrifice? Yet the sacrifice needed to be done.

"If you are sick of blood, then you are sick of Yahweh, and he of you!"

The Prophet's voice cold with rage and fury.

"You swore, Sha'ul. You swore an oath. Before the Elders and before the people. You swore."

Sha'ul's hand had groped as far forward as the handle of the scimitar. But his fingers would not close.

"I cannot do it."

"An oath, Sha'ul. An oath to redeem the sin of disobedience. Remember the oracle."

But the king was no longer capable, of speaking let alone recalling words. Whatever daemon had possessed him, that daemon had been exorcised. It was truly done.

So Shmu-El took back the sword. There was in his face a look of anguish more ghastly even than that of the departed daemon. There had always been a chance that it would come to this. He must have imagined it. He must have prepared himself. But he was exhausted after his struggle with the king. And now, now he must bear still one more unbearable responsibility. It was his duty as the Elder of the

Guild of Prophets, as the Mouthpiece of Yahweh, as the Guiding Soul of Yisra-El. Yet who ever did, with more unwillingness, a deed more terrible in all their lives? It is written, Shlomo, written in the Scroll of the Kings of Yisra-El, written in the blood of Yahweh - thus:

"And Shmu-El hacked Agag in pieces, before Yahweh in Gil-Gal."

Exactly thus, Shlomo. I witnessed it.

Parchment Six

I have been dreaming much about the old king lately. Sha'ul the Reluctant. Sha'ul the Insecure. Sha'ul the Jealous. All kings should acquire epithets – don't you think? What will mine be? Daoud the Dilettante, perhaps. Or Daoud the Deleterious. Are these not what men say of me? Daoud, King of Kings - that would be the style of Mitsrayim, the king writing his own epithet, meaningless but exalted. It is sorely tempting. Like all men, but especially kings, I yearn to set the record straight before I die, to write my own history and biography in advance, to circumscribe men's memories. It is simply a form of self-preservation, putting embalming fluid on the reputation, before the jackals descend. Men being what they are, my weaknesses will be set above my strengths, my scandals above my heroics, and I too will be deemed a failure, as all men are ultimately failures, but especially kings. Ah yes, but what a failure I have been! Daoud, Dreamer of Dreams. Daoud the Ridiculously Ambitious. Daoud of the Immaculate Failure!

And as to Sha'ul - no, I cannot say I loved him as a man; but that I respected him as a king - I mean, that I gave him all the respect, the honour, due to the person of a king - of that let there be no doubt. Oh, he was often a fool, his misjudgements were prodigious, his faults should be placed in a manual for the erudition of future kings. In particular, given the nature of his kingship, his inability to swap the lifelong habits of philanderous Ba'al and nymphomaniac Astarte for the wool-shirt asceticism of Yahweh was of a truly monumental order. But anyone can sit high in the amphitheatre and criticise the players. He was also the first, the experiment, the trial-run - you should have witnessed the disaster of the Civil Service when first we introduced it! And then, there is the human soul, and there is the public office, placed on a man's shoulders by the Almighty like hay-bails on a beast of burden. To criticise a king is to criticise the Almighty, who anointed him. To kill a king is to rebel against the Almighty, and we all know from Sha'ul what happens to such a man. So I shall make no further comment about Sha'ul's kingship, but only about the private man too frail to wear the holly-crown as it should be worn. It doesn't matter a damn whether he was a good king or a bad king, a good man or a bad man; he was Yahweh's choice, and that is all that counts. I have allowed my bitterness to get the better of me in these pages, and I repent this.

✡

Go back a few years. Shmu-El came to Beit Lechem Ephratah for the feast of the New Moon, and to sacrifice a red heifer so that its ashes could be used in the consecration ceremony for a new well that had been dug. It was an ordinary enough event, made out-of-the-ordinary for us only because it was Shmu-El who came to conduct the service rather than any other priest or prophet. My first sight of him was as he washed at the old well before the service. I had gone there with Eli-Av and Avi-Nadav and Shammah, my three eldest brothers, to water the flocks that we had brought down from the hills that afternoon for shearing, and there was some squalid old shepherd, dressed exactly like ourselves but worse, and he was washing at our well.

"Hey, you! This is a well of the Bene Yishai!"

The man who stood up and turned to us must have been well into his sixties, thin and gaunt and very frail, his long hair and even longer beard matted and grey. He could have been one of those vagabonds who sleep in ditches and break into the houses of the rich to steal their food. He stood there, looking us up and down, for several moments.

"This is a well of the Bene Yahweh," he did eventually reply, but my brothers just looked perplexed, as though some legal challenge were being made, or doubt cast on the fact that they themselves had dug it.

And then I realised who he was.

"The well belongs to the Bene Yishai, because they dug it," I said. "The water belongs to all who are thirsty. Please drink."

He did so, long and slow, from an old-fashioned goat-skin flagon that hung from the belt on his waist. Then he poured some water into the palms of his hands, to rinse them, and came towards me.

"How old are you?"

"Thirteen."

He put his hands on my head, so that the water spilled down my face. He looked embarrassed.

"Thirteen is a very important age. The age at which a boy becomes a man. Do you know what the first duty of a man is?"

Avi-Nadav giggled, and Shammah whispered something vulgar in his ear. But fortunately one of the ewes had broken ranks and gone off down the hill, which gave them the excuse to get away from such a dirty, fetid, slobbering old man. Whereas I was trapped.

"To learn the Laws of Abou Mousa," I replied.

"And have you learned them?"

"Some. I know it is an important duty to invite a stranger to share a meal on Shabbat eve."

Not that I was absolutely certain how pleased my parents would be with me for obeying that particular commandment so injudiciously.

If Shmu-El had been, say, a young woman of twenty-five, she might have accused me of flirting with her. And I suppose I was trying to impress him.

"You are generous. But I am invited to dine with the Elders tonight. Perhaps I will see you for the Shabbat prayers tomorrow?"

I smiled. Here was my real chance to impress him.

"You won't be able to miss me. I sing in the choir. And play the lute. My father, Yishai ben Oved, is the choirmaster."

This seemed to ring a distant bell.

"Please wish your father, and your grandfather, a good Shabbat."

And saying that he turned and left.

Retired from his retirement, Shmu-El was always travelling, town to town, shrine to shrine, to make sacrifices, to deliver sermons, to teach, to preach, to judge. Wherever he went he blessed people - it was part of the job. He didn't mean anything very specific by it, to you, as an individual - he simply put his hand on your head, and some fragment of his magic power was supposed mysteriously to transfer itself. It increased the sum of goodness in the universe, but because it came *from* him, and not because it came *to* you. To most people that was all it was - like being called to the annual reading of the Law; you say the blessing, the chazan reads on your behalf, and afterwards you are blessed – "in the name of our forefathers Abou Raham, Abou Yitschak and Abou Yah-Akov". People congratulate you, because it's a great honour. But since it's an honour that is bestowed eventually and equally on everyone, it isn't really so momentous as all that. But to me it was different. I had been blessed by Shmu-El, and it was not like any ordinary blessing, because it was not bestowed by any ordinary priest or prophet.

And there was the matter of the water - an old man's foolishness, of course, moving from washing his hands to giving the blessing, and simply not thinking to drain his palms. Yet mean it or not, he had anointed me. The water inside the blessing was rendered holy, a libation, my head the altar - there was no denying the symbolism, however accidental it may have been. The look on his face when it happened told me that he too thought it was significant - he who did not believe that anything was ever accidental. Yahweh had meant it, and time would explain why. It was evident in his face, his looking - not at me, but into me, as though seeking an answer to the enigma. For the first time my religion had acquired a personal dimension, as though I myself had dealt with Yahweh face to face. It opened up a part of me I did not know existed. And Shmu-El, I think, had recognised this also.

In the village they ribbed me about it for months afterwards, imitating the way I had said this or that, filling their palms with water and pretending to anoint me, going on and on about the two shepherds meeting at the well, "and one of them was the most important man in Yisra-El, and Shmu-El thought it was him." But I was proud. They could taunt me all they liked, but I knew it was only jealousy. And their envy elevated me still higher. I had held a conversation with Shmu-El, the greatest Prophet in the history of Yisra-El. And there had been nothing to it. You spoke to him just as you would speak to your brother or your friend. It was entirely natural. And he had liked the things I said. And he had blessed me.

His visits to Beit Lechem Ephratah became quite regular - simply because it was conveniently en route between Giv On and Teko'a, where he was establishing a new school and reviving the old shrine. He had, too, developed a close friendship with one of the Elders of Beit Lechem, who always gave him a guest-bed for the night. Often on the Shabbat or the Holy Days of Yahweh - obviously he would have nothing officially to do with the rites of Tammuz - he would come and preach (invariably against Tammuz worship, because it was expected, but in so gentle a manner you could hardly imagine his comments troubling the guardians of the shrine), or my father would take us to the shrines at Gil-Gal or Beit-El, or to Chevron where the patriarchs were buried, or to Kiryat Ye'arim of Giv-On where the

Ark was kept, to listen to him. Whenever he came to Beit Lechem he would hear me sing and play - he could hardly not, since mine was the only instrument accompanying the choir - and it was obvious from his concentration that he was listening with pleasure. And then one time - he was standing in the gate, talking to his friend, the elder Av-Raham ben Zev, and I happened to walk by - he put his hand out in front of me, to make me stop.

"And to think that, but for this young man, I might have cursed Beit Lechem for a town of unhospitable Tammuz worshippers and Bli-El and gone away."

Av-Raham ben Zev appeared less impressed than intrigued, and after giving me time to greet the Prophet respectfully and inform him that, yes, Oved ben Bo'az was indeed my grandfather, Av-Raham gestured to me that my continued presence was unnecessary, and asked to hear the story. As I left, Shmu-El again put his hands upon my head, to bless me, and I heard him say:

"I was washing my hands. I thought they were empty. When I put my hands on his head to bless him, I ended up anointing him with water by mistake. I wonder if it was an omen."

So I wasn't imagining it. Nor, apparently, was I the only one who had gone on wondering.

Av-Raham ben Zev laughed politely at what was obviously a most amusing anecdote, something he would be able to dine out on for months to come. But the word entered my consciousness, as the act had clearly entered Shmu-El's. An omen. Portending what? For he was looking at me, quizzically, interrogatively, as though he too were wondering if it had really been by chance.

That was the second meeting. The third was on the occasion of Nachshon's wedding.

Eli-Av and Avi-Nadav and Shammah were long married by this time, and their wives had added, between them, another nine mouths to the feeding-list, not to mention the space they all took up at sleeping-time. Since all three husbands were away soldiering most of the time, and the youngest of us boys and girls were happy enough to sleep on the roof through most of the year, and anyway were away flocking a good deal, there had been no question up till now of breaking up the clan. But when Nachshon's marriage was announced - father had found him a bride among the Bene Yehudah of Beit Horon, an excellent match - it was also clear we could not cope with any more additions. Father went to the Elders to ask for land, and we were given a small space adjacent to the market, close to where the camel-riders had their stables. It would be more than sufficient for Nachshon and his bride to start a family of their own.

The house was very basic, but it was all we could afford to build, and besides, a house for a bride-gift was a good deal more than the Bene Yehudah of Beit Horon were accustomed to; it was they in fact who started the rumour later on, of the great wealth of the Bene Yishai, and the bride-gift was the reason. All things are relative - in-laws included, if you'll forgive the awful pun. The truth is that the house was classic, standard, Beit Lechem mud-brick; large mud-bricks, made by setting them in wooden moulds, the way we learned to do it in Mitsrayim long ago! Have you ever watched them do it? It's well worth the trouble. They dig a hole in the ground and fill it with water, chopped straw, palm fibre, and bits of shell and charcoal. This is then trodden into mud - the worst job in the world, but someone has to do it. If you didn't have a slave, you had a youngest son. The mud needed to be soft and pliable, so it could be shaped into a brick. You - I on this occasion - trod for hours. My father did not possess a kiln, so the bricks had to be left out in the sun to bake. To build with them, you simply packed the bricks together with still more mud, and left that to dry out. The trouble is, the rain washes it away, and it can be terribly leaky in the winter, not to say vulnerable to any would-be robber who can carve himself a doorway as soon as he sees something worth the stealing.

Anyway we built it, and it was magnificent because we built it with our own hands, though it was really very ordinary, with the normal tiny slits for windows, and latticed shutters, and a flat roof for storing jars, and not even a balcony let alone an upper room or courtyard. The smell of camel-dung was everywhere; most of the usable adobe in the vicinity was really just composted camel-excrement, gathered over the decades from the stables and mingled with the sand and stony soil. Very warm in winter, though there was an awful tendency for seeds blown in the wind to stick to the soft surface, and take root there, so the walls of the house were decorated permanently by the most glorious wreaths and bouquets you have ever seen or would be likely to put together: aloe flowers and castor oil shrubs, bougainvillea and poinsettia, narcissus and nasturtium, fuchsia and lobelia, each one as lovely as its name.

The wedding itself was sumptuous. Because we were consecrating the new house as well as the bride and groom, the whole town felt entitled to attend. Father had gone to Beit Horon with Nachshon several weeks before, to agree the house in place of a mohar of money, and to sign the marriage-contract; and it was agreed that they would conduct the meeting of the bride and groom in the city gate, rather than have Nachshon travel to Beit Horon to the bride's house, and then all the family have to travel back again to Beit Lechem for the unveiling. So we raised the festivities right there in the gate, and the townspeople brought cakes and wines and gifts of furniture for the new house, and Achi-Yah ben Re'u-Ven, who was a priest as well as Nachshon's wedding-companion, went up into the watchtower above the gate, intending to blow the chatsotsra to announce the wedding as soon as the bridal party appeared over the horizon. The guards were furious and at first would not allow it, because of course the priests only ever blow the chatsotsra to announce camp movements during battle; but it had been Nachshon's instrument since childhood, and it was a wonderful gesture.

They were desperately late, of course - the bride always is, at a wedding of the Bene Yehudah. Achi-Yah and the other sons of the bride-chamber - myself among them - had been waiting at the roadside before the gate for nearly an hour when at last we saw them, and extraordinarily there was Shmu-El in his donkey-cart, riding up with two of his disciples, quite oblivious to the fact that half of Beit Horon was singing and dancing along a half a mile behind him, and the whole of Beit Lechem waiting in attendance at the gate. He was delighted. Old and ascetic he may have been, but he was also a Bene Yisra-El, and never yet was there born a Bene Yisra-El who would refuse the chance to eat. Except on fast days, obviously!

Rach-Yah was fourteen, and very lovely, even underneath her wedding veil. Nachshon had sent her any number of bead-necklaces - Tamar had given them to him before she died, saying they were to be kept until he married - which she had plaited into her hair and into the high head-band that held her veil in place. For a greeting gift, because the Bene Yehudah do not believe in nose-bracelets which make a bride into a chattel, he had given her a head-band made of coins and still more of Tamar's wrist and ankle bracelets; so that she was literally clattering like a pa'amon when the two of them finally came by torchlight through the gates, to the equally clattering music we sons of the bride-chamber were making. She had no gift for him - the proverb of the Bene Yehudah says, "a beautiful bride is herself a gift" - but her father had sent two servants as a dowry, and while she and Nachshon stood below the watchtower for the formal ceremony of removing the veil and laying it on the bridegroom's shoulder, they slipped away to set up the Tent of Sarah in the bedchamber of the new house; and we clapped and sang and danced them all the way to bed.

They weren't away long, but it was a happy return. Rach-Yah was not inclined to dance so soon after her deflowering, but Nachshon was wild like a billy-goat - no, not for more flowers. He was determined to play the chatsotsra at his own wedding, and not simply to rehearse the entire concert of military alarums that he had learned while soldiering. Renderings of every folk tune he had ever heard, from the polka to the set-dance, most of them in six-eight time which made them very hard to follow. So while Rach-Yah sat and watched and received the constant tribute of well-wishers, Nachshon and I and our other brothers assembled the familiar roof-orchestra of the Bene Yishai, and for once not a soul in Beit Lechem could complain about what was, in truth, a dreadful row.

Shmu-El's presence, as I say, was not by invitation, but simply a result of his turning up in Beit Lechem that night, en route as ever to Teko'a. He seemed as pleased as punch at the coincidence though. I had been playing the hallil and dancing, so I had quite forgotten he was even there, when suddenly I noticed grandfather Oved deep in conversation with him. The two of them were looking in my direction, and then pretending not to when they saw that I had noticed. I didn't exactly wander over, but put down my hallil and picked up my young niece Na'amah – Shammah's eldest - to dance with her. Given that she was only five, it wasn't difficult for our attempted circle-dance to turn elliptical, and to end up depositing her right into her great-grandfather's lap.

So that I simply couldn't help but hear their conversation.

"Then it is indeed true, as Av-Raham ben Zev has told me, that your line is traced directly to Abou Yehudah."

"Through Pharets. Indeed."

"'What profit is it if we slay our brother, and conceal his blood. Come, let us sell him to the Bene Yishma-El, and let our hands not be on him, for he is our brother and our flesh.'"

If grandfather Oved was looking bewildered, it wasn't for lack of recognising the allusion, but only as to Shmu-El's intent.

"Are you thinking of the king, Shmu-El? These massacres at Tsovah are not worse nor better than any others this past year."

Shmu-El returned no comment, only that slightly supercilious smile he always wore when his mind was engaged upon deep thinking, but not yet ready to divulge. Perhaps he himself did not yet know where his intuition was leading him.

"Yehudah was the only brother who did not resent the dreams of Abou Yah-Suph," he went on musing. At which precise moment Na'amah fell into her great-grandfather's lap, and Shmu-El saw me. "When all the other Bene Yisra-El were committed to murder, he alone resisted." He had done more than see me. He was staring at me. He was quite plainly speaking for my benefit. "And when Ben-Oni was found to have stolen the kiddush becher, the silver goblet in which the blessing of the wine was made, it was Yehudah who offered himself as bondsman."

I was more struck by his calling him Ben-Oni, instead of Bin Yamin, than by his pointing out the significance of the cup that Abou Yah-Suph had planted in his younger brother's luggage. But still, neither I nor my grandfather had the slightest notion where his thought was leading.

"Had they killed Yah-Suph, and not sold him into slavery, how would the brothers have fared when Abou Yah-Akov sent them down to Egypt to buy corn?" It was almost as if he were deciphering these mysteries for the first time, and still not sure himself of what they meant. "The last-born son of the direct line of Abou Yehudah. Yes, he, of all the brothers. Perhaps we misunderstood the oracle."

His hands were on my head, as though, like a blind man, he were trying to read me with his fingers. His eyes were closed.

It was tempting to stay silent. But it would have been dishonest not to disillusion him.

"My elder brother Eli-Av has two sons younger than me. And Shammah's wife's expecting. Perhaps she too will have a boy."

"But Eli-Av and Shammah are not the last-born of the last-born, Daoud," grandfather Oved corrected me. "You are."

Then my father came up, ostensibly to ensure his hospitality was being extended as it should, and to retrieve Na'amah who was becoming a nuisance.

"And this is the father of the prodigy, I presume?" Shmu-El laughed.

My father looked perplexed. Prodigy? What prodigy? My father was certainly unaware that any of his sons might be prodigious. Prodigiously lazy, possibly. Prodigiously expensive to feed, no doubt about that. What could the Prophet have meant by it?

But really, he was only making fun of me because of the incident at the well.

"Forgive me if I take my son away. He is needed to play out the bride and groom. It's late. They have announced their intention to retire."

He was upset. It was obvious to everyone. He must have been standing there watching for some time, had seen the looks exchanged, had seen Shmu-El bless me once again. And then those words. What did it all mean? But he never said anything.

At Beit-El, it must have been. The first time I heard him open up his thoughts in public and communicate the vision that had dominated half his life. He talked about the Patriarchs and their covenants and their visions. He spoke of his belief that all gods are really the same god, bearing different names and having different attributes, worshipped each according to their own Mysteries, but essentially the same One god. He spoke of what he called Fragmentation, by which he meant (I think) that in order to create the universe, the Omnideity had shattered the harmony of his being into a myriad fragments, rather like the explosion of a piece of crystal, and that these fragments had become trees, planets, birds, people, flowers - seeds of life. He warned us to be aware, not of false gods, because all gods were aspects of the One god - even Ba'al and Asherah, he said, were synonyms - but of false forms of worship, those apparent Mysteries that were really demon-worship - by which he meant (I think) those ceremonies involving deeds unnatural or dangerous. He talked about the land promised to all the Bene Yisra-El as a single people, the twelve tribes of Abou Yah-Akov unified under a common banner - the banner of Yahweh Elohim. He talked for nearly two hours, under a blindingly hot mid-day sun, so that by the end we were all dizzy from the combination of heat and uncomfortable sitting and thirst and hunger and the rhapsodic ululations of his voice and the huge quantities of incense floating across the shrine. Many of those assembled were drunk on pomegranate wine or dizzy from smoking poppies through a pipe and bowl. But it was Shmu-El's vision that had intoxicated me. Though I admit, I didn't really understand the half of it. One doesn't need to comprehend to be inspired.

The ribbing after the heifer sacrifice had not only not diminished, it actually increased after the whole town saw him bless me again at my brother Nachshon's wedding. When next he came to Beit Lechem, I waited by the well for the opportunity to speak to him. I knew I was being watched, and that I would be teased remorselessly about it - had Shmu-El himself not made reference to the way his brothers had mocked resentfully the pretensions of Abou Yah-Suph? - but I didn't care. When he passed by the well on his donkey, I threw myself prostrate on the sand in front of him. His servant Yazar-El was on the point of beating me with his willow-stick to get me out of the way, when Shmu-El stopped him.

"You are the lute-player who gave me water once?"

"Yes."

But hesitantly, stammering. I had made a dreadful error. And knew it now. The tone of his voice was white, hot anger.

"I asked you then if you knew the Laws, and I seem to recall you did. What is the Law concerning idolatry?"

"It is false worship, and therefore a sin."

"Indeed it is a most heinous sin. And if you know it, then why are you on your face before me in that manner? I am not Yahweh. You should prostrate yourself before Yahweh, and before no one else. Not even before a king."

"I'm sorry."

And as though it had never existed, his anger passed, and was replaced by the most soothing gentleness.

"I have a task for you. Consider it a means of expiating this sin of

200

idolatry. Will you do it?"

"If I knew what it was."

"There is a man who is very sick. Everything has been tried, every known medicine, every imaginable sacrifice and prayer. Nothing has worked. But he has a great love of music, and he finds tranquillity in the old songs and psalms. I have heard you play and sing. It would be a great act of charity if you were to go and visit this man, perhaps as often as once a week, and soothe him for an hour or two."

"Who is this man?"

"You know him well, Daoud. His name is Av-Raham ben Zev."

Indeed I did. But I was staggered to learn that Shmu-El knew my name.

Except when I was flocking in the hills, too far away to make the journey back to Beit Lechem, I went to the house of the Elder at least once every week for the next whole year. I took my father's lute, though Av-Raham possessed a very fine lyre of olive wood, a beganna lyre, with pegs and levers, such as the eunuchs of King Nimrod play in Bav-El of the Bene Kessed. I had never seen, let alone played one before, and I can assure you it is a much better instrument than our kissar-lyre, if only because the pegs stop the strings slipping; on the kissar you have to wind and tie them like wool on a loom, only lyre-strings need tautness, and you simply cannot play a whole song without losing harmonies. But argue that with Asaph, if you will - Yeditun won't even hear me on the subject. I have spent twenty years trying to persuade the royal choir to modernise its instruments, but you might as well try to teach an ostrich how to fly. Do you know I once had Nimrod send me a whole camel-train of instruments from his royal orchestra - psanterim, zummarim, a wonderful double-reed pipe they call the balaban...but this isn't what you want to hear.

Av-Raham's wife, Rach-El, was as talented a musician as any I have ever known. She played the harp and often accompanied me in playing for her husband. But it quickly became clear that, much as he loved and could be soothed by music, I had been sent to him for my benefit rather more than his. I was there to be educated, by Av-Raham in the Laws and by Rach-El in music. Nor was Av-Raham anything like as sick as Shmu-El had led me to believe. Or not physically anyway. He was a man who wept often. Certain laments could reduce him to sobs. If he was sick at all, it was in his heart - he suffered dismally from the disease of excess sentiment.

I knew hardly any of the songs that he wanted me to sing, and - let me admit it - in those days I played music more by intuition than technique. In the hills I spent hours singing, or making up my own songs when I ran out of any others, and playing reed pipes that I carved from willow-stems - until my father was made that present of a lute as a gratis for his services as choirmaster. But no one had ever really taught me. Mother gave us instruments as children and we banged or blew them. Those with an ear worked out how to make it sound like music. Those who didn't, didn't.

And as to the Laws. My father fully approved Shmu-El's idea of establishing schools for the teaching of the Laws, but we were poor shepherds - yes I know the official annals claim we were a prosperous and influential family, but that is by the by; what we had once had, my father's lack of success in farming, and the sheer size of our family, had mostly drained away. In some generations poverty is considered a boon, in others a handicap; to my father the written record of his poverty, the testimony to the parlous ruin of the line of Abou Yehudah, would have been tantamount to a disgrace. History, Shlomo, is in the eye of the beholder. So it is written, so must it have been done! We were not the poorest of the poor (have I not written about this already? my mind lapses, Shlomo), but we were still poor enough that, as the youngest son, my place was with the sheep, and not at school. I learned aleph-bet from my mother and the blessings from my father, the basic Laws like everybody else by rote; to which grandfather Oved added an entire encyclopaedic serendipity in addition. But now I was a scholar of the Laws, a learned man, a man who knew his zarko from his reviya, a man who could explain how Abou Raham mixed milk with meat before the angels and yet did not break kashrut. At the feet of the Elder of Beit Lechem. On the instructions of the Prophet. It was the most awful bore imaginable. I hated it so much I cannot even bring myself to write about it now. Ah, but the music, Shlomo. The music.

I learned the song of Abou Mousa at Pisgat ha-Har, at Mount Nevo:

"Give ear, O you heavens, and I will speak; and hear, O earth, the words of my mouth. My words shall drop as the rain, my speech shall distil the dew, as the light rain on the tender herb, and as the shower on the grass. I will make known the name of the Lord, I will exalt Yahweh. He is the Rock, his work is perfect. For all his ways lead to judgement; a god of truth and without iniquity, just and right is he..."

I learned the song of Devorah after the defeat of Sis-Ra:

"Speak, you who ride on white asses, you who sit in judgement and walk by the way. They that are delivered from the noise of archers in the place of drawing water, there shall they rehearse the righteous acts of the Lord towards the villages of Yisra-El; then shall the people go down to the gates. Awake, awake, Devorah, awake, awake, utter a song; arise, Barak, and lead your captivity captive, you son of Avi-No'am..."

I learned the song of the Lord when he appeared to Iyov in the whirlwind:

"Who is it that darkens counsel by words without knowledge? Gird up your loins now like a man, for I will demand of you, and you will answer. Where were you when I laid the foundations of the earth? Declare if you have any understanding, who has laid the measure of it, if you even know? Or who has stretched the line upon it? On what are the foundations fastened? And who laid the cornerstone, when the morning stars sang together, and all the sons of Yahweh shouted for joy? Or who shut up the sea with doors, when it broke forth, as if it had issued from the womb?"

And I learned the song and dance that Shmu-El was making about my talent, even speaking to the king about "the young prodigy with the beautiful voice and even greater skill as a musician", which was a remarkable synthesis of flattery with hyperbole. Av-Raham told me that Shmu-El had praised "the boy's religious fervour", that he had asked Av-Raham to take care both of my religious and my secular education, "because he might need it later on." Av-Raham thought he might be preparing me for a future in the priesthood, not that I would have wanted it, and anyway I wasn't of the Bene Levi, not that that mattered much back then. Rach-El I think was nearer the mark. Shmu-El was trying to persuade the king to establish a royal choir, of which I could perhaps become a member, if I worked hard, if I learned the liturgy in full. And if I smartened myself up, because you could be neither priest nor chorister dressed in the rags of a poor shepherd.

Unless, of course, you happened to be Shmu-El.

And it was, undoubtedly, extremely flattering, to think that a Prophet had noticed me amongst all the anonymous mass of Bene Yisra-El he must encounter every day. Me, or simply my voice, or the mysterious nature of an omen, any of which could be extremely useful in furthering one of his own ambitions. Every great man is perforce an opportunist. He seeks out occasions to advance himself, and he seeks the advancement of others in order to generate new occasions that he will then be able to seize on for his own advantage. Men you have made owe favours, thanks - and being yours, share your ambitions anyway. There is nothing wrong with this - quite the reverse, it is a necessary skill. So I became aware that Shmu-El was keeping an eye on me. And though I had no ambition to become either a priest or a chorister, though I had not the feintest idea what I did wish to become - as if there might even be a choice about the matter - still I knew I would not object to being something more than just a shepherd-boy, and that it was therefore sensible to make sure the reports were positive, and that he saw only what I wanted him to see. The opportunity was bound to arise eventually.

And then, one day, I was studying the theory of composition with Rach-El when Shmu-El arrived, and sat down to listen with great interest to her lesson. She was explaining, as I recall, the use of reiteration to emphasise a passage – "spoil of dyed stuffs for Sis-Ra, spoil of dyed stuffs embroidered, two pieces of dyed work embroidered for my neck as spoil", as Devorah puts it in her song - and the use of echo-lines for rhythmic effect – "Has he said, and will he not do it? Or has he spoken, and will he not fulfil it?", as the prophet Bilam had said to Balak ben Tsippur. After a while Shmu-El interrupted, saying how pleased he was that I was learning so much, and would I sing for him something of my own choosing. He meant to give me the opportunity to show off my party-piece - in those days that would have been the Psalm "Shaphteyni Elohim - Judge me, o gods", which I loved for the tremolos and vibratos in almost every line: "ve-riva rivi", "mey-ish mirmah", and the elongated pazer on "el-el simchat" - wonderful music! But I chose one that I knew less well, for it seemed appropriate to sing the song his mother Chanah had sung, when it was thought she was barren, and she called on Yahweh to give her a child. He had published it himself, in the first part of his scroll about his life, and Rach-El had taught me it:

"I am a woman of constant sorrow. I have drunk no wine nor strong drink, but I have poured out my soul before the Lord. Count not your handmaid for a daughter of Bli-El, for out of the abundance of my complaint and grief have I spoken. And you, Lord of the Hosts, if you will indeed look on the affliction of your handmaiden, and remember me, and not forget your handmaiden, but will give her a son, then I will give him to the Lord all the days of his life, and there shall come not a razor upon his head."

Shmu-El was grinning. Grinning? He was positively beaming. As I sang the last line I saw his hand go to his head - a gesture as unconscious as it was automatic - and he ran his fingers through that long, untrammelled lion's-mane of his. And as I finished, he began:

"O my Lord, as your soul lives, my Lord, I am the woman who stood by you here, praying unto the Lord. For this child I prayed, and the Lord has given me my petition which I asked of him. For this reason too I have lent him to the Lord; as long as he lives he shall be lent to the Lord."

It was a moment of the utmost poignancy. I don't believe anyone had ever seen Shmu-El weep before, except perhaps in rage, or in the tears he often simulated as part of the marvellous theatricality of his public performances. But there was no acting here. He was remembering his mother, thinking back on sixty years of living as a Nazir. And as he cried, he stared at me, and I knew that now I had won for all time the heart of the Prophet of Yisra-El.

"Shall I sing some more?"

"My mother's song of thanksgiving. Do you know it? You sang her petition so beautifully. I have never heard it sung. It is very strange to be the subject of a song. But stranger still never to have heard it sung."

Was it likely that I would have learned the first song, without also learning the second?

"My heart rejoices in the Lord, my horn is exalted in the Lord, my mouth is enlarged over my enemies, because I rejoice in your salvation. There is none as holy as the Lord, for there is none beside you, nor is there any rock like Yahweh."

Shmu-El joined in, his voice cracked with age and emotion. Nor had it ever been a very good singing voice. But he could hold a tune.

"The Lord makes the poor and the rich, he brings low and he raises up; he raises up the poor out of the dust and lifts the beggar from the dunghill to sit among princes and to make him inherit the throne of glory; for the pillars of the earth are the Lord's, and he has set the world upon them."

He was looking straight into me as he sang those lines, as though - omens and anointings – he had suddenly discovered a new meaning in them. Now, very slowly, his old bones creaking, he got up, and walked towards me, even as we were both still singing. This was the hardest part of the song, the triple stress that was so difficult to work the rhythm and the melody together on the lute and still manage to sing the words. But he was wanting to do the singing on his own now, to hear his mother's words of thanksgiving for her son's birth, to translate them into a thanksgiving of his own, to her, to Yahweh, and to me too, for giving him this opportunity. So I stayed silent, simply providing him a musical accompaniment for his own singing, aware that Av-Raham and Rach-El were both now present, and that they too were close to tears. And though I had done this out of simple vanity and flirtatiousness, it mattered not a jot. The old man was happy.

So he stood over me, and yet once more he put his hands upon my head, just as he had done that day beside the well, just as he had done at Nachshon's wedding. But looking quizzically at me, as though he still was not sure what it all meant. But triple-blessed. He had bestowed on me the triple-blessing. And it was by design now, not by accident. I bowed my head.

But Shmu-El took my chin, and lifted it. And now he sang the closing stanza, staring into my eyes:

"The adversaries of the Lord shall be broken into pieces. Out of Heaven shall he thunder upon them. The Lord shall judge the ends of the earth, and he shall give strength unto his king, and exalt the horn of the anointed."

Exalt the horn of the anointed!

It was as if the sun had been made to stand still, and the moon as well, as it did for Yehoshua ben Nun, that day at Giv-Yon and at Ayalon.

Parchment Seven

At that very moment, so people said, that moment when Shmu-El blessed me for the third time and thereby confirmed my anointing, at that very moment Sha'ul felt an evil spirit come upon him, that evil spirit which is the shadow that passes when the face of Yahweh turns aside and the priestly blessing is withdrawn. Not true, of course, though it makes for fine poetic symmetry - the symbolic handing-over of the kingdom by mystical transference. Good literature. Good poetry. Quite unconnected with history, however.

The truth is, Sha'ul had been feeling that evil spirit on him for several years already - it was what all those murderous wars had been about, after all. And the time of Gil-Gal was still a year and more away, when he would watch Shmu-El hack Agag into pieces, and I in the dark shadows of the tent would hear Shmu-El pronounce the oracle, his judge's finger pointing like an iron sword at Sha'ul, but his eyes gazing prophetically into the darkness, seeking me. Ah, Shlomo, there are evil spirits, and there are evil spirits, just as there is god, and there is god - no different from the so-called scientific explanations of the Bene Cheret and the Bli-El - metaphors, that's all. Useful metaphors. My "evil spirit" that led me to your mother. (Which of us dares to judge his fellow-man?) Your "evil spirit" that leads you to the daughters of Anat, twice nightly and in pairs (you thought I didn't know?). And what about Shmu-El's "evil spirit" - the extremity of religious fervour that led him ever more dangerously into fundamentalism? It terrified Sha'ul, as it was meant to. To think that all that blood-lust, that delight in killing, might not be an expiatable evil at all, but the genuine Will of Yahweh! It terrified him, because if it was so, then there would be no redemption, not even in She'ol. That was why Shmu-El's sacrifice of Agag was so profound in its significance - it demonstrated the paradox of paradoxes upon which this world is built; the central pillar of all wisdom. Shall I tell you it? I watched Sha'ul's face, Shlomo, that night in Gil-Gal; and the butcher of Tsovah was genuinely appalled. So was he meant to be. Because, you see, all this killing, all this brutal, apparently senseless killing, this cutting off of the hands of thieves, this stoning of adulteresses, this rope-and-scaffold justice, this eye for eye and tooth for tooth with a priest always in attendance - why, this is exactly what Yahweh wants, requires and expects of us. Yahweh the all-goodness, mercy and compassion. Yahweh the healer of the sick. Yahweh the shield of Abou Raham. Yahweh who blesses the years. Yahweh who destroys the enemies and humbles the arrogant, and in whose face, for slanderers, there is no hope. "Happy is the man," eh, Shlomo, "who dashes the little ones upon the rocks." And now Sha'ul couldn't do it. He wouldn't do it. He had been doing it for several years, knowing it was madness, but unable to prevent himself. Unable? Evil is more often than not a form of sloth and self-indulgence; a bad habit too easy to feed and too pleasurable to break. But he had done it because he liked doing it, even knowing it was wrong - indeed, knowing it was wrong added flavour, like putting mint on lamb. But now he had made the dreadful discovery that all this killing was not wrong at all. On the contrary, it was actually a way of defining goodness, sanity and reason, because it was precisely what Yahweh wanted. Say that last sentence over in your head, at least three times, until you have sucked the last drop of sour juice from it, until you have fathomed the entire truth of religious history past and present - future too, no doubt. Do you understand, Shlomo, what Sha'ul had suddenly understood? That this was not massacre at all; it was crusading. Not slaughter, but sacrifice. Not rape and butchery, but purgation. Not genocide, but holy war. In the name of Yahweh, everything is permitted. And precisely because he could no longer lie to himself about it being "madness", so also he could no longer perpetrate the acts. Therein lies Shmu-El's genius, that he multiplied madness with madness, until it equalled sanity. But at the cost to Sha'ul of his kingdom and his faith - yes, that too, for it wasn't only Yahweh who rejected Sha'ul that day, but Sha'ul who likewise rejected Yahweh. All gods. From the day of Agag's killing till that of his own death, Sha'ul would count himself, not among the prophets, but among the Bli-El. Ah, as my father would have said, for the joys of a simple life, in the quietude of the country, with a wife and eight children and a flock of goats!

But all of that was still more than a year away, and Sha'ul's evil spirit had nothing whatsoever to do with the symbolic anointing of the shepherd-boy Daoud, in an act of the most outrageous sentimentality, by the aged shepherd-of-Yisra-El Shmu-El. Sha'ul had heard of me, perhaps, in passing, as some parenthesis to another of Shmu-El's grand ideas - but by this time Sha'ul had stopped paying heed to the ideas, let alone the marginalia. No more than that. The story of the "anointing" - and it was very much an "anointing" in inverted commas, and not the full saga of the horn of oil described in Shmu-El's scroll by disciples sycophantic to the both of us – wasn't known by him till later, when (I confess) I told it to him myself to arouse his jealousy.

No, I first encountered Sha'ul some months after the incident of the song of Chanah, when I was summoned to the new royal palace at Gil-Gal by the king's new choirmaster, to audition for the royal choir. I went with gifts - an ass laden with bread, a bottle of wine, and a kid goat. These were Shmu-El's instructions. I have often wondered if they too were intended symbolically, thinking back to Sha'ul's coronation, or as a bribe for the royal auditioner. No matter. I was accepted.

And now, Shlomo, now I must make the decision I have been putting off for days. There is broadsheet journalism, which passes on the news and gossip, and believes our prurient fascination with the sex-lives of the rich and famous to be the same as "in the public interest" - have you heard, for example, Abba Choshe'a, who sings his wife's adulteries to the accompaniment of a lyre in the streets of Megiddo and Beit She'an, and sells parchment copies to make a living, and likes to pretend his own sad plight is somehow analogous of the spiritual state of the nation? Marvellous songs, mind you! "Set the trumpet to your mouth. He shall come as an eagle against the house of the Lord..." Where was I? Yes. Then there is biography, which attempts to piece together a logical and credible life out of the chaos of incomplete evidence. And there is history, which is written to suit the prejudices of the author, or the commissioner, or the age (history, Shlomo, as I'm sure I must have said before, is in the eye of the beholder), and which therefore omits or alters or distorts or misrepresents whatever does not suit the thesis. Three ways of pretending to be factual, precisely by pretending not to be fictional. And all three false on both counts.

Where within this does one pitch one's memoires? Do I give you the gossip, the objective evidence, the official version, or the truth the whole truth and nothing but those parts of the truth that suit my best interests, protect my posterity, and are unlikely to incriminate me in the here and now? Or, since there are already the official annals -

the Scroll of the Kings, Shmu-El's scroll about his life, the writings of the Chronicler of Ephrayim (I predicted this, you know. I warned Shmu-El when we agreed to open a school in every town and to teach the aleph-bet for uses beyond the study of the Law, I warned him that all this undirected literacy would make a nation of hagiomaniacs out of us. Do you know how many parchments are being published every year? The scribes, Shlomo - like hail in Mitsrayim! Everywhere you turn, another hopeless dilettante, trying to scribe his parchment!) - but enough contrived digressions to avoid this of all issues. The question, Shlomo. The question. Can I trust you to read an act of full confession, and to keep it secret, destroying the parchment after you have read it? Are you capable of that, Shlomo? And does it really matter?

For I have great need of making this confession.

Very well then. Let me gird up my loins for their ungirding.

The king had at last agreed the establishment of a royal choir, to be based eventually at Giv-On, so that the ceremonies of the Ark could be performed with a trained priesthood and an accompanying orchestra. Sha'ul had never really listened to the music of the liturgy, but when he did, like Av-Raham ben Zev, it turned out to be a wonderful medicine for what he liked to call his "migraines" (people never think of their own "evil spirits" as "evil spirits" - like sulks and tantrums, these are things that only "other people" ever have). The king approved the choir, but the choir never got to Giv-On. It was quartered instead at Gil-Gal with the king, and travelled with him to Giv-Yah when he summered there. The orchestra comprised shofar, kinnor, nevel, tof, minnim and ugav; there was also a corps de ballet, amounting to six young girls and six older ones, all virgins, the younger dancing with the tiny, palm-held, high-pitched cymbals, the older with the larger, louder ones. The choir, like the orchestra, was twelve, one boy picked from each of the twelve tribes, and afforded priestly status, even though we were none of us Bene Levi. All the choristers were musicians too, and sometimes we doubled up. We sang at royal banquets, at ceremonies of state and sacrifice; we accompanied the Ark on pilgrimage; and often we sang just for Sha'ul, attending him alone in his private rooms at Giv-Yah or Gil-Gal, or in his tent, a small band of four or five to soothe and entertain him when he was weary but couldn't sleep.

And sometimes he would send for just a single voice, which could have meant any one of us – but always boys, not girls; he would never compromise a girl by asking her to be alone with him. Just boys – usually just me. His favourite, his beloved, his "uncle", his "trouble-maker", why, even his "basket" and his "boiling-kettle" and his "cooking-pot" - if there was a pun he could make on my name, Sha'ul was bound to make it. Why me? Well, you have only to look at the words in the Scroll of the Kings and learn to read between the lines, where all great literature is made: "Behold, I have seen a son of Yishai of Beit-Lechem, who is cunning in playing, and a mighty valiant man, and a man of war, and prudent in matters, and a comely person, and the Lord is with him." The Lord being with me might well have been a major disadvantage even before the death of Agag. But honestly! "Prudent in matters"? Which matters? Now there's a phrase open to all manner of deliberate misinterpretations. And as to "a man of war, and a mighty valiant man"! I was just fourteen, my voice was in process of breaking - no royal choir requires baritones, Shlomo - and I had spent the whole of my childhood tending my father's miserable flock of goats in the hills around Beit Lechem. All I knew of war were the stories my elder brothers brought home with them, and of mighty valiance the darkness fraught with spiders in the cave of Adullam. No, the only true statement in that entire paean is that I was "a comely person". Reasonably cunning in playing too, I suppose, though it was not for that that Sha'ul summoned me. The false attributes concealed the real one. As Ben-Ayah has been overheard to say on more than one occasion - a good man, Ben-Ayah; I recommend him to you - a man may achieve greatness for many qualities, but those of his buttocks are the most certain. You understand me, I am sure.

But then again it isn't your understanding that I am seeking, albeit that I am couch-bound and confessional. There are, Shlomo, certain Laws of Abou Mousa, written in the Tablet of the Priests - you know the ones I mean, the ones referring to the Bene Chalev...no, this still is not the way to tell it.

Very well then. Spit it out. Sha'ul had a great penchant for teenage boys, preferably in their early teens, pubescent, girlish and compliant - there, I've said it. There is a certain point, rather like waiting for a fruit to ripen on a tree and plucking it - the still point of the turning world, you might say; that moment when the fruit ceases to be growing to maturity, when it crosses its zenith, when it begins corrupting. Sha'ul liked to get his boys at just that point - the soft down of hair on the flesh that wasn't yet the goat-skin of an adult male. The testicles dropped, the voice breaking, but the mind still unsatiated with onanistic fantasies, the libido still unfocused upon girls. That in particular. To take a boy at precisely that moment when he becomes aware of sexual stirrings, and to divert his thoughts away from girls, to seduce him, to render him up completely to his own kind, until the very thought of girls disgusted him. Put it down, if you must, as a further manifestation of his "evil spirit".

I was glad to serve – "to disobey", after all, "is tantamount to rebellion, which is a greater sin than witchcraft" - though I cannot claim to have enjoyed it. Nor was he able to render me up to men - I was fourteen, as I said, and past the point of rendering. But when the king says bend, you bend. Kissing him was like eating lamb with the fleece still on. He favoured bottoms, though his own was majestically inviolable, except by tongue. Round not flat for preference, and he rarely wasted time worrying if they were hygienic. I must say I never understood the fascination with bottoms, male or female. Sha'ul went in for sodomy and buggery in roughly equal measures, though I would say he treated sodomy as a way of hurting women, and buggery as a way of hurting himself through men. The amateur psychologist, I. But physically I never understood it. It was almost impossible to get the damned thing in without vast amounts of lubricating oil and preparation with the finger. I always thought the anus was designed for getting solid objects out, not for putting solid objects in. Practically any other orifice is preferable. And cleaner. My god, but the diseases he inflicted on himself! Well, what do you expect? A tight anus tears - especially if it's fourteen years old and virginal - and a mingling of blood and faeces is positively a witch's brew of illness and disease. No wonder Abou Mousa outlawed it as an abomination.

Why, then, did I submit? Why does Avi-Shag submit? Because a king is a king. Flagrant, naked ambition too, I am afraid - allied to the certainty of what would happen to me if I declined the royal invitation. But the truth is, I liked the power my position gave me at the royal court (why, you had only to whisper the name of a rival in the king's ear while your fingers were obeying his every command, and the rival would be gone by morning). I wanted the continuing patronage of the king so that I could advance further. And the only way that anyone like me got access to Sha'ul's patronage was in his bed. Men are just as capable of using their bodies to gain power as women are. Daoud ben Yishai, hetaerus to his majesty, prostitute prince to the prince of pederasts, catamite to the king, whore and darling of the Lord of the Underworld. Sha'ul She'ol. She'ol Sha'ul. Happy is the man who delights in human flesh, for was it not given to us, naked and unashamed, in Eden?

And so we enter the realm of myth and legend. There is a point, Shlomo, at which the need for public acclamation to enhance one's image and thereby secure the love and obedience of the people, a point at which that need subsides into the merest propaganda, into fantasy. And this is dangerous, not because the people are likely to suspect the veracity of your latest Labour of Shimshon - no, indeed, the people will believe absolutely anything, and the more so the more fabulous the tale, because that is the image and the likeness in which men create their gods. No, it's dangerous because, if you tell the lie often enough, you yourself may come eventually to believe in it. Has it ever occurred to you, for example, that if all the people who claim to have been present, let us say, when Shmu-El judged the people at Mitspeh, if they really had all been present, then they would have constituted an army of such size Shmu-El would not have needed to judge the people at Mitspeh? You take my point.

Then, with that rider and qualification, let me now reveal to you the truth about my greatest legendary feat, the killing of Gol-Yat of the Bene Gat, at Sochoh of Ychudah, near Azekah, in Ephes Damim. As it is written in the First Scroll of the Kings, the Scroll of Shmu-El (column seventeen, lines four five and six to be precise):

"And Sha'ul and the Bene Yisra-El were mustered, and pitched their camp in the Vale of Elah, to set the battle in array against the Bene Pelet. Their chief of staff was Av-Ner ben Ner."

There is another legend, also recounted in that same chapter of the Royal Annals, a rather absurd story of my going home just after the pitching of the camps before the battle, but being sent back by my father with an ephah of parched corn and ten loaves and ten cheeses for the captain of my brothers' thousand; a story which makes me appear rather young, insignificant, and decidedly ordinary-human, but which I am sorry to say is remarkably nearer to the truth than any Bene Yehudah wishes to admit. For it is what really happened.

I was sixteen years old. For nearly eighteen months I had been resident at the court of king Sha'ul. It was not the opulent lifestyle in which you grew up, Shlomo. There was a splendid home at Giv-Yah which was called a palace, though really it was just a fortified hill-house. Sha'ul had built it for his father, whom he worshipped. The nearest it came to being palatial was the cedar frames and beams, but the rest was plain adobe, and there were few furnishings. Next to it he had built a house for Shmu-El, but after the killing of Agag, when the two fell out completely, Shmu-El left the house to his disciples in the Guild. We spent the long summers in Giv-Yah. The dry heat of Gil-Gal made the shrine unbearable, and the density of salt in the air gave you an unquenchable thirst for water. But Giv-Yah was cooled by breezes off the hills, and the trees gave shelter. For the rest of the year we were lodged at Gil-Gal, where we lived in tents or wooden huts, and spent our days.

I know you think that last phrase is incomplete, yet it represents the sum of things. We spent our days. It is hard now to recall what precisely they consisted of - choir practices obviously, though even those were few and far between, for outside the liturgy, which we practiced by performing at the daily services, Sha'ul was not a king who banqueted, and Yisra-El was not yet a state that welcomed ambassadors and queens and magi. Entertainment came in the form of athletics tournaments, archery contests, wrestling-bouts - the symphonies of Asaph ben Zamar were, shall I say, not yet in vogue! You have to remember, Shlomo, though it was only fifty years ago, that these times were primitive (begging Shmu-El's pardon), without our contemporary modernities. An adolescent society follows adolescent pursuits - voyeuristic sex and ball-games. Sha'ul was a semi-illiterate cattle-farmer, unsophisticated, uncouth, uncultured, and quite out of his depth. The world has matured a long way these past fifty years.

We went to school, of course - rich man's school, not the open schools we now have. Each tribe that sent a choir-boy, a dance-girl and a member of the orchestra, also sent sufficient funds to pay for tutors. We were supposed to develop our knowledge of the aleph-bet into grammar, but this simply never happened - all we did was endless copying-out of psalms and prayers, as though we were in training to be scribes. Because most of us were destined to become Elders, we studied the Tablets of Abou Mousa to understand the Laws. However, as the school father was fond of explaining, any detailed examination of the text in any other way was "dangerous". After all, this wasn't literature made up by men. You couldn't question its subject-matter. You couldn't challenge its contradictions though there are enough of them to keep the lawyers busy for eternity. You couldn't argue against it. You couldn't express interest in the deeper meanings of, say, the names of people and places - grandfather Oved would have been sent to the school father for punishment several times a day! Better then not to study it at all, except for Law and handwriting. We spent a good deal of time though doing geography and botany - did you know, for example, that the avati'ach, the melon referred to in the Scroll of the Numbering in the Wilderness as one of the five species the Bene Yisra-El grew in Goshen, is in fact the red, black-seeded water-melon, and not the white-seeded yellow variety? Oh yes, amongst the many subjects in which I count myself as educated well beyond my intellect, is the fascinating scholarly erudition of gardening.

But what, you are losing patience, has any of this to do with Gol-Yat? I am getting there, Shlomo. I am getting there.

As soon as Shmu-El found out why the king had been so keen to establish a royal choir, and why the personnel seemed to change so often, he disbanded it. The royal choirmaster was sent home in disgrace - Shmu-El held him personally responsible, accused him effectively of procuring, but in all honesty there was little the poor man could have done but agree to Sha'ul's requests, or die refusing. Several of the priests of the shrine were mustered as a punishment for their collusion, and died trumpeting in battle. Shmu-El would have had us all sent home, but Sha'ul kept on several of his favourites, myself amongst them, granting some an honorarium and some a stipend to live at court. As for me, I was appointed as the king's personal lutanist and armour-bearer.

At Gil-Gal Sha'ul mostly occupied a tent. It gave him, I think, the sense of being a real desert-sheikh, like Abou Raham, rather than some tame, city-dwelling, pampered monarch like the Pharaohs of

Mitsrayim. Not that inhabiting a tent is in itself an abstention from pampering. He had a couch made from the softest sheep's wool, all draped with multicoloured silks and satins - rather like your mother's boudoir, it occurs to me - and the rest of the floor was covered with rush matting and a carpet of linen cushions likewise stuffed with wool. The narguileh took up a space in one corner, with the scribe's seat and the secretary's table to conceal it. His fighting wardrobe occupied the other corner.

For hand-to-hand combat he had a short-sword and a long-sword, both wrought in iron by smiths of the Bene Pelet. He also had a double-headed axe, heavier than I could lift or human head could possibly withstand, but which he with his massive frame had little trouble wielding. He practiced on tree stumps and regularly threatened to practice on unruly soldiers. Av-Ner was a bow-and-arrows man, but Sha'ul never had the coordination to master it - several times I watched him practicing in secret, but invariably the arrow slipped its line as soon as he pulled it past the tension-point. And his javelin throwing was proverbial. He could throw immense distances, but no matter what, you could guarantee that it would flatten out in flight, so that it landed horizontal on the ground instead of spearing. He was so consistent he was worth putting a wager on - the truth is, the man could be guaranteed to miss absolutely anything at any distance up to fifty paces, beyond which no one would waste a shekel betting anyway. Mind you, he was lethal at half a yard.

Fortunately I did not have responsibility for his weaponry - I say fortunately, because it was a desperately cumbersome load to carry, from tent to cart and back again, let alone into battle. My responsibility was his armour. Though he never fought at the front, he always carried a frontsman's shield, a large rectangle of wicker covered with leather, though in his case with the frame encased in bronze to strengthen it. The leather needed oiling almost every other day - forgive me the crudity, Shlomo; we all referred to it as "bum-oil", and there was always plenty of it in his tent - and because his hands were huge and clumsy, the leather handle on the inside of the shield was forever needing to be stitched. He had bronze greaves for his legs and a lower skirt of mail, and a breastplate of such heavy mail it was lucky we were always fighting on sand and rock and not in marshland, because he would have sunk to oblivion under all that weight before the enemy got the chance to scupper him. He put it on me once, for a joke, and I collapsed. Literally. Oh, and of course he had a bronze helmet, green as copper, with two half-moons for the eye-slits. Everything had to be kept clean and polished, so he could go into battle looking like a king. And when the polishing was done to the royal satisfaction.

"Play for me, boy."

Asaph ben Zamar, first royal choirmaster, removed from his post, reinstated a decade later by the new king (me), greatest composer and musician in the known world. All his life Asaph had travelled the length and breadth of Yisra-El, and well beyond, collecting liturgical hymns and folk-songs, orchestrating them, arranging them for trio, choir or quartet, using them as starting-points for his own orchestral compositions. Asaph ben Zamar, hero of the boy Daoud. It gave a sort of secret pleasure, a kind of vengeance, to sing his psalms before Sha'ul, and know that Sha'ul didn't know it.

"Ah but the gods are good to Yisra-El, to those whose hearts are clean. But as for me, my feet were almost gone, my steps had well-nigh slipped, for I envied the foolish when I saw how the wicked prospered."

"Why are all your songs so damned morbidly gloomy?"

He was in one of those moods again.

"No, don't stop playing. Just play something with some life to it. Your songs are like my cousin Av-Ner's military despatches. Why does no one ever have good news to report?"

There was a simple answer, of course. But did I dare to give it?

I dared.

"The psalms begin in gloom, sire, in order to end in happiness. If they began in happiness..."

"Yes? Go on. If they began in happiness..."

"They..."

"They could still perfectly well end in happiness too. Well couldn't they?"

"I..."

"Exactly. Now sing something cheerful."

"'In you, O Lord, do I put my trust, let me never suffer confusion.'"

"You see. You see. Not that putting his trust in the Lord ever did a man much good. But at least it's not morbidly gloomy."

Clearly this was the watchword of the week. There was always one.

The previous week it had been "hymns of blasted desolation".

"'For you are my hope, O Lord; you are my trust from my youth.'"

Armour-bearer to the king. Keeper of the royal bum-oil, anyway. I had three, theoretically different, yet in practice absolutely symmetrical functions in life. The first was to keep his armour shiny, so his ego wouldn't droop. The second was to play the harp and sing to soothe the royal distemper, to stop his spirit going flaccid - the blood-lust may have passed, but now he was a victim of "the most terrible", "the most desperate", "the most awful black-dog depressions". You have to envisage him describing it thus, with a wrist placed theatrically against his forehead.

And the third.

"Enough, boy. Put away your instrument and come over here."

The third was to play his instrument - solo virtuoso - for a similar erotherapeutic purpose. I was his "boy" when I polished his armour and played the lute, but in this I was even less, a nobody, a nothing, a mere set of orifices. The king didn't even look at me when he was fucking me, and if he looked at me when I was fellating him, it was only because he liked to watch himself being plated. He didn't see me - merely a clump of black locks and a mechanical mouth. Why did I do it? Because he was the king. Because I knew what happened to boys who refused. Because I was ambitious. Just because.

After the war with Agag, there had been peace for the best part of a year. There was, in truth, no one left to fight a war with, every one of our neighbours having skulked away from another of Sha'ul's blistering skirmishes. Not that he had won anything - neither territory nor treaty nor even security of borders. He warred the way a greedy man eats, shovelling in the food without tasting it, planning his next menu while he does so and salivating at the prospect, so that what seems on his lips to be present pleasure is in fact future anticipation. But he had demonstrated his strength. Those who tend to be impressed by the flexing of muscle, were duly impressed. Those who recognise that violence is actually a revelation of weakness, watched Shmu-El retreat to Ramah, and gradually regrouped their forces.

The Bene Pelet mustered in each of the Five Cities. Av-Ner's footmen were everywhere, collecting numbers mostly, though what

Sha'ul wanted to know was the extent of the iron weaponry being forged. Men who are frightened of large numbers are frightened of eternity. Whereas iron kills, now.

"There are local musters, in Neballat, Yehud, Beit Dagon, Azekah."

"Azekah? Then they threaten Beit Shemesh."

"There's a forward garrison at Yarmut. My guess is that they'll try to take Beit Shemesh from the west and south, and then move on through Eshta'ol towards Kiryat Ye'arim. There's a rumour that this time they wish to destroy the Ark for good."

This was patent rubbish, and surely Av-Ner knew it? It wasn't even a logical military ploy, since if it succeeded it would bring the whole of Yisra-El down on their heads in genocidal fury. And besides, the Bene Pelet are even more superstitious than the Bene Yisra-El. Men who believe in gods will fight men who believe in other gods, to prove their gods are superior; but the power of divine destruction remains with the divinity. Av-Ner was wrong - and Sha'ul knew it. This was not a war of aggression being planned, but a part of the gradual strategy of colonisation they had been practicing for decades, strip by strip of farmland, village by village, settlement by settlement. The forward garrisons were purely protective. The mustering was almost certainly a ruse.

"Have they gone as far as Zano'ah?"

Listening to the discussion was driving me nostalgic. This was my territory, after all. Yarmut, Sochoh, Zano'ah, Adullam - these were the Hills of the Shephelah where I had flocked for years, before the shepherd-boy was transformed into the choir-boy, and the choir-boy...I hadn't missed my home so much in ages.

"How nearly ready are they to attack?"

Av-Ner was a slow and thoughtful man, sometimes irritatingly ponderous. When you asked him a question, you watched the mechanics until you could see the answer slithering down the thought-channels, ruminated in the gut, passed through the liver to the heart, a lengthy tangling and untangling of entrails as it made the difficult journey from the heart to the brain, then down through his eyes until at last it reached his mouth. In the meanwhile he chewed his lips and tongue. He sucked his teeth. He nodded his head. He curled his lips and nostrils as though they tickled. He sniffed. He rubbed his chin. It was very rare that Av-Ner's answer came out wrong, even if it occasionally came out so late you had fallen asleep in the meanwhile or made your own decision. But this time he was badly wrong.

"I would say they're within a week. We could move at once, take them by surprise."

The triumph of Yavesh Gil-Yad had never left his memory.

So the little armour-bearer was about to be called upon to fulfil some official duties - of which the discovery that Sha'ul liked to be "soothed" before a battle as an aid to clarity of thought, as well as after it as an aid to clarity of sleep, was the least of terrors. It was the thought of battles that horrified me. I had no wish either to kill or to be killed. But the latter in particular. I was sixteen years old and there was still so much to do. My head was full of songs that one day Asaph ben Zamar – he had promised - would teach me to write down. My total experience of sex as yet included nothing of the topography of the female form. Life awaited me like an autumn vine. And as an armour-bearer I would be given no weapon of my own, but would be left in the tent to have my throat cut if we lost. In short, I wasn't prepared to give up everything for nothing, or not without first saying farewell to my family. There is a name for what I did, Shlomo, a technical term that describes my entirely healthy and rational response, a name that belongs not to philosophers or to star-gazers, not to metaphysicians or to priests, but is the exclusive provenance of those of us who have lived it, the true poets of the civilised human soul. The word is cowardice.

I fled.

That is the sordid truth, Shlomo. I ran away. While the army was being gathered in Gil-Gal, I went home to daddy. While Sha'ul was being dressed in his armour by Avi-Chai ben Amasa - and didn't even notice I was gone - my father was going against everything he believed in about how to bring up children, and was belting the living daylights out of me with a leather strap. While the Bene Yisra-El marched westwards across the hills to surprise the Bene Pelet in Ephes-Damim, I was being subjected to the full epic of the House of Yishai. It was all entirely predictable.

"Your brother Eli-Av fought at Aphek when he was barely seventeen. Wounded in the leg and never once did he complain. And do you think it stopped him mustering again?"

As I recalled it, Eli-Av won the national prize for moaning several years consecutively, parading his wounded leg around like a badge of honour every time he didn't feel like shearing sheep or sticking his arm up a goat's uterus to pull out a still-born kid. But memory is memory. Nostalgia is never what it used to be. My father had a point to make. Or a bag of clichés anyway.

"And where do you think your elder brothers are, right now? At the front, that's where."

This at least was indisputable.

"Eli-Av, Avi-Nadav, Nachshon, Shammah? What do you think they're doing now - gone on pilgrimage to Kinneret to take the waters? Is it? Is that what you think?"

It was actually worth enduring this, just to learn a new side of my father I had never seen before. While my mother just sat quietly at the quern, turning it single-handed, wincing and weeping.

"And Salmah. And Chetsron. Where do you think they are?"

He didn't mention Ram, of course. No one ever did. In times of war, being a cripple like my brother Ram was a family disgrace, for which the ordinance of the leper was the only proper expiation.

And as to cowards and deserters.

"I have six sons in the army. But my seventh son..."

That was when he reached his own nadir. Smacking me, he had known from the outset, would make not the slightest difference to my behaviour, though it didn't half make him feel better doing it! But now the very fact of omission brought him up with a start, and then he too began weeping, clutching me to his breast and sobbing openly. This was more like the father that I knew.

"And you the king's own armour-bearer."

I was sorely tempted to disabuse him of any illusions he might have add in that regard. Yet even the words in which I was thinking it - words like "sore" and "abuse" I mean - made me realise it was impossible. He wouldn't have believed me anyway.

"You'll go back, Daoud."

That was obvious already.

"You know the hills as well as anyone. You'll go to Sochoh. They say the army's gathering there. You'll take some food with you. Say you went to fetch it for your brothers. You'll go back, Daoud. You'll not disgrace us."

I could tell that, now that the expected tirade was done, now that the required sermon was delivered, he would more than happily have hidden me in a barn, all eight of his sons together, until peace returned. Had he not fought himself at Even-Ezer, all those donkey's years ago? No one hates war more than an old soldier.

I went back, but not directly. I roamed the wadis and hills west of Beit Lechem for two days and a night. I wandered through the woods into Ramatayim Tsophim, thinking to go and take refuge with Shmu-El, who I had heard from a shepherd was with his family. But he wasn't there, and at the entrance to the village there was a small platoon of footmen, gathering food and water - so I slipped away. I stayed two more nights in the cave at Adullam, staring at the rock paintings, unable to sleep. Fear mingled with the realisation of my cowardice. And then more fear, of being flogged to death as a deserter when I did go back.

From the hilltop above Elah I looked down on the two armies, and for the first time I appreciated what a magnificent yet terrible thing an army was. The constant sound of ram's horns signalled movements at both ends of the valley: long-shielded frontsmen building their vanguard walls, lines of archers and lancers and slingers, men gathering in their fifties and hundreds, the sun glinting on bronze or dulled by iron. At the very back of the lines of the Bene Pelet, a cavalcade of ox-drawn chariots stood like death in waiting, impatiently scratching at the dust. It was an awe-inspiring sight, and yet curiously passive. They must have been facing each other out like this for nearly a week now, yet neither army looked as though it was about to make war.

I had gone home in a royal donkey-cart, without permission obviously, but no one had stopped me because I went so brazenly and so openly that it was presumed to be legitimate - men only ever suspect stealth. So, now, remembering the footmen at Ramatayim Tsophim, I brought the donkey-cart back again - not the same one obviously, that was left in Beit Lechem. I "requisitioned" one near Adullam, and filled it with water-jars and vegetables and fresh loaves – I had eaten the ones my father gave me - and more cheese, and fresh fruit, especially pomegranates, the king was passionate for pomegranates. As though I were in service to the royal quartermaster. No point, I thought, dissimulating. I had spotted the king's tent from the hill, and I headed directly there.

"King's armour-bearer, bringing fresh supplies," I shouted to the camp-guards, and drove on. I was light-headed with fear, such that it manifested itself in a curious kind of bravery. So heroes are often made.

I stopped the cart and got out. Avi-Chai ben Amasa had seen me from the tent, and waved, to warn me in fact, though it seemed at the time like a welcome. I was literally about to call him to help unload the cart, standing there myself with an armful of cheeses, when Gol-Yat appeared on the high rock behind me, about to issue his now-famous challenge, and from the tent appeared, not Avi-Chai, but Sha'ul himself. There was the Chief of the Bene Pelet - no giant, I assure you, though a very powerful man, and by all accounts a very great general - there Sha'ul, king of the Bene Yisra-El, dressed in full armour (though not, I thought, as brightly polished as I would have insisted on). And in between them - I, Daoud, lapsed deserter, repentant coward, stealer of the royal donkey-cart - with an ephah of parched corn and a wagon-load of fruit and vegetables, like some greengrocer's delivery boy on his way home from the shouk. It was, in truth, extremely comic, though I don't imagine anybody laughed.

"Why are you come out to set your battle in array?" shouted Gol-Yat, in the formal rhetoric of pre-engagement. "Am I not the Chief of the Bene Pelet, and you the mere servants of Sha'ul? Choose a man from among you, and let him come down to me. If he is able to fight with me, and kill me, then we will be your servants. But if I prevail against him, and kill him, then you will be our servants, and serve us. I defy the armies of Yisra-El this day. Give me a man, that we may fight together."

Huge, bearded and fearless, he stood clutching his sword-handle, entirely alone on that hilltop. Sha'ul was clearly terrified, but for me it was a moment of revelation. There was Gol-Yat, issuing his customary challenge, repeated every day for the past week without response, and me loaded down with enough bribe-goods to feed every officer in the army breakfast. I couldn't move without being noticed - for it was clear that, so long as I stood completely still between them, Sha'ul simply wouldn't see me through the haze of his own terror and bravado; and Gol-Yat wasn't looking. So I stood, and looked at each of their faces. And then, slowly, almost reluctantly, a question worked its way upward from my own shriven bowels into my by-now-highly-active brain - why was Gol-Yat issuing such a challenge? For it sounded like brazen arrogance from a man who knew he could achieve victory by any means. And yet. And yet. If he was that self-confident, why take such a risk, why stake his people's future on the uncertain outcome of a single combat? Were we not named Yisra-El, after all, precisely because of an improbable victory in an unequal single combat? I had seen his chariots from the hilltop. I had watched his archers and lancers form their lines. Did he not trust his own strength? Did the reputation of the butcher of Tsovah work that much magic? Had he mis-read the name Sha'ul, thinking it named him She'ol, Lord of the Underworld, Lord of Death? No, he couldn't read. But he had issued the challenge – underline this, Shavsha, but be careful not to tear the parchment – he had issued the challenge *precisely because he anticipated defeat*.

And Sha'ul, conscious only of his own frailties, simply couldn't see it. The man was effectively suing for peace. And Sha'ul couldn't see it. What sounded like an arrogant threat was really a concealed plea - we cannot defeat you in battle, but perhaps, in single combat, we might yet. And Sha'ul couldn't see it. The Bene Pelet were expecting to lose, and looking for an honourable way to retreat, while keeping the few fields and villages they had taken on the way. And Sha'ul couldn't see it. And my own fear of battle, the absurdity of my predicament, the strangely quizzical look on the king's face as he suddenly recognised one of his catamites standing in the midst of the battle-field with a picnic in his arms, induced me to add absurdity to absurdity.

"Sire," I made it sound as brave as possible, putting down the groceries as I did so, "I have slain lions and bears..."

And took my sling out of my tunic, to demonstrate.

Sha'ul roared with laughter - louder than a whole pride of lions and bears. Gol-Yat especially roared with laughter. So thoroughly comic was it, the two could have been united in friendship over the shared joke. But it was not a joke.

Then Sha'ul said: "No. You are a boy, not a man of war. I will not see my people delivered into the hands of the Bene Pelet because of a mere boy."

But the sling was in my hand, and fear and absurdity were conjoining in my bowels. I picked up a stone. And I threw it - yes, at Gol-Yat, but really anywhere, a gesture, I didn't even sling the stone, just threw it, to get me out of this ludicrous predicament, to attempt to shatter the glass wall of illusions that prevented Sha'ul from seeing what was so obvious, to knock down the paper skittle which was all that Gol-Yat really was. And damn me if a whole bevy of stones didn't hit him bang in the middle of his forehead. Knocked him out cold. It was a most appalling breach of the moral etiquettes of warfare, the civilised chivalric codes that men stupidly pretend to before they go out into the battlefield and perpetrate the most ultimate acts of cannibalistic barbarism, one against the other. Yah-Natan had placed a battalion of slingers in his front rank, the very best he had in an army whose slingers had long been their elite command. Just as Gol-Yat had been coming out to issue this absurd challenge for several days, so Sha'ul too had been procrastinating. He could not take up such a challenge and risk his kingdom in a single combat, yet neither was he ready to commit himself to battle. So Yah-Natan had prepared his own answer, just as he had done previously at Geva, and at Mishmash, to force his father's hand; and I happened to provide the useful pretext for what would have taken place without me anyway.

As I raised my arm to throw my stone - miles off-target, into a ditch somewhere - Yah-Natan had already given the order to his men to arm their slings. My stone fragmented into a thousand stones, and they shattered the giant's skull. But I didn't kill him. In the shock of that unexpected happening - how dare anybody cheat at the noble sport of war! - and believing their champion to be dead - when in fact he was merely wounded - the Bene Pelet prepared to flee, and the king of Yisra-El unsheathed his sword, realising that the lost battle was not a foregone conclusion after all. Av-Ner ben Ner, the king's commander, handed me the sword of the stricken Bene Pelet champion. His look told me, that now I had the chance to prove myself. Cut off the giant's head. (Or perhaps he meant, hack it into pieces, like the head of Agag?) But I couldn't. I held the longsword out in front of me, like a man pushing a broom. But lift it over my shoulders I could not. For the first time in my life I was holding an implement that could sever the knot of human life. And I couldn't use it. My fingers that were so accomplished at prick and lute, that were accustomed to sharpening a knife against the umbilicus of a lambing ewe, had turned arthritic. My bowels had shrivelled up inside me. My scrotum had likewise become a hard, tight mesh of fear. I was swallowing, trembling, sweating. But I couldn't do the deed. And then - but this is unrecorded, you will have to take my word for it - the king's son, Yah-Natan ben Sha'ul, himself stepped forward, took the sword out of my hands, and took off the head.

Then Yah-Natan pressed the sword back into my hand, lifted my arm into the air in triumph (blood dripped along the hilt and down my sleeve - it was utterly revolting), forced on me the glory of his act. And whispered:

"You must take the credit for this. I dare not. You will be rewarded."

Suddenly I had been lifted onto someone's shoulders. Banners were being unfurled about me. They carried me like this to the hilltop to watch the Bene Pelet flee, Sha'ul in pursuit and bodies falling everywhere as the retreating army was cut down, all the way to the gates of Ekron. The old madness was upon us once again, revisited, restored - yet justified this time, for this was not a war Sha'ul had sought. Once engaged, however, the requirement of the gods was sacrifice. Wherever the Bene Pelet had pitched their tents, wherever they had established forward garrisons, wherever they had settled families on Bene Yisra-El land, Sha'ul sent his men to slaughter them – Sha'arim, Gat, Shalvim, Beit-Dagon. The air was rancid with the taste of blood.

Meanwhile, the fields of Ephes-Damim were being emptied of the living, and you could not see the dust for men. I held the royal banner in my two uplifted arms as I swayed now upon Prince Yah-Natan's own shoulders in the midst of maybe forty of his men.

"Form sixes."

There was a smile on all their faces, a new mood of excitement, as this order was received. I had the feeling, and afterwards Yahni confirmed it, that this was the first time for something special, something they had been practicing, something they had been waiting for the right moment to try out. So, now, it happened.

The men - exactly thirty-six of them - formed into six groups of six, making a protective circle around us - around me. Each group lined up in a circle, facing inwards, one sword-length apart.

"Swords."

Each man took out his sword - a longsword; they hadn't yet perfected it enough to try the trick with shortswords - and held it horizontally before him. Each sword was raised - the six passing so close they could easily have touched and spoiled the show - until it was held flat and vertical against the chin. Each movement choreographed, balletic, awesomely precise - as beautiful to watch as set-dancing. Yet to what end, unless to demonstrate the quality of their training, the fervour of their loyalty to Yah-Natan, the power he was capable of wielding in Yisra-El? To what end? To the very end of destiny, where men take hold of fortune and subdue it to their will. To that point at which war and poetry are one.

"Lock swords."

With little more than a controlled clatter and a set of arms spinning like the flaming sword itself, the fire-wheel of Edinu which the Bene Kessed call the swastika. How did they do it? In a marvellously complex movement which to this day, Shlomo, I still have not really fathomed. But lightning fast. And tight as Gordius' knot. Till at its end the men stood locked like an iron hedge, impregnable around us, a single shield enclosing them in the shape of an iron star. Until Yah-Natan and I were completely surrounded by a defensive wall of soldiers, their swords interlocked to make a shield. My victory-tribute. My shield. My symbol. My destiny. The shield of David. Magen Daoud. The star of swords. The perfect symmetry of the thirty-six good men. But also my debt. For properly it was never mine, though it did truly belong to the one who threw the stone, the one who cut the head from off the shoulders of the giant. The Star of Yah-Natan.

"What is your name?"

"Daoud ben Yishai."

"Yes, I recognise you now. You are one of my father's...choristers."

His tact was marvellous. But then, he owed me his life. Though I did not yet know it.

"This must remain our secret, Daoud. The victory belongs to the king. We are his loyal subjects. We shall take him back in triumph to Gil-Gal, and the men will sing that Sha'ul has slain his thousands." He paused, wondering perhaps how much it would be sensible to tell me. But we were bound to each other now, by ties beyond blood. There could be no secrets. "At Geva they added a line, that Yah-Natan had slain his tens of thousands. He will kill me if they sing such words again."

He took my hand and placed it under his thigh - not as his father would have done, however. Simply the conventional method of swearing a solemn oath.

"Our secret?"

"I promise."

"I shall make you a hero for doing this."

I wasn't sure I wanted to be a hero. Perhaps, after all, a priest or chorister were not such terrible occupations. And as to flocking goats.

"I swear."

"Then we are now brothers."

We stayed like that for more than an hour, prisoners inside our shield of glory, merely watching the last stages of the battle so that men could grumble afterwards that Yah-Natan had done what generals always do, leading from the rear in order to protect their own. While I was the triumphant hero, borne about like Abou Mousa's banner of Nechushtan to inspire the troops, absurdity elevated and exalted to the apotheosis of absurdity. It would be written that I had slain Gol-Yat, lopping his head off with his own sword after felling him with a single stone. Written down! It would be trumpeted, on Yahni's orders, in every town from Dan to Ber Sheva, until Shimshon himself turned green with envy. But none of that could make it true. Gol-Yat was killed, yes, but not by me - only I was seen, later on, at Gil-Gal, after the triumphant procession, holding Gol-Yat's severed head above my own as a trophy (blood still dripped along the chin and down my sleeve - but it was becoming less revolting), and wearing his armour that had been brought to "my" tent. It was a pantomime - the armour especially, large enough that I could have fitted into it twice over and still had room to spare. But it was enough to generate a legend. From royal catamite to abject coward to national hero in a single afternoon - the wages of my desertion! Yet even as I sat there, raised on shoulders almost as powerful as Gol-Yat's, the taste of blood was coagulating in my mouth - far less salty, far less unpleasant, than the taste of semen - and the memory of my own absurdity rose up again to shame me, so that I felt again that tightness of the scrotum that is undiluted fear. Gol-Yat did not die that day, except physically; denied the tranquil oblivion of the defeated, he too was raised into legend, which requires both a victim and a hero. But the shepherd-boy Daoud, psalmist and lute-player, protégé of a Prophet, he died - most abjectly. From that day on, for Yahni's sake, because I had sworn a solemn vow, I had no choice but to become my own fairy tale, for there was no one else left for me to be. Yedid-Yah - the beloved of Yah and of Yahweh, child of the celestial pair, resurrection of the royal line of Yehudah! And know this, Shlomo. I have despised myself at every minute, hated myself for every vainglorious and hubristic attempt at living it. There, Shlomo - now you know it. The truth is far more sordid than the legend. And more sordid still, the truth of my attempts to live that legend.

Parchment Eight

Apotheosis followed apotheosis, but with each epiphany another sign that something untoward might follow all this undeserved ovation. Undeserved - but irresistible. The triumphal procession through the villages of Ephrayim to announce and celebrate the victory. The private ceremony in the tent of the generals, when we all got drunk on honey-wine and I was dressed in Yahni's robes. My appointment as captain of the men of war. The fury, born of envy I suppose, which did gradually turn into the grudging admiration of my brothers.

And then the formal triumph at Gil-Gal. The singing and the dancing and the tabret-players - the women falling at my feet as if there were some kind of national conspiracy to rescue me from Sha'ul's clutches. The sacrifices. The futile waiting for Shmu-El to come, and then the rages when he didn't. The athletics contests in which I was made to participate by Yahni's men, all of them quite literally falling over themselves to let me win - fortunately I could put to good use my years of slinging stones at snakes and scorpions, and won that contest fairly. Sha'ul calling and calling for his favourite lutanist, threatening to stamp his foot and call off the celebrations, refusing to accept that his favourite lutanist was the same boy who was standing there before him, holding the embalmed head of Gol-Yat on a spear, while his own soldiers danced round and round us, cheering. And then - it chills me to remember it - that terrible, portentous chanting that Yahni had so rightly feared:

"Sha'ul has slain his thousands, but Daoud his tens of thousands."

Had it not been prophesied that he would lose his kingdom to a companion, one who was dear to him, one who sat close to him, one he knew well? Was the Lord not tearing his kingdom from him, even now, so that like a man in mourning he was constrained to rend his cloak? Such terrible, appalling jealousy. And of what - a chimera! The king who had overcome one form of madness, was plunging into another quite as dangerous.

And the source and the object of that madness?

Me.

All of those events, Shlomo, should form part of my tale. Yet I feel no urge to speak of them. (Yes, speak. After that last collapse I have been forced to give up writing. My arms are as numb as my lower body. Yet my brain is as lucid as it ever was - lucid, that is, but for still more lapses of memory. It is strange though, that I forget what happened just moments ago, hours ago, days ago, yet what took place years in the past is as fresh and clear as if it happened yesterday. Can a stroke that paralyses only half the body, also paralyse just some parts of the mind?)

✡

Kish ben Avi-El, Sha'ul's father, died in the year of Sochoh, and was buried in an elaborate sepulchre on the hill at Giv-Yah. Sha'ul had lived all his life in the shadow of two older men, his father and the Prophet Shmu-El, and now one of those two shadows - the brighter yet the less illuminating - was passed.

"Stay with me, boy. I want it to be you who shuts my eyes."

Even kings are still small boys to their parents! It can be most demeaning! I like to imagine Rivka, shrieking at the twins because she was fed up to the back teeth with them squabbling all the time, especially that Yah-Akov, whatever are you up to in the kitchen, making such a mess of all that potage? Or Sarah, taking away Yitschak's privileges, because his tent was so untidy. Or Abou Mousa, grounded by Pharaoh for insolence, or for breaking out through a rear window of the palace to meet some illicit girlfriend of the Habiru. So even on that last night of his life, when death was closing in on him, Kish talked to Sha'ul the king as though he were some child of eight or nine. It was how he had always treated him.

Sha'ul stayed. It was indeed he who closed his father's eyes, and went on sitting even while the women washed his father's body and wrapped it in strips of cloth for burial. Being worshippers of Shet, they would not allow wailing over the corpse. But outside, in the streets of Giv-Yah, the women of Yisra-El poured out anyway the misery of everymother, lamenting the death of every beloved son in the eternally repeated death of Adonis Adonai. It was extraordinarily moving.

The sepulchre had been in the building for several months, and the resting-place was well prepared. Sha'ul may have been refused a dynasty by Shmu-El, but Kish ben Avi-El was still the father of the king, and due the rights of kingly burial. The entire household was summoned to see him placed on a wooden stretcher and carried with lugubrious slowness up the hill, through the acacia copse to the Cave of Giv-Yah in which the sepulchre had been erected, all of us wearing our most uncomfortable clothes, as was the custom, walking barefoot, our heads sprinkled with ashes, the older men unbearded.

It was a magnificent tomb, and fully worthy. Down through the solid rock a stairway had been cut to what must have been a tiny cave within the cave, a rock-pool probably, to judge from the damp moss on the cave wall. Slaves had spent months upon the task. Slaves, Shlomo! Men of the Bene Pelet and the Bene Cheret mostly, war-captives who had been retained. Like kings and palaces, a new phenomenon in Yisra-El. Nor did Sha'ul count them as deserving recipients of the mercy laws of the jubilee. Abou Mousa would have turned in his grave!

From now on the court lived almost permanently at Giv-Yah, and the sound of builders' hammers was so perennial we quickly ceased to notice it. Shmu-El's house was given over to the scribes and prophets, and on the hillside a dozen new houses were built, for generals and secretaries, for slaves and servants, for the harem, for his sons. But Daoud ben Yishai, the hero of the Bene Yisra-El, continued to sleep on lamb's-wool cushions at the foot of the king's bed, and most nights clutched his lute for loneliness, and some nights the king's hand.

He threw his javelin at me - did you know that? Twice, in fact. The first time took everybody by surprise. We were in the great room at Giv-Yah, General Av-Ner and the chiefs of staff, Yahni and the other princes and princesses, a coterie of courtiers. It was approaching the end of winter, but still cold. A great fire raged smokily in the centre of the room, spitting as a joint of mutton dripped its fat. Literally hundreds of wax-candles failed to simulate daylight. The narguileh was being passed around and a kind of tea made of mint and cinnamon leaf was boiling in a pot. Sha'ul had brought from Gil-Gal a young priest named Yitschak ben Gershon, a former chorister who had been kept back by the king when Shmu-El broke up the choir. Yitschak was seventeen now, handsome, olive-skinned and clever. He sang in a strong tenor, and knew how to ululate like a veritable hoopoe. But he was also vain, and thoroughly effeminate - a trait that usually put Sha'ul off. The king sat holding my hand all evening. Yet at every opportunity he also had a dig at me, throwing out some passing witticism with the deliberate emphasis of a ham actor.

"This wine has a good head, father."

Melchi-Shu'ah, probably. Drunk on half a sniff, and too simple-minded to know it was brew, not wine.

"As good a head as Gol-Yat, would you say?"

Royal jokes do not need to be funny, since they already have the distinction of being royal. But the gods help the man who could not compete with Sha'ul when it came to raucous, roaring belly-laughter. He would have split their sides.

And at every opportunity he sought out ways of praising Yitschak.

"Now what we need is someone who can sing a song about the ancients. Someone with a good voice and nimble fingers. Someone who has learned the sagas of the gods. Come, Yitschak, entertain us."

Squeezing my hand just that little bit tighter. As if to say - well, two things really, simultaneously. As if to goad me into competition with my rival. As if to warn me he could crush more than just my hand, and never even blink at doing it.

"What tale would his majesty hear?"

No one ever called him his "majesty". The damned little shit was sycophanting.

But Sha'ul had no idea at all what tale he wanted. Just to make the pointless point now made.

Then somebody of little wit suggested:

"Abou Mousa promised us a land of milk and honey. There's a very funny song the soldiers sing, you know, the milk's gone sour, the sow's a runt, and as to the honey..."

Yah-Natan was looking at his feet. General Avi-Yam, who had been with Yahni that day in Mishmash, began poking at the fire. Sha'ul's cheeks were turning red. Bad enough to have uttered a vulgarity when the king was making love to two boys at the same time. But to mention honey! Had somebody been idiot enough to mention honey? Were they now going to take his jest about the head of Gol-Yat, and transform it into one about the head of Agag?

I did what I had originally been employed to do. I tried to soothe the raging of the king.

"My grandfather told me that it's called the land of milk and honey, sire, because these are the only perfect foods the gods have made. Neither requires preparation nor purification. Both can be eaten raw, yet taste cooked. Like the sap and the dew, they are nutritious in themselves. No process is needed, no hand of man. They are the food of the gods, sire, ambrosia..."

Each word more difficult to utter than the last, as the pain seared through my fingers and into my wrist, my lower arm, my elbow. It felt as though he were trying to squeeze my hand to see if he could make it pop out of its socket. Yet the look in his face told me not to stop speaking, lest my silence induce worse.

"I asked Yitschak to sing, not you to lecture us."

"Sire, I..."

"Since you are so know-it-all about absolutely everything in the universe, you can tell us more. About milk, not honey. Stand over there. Where everyone can see you."

He was mocking me, trying to humiliate me. But also showing me off, goading Yitschak into rivalry as he had previously goaded me.

I stood by the door, where he was pointing. Lined up, like a target. But what was I supposed to say? Without closing my eyes, I conjured up the spirit of grandfather Oved, and found something suitable.

"When the goddess Yah was feeding her beloved son" - I studiously avoided naming him – "some of the milk splashed and made the stars; and that is why they are called the Milky Way. The Bene Cheret call the universe 'galaktos' or 'the galaxy', which in their language is the word for milk."

I was babbling automatically, concentrating on Sha'ul. So that I saw it coming, fortunately. He was well into his fifties, after all. Even standing upright he was slow and heavy in his movements, but from a squatting position he was sluggish as a snail. The javelin scraped on the hard floor as he picked it up. Several pairs of startled eyes snapped in his direction. Foolishly, Yahni put out a hand to stop him - yet one more betrayal for which his father would never forgive him. The door was not tight shut. I ducked instinctively as the javelin flew, so it speared the door, not me, and quicker even than a javelin I hurried out. The shrieking of the king - a raging tantrum that tried in vain to require my immediate return and apology - pursued me down the path, and did not grow silent until I had climbed right down into the cave where Kish ben Avi-El was buried.

Why there? I hadn't meant to go there. To flee Sha'ul by entering She'ol! Irony, or prophecy? Each man, Yahni said to me later, showing me the catacombs that ran even below his grandfather's tomb, each man must harrow hell, and emerge the other side intact, or never grow his adult self, never become whole. But which of us ever does become whole anyway? A man, it seems to me, is little more than the sum of his wounds, and the itching as the skin grows back. Yet it seemed to me that this was truthfully the one place in the universe that Sha'ul in his rage would never follow me. For fear of his own father's shade.

That night, when I crept back, I saw Yitschak sleeping on a rush mat in the courtyard. Even by moonlight you could see the bruising round his mouth and eyes. I said a prayer for him to Yahweh.

✡

That same week, Yahni left Giv-Yah for the desert, and no one wasted breath discussing the coincidence. Had he been sent away, or found a pretext? - that alone was the question being asked. Probably the latter - he was very wise in all things, but when it came to self-protection he could be oracular.

For myself, I had taken refuge in politesse and courtesies, bowing and scraping, yessing and noeing, keeping my tongue well out of harm's reach, either from sycophancy or a misplaced word. It seemed the only sensible strategy.

But the king's eyes were on me. And not only the eyes in his head. Footmen and palace guards were being trained in all manner of activities unlikely to have elicited the approval of Abou Mousa. There were rumours that a ba'alat ov had been summoned from Ein Dor, whether to make prophecies for the king, or to teach him certain herbal remedies. Asher ben Elias, Yahni's armour-bearer who had gone with him to Mishmash, had fallen from a rock and smashed his head. One of Achi-No'am's women told me outright that Sha'ul had planned to have me poisoned after Sochoh, but then drew back.

Why?

"Daoud is the beloved."

Too easy. Everyone played games with the meaning of my name. It told me nothing.

Why?

"Daoud is wise in his behaviour. He is beloved."

Dropping the definite article. You cannot play word-games with a poet and expect him not to notice. Beloved of whom?

"Of all Yisra-El, and of the gods. Daoud is the slayer of Gol-Yat."

A protective cloak of legend. Yet even as she recited the formula, her eyes were giving a quite different answer - but that was true of all the women of the harem. Surely she didn't also mean..?

"Sire, Prince Yah-Natan leaves this morning to take the slingers and lancers into the desert for exercises. As captain of the men of arms, I ask permission to accompany him."

My title had been honorary, a necessity in the wake of my heroism at Sochoh. Sha'ul had never intended me actually to carry out the role.

"Why did you allow that feeble priest to make a fool of you?"

"Sire?"

"Don't act as if you don't know what I mean. A whole evening I wasted, preparing that pathetic Bene Levi to be taught a lesson by you, and what do you do? What do you do? I will not be treated this way by you, Daoud. Do you hear me?"

I heard, but not a word did I understand. Were Yitschak and I then rivals for the favours of a courtesan, and not the mere faithful and obedient servants of a king? It was too absurd.

"Sire, I wish only to please you. As captain of the men of war..."

"You may not go. I need you here, Daoud."

The speaking of the word "need" with his voice was as nothing to the way his eyes pronounced it. Two dark moons, like those of Achi-No'am's woman.

"Shall I fetch my lute then, sire?"

"Yes. That will help a great deal. Go now."

I turned to leave. Then it occurred to me to press my case. It seemed I had reached a crossroads, and must now decide. To take up the burden of the hero of Yisra-El, whom Sha'ul hated precisely because he was beloved. Or to go back to what I had been before. His "boy". His lutanist. His catamite. And in a year or two years' time, when my beard grew, and I sought a wife?

I turned around. The king was leaning to one side, stretching for his javelin. Our eyes met, and froze, but his hand did not stop moving. I could feel my entire body shaking with trepidation. I wasn't more than a javelin's length away from him. He wouldn't need to throw it. A mere lunge would suffice. Yet now he froze.

"I will kill you, Daoud, if you do not stop killing me."

How does one give lucid answers to a man whose sanity is lost?

"Let me go to the desert, sire. You appointed me as captain of the men..."

"I appointed you to go and fetch your lute. Now go!"

The sound of the javelin penetrating the olive-wood door coincided almost perfectly with its shutting. The sound of the king weeping followed not much behind it. I didn't go to fetch my lute. The king behaved as though my absence had gone quite unnoticed, when Yahni and I returned with the soldiers three weeks later.

In the wake of the Battle of Sochoh, Yahni and I had become fast friends. The difference in age was nothing. I as the youngest of eleven had long been used to the company of elders, and he, obversely, the oldest of six, was well accustomed to playing the father-role to younger siblings. Such were the terms of our friendship. He was my self-appointed friend-protector. I was his buttress against his father. And were we not both princes?

"I want to teach them archery, Daoud."

"Does your father agree?"

"No, but Av-Ner does. Father has permitted three thousand permanent troops, but it isn't enough. We've doubled each of the three units, and I'm creating a fourth which we'll probably base down your way, if not Beit Lechem then Manachat or Netophah. We need a complete circle of defence."

"And archery? Now that we've destroyed our enemies, are we to hunt the wild boar instead?"

Yahni laughed and scowled simultaneously - a familiar expression.

"When we made the triumph through Asher and Naphtali, I slipped across the border into Tsur of the Bene Cheret and met their king. Eshmun-Azar by name, though they call him Hu-Ram. I took him the gift of a scroll of Abou Mousa, hand-written in the new aleph-bet of Ugarit."

"Shmu-El told you to do this?"

"You're quick, Daoud. They told me you were. Yes, I've seen Shmu-El many times these past months. He always asks after you. All these things are our secrets, yes?"

"Of course."

"Eshmun-Azar's people have been enemies of the Bene Pelet since long ago in history. They wish to help us. They have developed the use of bow and arrow so that it's no longer just a hunting-weapon. Put two or three hundred soldiers in a line, behind a fence of javelins angled outwards. When the enemy charges, you rain down arrows, and any of the enemy who get through the storm to attack you are impaled on the javelins. A double-strike. Put a row of lancers behind the row of archers, and the fence is double-barbed. He has a son your age."

The non-sequitur eluded me.

"Who has?"

"Eshmun-Azar. They say he knows even more about the ancient gods than you do. Can't sing though. He has a passion, they say, for architecture. Builds entirely in wood. One day you must meet him."

We marched the soldiers, all eight thousand of them, south into the lands of the Bene Yehudah, to Wadi Tse'elim near Ber Sheva, where Yahni wanted to establish a permanent training camp. From Giv-Yah we went along the Route of the Spies towards Chevron. The name was Yahni's invention, though everyone knew that this was the road Yehoshua ben Nun had taken when he came into the land to find it out for Abou Mousa.

"We need to instil a sense of history in them, Daoud. It's not enough to toughen their bodies and sharpen their fighting skills. Men have to know why they are fighting, as well as how to do it. If they care enough, they won't need exercising. The heart is always stronger than the sword. If they see themselves as the natural heirs of Yehoshua and Abou Mousa..."

This was why he had wanted me with, of course. To use my reputation as the giant-killer to help him teach the men his own idealism. But it turned out that he needed me first for something very different. To convince the Elders of the Bene Yehudah to let us cross their land.

"Does Sha'ul now send soldiers against his own people? Are we to be subdued, like the Bene Gil-Yad, or eradicated, like the Bene Amalek?"

"You are to be honoured, as the Bene Yehudah," Yahni pushed me forward into their midst. "Is the slayer of Gol-Yat not the last son of the last son of Abou Pharets? Do the Elders of Yehudah not know their own royal prince, who captains the men of arms?"

Flattery, of course, is the beginning of diplomacy.

"Daoud is welcome. He has honoured the names of his grandfather Oved and his father Yishai. But the son of Sha'ul is not of the Bene Yehudah."

Tribal rivalries! Forever tribal rivalries! There is a part of me, Shlomo, a small but niggling part of me, that fears deep down that any forced confederation of unwilling peoples must eventually collapse in bloodshed and recrimination. One day, if the king is weak enough, it will slip from his grasp into civil war.

"Sha'ul the king of Yisra-El is Nasi of all the tribes, and we have brought soldiers to train in the wilderness, the better to defend the tribes of Yisra-El against our common enemies. Will Yehudah bar our route?"

Unlike me, who has always preferred to talk to politicians as though they were human beings and not scribes taking dictation, Yahni had mastered the formal rhetoric of diplomacy. He talked it as well, as naturally, as a chisel on a clay tablet.

We crossed the hills of Adorayim by route-march, forcing the men in six-hour shifts, in full daylight, then making camp by night. Not to sleep however, or not for more than three hours any night. In full armour, or clad in ever-increasing layers of goat-skin to build up weight and sweat, and holding an iron javelin in two hands above their heads, they ran, up and down and up and down hills mined by rocks which sheep could barely clamber over, until they were almost dropping to their knees.

And the extraordinary thing was - the men seemed to enjoy it. To me it was akin to laying down on thistles or being locked up in a pit with Natan and a ban on silence - and I was doing none of it. Like all those facile athletics competitions, the proving of physical prowess has never seemed to me important. Give me a lute or a beautiful woman, and I will fulfil the physical. But this! Running till the muscles in their calves and thighs were turned to balls of stone. Lifting till their shoulders emulated Shimshon's. Charging with their lances into bags of sheep's intestines and howling as they plunged their iron manhood into the ruined belly. Firing arrows into oblivion, for a prize not worth the winning, though clearly they thought it was - a mere word of praise from General Yah-Natan, and the honoured camaraderie of their fellow masochists. Shlomo, I hate soldiering, I hate war. I have spent sixty years of my life doing little else, and yet...ach, I shan't even waste breath on saying it.

But Yahni was supreme. He worked them for three full weeks, till they had nothing more to give, yet still marched them home in close formation, six-hour forces just as we had come. They cheered him every time he passed them, going up and down the line on camel-back. If ever a man were made to command soldiers, it was he. There was nothing they would not do for him - and then still more. So he took eight thousand men - eight thousand obstinate, self-opinionated, stiff-necked Bene Yisra-El - and made of them an elite fighting force to rival any in the history of the world. He taught me everything, Shlomo, every last detail of my so-called military genius. I have only ever had one strategy in all these years and years of fighting. To ask myself - what would Yahni do? It hasn't failed yet.

But it also served to make Sha'ul more envious of me still, even afraid of me now that I could claim the loyalty of a professional soldiery. When Av-Ner made public the doubling of the permanents and the garrisoning of Manachat, the general was awarded lavish honours and hailed as a hero of the Bene Yisra-El. Though officially, of course, it was made clear that he had only been carrying out Sha'ul's orders, based on Sha'ul's insights into military necessities. Yah-Natan on the other hand received absolutely nothing, not even private thanks. But I was rewarded with a promotion. He took away my captaincy of the men of war, and put me in charge of a thousand. In reality it was a demotion, except that it carried with it a grace-and-favour home, one of the new houses behind the royal palace - yes, he called it that now - in Giv-Yah. Yahni was sent to command the garrison at Manachat, actively encouraged to take his wife and children, to set up for a long stay. Avi-Yam and I shared house and duties at Giv-Yah. And Sha'ul found new ways to pursue me.

"You and my son are close friends."

Yahni might as well have been in Giv-Yah as in Manachat, so potent was the shadow of his presence. Or on the far side of the galaxy.

"Prince Yah-Natan has honoured me with his kindness."

No, I lied before. With Sha'ul I was perfectly capable of using the language of diplomacy, clipped and formal. You could almost feel yourself bowing as you spoke.

"Do you sleep with him?"

"Sire!"

"No, I don't suppose my son inclines that way. He's far too masculine for that. But you would do so if he asked you?"

"Sire, I was raised a shepherd-boy in Beit Lechem Ephratah of Yehudah. I am a servant of the anointed king."

"In other words, yes."

It was, I have to admit, a rather mealy-mouthed answer that I had given. But the thought - and I have had years and years of rumouring and gossiping to make me think about it - the thought of Yahni with a boy was unimaginable. Some men quite simply don't.

"I believe, sire, that you were right in what you said before. Prince Yah-Natan is devoted to Acholi-Bamah his wife."

"As am I to Achi-No'am his mother. So what?"

From the high windows of the upper floor of the palace, you can see over the roofs of the acacias, down the long hillside into Wadi Farah, and beyond it, climbing steeply on the other side, the slopes of Almit terraced with grafted vines and olive trees. How far beyond that to Anatot, Wadi Salim, Wadi Shalem, hills rising and falling as steep and sharp as the king's moods? And then, still further south, the city I had stared at year on year, the horizon of my childhood, seen then northwards from the flat roof of my father's house in Beit Lechem - the Hill of Ophel and the Plain of Rephayim, the Brook of Silo'am and the Pool of Gihon. Yiru-Sala'am, City of Peace, the Holy City of Tammuz-Adonis, where Our Lady of Sorrows Mor-Yah wept for her beloved son upon the hill of sacrifice and by the tomb of resurrection. How many nights had I recalled grandfather Oved's tales of Abou Yehudah, the birth of Pharets, and dreamed of restoring the House of Yehudah to the royal throne? I haven't admitted it before, Shlomo, in telling you this tale of my life. And if I haven't, it is because this was the moment at which it first struck me that my dream might not have been a dream at all, but prophecy. For how else can a man become a king, except by harrowing hell, by facing his ordeal, and triumphing. Gol-Yat the Giant had been slain.

Thus the first oracle. Sha'ul the king of hell had summoned me to his tent, a lifetime ago, and asked me to do something that I found disgusting, and forced himself on me, again and again, until I had learned precisely how he wanted me to do it. Why? Why did I yield? Because it was necessary - the second oracle. And now he had asked me, had I slept with Yahni? And I hadn't. But I would have done so, had he asked me, had the oracle required it. I knew as well as the king did that this was the truth of it. And why? Why? It still disgusts me to remember what I did, and let him do. I would not have let a madman by the roadside rape me, even with a knife held to my throat. But a king, a prince? It was necessary, Shlomo. It was my ordeal.

My first ordeal, at least. There were many more to follow.

"Sire, Prince Yah-Natan has offered me the hand of friendship, and for this I am as grateful as a humble shepherd-boy can be. He has asked for no more, and I have offered no more. I have duties, sire, with the garrison."

But Sha'ul grabbed my hand even as I turned to leave.

"You don't sleep with him. But you won't sleep with me either. The hero of Sochoh is too god-like to share a couch with a mere king."

He was like a hysterical, teenage girl. It would not have been surprising if he had taken to starving himself, just so we would all take notice.

"The people say: 'Daoud behaves himself wisely in all his ways.'" His voice was heavy with sarcasm now. "'All the Bene Ephrayim and the Bene Yehudah love Daoud, because he goes out and comes in before them.' From what my footmen tell me, you go out and come in to the women of the harem nightly. You know, I trust, the punishment, if this should prove to be the truth?"

Squeezing my hand, till the knuckles ached. By the gods that man was forever doing something with my hand. Only me - others he took by the ears, or throat, or hair. But then, only I needed my fingers to play the lute.

"It is untrue, sire."

"No, it is not untrue. You are scrupulous about which women you choose. But choose you do. Touch any that you shouldn't, Daoud, and I will place your head on a spear-point, next to those of Gol-Yat and Agag."

The accidental understudy had outshone the star - or was it, oracularly speaking, that the waxing moon had eclipsed the sun, that the runaway slave had got his fingers on the golden bough? But it wasn't this that hurt him, any more than it was really my friendship with Yahni. What difference my pleasures in the beds of concubines he had acquired in treaties and then never touched? No, what wounded him was that I was the companion, the one Shmu-El had indicated, that night in the black tent. I was the one he had anointed, three times over. I was chosen to succeed him, to inherit his throne. We both knew it, and he couldn't bear to watch his own supplanting. A mere bum-boy take his throne! A third-rate cock-sucker who made it clear he didn't even like what he was doing - that such a one should take his throne! And now, worse, worst of all, that I would no longer let him take me to his bed, and he did not have the power to coerce me. No, not worst of all. There was something else, something worser even than this worstest of all worsts. Something sad, pathetic really. Now that he had noticed me, now that I had become a hero, like everybody else in this silly, goddess-worshipping confederacy, he needed to express his adoration sexually. But there was one key difference between him and all the rest. I had not been kept back in Giv-Yah now, in Gil-Gal previously, by chance. Nor was it my limited erotic skills that had made me his favourite. Achi-No'am's girl was right. The silly old fool had gone and fallen in love with me.

So had Michal, his younger daughter. In those days everybody was in love with me. Take a hero to bed and you touch the quick of him; perhaps the contact will endure to give you contact with your own quickness. It is the most basic human superstition, a kind of natural magic. Sadly it doesn't work.

Michal was fourteen and I was seventeen. Tall and thin, with the most beautifully flowing, dead straight hair, and legs that started at the ground and ended somewhere around her neck, she was also completely flat-chested, extremely late in reaching puberty, and having been very ill - almost to the point of death - when she was younger, the chances were, and so it later proved, that she was barren. There was a young girl's charm about her nonetheless, which made her extremely popular at court. No one wanted to marry her. No one wanted to sleep with her. She was the kind of female who brings out the protective instinct in men, who want to put their arm around her shoulder and take sufficient care of her that, self-satisfied in their fulfilled paternalism, they are now guilt-free enough to curl up in her lap, tell her all their secrets, and then sleep rather like an infant in its mother's arms themselves. She was everybody's best friend, including mine, and she knew more of the intimate secrets of the court than any other person, including Sha'ul's footmen.

Michal, as I say, was fourteen, and a royal princess at fourteen is due to marry. Sha'ul had spent several months in his usual procrastinatory manner, trying to make up his mind about which of several possible marriage-alliances would suit him best, when Michal crept into my room one night and slipped between the sheets.

"What does it feel like?"

"What does what feel like?"

"Having a man put his thing inside you."

"Please go away, Michal. If they catch you here, we will both be killed."

"No we won't. I am needed for the treaty with the Bene Mechollah, and you are too important to be gotten rid of."

"I thought Merav was due to marry the Bene Mechollah."

She curled her face up in disgust.

"Didn't you see his face when they were brought together for the signing of the marriage contract? No one's going to marry Merav unless they're very desperate or very ambitious. Well, it's true, Daoud, even if it is cruel. Don't look at me like that."

There are some forms of ugliness that should be illegal - so she had said one previous conversation, also about her elder sister. Yet so playfully, with such innocence of intention, it was positively endearing. And now, in the moonlit darkness and her slender body pressing against mine, I was remembering in detail Sha'ul's threats, listening in case Avi-Yam or his family, let alone the palace guards, had heard us.

"Well, you might be needed, but I am certainly not. I sometimes think your father would prefer to have me out of the way altogether. And I am not about to give him a perfectly good excuse. Now go home."

"What's it like?"

"How would I know?"

She put her hand on me.

"I think it's disgusting what my father makes people do for him." And then, after a pause: "Will you put it into me, so I know what it's like?"

"No."

"You did it to Devorah bat Edna."

"She isn't a royal princess who needs to be a virgin on her wedding night."

"You can't tell anyway, not really. With some girls it breaks open just like that. Merav's broke open one day when she was out riding."

Was she deliberately trying to embarrass me, or was it just her natural naivety? I was very embarrassed.

"I don't want to marry Adri-El the Bene Mechollah. I don't want to marry anybody. I want you to put it in just one time, so I know what it's like, and then I'm going to go back to being a virgin for the rest of my life."

I laughed.

"It doesn't work that way."

Her hand rubbing against me all the while, with total lack of expertise or inhibition. She could have been trying to milk a goat.

"Merav says you're a virgin with every new man you take to bed. Virginity isn't physical, it's spiritual."

But there was nothing spiritual about the way she was starting to lick my ears.

"I'm supposed to be starting as a novice at the shrine of Anatot, and you don't have to be a virgin for that. On the contrary, you need a lot of experience. The priestesses have to serve as sacred hetaerae, even if they're married?"

"Only once, to fulfil the duty."

"My mother served at Shechem. They anointed her May Queen one year and she had to do it under the trees with this gross old man who couldn't keep it hard. The whole town was there to watch and she had to lie with her legs apart for four hours till he finally produced some seed. So much for the Green Man bringing fertility. I bet they had a famine that year."

It was far from clear whether she was trying to turn me on or off. But she was simply, naively, fascinated by the mechanics of it.

"She was still a virgin afterwards."

I laughed.

"The sacred hetaerae are always virgins afterwards. That's the whole point of the ceremony. It isn't them who's doing it, it's their bodies being used as surrogates by the god and goddess. That's why the father's name is never known, and the mother always bears the title of the goddess - at Anatot you'll be named for Yah, either as Mir-Yam or Meri-Yah. That's why the child they produce is always dedicated to the Temple to be brought up. It doesn't belong to the human parents. It's a holy child. A lot of barren women offer themselves as hetaerae, in case the barrenness comes from the husband not the wife. Shmu-El, for example, was such a child."

She wasn't listening, or not to the words anyway. Only to the sound of my voice, allowing it to mesmerise her senses. And in the meanwhile, from licking my ears, she began to nibble them. Her breath was hot as she whispered:

"If you don't put it into me right now, I'm going to call the guard and claim you tried to rape me."

But saying it as though it were meant to excite, not threaten me. She was already hitching up her robe and climbing on top of me. I suddenly had the feeling that she had done something like this before, and wondered in what circumstances she had learned to be so forward. Yet she was most definitely a virgin.

Like Giv-Yah, Manachat was a hill-town that had been gradually but incompletely fortified over several generations. It commanded the heights to the south-west of Bin Yamin, on the borders of Yehudah, but more importantly it protected the underground springs at Mey Nephto'ach, Ben Hinnom and Berot, which were the main sources of drinking water for the towns for miles about - Beit Lechem, Beit Ha Kerem, Yevus in particular. Choosing Manachat over Netophah or Beit Lechem as the fourth garrison was only logical, but there were family reasons too. Yahni was as devoted a Bene Yamin as was I a Bene Yehudah. The Bene Yamin had always made Giv-Yah their capital, but when the Bene Pelet first tried to settle in the land, they had evicted the Bene Yamin for a period from Giv-Yah, and Echud had taken the royal family into exile until he could win the city back. He had found refuge in Manachat.

Yahni had completed the fortification of the town with a high wall on three sides. There was no need to wall the upper slopes, since to attack the town from over the hill required a climb through rocky screes no army would ever attempt, nor any raiding bandits reckon worth the booty. It was on these upper slopes that he had taken a house of his own, terracing the hill behind it so that he could undertake his other love - wine-making. Strange hobby for a soldier, yet where better to find the silence needed for deep thought than in the quietude of husbandry. The arts of generalship are little different from the arts of poetry. And speaking of husbandry.

"I want to marry your sister."

It must have been obvious all afternoon that I had not come such a long distance to discuss matters of indiscipline among the troops.

He was leaning over a rod of black grapes, as tiny as currants still, pinching out the lateral vines, thinning out the trusses. Two of his small children kept putting fir cones under his feet, but he didn't seem to mind.

"Merav? You are either very desperate, or even more ambitious than I had realised. I cannot imagine you are that desperate."

So Michal had said. I wondered now if she had been quoting. Yet there was a sharpness in his comment that would not have made good wine.

"I meant Michal."

Thumb and forefinger teasing out the smallest clusters, an operation of enormous delicacy.

"When the shoots on a spur get to finger-length, you rub out all but the strongest two. Then, when they've doubled their length, you get rid of the weaker of them too. I often find myself wondering whether we couldn't learn more about war and politics by examining the ways of nature."

It was not like Yahni to speak in riddles.

"Do you mean your sisters, or you and I?"

"Knowing my father," he laughed, "probably both. But I meant you and I. He will happily take you for a son-in-law, because having you as an insider makes you much less of a threat. Family loyalties. That sort of thing. Left on the outside you are not so easy to control. But it puts me at greater risk."

In the stifling heat of early summer, the cooling breeze that seemed to come from nowhere made of Manachat a veritable oasis. I had thrown off my cloak, and was squatting on my haunches, leaning for support against a vine-stump. Yahni's children were playing marbles now, rolling large, rounded stones through a three-arched wall to knock down skittles. On the roof behind us, Acholi-Bamah, Yahni's wife, was weaving with a group of soldiers' women. Yahni never tired of finding ways to keep the good faith of his troops.

"Will you speak to him? Yahni? Tell him I want to marry his daughter so that I shall be even closer to the king, to serve him. Something like that."

"I know what he'll answer. Yes - until he realises you want Michal, not Merav. She's his eldest, and not easy to find a willing husband for. Think of Abou Yah-Akov."

"I want Michal, Yahni. It's not just ambition. I want her for my wife. And no, I am not prepared to wait for seven years just so that he can cheat me."

I had come to Manachat on official business. There had been an on-going squabble in one of the barracks of my thousand, and eventually a man had been killed - stabbed below the fifth rib to show it was a cherem, a blood feud. The affair was tribal, personal, which made justice all the more difficult. Avi-Yam and I had agreed to ask Yah-Natan's advice. So the matter of marriage was dropped while we walked the new walls together and argued, as only friends can argue, about the nature of justice in the abstract, in order to carry out justice in the concrete. We agreed to send the accused back to his tribe, to let his own Elders pass judgement. So we ended up discussing matters tribal, and came back, circuitously, to where we started.

"My mother is not Bene Yisra-El, you know that, don't you? She's a Kena'ani woman. It's one of the great ironies that nobody seems to have realised. Even if Shmu-El had not ruled against a family succession, no one in the twelve tribes is ever going to accept a king whose mother isn't Bene Yisra-El. There couldn't be a dynasty."

"He could take a second wife. Father more children. He's still young enough."

Yahni was not thinking of his father though. He was thinking of himself.

And looking, very deeply, into my face.

"We will always be best friends, won't we?"

"Of course."

"No matter how high you rise in the world?"

"No matter what?"

"Even when you become king?"

"That will never happen."

"It will if I make it happen."

"How?"

"I made you a hero. I can make you king."

"On your behalf?"

"Why not? You're a Bene Yisra-El."

"My great-grandmother was Bene Mo-Av."

"Three generations, Dodi. It doesn't really count. And anyway, her sons married Yisra-Eli women. You are a Prince of the Bene Yehudah."

All the while I had been wondering, how much of this conversation is Yah-Natan, how much the voice of Shmu-El, speaking through him? Now I knew.

"Your father would never name me for his heir."

"My father isn't going to have any say in the matter. Have you not understood that yet? The dynasty has been refused. There is an oracle. The next king will be chosen by acclamation of the Bene Yisra-El and through the mouth of the Prophet. Who is the favourite of the people?"

I laughed.

"Yah-Natan ben Sha'ul."

"Perhaps. And who is the favourite of Shmu-El?"

"He has no favourites. He is completely scrupulous about that."

"I shall make you king, Dodi, believe me. I have no other useful role in life except to make my best friend king. And to do that, you must be of royal blood, for Yisra-El, not just Yehudah. I will speak to my mother about Michal. Then it will reach his ears, and it won't have come from me. He will like it best of all if he thinks it's his own idea."

Royal blood, he had said, for Yisra-El, not just Yehudah. That sentence suddenly alarmed me, made me realise what I had been too vain or too preoccupied to realise at the time. That when I had done what Michal asked me to, and though it was obvious that she was still a virgin, there had been no blood of any sort, royal or otherwise.

So much for dynasties.

✡

Sha'ul summoned me one evening and formally offered me the hand of his eldest daughter, Merav. We were in the great room at Giv-Yah, surrounded by the entire court, such as it was. Publicly he stated how much it would mean to all the Bene Yisra-El, if the heir of Pharets and the hero of Ephes-Damim would accept the honour of marriage into so humble a house as that of Sha'ul ben Kish. How pleased he was, with himself I mean, for having thought up such a clever ruse, to get rid of a daughter and a threat in one move, to kill off two cuckoos with a single stone. It was unimaginable that anyone should so insult a king, but I declined the offer.

"Sha'ul is generous, and does me a great honour. But I am a shepherd-boy of Beit-Lechem Ephratah in Yehudah, and I am seventeen years old. The king's daughter is a royal princess, and she is sought in marriage by a sheikh of the Bene Mechollah, while I am sought at home where my mother is sick."

No one who saw Sha'ul angry that day will forget it in a hurry. It was one of his very greatest rages. He had no javelin with him, or someone two feet either side of me would have been killed. But how he raged! At one point he managed to stamp both feet simultaneously. He called on Ba'al and Anat to avenge him. He called, more pertinently I thought, on Shet ben Adam, though I don't suppose he had the faintest notion of the significance. He called on Geb, the patron god of the royal city, asking him to shake the physical foundations of the world - a wonderful figure of speech in the circumstances, for Sha'ul was causing such tremblings himself, there would have been little left for Geb to do. He failed to invoke Yahweh, which was not without significance itself. And when he had finished raging, he formally pronounced my eternal and perpetual and irrevocable banishment from the court.

"Go home to your sick mother, and may she be glad of you."

I wanted to assure him that she would, but held my silence. I made a wager in my mind that I would be back within the month. I was wrong, but not by much.

✡

Merav was given, as had already been contracted, to Adri-El the Bene Mechollah, a political marriage more useful anyway than partnering her with me. A month later, while I was sitting at my mother's bedside in Beit Lechem – "look after your older brothers, Daoud. It has become hard for them since you became so exalted"; wise advice; though wiser still the reminder that I had gone to court a psalmist, to serve Yahweh not the king - a month later, as I say, the princess Michal was betrothed to Ma'och ben Shimshon of the Bene Pelet, king of Gat, an even more sensible political marriage in which I suspected the hidden hand of Shmu-El, working through Yah-Natan, working through his mother. Such are the labyrinthine ways of politics.

The wedding by all accounts was sumptuous, as Merav's wedding had been previously. But on the morning following the nuptials a disgraced Michal was delivered back to Giv-Yah on a donkey, and the envoy of an outraged Ma'och summoned Sha'ul to war.

Not half so outraged though as was the Sha'ul who sent Avi-Yam, personally to deliver me in chains to Giv-Yah.

"It would appear the Princess Michal is already married."

It could have been one of those rhetorical statements that require no response. Certainly it was a lot easier just to stand there, in complete silence, and await my fate.

"I will not have it published abroad that a member of the royal family shared a bed with Daoud, the chorister of Sha'ul."

The chorister of Sha'ul - now there was putting me in my place! And anyway, which member of the royal family was he referring to - his daughter, or himself?

Nevertheless, I sighed internally with relief. A member of the royal family had shared a bed with the chorister of Sha'ul – was there not something spurious in the order of precedence of that remark? Should it not have been that a chorister of Sha'ul had shared a bed with a member of the royal family? Subtle distinctions, but significant. Hearing it phrased like this was to hear a jury pronounce my acquittal. That he was jealous of Michal I understood. Yet did he really not know that all the world already knew about his peccadillo?

"It would never have been spoken from my lips, sire. Of that you could have been assured."

He was banging the arm of the throne with his fist, methodically, almost manically.

"It didn't need to be spoken, damn it! It spoke for itself. The girl was not a virgin."

Since he had declined simply to outface Ma'och on this matter, what choice did I have but to teach him his error, by outfacing him. But Shlomo, I swear, I never sought these battles.

"Sire, it is well-known that the hymen may break open of its own accord..."

"Perhaps. Perhaps. But I am speaking of the honour of a royal princess."

"Daoud," Yah-Natan was shaking his head at me from his father's side. "She has confessed it."

Av-Ner on the king's left, Yahni in the seat of honour on his right. As always, when one of us was in disgrace, the other became Sha'ul's favourite. So, now, it was Yahni's time.

Sha'ul leaned down towards him and they whispered heatedly in each other's ears. I was hoping for a sign, a signal, a gesture - but nothing came. Then Sha'ul nodded to the guards, and my ropes were taken away. They had only ever been symbolic anyway.

"My son reminds me that, though you are of royal descent, you are not from wealthy parentage. You cannot marry a princess without paying a full bride-price. And I, in the meanwhile, must answer the summons to war of Ma'och ben Shimshon, who my son also advised me would make a peace-ally through my daughter Michal. You are the captain of a thousand, are you not?"

Unroped, and reinstated.

"I am, sire."

"And you are the hero of the Battle of Ephes-Damim, are you not?"

Reinstated, and still loved.

"So it is said among the people, sire. But the victory was yours..."

He waved his hand dismissively and leaned over Yah-Natan again, whispering in his ear. Whatever he was saying, it was clearly the funniest thing ever. The famous belly-laugh was struggling to get out. He was snorting like a donkey through his nose. I tried to meet Yahni's eyes, but he was studiously avoiding me. I saw him nod.

"Then I suggest, Captain Daoud, that you take your thousand down to Gat, and answer the summons of Ma'och of the Bene Pelet on my behalf. If you return" - o, he enjoyed that bit – "the king will require a dowry of one hundred foreskins, to satisfy the honour of his daughter Michal."

And now he let the belly-laugh rip, looking round from courtier to courtier, until he was quite sure everyone was laughing with him.

Even Yahni, though to his credit he did little more than grunt.

But Sha'ul was delirious.

"Captain Daoud, you are dismissed."

A dowry of one hundred foreskins! It was difficult not to share in what was, it must be said, a very funny joke. I had never previously credited Sha'ul with a sense of humour. But what a marvellous joke it was. Yahni must have thought it up, and fed it to him, probably through Michal. I could just imagine Sha'ul asking his daughter what she would like for a wedding-gift, and her giving that answer. Ma'och, after all, was the son of Shimshon. Not *the* Shimshon of course, but his father had been named in honour of the sun god of the Bene Pelet, for he was their hero long before he became ours. Hu-Ram's people call him Herakles, which is Yah-Chavod in our language. And just as the king of the underworld sent Herakles to perform his labours, each time thinking that this ordeal would finally defeat him and thus rid the king of him, so Sha'ul sent me to Gat to deliver up the unimaginable. Or to die trying.

Yah-Natan came out to find me.

"What did he whisper?"

"'I will give him to her, so she can be a snare for him. He is the cause of this. So let the hand of the Bene Pelet be against him.'"

"He wants me killed. As I thought."

"Then you had better not be."

"Because you want your regency?"

He didn't answer - I don't blame him; what I had said was bitter and unkind. He simply turned and went back to the king. Just how much of this had been his doing, I wondered? Had he sent Michal to me that night to render her unmarriageable, except to me? Was he really capable of playing such a dangerous game? And yet he was the hero of Geva and Mishmash, the hero in fact if not in name of Sochoh, a brilliant military tactician, a man with a profound understanding of human nature. Certainly he had the capability to think up such a ploy. And the saddest part of it all was that he would have made an outstanding king, if only he had been given the opportunity. Yet was he really prepared to risk my life, just so that he could become the king-maker?

✡

253

Sha'ul wanted me killed, and in a sense I did die, just as I had died and been reborn that day at Sochoh. Not literally; I don't mean literally. But what else is growing up except a series of little deaths from which we are reborn, wiser, tougher, other? Shall I tell you?

We went down to Gat, I and my thousand. I camped them well outside the town and took just a small number with me to the city gates. We must have looked like an embassy rather than a war-party, because no soldiers came to meet us, only the sentries in their watchtower above the gate, and a delegation of the city Elders. They had heard about my difficulties with Sha'ul - ballad-singers were already telling how "the beloved son was bound in ropes and dragged from Beit Lechem to Giv-Yah" - and perhaps they thought I was coming to seek asylum, even to invite an alliance against him in the war they had just declared. But I was buoyant with my own false glory. Fame had rendered me arrogant - fame, and my sole guardianship of the truth about its falsehood. The taste of coagulated blood still resonated on my palate. I told the Elders - the phrasing was deliberate - that Sha'ul had sent me to make peace with Shimshon.

We entered the town and found the marketplace extremely busy. Grain that was scarce locally had been imported from Sharon and Dan in huge amounts, and was being sold at cut-throat prices. The pomegranates were wonderfully sweet. Black and green olives in abundance. But I was looking for a pretext, and the grain offered me one. I seized a bag of Sharon grain and tipped it out on the floor, crying loudly that this was stolen goods. My soldiers immediately surrounded me, forming two stars, one on either side. The whole market stood frozen, transfixed by the splendour of that piece of artistry, paralysed by the impossibility of conflict. Here was Daoud, hero of the Bene Ephrayim, slaughterer of Gol-Yat, envoy of the king of Yisra-El. They could have killed me easily, but at what cost! Deaths aplenty now, and the consequence unthinkable. Sha'ul's vengeance would have been nothing less than the razing of the whole town. Yet they couldn't let me get away with this. So they surrounded me - elders, market-traders, soldiers. And I, arrogance personified - but trembling inside, dissimulating arrogance outside - took out my dagger and slashed open a second bag, spilling the grain onto the floor. Gasps of shock. But no movement from the soldiers. I slashed a third bag, a fourth, spilling into the fetid gutter what was a lifeline to hundreds of people, irreplaceable and highly expensive grain. The taste of power was compulsive, and already it was beginning to wash away the taste of blood. The dagger felt light and natural in my left hand, but my right was already edging towards my sword. And as the soldiers stood, wanting to have the courage to kill me but quite immobilised, the rest of my thousand were quietly entering the distracted town, until the whole place was surrounded.

And then I drew my sword. Shlomo, I am not proud of what I am recounting here, but it is the truth, and like all truths the telling of it is essential to my story. On this day, this afternoon of terrible chamsin in Gat, this day of false peace and false war, on this day I stood upon the very threshold, and did what few are capable of doing - I made the crossing. It was dark, damp, dirty - dreadful. I climbed upon the back of She'ol and whipped him like a racing camel until he carried me across the teeming, brackish waters; and I did not look back. Yet already my heart was turning into stone, and I knew the rest of me would follow soon enough - no, this is not the place for metaphors, for poetry. This crossing was literal, physical, a matter of skin and bone and blood. I crossed. And once across, there is no returning.

Standing close to me, whittling willow on a barrel, was a boy of maybe twelve or going on thirteen. I seized him by the neck. Even then I was half-aware that I was choosing him deliberately, because he was exactly as I had been the day when I was first sent to Sha'ul - pubescent, innocent, black-haired, beautiful. I had fixed my eyes on him and chosen him almost as soon as I entered the shouk. He would be my first victim, and in sacrificing him I would effectively be sacrificing my previous self. Yes, I know you hate all this symbolism, but all my life I have been ruled by symbols, and I believe they are the harbingers of our fate. I seized the boy around the neck and pressed my dagger to his throat. I who had been unable to kill Gol-Yat. I who had fled the field of battle even before the battle had commenced. I who had hidden under rocks when once a wild boar attacked my father's flock. I who had always climbed cautiously, even through the foothills, for fear of encountering a scorpion or snake. I who had fainted the first time I had had to help a goat-kid that was breach-birthed in its mother's uterus. (I who told my elder brothers tales of mountain lion I had fought, of bears I had defeated!) I held this boy - this Azaz-El, this Ram of the Akeda, this Paschal Lamb: the symbols matter, Shlomo, the symbols are what bind us to the universe. I held him by the throat, and trembled twice as much as he was. I breathed in, deeper and deeper to retain my calm. Or simply to convey a credible illusion of serenity. As my men completed the encirclement, and women began to scream as they realised they were trapped. The fear of rape and slaughter was almost palpable.

The boy - in my memory I always imagine that he too must have been named Daoud - the boy began to struggle, and in leaning forward his Adam's apple pressed so close against the blade it could have shaved him. We both screamed. And blood seemed to spurt from his throat like water from a fountain. I had done the deed - or it had happened, despite me. Daoud fell to the ground, mortally stricken. But it was all my imagination – he had simply thrown himself down, hoping to escape. Two of my soldiers pressed swords to his throat, and he ceased his struggling. I leaned over him, ripped away his clothing, and took his tiny penis in my fingers, holding it precisely the way Sha'ul liked to hold mine, in his case slavering over it, drooling over it, secretly wishing to cut it off in surrogation for his own. Ah yes, Shlomo, that was the revelation of that moment. In every crossing of the threshold there is a moment of epiphany, of revelation, and this was it. Sha'ul the fucker of young boys had a deep, secret desire to cease to be male, a wish for self-castration. But this was not the time to dwell on thoughts like these. On his behalf I did the deed. I, Sha'ul, the boy, Daoud, by process of symbolic, symbiotic surrogation. I cut it off. I drew the prepuce forward over the glans, and cut it off. Only the foreskin mind, the king had not asked for more. But I cut it off. In vengeance for what his had done to me.

The townspeople no doubt expected wholesale slaughter. But that was not why we had come. The young boy was a mere sacrifice, Abou Raham's ram. Give him a few days and he would recover. But we were here for Yah-Akov, as well as Abou Raham; we were here for Shechem, and Mor-Yah. As the sons of Abou Yah-Akov had done at Shechem for their sister Dinah, so we for Michal ordered the circumcision of every male in Gat, until we had done far worse than rape or slaughter their bodies, than raze their town – we had snatched away their souls, and ravaged their identities. No longer were they Bene Pelet, men of Shimshon, men of Gat. Sons of Abou Raham they were now, bound by the covenant of Brit Milah. We had given them to Yahweh.

One by one they stepped forward, pushed by my soldiers, some of the unwilling dragged in chains. From the temples the teraphim had been brought out, statues and statuettes and figurines of Dagon, Sib'ani, Etrah, the founding gods of Sahar and Sala'am, ikons of Ba'al and Asherah. The priest of Etrah had been brought out too, in all his finery, and him I made stand on a dais before the people, made him recite the words from the Tablets of Abou Mousa that admitted his people to the covenant (Ma'och had fled, or was in hiding - else I would have had him do this):

"'I am El Shaddai, god almighty, walk before me and be wholehearted. And I will make my covenant 'twixt me and thee, and multiply thy seed exceedingly'. And Av-Ram fell on his face, and the Lord spoke with him, saying: 'As for me, behold my covenant is with thee, and thou shalt be the father of a multitude of nations. Neither shall thy name any more be called Av-Ram, but Abou Raham, for the father of a multitude of nations have I made thee. And I will make thee exceedingly fruitful, and I will make nations of thee, and kings shall come out of thee. And I will establish my covenant between me and thee and thy seed after thee throughout their generations for an everlasting covenant, to be a god unto thee and to thy seed after thee.'"

Convoluted, repetitive and anachronistic. But the priest, the Bene Gat, were gradually beginning to understand. Instead of slaughter, their lives were to be spared, but on condition. They were to become Bene Yisra-El, and transfer their loyalty from Gat to Giv-Yah, from Ma'och to Sha'ul. They were to abandon their gods for Yahweh. And why not - their gods, their king, had abandoned them? As realisation dawned, the townspeople rushed to claim their share of mercy. One by one they stepped forward, some white-faced with terror of the knife, others affecting bravery. The priest of Etrah was given the task himself - this was an act of holiness, not barbarism. Their pricks on the table one by one, and chop. Just the foreskin, mind. El Shaddai had demanded foreskins, only foreskins. Sha'ul too - foreskins, not eunuchs. What better representation of the slighted sexual honour of his daughter. The Bene Gat understood that. We collected the pieces in a leather pouch.

But there remained the problem of making our departure. Ma'och ben Shimshon had fled to Ekron, but only to bring help, and even now he was coming towards us as we left the town. A thousand against a thousand, and my men fraught with bottled-up energy from having to restrain themselves, policing without violence, tested for the first time ever in their professional resolve. They had done well. They had done exactly as they had been trained, and ordered. But now they were champing at the bit. When they saw the Bene Ekron forming ranks on the horizon, it was almost impossible to contain them. Mayhem was inevitable. I led the charge myself.

Ah, Shlomo, the feel of the sword in your right arm, making its precise arc, notching its precise cut! Hack, slash, sever, stab! Like Sha'ul at Mishmash, like Shmu-El when he circumcised the neck of Agag, I was learning for the first time the pleasure that could be found in butchery. Hard to write those words, but true, but necessary. Let me repeat them, because they matter very, very much. I was learning for the first time the pleasure that could be found in butchery. I was enjoying this pulse of power. Having watched the hacking off of several dozen foreskins, now it was my turn, and I could not stop. It was as addictive as any drug, as sex, as prayer, as poetry. And besides, I longed to see what effect my butchery would have, on Sha'ul, and on my legend. We slaughtered seven hundred in the field that day, and lost fewer than fifty of our own. For three days more we hunted down as many as we could find of those who fled.

And then, Shlomo, I did what I did, and it sealed my fate with Sha'ul, but it felt very, very good. From among the prisoners of the Bene Ekron I selected precisely one hundred, the most masculine, the ones most suited to the tastes of king Sha'ul. Hand to hand and leg to leg we chained them, and we led them back to Giv-Yah. Even as we came along the valley, camel-backed, the sounding of the shofar reached our ears, trumpeting our victory, and soon enough there was Sha'ul himself, standing on the barbican, looking down.

"I have come to claim my bride, Sha'ul. I shall marry her in my mother's tent, as Abou Yitschak married Rivka. Send her down to me. My friends and I are travelling to Beit Lechem."

Sha'ul with his hands on his hips and Av-Ner at his side. The gates of the town were open, and I could see a crowd gathering in the market-place, among them Michal with her maid Timna. She ran down the hill to meet me, Timna following with a goat-skin bundle in her hand, containing no doubt a few belongings, though the thought occurred to me that she might be stealing her father's teraphim.

"Where is my bride-price, Daoud ben Yishai? A king's daughter cannot be purchased with mere prisoners-of-war. I asked for a hundred foreskins."

Without him being able to see me, I took the leather pouch from my pocket and handed it to Michal. She looked inside, turned white, and for a moment I thought she was going to vomit. But she took my hand and climbed onto the camel behind me, clutching her trophy. One of my soldiers gathered Timna on his camel with her bundle. I gathered in the reins and prepared to leave.

"When I go to war as a Captain of Yisra-El, Sha'ul, I go for Yahweh, not for slaughter." I indicated the roped prisoners. "There are your hundred foreskins. If the king requires them separate from their owners, then let the king cut them off himself. Here is my dowry."

And holding up Michal's hand with the leather pouch in it, I wheeled my camel round, and rode off to the cheering of my men.

Parchment Nine

Ah, what a wedding it was! Shlomo, you have never seen such celebration, such joy, such plentiful honouring of the goddess! Wine and meat, music and dance, and love of course – we had found a passion for each other that night in Giv-Yah, and it was truly inextinguishable. We stayed at Beit Lechem the full month to honour the goddess properly, and though the king sent messengers, we politely dismissed them. There was one lovely irony – asking Yahni to be my companion. Not that he accepted, but he enjoyed the joke as much as me, albeit in his usual dry and sober way.

But she was the king's daughter, and I the captain of his thousand at Giv-Yah, so like it or not we had no choice but to go back to the capital at last. Avi-Yam and his family had been given a new house in the palace complex, so we had ours all to ourselves, save only Timna and my body-servant. Michal did – whatever it is that royal princesses do, aged fourteen, and married. A good deal of priestess ritual – she was now in formal training and spent a lot of time at Anatot and Zelzah, the women's shrines. I trained with my men, learning the arts of war as we marched up hill and down wadi, practiced with bow and arrow, or pored over Yah-Natan's latest brilliance – contoured maps, drawn on goat-skins, based on the most rigorously detailed reconnaissance. Drawing a defensive ring around the garrison-towns and the major shrines – a radius of never more than twenty miles: the whole, in truth, of Sha'ul's kingdom – he had sent his footmen to study every inch of land within that ring, marking copses, rock formations, underground caves and springs, burial sites, everything. From such maps do men defeat their enemies.

"What we need to know in addition, is the ownership of every strip of land, and its loyalty."

In short, a census. But he wouldn't dare.

"There are Bene Chor, for example, living between Beit-El and Giv-On. Can we rely on their support?"

Sha'ul was never present at these discussions. Yah-Natan, Av-Ner, Avi-Yam, sometimes Re'u-Ven ben Tu-Va'al who commanded the chariots, sometimes Imnah ben Raphu, the captain of the footmen. Myself, of course.

"We really need to know their allegiances as well as their loyalties."

Avi-Yam's subtlety this. Even Yahni was at first perplexed.

"If we are attacked by the Bene Pelet, the Bene Chor will fight with us. But if the Bene Ammon come down from the Heights of Gil-Yad, we cannot be so certain of them. They might side with the Bene Ammon against us. There are ancient marriage-ties."

"Then we must have detailed lists. Town by town, clan by clan, family by family."

Yes, Shlomo, that census. The one I undertook decades later – and look at how much trouble it has caused me. It was an impossible undertaking, of course; even more so back then than now. Even within families, loyalties and allegiances vary. But we started the process. Footmen and scribes, working throughout Bin Yamin and Ephrayim, mapping and recording, mapping and recording. It was rudimentary, incomplete, haphazard. But if nothing else, it rendered Yahni indispensable to Sha'ul.

And thanks to Yahni, and to the fact that I was now his son-in-law, we too were briefly reconciled, Sha'ul and I. Very briefly. A matter of appearances. And what did "reconciled" mean anyway? That his hand was restrained from killing me, because the king could not murder his own son-in-law, however many pretexts might be given, however tremblingly his hands were yearning to do so. But his not killing me was not the same as my not dying. It was simply a matter of seeking a better means to achieve my death. Hu-Ram tells me that King Eurystheus sent Herakles on twelve labours, one each month, in hope of killing him; and failed. But I was no Herakles. It should not have been hard.

After the defeat of Ma'och of Gat – my first labour, you might say; or third, if you count the previous ordeals - Sha'ul wisely called a general muster of the Bene Yisra-El, reinforcing the eight thousand many times over, though essentially it was an army of Bin Yamin and Bene Ephrayim, with a contingent of Bene Yehudah and a handful of Bene Gad. He divided it between the three of us – Yah-Natan, Av-Ner, Daoud: son, cousin, son-in-law – himself retaining overall command. I was given the slingers and the foot-soldiers, and it was obvious to everybody why. Slingers and foot-soldiers were exposed in the front rank, but, unlike Yahni's archers, they did not have the protection of a row of lancers at their backs. The slingers carried swords or daggers on their belts, but they could only use them in their weak hand, if at all – the strong hand being needed for the slinging, and the weak hand for reloading. Foot-soldiers carried short-swords and flat-shields, and marched as fodder before the army. To command these troops was my "right" and "privilege" and "honour", for it was with a sling that I had struck down Gol-Yat, and it would have disgraced me to promote another over me! To command these troops was nevertheless to command the most vulnerable and the most often sacrificed, an adult infantry, so to speak. In pitched battle my chances of survival were severely limited. Ah, how convenient it would have been, if the national hero, now doubly national hero after Gat, should die a hero's death in battle! The king could even have faced Michal with pride and genuine grief at such a dreadful, dreadful piece of news. (And yes, Shlomo, I know what you are thinking: as I faced your mother, to tell her the fate of Ur-Yah her husband. Leave that for now.)

As expected, the Bene Pelet attacked us, seeking vengeance for what we had done at Gat. But their preparations were slow, and public, so we were able to pre-empt and out-manoeuvre them with ease. Where just a few years earlier they had held supremacy with their iron and their chariots, now we too had iron and chariots, but in addition we had a standing army, highly trained, and maps, and strategies, and in Yah-Natan a chief of staff of real brilliance. And bows and arrows – what use a sun-chariot, in a boggy field of battle, under a pouring rain of arrows?

They attacked us at Lod, at Gimzo, at Yarmut, in the north-west at Timnat-Serach, in the south at Migdal-Gad, thinking they could do better by attacking outlying towns rather than confronting an army face to face, thinking they could do better with small forces moving quickly over a wide terrain than a single, concentrated corps. But footmen travel fastest of all soldiery, and men who have been trained by forced-marching do not fear distances. We were there before them every time, and every time we defeated them with arrow and with stone, Yahni's men and Dodi's men, and Av-Ner's chariots needed only to pursue the cowards and deserters, and to round up the prisoners of war. Oh yes, we took prisoners now – those days of butchery were gone. We took, circumcised, and sent home. Even Sha'ul had recognised that the best strategy of all in holy war is superstition. No Bene Pelet ever raised his sword again, once he had been initiated into the Fear of Yahweh.

So I survived, Shlomo. So I evaded the hurled javelins of fate. But there are always more, and still more such javelins, and not all of them miss. After we had won another, and then another handsome victory, the people began to sing again, openly now, what Yah-Natan had feared and predicted – that Sha'ul had slain his thousands, while Yah-Natan and Daoud had slain their tens of thousands. The praising of Yahni the king had learned to take, with pride even in his son's achievements, with certainty that it posed no threat. But me? Daoud the Beloved? Daoud, husband of the moon-priestess Michal? Daoud whom Shmu-El had thrice anointed? Daoud the Companion. He sat on his "throne" in the great room at Giv-Yah – that dark, mournful, lugubriously shadowy parody of a royal palace, a stink of mossed mud-walls and uncleaned dirt and grime and soot from fires lit in peat-holes in the floor. He sat on his "throne" in the great room at Giv-Yah – so Michal informed me – rocking backwards and forwards like a woman sitting vigil for the dead, wrapped in his goat-skin like a shroud. No fire was kindled, no lamp lit. In darkness, Sha'ul mourned his victories, for they had failed to secure his kingdom against the only enemy that mattered. So now he spoke his certainty aloud.

"The Bene Pelet have fled Migdal-Gad, Sha'ul. The town is spared."

"Is there any news of deaths among the generals?"

"None, sire."

The ambiguity of his question echoed in the answer he received. Yet his anger at the steward was only an expression of his yearning.

"No news, you idiot? Or no deaths?"

"No deaths, sire."

Another moment of false hope. Yet he couldn't seem to be disappointed. So false too, the moment of rejoicing.

"Where are they now?"

"They have entered the town, sire. There are celebrations."

Dare he? Dare he tell everything? Or compel Sha'ul to force it out of him?

"They sing, do they? The townspeople? They sing?"

"Sire, they do sing. They sing that Sha'ul has slain his thousands."

Sha'ul, who was not even present.

"Go on. Tell me. Tell me what else."

Because sometimes the best way to make pain stop is to press and press upon the wound, and then upon the bruise, and then upon the scar. Until pain itself has been transcended. Until you are numb to it.

"That Yah-Natan has slain his tens of thousands."

An almost-smile, flickering in darkness.

"And Daoud? Do they sing this of Daoud as well?"

"Sire, they do."

"And what beyond this, except the kingdom?"

Those words, Shlomo. Those precise, prophetic words. In his mind, as in mine, the conviction now that I was indeed the Companion, the one Shmu-El intended. So it mattered little if I had or had not slain Gol-Yat, let alone my tens of thousands. I had driven the soul of the king deep into the darkness of the underworld, into the land from which there can be no returning. As the moon steals the light of the sun when the sun is driven to the far side of the universe, when it is night, when it is winter, so I Sha'ul. Sun and moon cannot rule together, but must contest the kingdom of the heavens. In such a contest, there can only be one outcome, one victor. So we were locked now, horns to horns. So began the years of flight and persecution, the fatuous game of cat-and-mouse we played from one end of the kingdom to the other, exactly as Shet pursued Osiris and the boar Adonis. So the time of the fulfilment of the prophecy drew nigh.

Now there was no question – Sha'ul wanted me dead. Not in a moment of lost temper, but calculated, deliberate, obsessive persecution. He had already tried to kill me after Sochoh. He tried again when I refused Merav. And now, after I married Michal, it resumed. He threw his javelin at me again – these days he was never without his javelin at his side, like Yam the sea-god with his trident! He missed, I am glad to say. Then he sent men to watch my house, with orders to murder me – I never did understand why he didn't simply adopt the methods of the Bene Kessed and the Bene Mitsrayim, and poison me; the gods knew he had his own personal ba'alat ov who was expert in all matters of fungus, herb and venom. But Yahni saved me – again. Sha'ul simply couldn't keep his secrets to himself – or perhaps Yahni paid the king's footmen better even than the king himself. However he found out, he always warned me, or talked his father out of it. So many times. But peace never lasted long between us.

He went to Yareyacho for the New Moon ceremonies, where some poor beggar asked for alms, held out his hand, and said:

"Daoud would have given ten agorot, why does the king give only five?"

He made a great feast at Giv-Yah for the Spring harvest, but Daoud was "too high and mighty", he "preferred" to play his lute and sing in the choir at the Tammuz festival at Beit Lechem, compounding the felony by "depriving the family of Michal".

He received an embassy from Lagash of the Bene Kessed, among whom a magus who asked specifically to meet Oved ben Bo'az, grandfather of "the prince" Daoud.

He joined the Pilgrimage of the Ark, but first the priests of Mitspeh admonished him for riding.

"A king does not walk."

"Sha'ul is no longer king in the eyes of Yahweh. And in the Pilgrimage of the Ark, all men walk."

And then sent him away altogether when he continued to insult and protest.

"Sha'ul has foresworn Yahweh and contracted ritual impurities. He may not follow the Ark until he has been purged."

Purged? Not simply purified? In his fury he continued following them, but at a distance, far enough away that every pilgrim on the road could hear his shouting.

"What impurities? That I ate forbidden food? That I have taken wives and concubines from the Bene Kena'an? What impurities?"

All Yisra-El blushed with the embarrassment of the king's hysteria. But the Guardians of the Ark were well used to him by now.

"The sin of abomination."

There. It was spoken. What all Yisra-El knew but none had yet dared speak. And now it had been uttered, on the public highway, before the Ark of the Covenant. In the mouth of the Guardian, Eli-Azar ben Avi-Nadav himself.

"A king of Yisra-El may not perform the rites of Shet and Asherah. As the elder brother forfeits his birthright to the younger, so too Sha'ul. So it was with Kayin and Hevel, so with Yishma-El and Abou Yitschak, so with Essav and Abou Yah-Akov, so with Zerach and with Pharets. The red-headed first-born who is the sun must yield to the dark-haired younger brother, the beloved of the moon. So Shet gave way to the reborn Osher. So the one to be anointed king of Yisra-El will come from Beit-Lechem Ephratah, the House of Tammuz, the corn-god of the Euphrates, home of our forefather Av-Ram, and raise his Temple on the mountain of Mor-Yah, to dry the bitter tears of his Mother. So the oracle has been pronounced."

That was all it took, and there were incidents like that almost daily. Some involved my name explicitly, others simply alluded to an obscure reference that might be interpretable as me. But it made no odds. He had been chosen as king, but his people did not love him. Love him? You would have been hard pressed to find a soul in all of Yisra-El who even liked him. His own wife, Achi-No'am…no, Shlomo, this is becoming improper. Let me return to my tale.

There were, as I say, incidents of some kind almost daily, reminders of Shmu-El's pronouncement, words or actions of my own. I could do nothing right, even if I did not do anything particularly wrong. Hatred works that way, just as love does. Everything, everything arouses, like an allergy. The way you blow your nose or scratch your ears. The tenor and timbre of your voice. Your clothes, your opinions, your very existence. Sha'ul flew from rage to incandescent rage. But when finally he sent his murderers to kill me, it was carefully premeditated.

They came at dead of night, as messengers of the underworld are meant to come. They came, indeed, over several nights. My house at Giv-Yah was towards the rear of the palace complex, built on natural terracing where the granite cut away to form a narrow plateau. You could not approach the front of the house unseen, but the back was enclosed by acacia woods and shingle screes and great outcrops of granite large enough for several men to hide behind. A haven for spies and burglars, but also for owls and partridges and jackals. The owls had been particularly busy for several nights.

"I heard something."

"It's only the jackals making love."

"Footsteps."

"The plodding of small badgers."

"Dodi, don't make jokes. There's somebody out there."

"I know."

Our bedroom was a tent of linen on the roof, and if we had not still been so newly-wed that we kept ourselves awake all night, the mosquitoes would have done the same for us. Or the Lilim, the night spirits, pursuing Tohu and Bohu through the dark.

"Please, Dodi, don't make jokes. There's definitely someone out there. I'm frightened."

Any excuse to wrap her arms and legs around me yet again.

"Do you think they're robbers?"

"No. Your father's men. There are three behind the rocks, another two behind the big acacia, and one who's been trying to scramble down the scree unheard for the last half-hour. I can't work out where the last one is. Av-Ner always works his spies in sevens."

Even then another crack, though whether of bone or twig it was difficult to be certain.

"What do they want?"

"My life, most likely. Or to listen to us making love."

She had a sense of humour, Michal, quite as wicked as my own. Especially in matters sexual.

"I'm going to explore. Make noises. Make lots of passion."

Giggling like – well, like newly-weds. She made, it must be said, a good deal more noise with me than she did without me. But it served its purpose.

"Yah-Achim ben Chadad, if I am not mistaken."

The man who was testing the sharpness of my dagger with his throat was standing in the shadow of the trees, so it was easier to creep up on him unnoticed than to be certain who he was. But he was more than willing to confirm his own identity.

"There are seven of you bound for garrison duty at Shalbim. General Av-Ner will not be pleased to learn how much of his careful training has been wasted. Now tell me, what precisely are you here to learn?"

"Your habits, Daoud. What time you go to bed, what time you rise. And your servant."

"That is all?"

"Yes, Daoud."

"And have you informed the king?"

"Not yet, Daoud. We were told to watch for seven nights and then report. This is only the third."

"The fourth."

"Daoud is right. The fourth."

"Daoud is also a late sleeper, is he not? Daoud does not go to bed until the early hours, and makes his servant stay up in case he needs him. So the house is hushed till after dawn. Is that correct?"

A dagger held to the throat and the threat of garrison duty at Shalbim of all unholy places, was a marvellous aid to understanding.

"Is that correct? Say it."

"It is correct, Daoud. It is as Daoud says."

"You use the signal of the owl. Summon your men. Brief them. Complete the full week of watching and then report what I have told you. And Yah-Achim, take note. Daoud will not be murdered in his bed. And not because of your incompetence or his cleverness, but because it is not written, it is not the will of Yahweh. Am I understood?"

Superstition, Shlomo. The sharpest weapon we possess.

They came four nights later, exactly as we were expecting, an hour before dawn. But not through a window. They came straight up to the door with an official warrant, and their swords were glistening like the tongues of hungry dogs.

"Messengers from the king for Daoud ben Yishai. Open up!"

"My husband is sick."

They would have pushed past her and gone to see, but this was no mere peasant-woman who could be treated as they wished. The princess Michal had blocked their entry. So they would report in all faith to their king.

Who sent them back.

"Sha'ul requires the presence of Daoud ben Yishai in the great room."

"My husband is still sick."

"Then if he cannot walk, we are instructed to carry him in his bed. Make way."

Their arrogance was Sha'ul's arrogance. They had the manner of bully-boys and secret policemen, who have forgotten that they serve the Law, who have come to believe that because they represent and carry out the Law, they themselves remain aloof from it. A despot is only as tyrannical as his agents. And even they require the willing subservience of the people. But Michal was not made that way. She held her ground.

"My husband is sick and may not be disturbed."

"We act on the king's orders, lady. If you will not grant us entry, we shall have to insist. Step aside."

Escaping through a window was hardly dignified, but so I had done two hours before dawn, Michal letting me down on a rope to the plateau where the spies had watched us. I took only the barest essentials with me – a bundle of clothing, my sword and dagger, my father's lute. Unlike Yah-Achim ben Chadad and his men, I made my way through the acacias without disturbing so much as the dew.

"As you can see, Daoud sleeps."

Wrapped in blankets that covered my head completely.

"We shall send guards to transport the bed."

It being far beneath their dignity to do so menial a chore themselves.

But what turned up was Sha'ul himself. Presuming his men to have done the deed, unaware of their continuing difficulties, he had wanted to be the first to commiserate with his daughter and mourn with her the tragic death of his beloved son-in-law. No doubt he had composed his face correctly as he climbed the path, and rehearsed in his mind all the most appropriate phrases. He had even made a tear in the collar of his cloak – which now he would have to pretend was just some nail he had gotten caught on, dressing in a hurry to console his daughter.

"Father! I have told your guards twice now. He cannot come. He is sick in bed."

"Sick?"

"Something he ate last night, I fear. O, daddy, I'm so worried about him. He's been moaning and groaning all night long. He's vomited three times. Don't go into him."

But go into him he did. He knew Michal too well not to recognise that she was acting – or was she simply that unconvincing? He went in and checked, and there I was, all curled up under the blanket, still as a corpse. But not a moan nor a groan; not even the sound of gentle breathing.

"Sick, is he?"

Words like deceit and betrayal were on his lips. But it was enough to speak them with his eyes. Throwing back the blanket, this was how Abou Lavan would have looked, had he thought to make Rach-El get down from her camel. But Abou Lavan was more trusting, more naïve than Sha'ul. A large, stone teraph lay in my place, its face

269

sneering jubilantly, its eyes lit up. It was the oldest trick in the book –
but it hadn't fooled the king. Now Michal stood there, terrified. He
had not struck her since she was a child, but what she feared was
more than just a slap.

✡

Of all the shrines, none compared with Ramah for its atmosphere
of quietude and contemplation, its aura of serenity – the prototype
Kiryat Sala'am from which Yiru-Sala'am derived. O yes, I make no
claim for originality in the city of my dreams. Shmu-El invented it,
not me; his the male role, seed-planter; mine the female, hatcher of
the fertile egg. So Yah and Yahweh rule the universe. So Shmu-El's
village, and our city, Shlomo. What is Sala'am, after all – not simply
peace, but wholeness, harmony, perfection, order, beauty? But what
is right and proper and how it is supposed to be. A place of study,
creativity and civilised behaviour. A place of love and friendship. A
place where all the gods can live together without strife. A dream – of
course a dream. The apotheosis of naivety – such is my City of Peace.

In Ramah it had a great deal, I think, to do with the quality of the
light, and more with the pallor of the yellow sandstone quarried from
beneath the hill – a fine, delicate, crumbling stone so gently yellow
the townspeople rarely whitewashed it, but preferred to leave it open
to the elements. Light refracted on it, dipped in gold. Rare enough to
find a town in Yisra-El with more than a few houses made of stone,
but in Ramah they predominated. It was a sign of status to build in
stone, and even some of the poorer mud-houses were dotted with
occasional large stones – a buttress here, a cornerstone there, a
window-sill or door-lintel propped up by a handful of jagged flakes
of stone that would have been little more than ornamental were it not
for the statement of solidarity they made. It was like stippling in gold.
And gold, of course, is the radiance of Heaven, the jewel of Yahweh,
the sun-ring on the wedding-finger of the universe. To build in stone
was a sign, not of social status, but of religious. Sadly lost, Shlomo, in
latter years. All gone now.

The serenity and the devotion came from Shmu-El, whose town it
was, though it had been a shrine to all the gods for centuries before
Yahweh conquered it. How can I explain this without becoming
didactic once again? Our religion, Shlomo, founded on the Laws of

270

Abou Mousa, does not permit art or intellectuality outside the realm of faith – it is our greatest weakness, though it may serve our greatest strengths. Yet men are born with an urge to creativity, the need to dream, and an infinite capacity for asking questions. No faith can hold them which fails to channel and encourage and assimilate these gifts. So Shmu-El knew and understood. In Ramah he had established the greatest school in all the world, a centre for the study of the Law, at which he was training those who would run his other schools throughout the tribes of Yisra-El. But in Ramah he had also brought together every artist and intellectual worthy of the name, and they poured their creativity into psalm and song and musical composition, into the writing of Law-scrolls and the collecting of legends, into codifying and interpreting the Law and chronicling the histories of the gods and tribes, into the designing of buildings for schools and shrines, into the detailed explanation of the workings of the heavens, into every intellectual activity worthy of the mind of Man. And around Shmu-El, as Bedou merchants selling silks will gather round the camel-sales of Chatsor and Megiddo, so did Ramah acquire its colony of artists, breachers of the faith each one, yet welcome, though they were the germs of Ramah's dissolution. Makers of graven images – pictures imagining Abou Raham at Mor-Yah or naked women, the families of local dignitaries or the details of the wings of butterflies, carvings of teraphim in stone and wood. And with them every blower of glass and reader of palm and horoscope in Yisra-El, every clown and acrobat and singer of bawdy ballads and actor of mime-plays and seller of herbal cures and aphrodisiacs and "genuine" relics of the shrine and empty vials of nothingness made valuable by the name of the designer or the autograph of the celebrity on its side. All gone now, Shlomo, all gone   the bad with the good. A brief age – literally, from the stone, a golden age. And Sha'ul scarcely even aware that it was taking place.

Fleeing from the king, where else should I seek refuge but in Ramah? I came on foot, alone, as far as I knew unseen until an old woman washing her feet in the libation bath outside the shrine looked up and greeted what was, to her, a total stranger. I nodded back and went on, into the courtyard of the shrine. Feeling something like an actor performing the movements of his own life – so conscious was I that her eyes never left me for a moment – I took off my bernous and circlet and laid them on the ground with my

271

sword and dagger, set my sandals beside them, knelt, prostrated myself, asked aloud for the Lord's protection. But it was the old woman's ears that counted, not those of the divinity. I went inside the shrine, confident that she would know what was required.

It must have been an hour later that a younger woman came in, bringing pitta bread and drinking water. She didn't speak, didn't even look at me from underneath her veil; merely she placed the bread and drink beside me, and went away. Later still another woman – or it could have been the same woman; all women look alike beneath the veil – brought me a goat-skin blanket. Otherwise I remained alone. The high stone ceiling and the stuccoed walls intensified the coldness and I was grateful for the goat-skin though it was rife with fleas. I sat on the paved ground, leaning back against the altar, watching the procession of ants across the stones and wondering – daft thoughts bred in boredom – if they too were perhaps making a pilgrimage of some sort around the altar, worshipping the Ant of Ants, the great four-winged divinity who made all the little ants in his own image and likeness before resting on the seventh day. So too I pulled out tufts of grass from where the mortar had eroded, and learned the patterns of the spider-webs and cracks along the walls. There was nothing else to do, but this, and wait. Soon enough the kindling priest would come to set the night-fire in preparation for the morning offerings. Soon someone would come, whether to kill or rescue me. I anticipated the former.

Then, at last, but hours later, there came from behind me a familiar voice, a deliberate, affectionate echo of my own voice, aged thirteen.

"The first duty of a man," it said, "is to learn the Laws of Abou Mousa. Do you know what is the Law of the refuge cities?"

Without turning round I answered, imperfectly I was sure, but as well as memory recalled:

"When you have occupied the land, and dwell in cities and in houses, separate three cities in the midst of the land, so that any man who slays a man may flee there, and find refuge."

Like actors, as I say, performing the events of our own lives. Sometimes the audience one is conscious of is posterity.

"And is this one of the three cities?"

"No, Master."

"Then why are you crouching here before the altar, clutching at the horns? Have you slain a man?"

272

I had slain rather more men than I cared to think of. But no, in the sense that he meant, I had slain no man.

"There is one who seeks to slay me. Three times he has tried and failed. And now I am in need of sanctuary."

In the silence that followed, I sensed that he was waiting for me to stand, to turn, to go to him. But I remained where I was. Perhaps this way of greeting me was intended to tell me I had been wrong to flee. Perhaps the fates required me to endure the persecution of the king, even as Abou Yah-Akov had striven with the angel at Penu-El. Perhaps evading death was my equivalent to Shimshon's labours, and I still had several more deaths to evade. My intuition had no answer. I waited for the oracle himself to tell me.

"Well might he wish to slay you," the answer came at last, "for you have broken his heart repeatedly. And soon enough you will break his kingdom too." I felt his presence looming closer now. His shadow was directly over me. His hands were reaching downwards, but they came to rest, not on my head, but on my shoulders. "Come, Daoud, come eat with me. There are people here, anxious to meet the Lord's beloved."

So openly did he now speak it. So certain of his oracle.

I stood up and turned around. His arms were open, inviting me into an embrace as huge as any mountain bear. Yet even as he held me, I could feel the frailty of his arms, could hear the grating in his lungs each time he breathed. For all the appearance of vigour, this was a Shmu-El grown old. Death could not be very far away.

Fleeing to Shmu-El at Ramah, I had taken a vow in my heart that I would have nothing more to do with politics and warfare and the royal family. A priest and a chorister, Shmu-El had said, when he sent me from the house of Av-Raham ben Zev to serve at court. Then a priest and a chorister let it be.

My resolve was short-lived though. For one thing, I missed Michal beyond enduring. For another, this simply was not for me. I had gone from shepherd-boy to chorister to soldier in the king's army to prince of the Bene Yisra-El. I was just nineteen and had lived fully enough lifetimes for a man of ninety. A student at the school of prophets was too many mountains back to climb.

I was given a room among what they called the nayot, little more than habitations really, shriven and sparse and frugal as the cells of prisoners. A single, extended house, built on four sides of an open courtyard, divided by adobe walls, each cell with a bed-platform, a single oil-lamp, straw mats for four. We ate together in the great room where the singing and studying and scribing and discussing and praying and prophesying went on uninterrupted day and night, according to the strictest rule and regimen. Each talmid navi had his scroll to write, a lifetime's undertaking with blue dye and feather quill and parchment, hour after hour setting it first to memory – young men ceaselessly strolled around the courtyard with their madrich, their guide or tutor, ululating tremulously, reciting the same tales – then from memory to parchment, with not a single blemish tolerated. Err, and the whole task must begin again. Each talmid navi had his duties in the nayot, sweeping, washing floors, preparing food, making wicks for lamps, weaving tunics, sharpening quills – mundane tasks whose purpose was humility. Each talmid navi had his priestly role, lighting evening fires, officiating at services of prayer or sacrifice at the shrine, going out into Ramah to attend the sick or bury the dead, to perform marriages and circumcisions. Each talmid navi had his prophetic role, observing the heavens from the watchtowers, signalling the dawn star and the evening star with tekiyot on the shofar, recording the juxtapositions of the planets and the movements of the constellations and deciphering their meanings, counting the days of waxing and the days of waning of the moon, preparing the poppy seeds and herbs and toadstools for the Mysteries. No one ever slept more than three hours in any twenty-four – like Yahni's soldiers. No one ever seemed to know or care what was happening outside these walls. We were expected to live like nazirim, a life of piety and study without wine or rich food, without women or – I was proven wrong only in this latter – music. It was, no question, a most admirable way of life. Each cell had a small window, overlooking the courtyard and the shrine we served. I have to confess that, after three days, I was beginning to think it might not be terribly different from torture in one of Sha'ul's prisons.

My "companions" – that was what they called each other, though the term was full of delicate connotations and hardly ever spoken in my presence – had all chosen this life, and were clearly happy with it. They spoke constantly of chayey nephesh, the life of the spirit – a phrase which always rouses me to sarcasm, for it seemed so utterly dead to me. As I must have seemed to some of them. Still I was accepted, as a welcome guest, for a short period, without conditions. It was not expected that I would stay for very long.

✡

To my delight I found again several of my former companions from the royal choir, whom Shmu-El had brought to Ramah. And amongst them, delight of all delights, my old choirmaster, Asaph ben Zamar.

Asaph was short of stature, gaunt and thin, with great sacks of flesh hanging below his eyes, and worry-lines all over his face. He kept his face clean-shaven, which in itself made him stand out from the rest in a world where everyone was bearded, or at least moustachioed, and he refused to wear the traditional bernous and circlet, going bare-headed indoors and putting on a kind of coloured cap he called a fez outside – he had brought it back from one of his long journeys and had never minded people laughing at him for it. His eyes were small as sheep's eyes, and he was growing ever more desperately short-sighted with each day. Terse, curt, brusque and eccentric, yet also marvellously gifted, he was the most inspiring man – the third of my trinity of heroes, after grandfather Oved and Shmu-El.

It is strange, Shlomo, that all the world knows and loves his anthology of songs, yet few are even aware of his name, let alone his life. Perhaps, then, this is as good an occasion as any to tell what small amount I know of it. He came from the hill-country of Korazim in the Galil, was a Bene Tsava of the Bene Naphtali whose real name – Asaph ben Zamar was an affectation as you might have guessed – was Bela bar Tohu in the tongue of the Amoritic Bene Tsava, Bela ben Baruch in Habiru. His father was a Bedou from Iglau in the Charan who had come down from the hills to sell wine in the markets of Kfar Nachum and Beit She'an, a pauper because he saved every agora he could to ensure the musical training of his extraordinary son.

From his youth onwards he sang and collected songs – whence the name Asaph ben Zamar. When he had learned more than even his prodigious memory could store, he began to write them down. How many times did I hear him lamenting our lack of a simple means of writing music, a form of notation that expressed notes as notes? How many failed attempts did he make during his lifetime to invent one? Of necessity he used the best system available, writing the words down in aleph-bet, annotating them with symbols above and below to indicate phrasing – the Shaleshet and the Pazar, the Munach and the Dargo; and the Selah to indicate the ending of a stanza and a musical pause, but which, for some absurd reason, people today insist on singing as though it were itself a word out of the song. Proof of the inadequate notation, I suppose. He collected thousands of songs, from every tribe in Yisra-El, from amongst the Bene Ammon and the Bene Mo-Av; he travelled into the lands of the Yavan and the Bull-Mountains of Anat of the Bene Chet; he went one long journey east to the lands of Hodu which my grandfather Oved had spoken of so much, and where they have a song-form called the Veda that uses techniques identical to ours; he even went down the river of Mitsrayim, into the lands of Cush and Chem, and brought back new rhythms, new forms of hollow drum and lyre, new ways of sounding them.

And of course he wrote his own songs, and orchestrated them. The first, written before he underwent circumcision and became a follower of Yahweh – Shmu-El would not allow him to become royal choirmaster otherwise – was dedicated to the Nephilim, the primordial demi-gods. Then several founded on the songs he had collected for the shofar and chatsotsra, and several more based on the liturgy of the Bene Kena'an for the ritual sacrificing of the first-born ("Happy is the man who dashes the little ones against the rocks"). For Sha'ul he had begun, and now, at Ramah, had dedicated his life to finishing, that extraordinary cycle of hymns of praise to Yah and Yahweh – his greatest works – songs of the fertility cycles of the earth which he didn't finish until I myself reappointed him as royal choirmaster, songs which the whole nation sang in joy as we carried the Ark to Tsi'on.

"Hodu l'adonai ki tov, ki le-olam chasdo. Give thanks to the Lord, for he is good; his mercy is eternal."

There were other brothers and sisters, and Asaph always maintained that one elder brother, who died in his twenties, was an even greater musician than himself. But it cannot be true. He himself played every instrument by natural gift and with a perfect ear, and he had a genius for harmonies. Where every other musician believes it is only possible to demonstrate skill by playing incalculable strings of notes in complex consequence – a mechanical aptitude little different from juggling balls – Asaph's genius lay in scoring remarkably few notes, but orchestrating the widest range of harmonies for the accompanying instruments, and creating the most exquisite tension by holding every note as long and slow as possible. The challenge to any performer was to see how long you dared to hold each note, before the tension snapped and took the mood of the piece with it. I have played the songs of many men. Some write to fill the inside of a tavern, some the great room of a king. But Asaph wrote for shrines and temples, and the architecture of his music mirrors theirs.

✡

At Ramah, Asaph had built a new orchestra, though its members were entirely the sons of those who could afford to send them, its single task the performance of the works of Asaph ben Zamar. No, that is unfair. They played other music too – rich patrons could hear practically anything they pleased, since their patronage was also the livelihood on which the shrine depended – though there was so little of equal quality that they did not play much of it. Shmu-El had asked Asaph to train musicians, and this too continued day and night. Among the players and singers, any number of would-be composers emerged from under the inspirational shadow of the choirmaster. In the greyness of my cell, after we had worked all day without a break rehearsing Asaph's great hymn "Al Tashchet – Do Not Destroy", and with that melody very much still in my head, I wrote the song "Deliver Me From My Enemies", and dedicated it to Asaph.

"Deliver me from my enemies, o you gods; defend me against those who would strike me down. Deliver me from the agents of wickedness and the instruments of blood. For, see, they lie in wait for my soul; cruel men dwell by me. Yet I have done no wrong, Lord; I have committed no sin. For all that, they run to ready themselves; awake, Lord, hearken to my call. For you are the Lord, god of gods, Lord of Hosts, Lord of Yisra-El. You are he who visits all the nations. Lord, do not show mercy to the merciless."

There is more, much more – I hadn't written anything for months and months, and now, with all the joys and tensions of those weeks, entire quarries of unmined emotion seemed to cut and carve themselves into poetry. Some of my most angry lines:

"At evening let them return, and let them make the noise of dogs as they scavenge through the city. Let them wander up and down for meat, and groan if they are not satisfied."

But also some of my most gut-felt:

"But I will sing of your power. Yea, I will sing aloud of your mercy in the morning. For you have been my defence, and my refuge in my day of trouble. Unto you, O my strength, will I sing, for the gods are my defence, the gods will give me mercy."

Three times Sha'ul sent messengers to bring me back, but in the presence of Shmu-El they were rendered incapable. We had great fun with them, to tell the truth. As soon as we got word that they were on the way, Shmu-El set up a shi'ur, a teaching session. The messengers would come storming in, demanding to see him in order to demand he hand me over. But Shmu-El would never interrupt a lesson, and they would never dare to challenge either him or me while he was teaching. After all, this was the word of Yahweh, and he the Prophet. And their swords and daggers left respectfully at the doorway of the shrine.

"Come sit with us and learn. There is space on the floor, right there, beside your General, your Prince."

The messengers sat, sweat-soaked and slaked with dust from their long ride across the dry plains, uncertain whether to salute me as they crouched down at my side or to defy the sanctity of the shrine and risk their own eternities by strangling me on Sha'ul's behalf. This was not as they had imagined it would be – a formal reception honouring their status as royal envoys, pitta bread, watered wine, honey cakes; and then a bath in the hot springs below Ramah, a night's whoring in the town, and finally the triumphant dragging of the prisoner homewards after they had slept long and late into the second morning. Instead of which their thighs were suffering the most awful cramps from sitting cross-legged on the floor – and this after straddling their camels for several hours immediately beforehand. Shmu-El made one of these shi'urim last seven hours!

"We shall examine today the question of capital punishment." He always chose his texts deliberately. "For which crimes does Abou Mousa decree the death penalty?"

In addition to Shmu-El himself, and Natan ben Ayah his favourite, there were some eight of us studying with him that day, sons of the aristocracy, the eldest and second-eldest of Asher and Re'u-Ven, a brother of the Aluph of Givat-Arayim, others of the same rank and order. They had been at this for months, in some cases several years. For myself, I was in a state of ignorance comparable with that of the three messengers. The young Natan – young, that is, by comparison with Shmu-El, who was well into his seventies by this time – was the one who stood out as the master of esoterica, the natural successor when the time came. He knew it too, and kept an arrogant silence.

But eventually he was made to speak. When all the rest of us had reached the limits of our knowledge.

"You shall not suffer a witch to live."

"Good. What else?"

"Whosoever lies with a beast shall surely be put to death."

"Excellent. And what about men who lie with men, Natan?"

"It is not stated what the punishment should be. It is merely declared to be an abomination."

Shmu-El's eyebrows wrinkled in perplexity.

"Not stated? Not stated? It most certainly is stated. You will peruse the scroll Shemot once more this afternoon and provide us with the text and exegesis by tomorrow morning. Is that understood, Natan? Not stated, indeed. There is a most clearly defined punishment for the abomination of a man who sleeps with his own kind."

Had it been scripted and rehearsed, the point could not have been made more pointedly.

"And what else? What else is punishable by death?"

Now it was my turn. But utterly, utterly irresistible.

"He who sacrifices unto any god save unto the Lord Yahweh alone, he shall be utterly destroyed."

Even the god power. Even the god lust. Even the demi-gods jealousy and envy. Especially the royal favourites Asherah and Ba'al and Shet. And as for the sacrifice of a mere shepherd-boy who had got rather too big for the king's boots.

"You, what is your name?"

"Yerach ben Nachri," the man, the least of the three messengers, replied.

"Ben Nachri?" Shmu-El was taken aback. "There are no Bene Ephrayim or Bene Yehudah who are Bene Nachri. What was your father, a freed slave?"

279

One learned so much more than just theology at Shmu-El's feet. The power of language, for example. As he had just demonstrated, by reducing a man of considerable self-importance to a state of shamed self-deprecation.

"So now Sha'ul has deemed it fit to use the sons of freed slaves to do his dirty work. Bene Aram, by the swarthy look of you. Are you circumcised?"

"Yes."

There was a long delay, long enough to allow us all to wonder whether he were lying, or remembering the pain of it, or simply considering if such a question, in the presence of the hero of Gat, were more than a coincidence. But none of these were the explanation for the awesome darkness of Shmu-El's eyebrows, that seemed to swell and close together like – like the closing waters of the Red Sea. Until there was the messenger of the king, assuming his rightful position in the Universe, that of squirming worm-like on the end of Shmu-El's long hook.

"Yes – Master," he made his answer complete at last.

And Shmu-El's eyebrows withdrew – deflating as the nostrils of Yahweh are said to deflate, when soothed by the incense of sacrifice.

"Let us study the laws of circumcision for a moment. Let us consider what rights, if any, a convert is granted under the Law."

Are Prophets of Yahweh meant to take pleasure from making the servants of their renegade disciples grovel? In humiliating a king, long-distance, and by proxy? Ashrey ha ish, eh, Shlomo. Ashrey ha ish!

How much of all this the messengers reported back it is impossible to say. What is certain is that eventually Sha'ul came himself. He came in state too, with all the trappings of royalty – a liveried bodyguard, a high-backed ox-cart looking like a pageant-wagon for the harvest festival, soldiers fore and aft in full helmet so that they looked like the bow and sprig of a Bene Pelet long-boat. Trumpets a half a mile ahead of him. Guards of honour in the villages. The soldiers had come to Ramah half a day ahead, to bully and cajole the town until there was scarcely a soul not on the streets that morning waving and throwing confetti of white flowers. But it was all to no avail. Shmu-El had done with him by this time, had rejected him as king, was simply waiting for the right moment to dismiss him altogether and name his successor. How Sha'ul acted in his temporal role was no concern of Shmu-El's – though he visibly turned his nose up at the smell of perfume, kohl and henna. He had taken back upon himself the governance of the spiritual realm, and his "throne" was a paved floor at the shrine of Ramah. Fine clothing and braided hair and painted wagons did not impress him. His own courtiers were acolytes who wore plain white tunics and sandals on their feet. He treated the king exactly as he had treated the king's messengers. He even forbade those of us who inhabited the shrine to go out into the streets and honour "the false king's" arrival. We stayed indoors, and worked a normal day.

The shi'ur, as I recall, into which Sha'ul came thundering, was Yitro, and specifically those verses in which Abou Mousa's father-in-law asked him: "What are you doing to the people? Why do you sit alone, and all the people gather around you from morning until night?" Then Abou Mousa answers: "Because the people come to me to enquire of Yahweh; whenever they have a problem, they come to me, and I judge between a man and his companion, and I make them know the statutes of Yahweh, and His Laws."

"What do you make of these lines, Sha'ul?"

The king was loath to answer, not because he didn't know the answer, but precisely because he did.

"I am not trained in the Law, Shmu-El. I wasn't chosen to be king because I knew the ancient scriptures. As well you know."

It was a kingly answer. But insufficient.

"But I do know the ancient scriptures, Sha'ul, and I know that it is upon the words of those scriptures that you were anointed king. And the people gather around me too from morning until night, and they enquire of me of Yahweh, and I judge between a man and his companion, and I make them know the statutes of Yahweh, and His Laws. I, Shmu-El, and not the king, who rules without a Prophet at his right-hand side to guide him. I who judged that there should be a king, albeit most reluctantly. I who judged, and perhaps it was in error, that you should be that king. I who can be called upon by Yahweh to replace you with another who fears Yahweh, and who does not turn aside to commit abomination and make sacrifice to other gods. Do you understand me, Sha'ul? Shall we call upon Yahweh now, as we did that day in Geva, after you had met me at Zelzah? Now that you would have me judge between a man named Sha'ul" – a man, he called him, not a king – "and his companion

Daoud" – the third time he had used, deliberately surely, that word "companion"; you could almost witness Sha'ul flinch – "shall we call upon Yahweh and ask his judgement? Or are you fit to judge, not needing the guidance of the oracle, being like Yitro to Abou Mousa, in the position of father-in-law?"

By the gods, that man was so clever he should have anointed himself king. He taught me far more about politics than he ever did about theology, and Yahweh knows how much he taught me about that.

"What would you have me do?"

"Join me in the performing of the mysteries."

He stayed with us a full twenty-four hours, half-naked and prophetic, like any young initiate to the Guild of Prophets. And when he got back on his camel the next day – the ox-cart of the royal pilgrimage had been subtly magicked away to spare his shame – it was to return quietly and unnoticed to Giv-Yah. But word was already out of what had taken place. He had been humiliated. Again. In every village people came out into the streets, but where they had cheered two days previously, now they openly laughed at him. And at the well of Sechu, the caravanserai where he stopped to let the camels drink, one of the Bedou actually had the nerve to walk right up to him, and prostrate himself at the king's feet.

As I had done to Shmu-El at Beit Lechem.

"Get up!" Sha'ul called down to him, outraged. "Why are you prostrating yourself like this? It is not the custom of the Bedou. It is undignified."

But the young man remained with his lips pressed to the dust for several minutes, his black robes turning ever whiter as the dust blew over him.

"Why are you worshipping me like a god. I am not your king."

The young man looked up at last.

"No, sire. But among my people it is customary to prostrate oneself before a man who is a Prophet of the gods."

Just as at Geva all those years before, when they asked, "Is Sha'ul among the prophets?" To be the king that Shmu-El wanted, the messianic avatar of Yisra-El, was to incur the mockery and derision of the people. Yet to be the king the people wanted, an earthly lord of pomp and majesty, was to receive the condemnation of the

Prophet, and to lose his throne. Not a man for such conundrums, Sha'ul knew only that his position was untenable. Inevitable that such turmoil and confusion would require someone else to take the burden of his suffering, and who closer at hand than this young Bedou? The king turned sharply to his steward, and ordered the insolent reprobate to be whipped.

And then, in full hearing of the people, the kingly gesture of magnanimity, which re-established him.

"Go back to Ramah, Eli-Ezer ben Avi-Tal. Go back to Ramah with this message for my son-in-law. Let him know that the king has forgiven him. Openly and publicly his lord the king has granted clemency. Tell him the king is concerned for his daughter Michal, who has been left husbandless too long. Tell him that the king is planning to celebrate the New Moon of Sivan with a banquet at Giv-Yah, and awaits with longing the singing by Prince Daoud of the blessings after the meal."

When Eli-Ezer brought the information to Ramah, I will not deny that the word poison crossed my thoughts, if only for a moment.

✡

"What's he up to, Yahni?"

"I'm not sure."

We had met secretly, by the spring in Wadi Manachat, two strangers in conversation about the sheep and sand while filling and refilling their gourds. Yahni was in full uniform, apparently conducting a private tour of inspection of the out-lying defences, myself inconspicuous beneath the folds of my bernous. Seen by Sha'ul's spies, they would have laughed at General Yah-Natan taking counsel from a shepherd.

"If I knew what precisely I had done wrong, I could defend myself. But how do you resist the interpretation of an oracle? He simply wants me dead, Yahni."

"Chas ve chalilah."

Yahweh forbid!

"At least if there were specific charges. I would be a lot less uneasy if I had something genuine to feel guilty about."

Making jokes was always my way of dealing with it.

"We must be the only nation on Earth which doesn't have a

283

treason law. If you could persuade him to introduce one..."

"Please, Dodi."

"If I am to be allowed to choose my way of death, tell him I want a javelin, at five paces. But only if the king throws it himself."

"He doesn't want you dead."

"How can you be sure of that?"

"Because he never makes any decision, no matter how trivial, without consulting me first. He hasn't spoken a word against you since you came back from Ramah."

But the footmen were once again inhabiting the scree by night. But things not where they should have been suggested uninvited visitors to my house. But my presence in the great room constantly required, for banalities, absurdities. But an atmosphere around Giv-Yah as though the earth were quaking somewhere still a long way off. I should have stayed in Ramah.

"He knows we're close, Yahni. If he's intending to kill me at the New Moon banquet, this is precisely the one thing that he wouldn't discuss with you."

No disagreement this time. Not even the slightest shaking of his head. Just:

"What do you want me to do?"

"Cover for me. I'm going to skip the banquet. Tell him there were rumours of Bene Pelet gathering at Tsemarayim and that I went to spy. I'll go into hiding for two or three days. Let me know how he reacts. If he takes it calmly, fine, I come out of hiding. If he's angry, then we know I was right."

"And if he thinks we're in collusion, then what?"

We made a formal pact, right there and then. We went into the nearest field and found the largest stone we could, to serve as an altar. Other than pouring a libation from our gourds, we had nothing for a sacrifice – but both of us knew it was unnecessary. The bond of our friendship was already sealed, even without the formalities. Yet the formalities are important too.

"Adonai Elohey Yisra-El..."

The oaths we swore were trite, poorly worded, sentimental – like adolescent boys playing a game of hoods and blood. Hands clasping hands, almost to the wrist. Hands placed under thighs. Embraces. Kisses on both cheeks.

"Do you know the stone of Ezel?"

"Yes."

"Be there in three days. I shall shoot three arrows into the field, as though I were practising by aiming at a mark. Then I shall send a boy to fetch the arrows. If I send him to the stone, it means you're safe. If I send him to the stream beyond the stone – you know what Ezel means?"

"Depart."

"Precisely. Daoud?"

"What is it?"

"There's one thing more I want you to swear."

"I know. I was expecting you to ask before."

"Will you swear it?"

"If you'll do one more thing for me." From my tunic I pulled out an ivory comb, studded with agates. "I had this made for Michal. For her birthday. Will you give it to her?"

He took the comb and I put my hand under his thigh once more.

"In the name of Yahweh, the One god, Omnideity and Lord of Yisra-El, if it should fall out that I am indeed the companion who supplants the king, if my three days in hiding should prove to be like the three days of darkness between the waning of the old moon and the appearance in the heavens of the new, then I vow that the Prince Yah-Natan ben Sha'ul shall fulfil the destiny of his name, for Our Lady has given him to sit at my right hand, to rule with me, in fact if not in name."

Trite, melodramatic, pseudo-mystical. Yet true.

He put his arms around my neck and held me for a moment.

Then I was gone.

The arrows were fired into the stream. You could hear the whooshing sound as they pierced the air, and then the disappointing plop into the water. What could kill the body could also kill the spirit.

I watched the young lad cross the field – stunningly blue with linseed flowers – and found myself thinking crudely that Yahni should protect the boy from Sha'ul too. Of Yahni himself there was no sign anywhere. The boy went tentatively through the grass, looking down at the ground as though in fear of snakes, until one by one he found the arrows and retrieved them. Returning whence he came, his feet bent back the linseed, leaving a trail that I began to follow, all the way to the far edge of the wood. A weasel hiding in the grass ran out in front of me. I waited, until the boy had given back the arrows, and been told to go on ahead. Yahni was standing there, white as the tents of the Bene Yah-Shachur. Except around the eyes, which were sore from crying.

"I have been disowned. He has made an edict that I am no longer a Prince of the Bene Yisra-El."

"Oh, Yahni!"

Then he laughed, that laughter that tries to make light of desolation, which he so complained about in me. But now he too had touched its source.

"He called me 'the son of a perverse, rebellious woman', which has to be the most unlikely insult anyone ever threw. As though it were all my mother's fault!"

And perhaps it was. Had she been Bene Yisra-El, and not Bene Chor...

"Are you banished?"

"For as long as you are alive. Or next Shabbat, whichever comes sooner. You know his tantrums."

"I'm sorry."

"I am still a Prince of the Bene Yamin, and governor of Manachat. He threw his javelin at me – he really is the most incredibly poor shot."

I put my arms around him and held him tight against me. Dimly the thought entered my consciousness, the recognition, that it was part of my strange destiny to be the comforter as well as the destroyer of this family. In very different ways, I had now held three of them in my arms.

Yahni dried his tears and looked up at me.

"What will you do?" he asked.

As though my plight were of greater concern to him than his own.

"This is the stone of Ezel, isn't it? You didn't choose it by accident. For everybody's sake I shall flee the kingdom. Someone will give me asylum. And if not, there are always places to hide."

He didn't argue, for it was obvious that this was right.

"Go back, Yahni. Go back and make your peace with him. We have sworn an oath. But neither of us is any use to the other dead or banished. Go and look after Michal for me."

Ah Yah-Natan, my Yahni, what will posterity say about us? Our god does not permit the sort of abomination with which they will wrongly presume our love to have been consummated. The world is too scared to accept male love, male brotherhood, male friendship – Hu-Ram calls it agapao - without winking and nodding and scribbling their sordid and prurient broadsheets.

Parchment Ten

After Yah-Natan and I parted company, and remembering Shmu-El's admonitions when I turned up in Ramah, I fled to Nov, to the refuge-city of the priests of the Bene Yevus and the Bene Anat. It was desperately close to Giv-Yah - what? two miles south-east across the Wadi Salim - but I didn't reckon my chances of reaching any other tribal sanctuary, and anyway Sha'ul would never think to look that close to home.

Nov was magnificent then, not the sanctuary itself, which was just a few adobe houses and the tiniest of temples, but the hill, the panorama. There were fewer olive trees - you would never have thought to name the mountain for the olives then, as they do now - but the ancient gravestones were more visible. You could hardly walk five paces without tripping over another flat slab or vertical stone, another dolmen or menhir, another henge or barrow, whether carved or half-eroded by the years; and every imaginable form of barrow too, bell-barrows and disc-barrows, pond-barrows and bowl-barrows - they took great care in their burials, the ancients did. When the dead rise at world's end, they will swamp Yiru-Sala'am by sheer weight of numbers! Aye, but what a view they will have, once you have raised the Temple on the Hill of Mor-Yah facing them!

The High Priest, Achi-Melech ben Achi-Tuv, turned out to be an old friend of my grandfather. He was a good, gentle man, an initiate of Moloch as his name infers, but one who had "come across" to Yahweh - I use the phrase advisedly as it was very much a political switch and not a religious conversion – who had happily accepted circumcision, married a young woman of the Bene Menasheh, and studied the full seven years it takes to become a priest of Yahweh. He had been inspired to do this by the preaching and teaching of Shmu-El's disciple Yeshiahu ben Dani-El.

The Ark had been taken to Nov for this phase of its annual peregrination, and there had been an enormous celebration of the New Moon of Sivan. I hadn't eaten for three days because I had been in hiding, and the smell of incense and roasted meat that hung over the entire region was almost more than I could bear. So I came to the door of Achi-Melech's house, as casual as any invited visitor, and when his servant came out, I adopted my most authoritative manner.

"I am Daoud ben Yishai, the king's son-in-law. I come in great secrecy. Give me something to eat."

But it had all been consumed, whether by gods or men. If I wanted meat, I would have to eat air.

The servant turned away, and almost at once Achi-Melech himself appeared.

"There is nothing here except challah for the kiddush."

"Then let me eat challah."

"Why are you here, alone, without a bodyguard?"

"The king has sent me on a secret mission. Give me bread."

"Are you clean?"

"Ritually pure. I bathed in the spring at Wadi Salim."

"Have you kept yourself away from women?"

"Three full days."

"Then eat."

The hill behind the High Priest's house was barren save only for the olive trees and the sacred courtyard of the shrine. Low walls of pudding-stone, lime-plaster floor as hard as granite, egg-shaped holes in the mud floor where feet had chipped away the plaster - the remnants of still more burials dating back the gods know how many millennia - and in the midst of all this the great obelisk, surrounded by any number of smaller obelisks, like a Prophet encircled by his disciples. The place was littered with offerings from the visit of the Ark - brooches, amulets, ceremonial knives, gold necklaces, hand-carved teraphim, clay pots, the clothing of dead children, spikes of chipped bone, coloured silks. Most of it hung from, or worshipped the feet of the great obelisk, but all the pillars were generously adorned. On one of them, some wag had carved "Yah-Akov ohev et-Lc'ah" with the point of a knife, then scratched through the word Le'ah and carved Rach-El in its place. Amongst the yuccas and cactuses by the northern wall, a piece of rag whose redness suggested menstruation or the loss of virginity by someone with less than proper respect for a shrine that was neither to Hat-Hor nor to Ishtar, though Achi-Melech told me later it had once been - hence perhaps the waggish graffiti. He called the obelisk "Our Lady of the Olive Trees". You had to press your thumb deep into the pole to realise that what appeared to be a man-made wooden column was in fact the trunk of some ancient breed of olive, tall and stately and undomesticated as any wild cedar.

"How long will you remain with us?"

"Not long. A day or two at most. I am charged with a duty by the king. I await a message from Prince Yah-Natan, then I shall depart."

It was obvious that he knew about my troubles and did not believe me. But bowed, humbly. Whatever lies I may have told about my duties, his were to the shrine alone, and he would neither question nor betray me. He led me to the altar, blessed me once I had prostrated myself and recited the Shema, then opened out his hands as if to indicate my welcome, and my freedom of the village. When he had gone, I lay down on the brow of the hill, desiring nothing but to stare across the valley, to gaze upon the beauty of Mor-Yah, and dream, and plan my destiny, and watch the new moon rise above Yevus until I fell asleep.

Sha'ul's chief herdsman, Do'eg of the Bene Edom, was also in Nov. I saw him from a distance, by the well at the foot of the village, when I came down in search of breakfast in the morning. He had brought an offering of the king's flock for sacrifice, and had stayed on to negotiate for pasturing across the wadi. I knew the man passably well. He was a swarthy, unpleasant creature with a hooked nose and a smarmy grin that revealed several rotten or broken or missing teeth, the sort of man who hated the world because he didn't know how to get on with it, and who preferred hating others to hating the person he really did despise - himself. People said he loved his sheep rather better than was virtuous, but the truth was that Do'eg loved no company at all except his own. It was fortunate for him that he did enjoy his own company, for no one else could tolerate it.

The sight of Do'eg alarmed me. My life was in danger everywhere except within the walls of the refuge city, but now even that was compromised. That Do'eg would report back that he had seen me was not worth the wondering about, and then my departure would become impossible. Nor did I have any doubt that Sha'ul would happily breach the sanctity of the Law of Sanctuary, and arrest or even murder me within the shrine. I went to Achi-Melech. He hadn't yet returned from morning prayers. I waited half an hour, then pursued him to the shrine. He had gone to the mikveh, to bathe a priest whose wife had given birth with his help that night. I pursued him there, but he was gone to the priest's house, to bless the child. I began to have the wildest suspicion that the High Priest was trying to avoid me.

But other than escaping through a window, he could not avoid my standing sentry at the priest's front door.

"I need a sword. The king's business requires greater haste than I had anticipated, and I have no weapon with me but my sling."

"There is no sword here. This is a refuge city."

But I knew the sword of Gol-Yat was in the shrine, hanging from the wall like one of those elongated crosses they use to brand the foreheads of sacrificial bulls - another of those superstitious talismans that Sha'ul in his atavism had agreed to despite Shmu-El's condemnation. No man in Yisra-El would dare to touch that sword, the icon of iron that recalled the shame of Even-Ezer and the humiliation of Aphek. No one, save only Daoud ben Yishai, whose claim that it was now his sword was surely irrefutable? With much reluctance, and insistence upon my immediate departure, Achi-Melech ben Achi-Tuv gave me the sword. It was strange holding that vast implement of iron in my hands again. Stranger still the discovery that I could now hold it with considerable ease.

But his reluctance engendered mine.

"No. I shall not take it."

In truth, I feared the weight and size of it would encumber me in flight. And no small measure of superstition too.

"But I cannot go unarmed."

"I will arrange for you to be met at the city gates. Sword and dagger will be provided. I will ask my son."

Avi-Atar of the golden hair. Avi Atar who had befriended me in the nayot of Ramah. Avi-Atar who had spoken with such excitement of the hints Shmu-El had been continuously dropping, hints that the time might soon be right to build the Temple, that the appointed time was nigh for which all Yisra-El had waited these three hundred years. No priest in Yisra-El was more opposed to Sha'ul than Avi-Atar. If I hadn't thought to ask after him, it was because I hadn't reckoned he would be in Nov. But he too, and of course I should have thought of it, had gone home for the New Moon of Sivan.

"Avi-Atar!"

"Daoud, you put the very lives of the stars and planets in jeopardy when you move about the universe. Why did you have to come to Nov?"

It was hard to tell if he was serious or joking. He ought to have been deadly serious. But who can predict?

"Where will you go now?"

"It's better that I don't tell you. That way Sha'ul can't force you to tell him."

"Sha'ul doesn't know you are here. Nor is there any reason to think that he will find out."

I named Do'eg, nodding in the general direction of the sacred grove where I had last seen him, curled up fast asleep beneath a tamarisk, surrounded by his sheep.

"He will say nothing," Avi-Atar was a great deal more certain of this than me. "If he has even noticed you. He is not a man who speaks to anyone. Even his dog has had to learn sign-language. Here, take this."

It was a letter, closed under the seal of Yah-Natan, delivered that morning.

"Clearly there is one who knows where to find you. One who is in close counsel with the king."

I shook my head.

"He and I are sworn. Can you get a message to him - very discreetly?"

"Through the priesthood it isn't difficult to pass a message. But whether you can trust the messenger?"

"Let Yah-Natan send for his arrows, every week before Shabbat goes out. Let him look for what is carved on the stone, and then depart."

As cryptic as an oracle, so clear yet so obscure that he alone could never miss the point.

We said goodbye like friends, Avi-Atar and I, like friends who were not sure they would ever meet again, but hoped to. I had given no clue as to where I might be going, because frankly I hadn't a clue myself. Ammon, Pelet, Midyan, one of the northern tribes perhaps? I thought of Mo-Av, but Av-Ner had taken the army down into the desert by the Salt Sea for exercises, and I did not want the risk of being seen when there were soldiers close enough to take me captive. And besides, Mo-Av was far too far, unless I could find some way to take my entire family with me. Because they too were at risk, my parents, my brothers and sisters. He wouldn't touch Michal, but Sha'ul was not above pulling my brothers out of the ranks and holding them hostage against my surrender. If I was to rescue them, I needed a safe haven; and I needed it close enough to home to be able to operate. Surely my own tribe, the tribe of Yehudah, would not abandon their last prince?

It was a moment of sheer madness to set out across Yehudah when I did. I had no clear idea where I was going anyway. Just south. Towards the desert. Grandfather Oved had told me about the labyrinth of King Minosh of the Bene Cheret, in which a man could become lost forever; but no labyrinth, however complex, however many walls you build and paths you make, can ever be so hard to find a man in as the desert. South then, to where emptiness would conceal me, and dust-storms cover my tracks. Time enough then to decide what I must do next.

But it did not fall out that way. Scarcely had I left Beit Lechem - I couldn't flee without first kissing my father and mother - than a raiding party of the Bene Pelet ambushed me. A solitary man on camelback was not a sight to be ignored. They had spotted me - a cloud of unexplained dust some way in the distance - and lurked in silence behind rocks to await my passing, no doubt thinking I was some footman of the king's who would be worth seizing for a ransom, or at the very least murdering for a ring or two of spoil. How easily they took me - like plucking a feather off a bird! Simply they broke out of hiding as I sauntered by, lost in thought and singing some song of Asaph's loud enough to entertain a valley full of Bene Pelet. Swords, daggers, and one vast kaf-shaped scimitar blazoned in the morning light, a ring of brightness like the sun's aureole. I was surrounded, forced to dismount, searched for valuables, bound hand and foot, slung belly-down over my own camel, and led to their hidey-hole. How ironic that in trying to escape capture, and failing, I should end up, not in the hands of Sha'ul, but of men just like myself - outcasts, bandits, wanted men. For it turned out they were not a raiding party at all, but a gang of brigands who lived by robbery and kidnapping. And I, no doubt, would bring a tidy ransom. I felt as Abou Yah-Suph must have felt, after his brothers had abandoned him, when the Bene Midyan took him from the pit and sold him to the Bene Yishma-El.

"The cloak's a garment of the priests of Nov, but the ring's a turquoise of the Bene Yehudah."

"Then he's the king's man. This'll double him."

"The camel alone's worth a hundred shekels."

"No. It's got swellings on its shins and the knees are raw. It's been over-ridden for many years. It'll fetch a price for meat in Ber Sheva, but little enough for riding."

Every craft has its experts, its specialists, its minutiae of esoteric knowledge. Even thievery. Even kidnapping.

"If it's that badly used, then it must be one of General Yah-Natan's."

Much laughter. I was wondering if I would be subjected to the same close bodily scrutiny as the camel, and if so, what they would conclude.

"What's your name, boy?"

No one but the king had ever called me boy like that. It roused me to resistance.

"Abdul Chara ben Chalev," I replied, and received back, for my insult, a slap across the cheeks. No dog-turd likes to be told he's a dog-turd.

"You're a man's son, and a woman's. Name yourself."

"Like you, I'm the son of your father's fifth wife."

Another slap. But damaged property is worth fewer shekels. They would add the insults to my price.

"It's no matter who you are. The king of Yisra-El has many nameless slaves who run away. There are chains for many more."

Of the seven men, six were garrulous but the seventh sat entirely in silence, staring not at me but right through me, squatting on his hams, counting the tassels on his bernous in the way the women of Anat count their beads. His eyes never blinked and his expression never altered. It was like having your soul read by a necromancer. When he did eventually speak, it was in a dialect of the Bene Pelet that I didn't understand. But what he said impressed them. Their faces earnest with intensity, all now smiled at me, and nodded their heads. It was clear that their captive was no longer nameless.

✡

They took me to Gat - the Vale of Foreskins, as Uzi ben Chokat, the commander of the king's bodyguard, once named it. It was obvious, really. Sha'ul was unlikely to pay much for me alive or dead, whereas the Bene Gat might well be keen to take revenge for what I did to them. Every human word and deed holds out a debt to fortune. So mine was about to be called in.

Entering Gat that first time, I had known fear in the very tightness of my stomach. But that was nothing as compared with this. Here, I had no doubt, my life would end. They would mock me, abuse me, spit at me, tear me with knives. I pictured every detail in my imagination, as though somehow this might prevent it happening. But worst, worst of all, they would seek justice foreskin for foreskin, as the Bene Abou Raham had been taught to do. How would they do it to one who was already circumcised? I could not imagine it - but knew that they, eventually, would find a way. With burning oil? With sharpened knife? Allowing every male in Gat who had been circumcised that day to take his personal revenge? Even as we entered the market, and I still belly-downwards across my camel like a sack of stolen grain, I could see not only the places that marked my last visit, but faces too, recognisable faces. I found myself wondering who was and was not circumcised, and whether their fear of Yahweh might protect me. A boy of thirteen or fourteen was whittling willow on a barrel. He looked up, recognised, spat at me. Then the whole town descended like vultures to consume my bones. But that too was just imagination. The market square was actually deserted. The bandits delivered me to the prison door.

"You are Daoud ben Yishai, the king's son-in-law?"
I let my head loll to one side, in the posture of a dead man on the scaffold. My arms hung limp at my sides. My legs refused to take my weight, so two guards had to hold me upright.
"Answer my question!"
"Daoud is beloved. Yishai Yehoshua the anointed son of Yah. I sing the praises of the One and Only god."
"He's mad, captain. They found him singing his head off in the desert. Too much sun, you want my view. He may have been General Daoud once. He ain't no more."
An effigy of Adonis, hanging in the noonday sun, ithyphallic carrion crumb. Blessed are you O Lord our god, who gave the crows

beaks to peck our flesh.

"What were you doing on the road to Teko'a, General?"

"Teko'a - tekiya. Shevarim. Toot-de-de-toot. Toot-toot-de-de-toot-toot. Tekiya. Teruah. Shevarim."

Even as I was doing it, the madness I was feigning gave birth to a truly sane idea - the use of the Rosh Ha Shana trumpet calls as a code of communication. Combinations of long notes and short notes representing letters of the aleph-bet, but ciphered, combined in trumpet-calls to make whole words, communicable by heralds from hill-top to hill-top across the whole of Yisra-El. I could hardly wait to share the idea with Yahni. If I survived to invent it.

"Teko'a, General. Your colleague General Av-Ner has taken seven thousand to Ein Gedi. General Yah-Natan is in Wadi Tse'elim. And you, alone, scouting on the road south to Teko'a. King Ma'och will forgive many things, in exchange for the plans of the Bene Yisra-El for their next assault. When will it come?"

"Not on Shabbat."

"No. Of course not. On which day then?"

"The first day is the sun's, the second is the moon's his wife, the third belongs to Narag-El and the fourth to Nevi. The fifth is Ba'al's day, and the sixth Our Lady's. Narag-El is the god of war. I warn you to beware the oracle of Narag-El."

"He is, Captain, he's stark raving mad. Let me hang him from a pike for a few hours and see if that don't turn his wits around again."

"No. The king wants him whole, to trade with Sha'ul ben Kish."

I could just imagine that negotiation!

"Let him stew for a few hours."

They put me in the darkest, dirtiest, most olid cell they had, a prison even for the rats who already inhabited it. I sat, slumped against a wall, trying not to retch, certain by now that death was not the destiny awaiting me in Gat, biding my time, continuing to feign madness.

"Yonat elem rechokim." Sung with intense slowness, plaintiff, lugubrious, each syllable extended to its limit, vibrato, ululated - as Asaph would have written it, in tense intense adagio. "Yo-o-o-o-o, na-a-a-a-t, e-e-e-le-e-em." And then the dying fall: "re-chok-im." The dove is alone, imprisoned, exiled amongst foreigners. Be merciful unto me, o gods, for men would swallow me up. Every day they wrest my words. All their thoughts are against me for evil. In the gods I have put my trust. I shall not fear what men can do to me. For you have delivered my soul from death. Will you now deliver my feet from falling, that I may walk before you in the light of the living? Yo-o-o-o-o, na-a-a-a-t, e-e-e-le-e-em."

My prayers were answered, though it took more than a week. And though my feet were indeed delivered from falling, still they wobbled, and shook, and it needed the support of a guard on each arm when I was taken at last out of that prison cell and marched across the square to the palace of king Ma'och. Palace indeed! A suite of rooms in the tower by the gatehouse. An apology for a palace to house what was a very sorry-looking king.

Yet who could have imagined that the townspeople of Gat would cheer me as I passed, would hail me as a hero? They sang my praises in the streets. They showered me with confetti of rose petals. I, who had deflowered the men of Gat. I, who had slaughtered the army of Ma'och on the road to Ekron. I, who had humiliated the priest of Etrah. Where I had anticipated curses and revenge, I received honours. Perhaps my feigning madness had infected them.

"Daoud ben Yishai," the king stood to address me, as kings do only in the presence of other kings. "I have sent to Sha'ul for ransom. What price do you imagine the king of the Bene Yisra-El would offer for his son-in-law?"

Continue mad, or recover sanity? Make the wrong choice, and my life might still hang by it. Unless, perhaps, there was a route between the two.

"The price of a good woman is above rubies', so says the proverb of the Bene Zvulun. But in the whorehouses of the Bene Gat, a good woman may be had for agorot. Of good men, let alone bad men, I cannot speak."

Ma'och was a tall man, a head taller than me, even without his crown. The Bene Pelet always regarded height as the principle virtue of kingship, as the Bene Cheret reckon athletic prowess and the kings of Chem their ability to be their father's eldest son. None of them good reasons to select a king, but all of them surely better than Shmu-El's reasons for selecting Sha'ul. Yet it was Sha'ul whom they all feared.

"When king Sha'ul laughs, is it a laugh that other men enjoy?"

"It is a great big belly-laugh, Ma'och. It is contagious laughter. Except when it is as sour as vinegar."

"He laughed, General, at the very suggestion of your being ransomed. He asked for your head, without the body. He offered my ambassador his javelin to spike it on."

"Then I hope your ambassador has a better co-ordinated eye than Sha'ul. Else the javelin will be returned, but still no head."

"Since my people have learned that you are now the enemy of the king of Yisra-El, they wish me to take you into my service, and have you fight with us. But I shall not do so, Daoud, because I do not so easily forget what you have done to me. I wish no feud, but I wish no friendship either. I will neither help nor hinder you. Know that you may leave Gat in peace. What you did to us that day is nothing compared to what Sha'ul ben Kish has spent years doing to my people daily. Take your life, and go."

I bowed, as low as my aching back and legs would let me. I could barely cross the market to the city gates for all the people desperate to touch my cloak and honour "he who has defied Sha'ul". In Gat, Shlomo! In Gat!

So I was free. As free as any band of brigands, condemned to roam the land of Nod, forever looking for a place to hide. So the very thought made clear what I had no choice but to do.

I went to the stone of Ezel on the next Shabbat. It was cold, and raining, and I feared that my absence for three full weeks might mean that Yahni would not come. But the cactus flowers were in bloom, golden orange as the sun, and I took this for a good omen. When I was certain that the place was quite deserted, I took a sharp-edged flint and carved on the cairn-stone the words Me'arat Adullam - the Cave of Adullam - and the letters lamed-hey-chaf-tav, hoping against hope that Yahni would understand. Then I wrapped myself tight in my bernous, and vanished.

"Once upon a time" - Grandfather Oved, squatting on his haunches on the edge of my bed-platform, his white beard luminous in the oil-light, a baby lamb curled up on either side of him for warmth, the squabbling of my elder brothers on the roof above. "Concentrate, Daoud. A good story must never be interrupted. A good story is an act of magic. Break the telling and you break the magic."

"I'm listening, saba."

"Once upon a time, in the southern desert of Kena'an, on the Plain of Shephelah, there was a royal city which bore the name Adullam. Adul-Am - the Justice of the People, for it was one of the cities where the kings sat in judgement, and pronounced the destinies of men. One day Abou Yehudah, the fourth son of Abou Yah-Akov, came to Adullam to visit his friend Chirah, bringing with him his entire flock of sheep, which Chirah had promised to help him shear. As they sat drinking together, Yehudah saw the beautiful Shu'a, and fell in love with her, and soon enough her father and his agreed the two should marry. So Yehudah came to settle with his wife in Adullam, for in those days it was still the custom of the Bene Kena'an that the husband settled with his wife. And over the next few years she bore him Er and Onan and Shelach.

"So the years went by, and Er was old enough to marry, and Abou Yehudah brought him Tamar, the priestess of the date-goddess of Timna, Our Lady of the Tamarisk, and they were married. Then Er died, and because it is the Yabam, the Law of the Levir, Abou Yehudah said to Onan his second son, 'Go in to Tamar. Father a child for your dead brother's sake. Otherwise he will have died and left no seed, and will have broken the first commandment. Go in to Tamar, lest your elder brother spend eternity in She'ol.' But Onan knew the child would not be his, and so he spilled his seed rather than impregnate her, and he too was struck down for the sin. Poor Tamar was left, widowed and childless, and yet a priestess of Our Lady. But Shelach was too young to be sent in to her, and she was not free to take another husband. So she too was in danger of sin, for being no longer virgin she could not attend the shrine, but as a barren wife she stood disgraced before her people. 'Be patient,' Abou Yehudah counselled her. 'My third son Shelach will come in to you when he is fully grown.'

"So the long years of waiting began, until at last Shelach was old enough. But Yehudah did not send the boy to her, and when she begged him so to do, he looked silently at her, and felt sorry for her growing years, but offered no excuse. Again Tamar faced the sin and the disgrace of barrenness, but she was a priestess of Our Lady, and when the time of the sheep-shearing came around again and the priestesses offered themselves as hetaerae to the shearers that the goddess might bestow fertility upon their flocks, Tamar went out into the road to wait for her father-in-law, wrapped so tightly in her gowns and veil he could not possibly have recognised her. But she offered herself to him in exchange for a kid of the flock, as it was holy and proper for her to do, and he fathered on her his twin sons who were also his grandsons, the first-born Zerach, and the younger Pharets."

Strange tale for a grandfather to tell his ten year old grandson. Strange legacy for a royal prince to inherit. Yet is there not more to this tale than meets the ear? Grandfather Oved never told any tale that did not have at least three meanings.

And as to the letters lamed-hey-chaf-tav. Numerically, lamed-chet spells thirty-eight; chaf-tet spells twenty-nine. The twenty-ninth verse of the thirty-eighth column of the First Tablet of Abou Mousa, the Creation Tablet, goes like this:

"And it came to pass, as he drew back his hand, that behold, his brother came out, and Tamar said: 'How have you broken forth? This breach be upon you.' Therefore his name was called Pharets, which means to breach, to break forth, to rupture."

Yahni might not be aware that Adullam was the royal city of my ancestors - and as such what better place from which to launch my campaign for the throne? - but he knew my claim to be the heir of Pharets, and he would recognise my signature at once. But he also knew the old army expression, "amod ba pharets - stand to the breach" - the gods know he shouted it loud and often enough in the battle for Yavesh Gil-Yad - the term used when the siege is down and the bravest, the ones most willing to court danger, are competing to be the first ones through the breach. Surely he would understand the hidden message of these words, a call to violence, rebellion, mutiny, the raising of a band of heroes. Signed in the name of the illegitimate son and grandson of the patriarch, one of a pair of equally bastardised twin brothers. Surely Yah-Natan would decipher my riddle and respond.

He did, and with such speed he must even have anticipated me.

The first man into the cave was a captain of cavalry, a thin, effeminate creature who had been demoted because he refused to punish a man for hiding a milk-lamb he had captured in a raid, and who had gone awol rather than stomach the disgrace. The next three were little more than brigands, hero-worshippers looking for the chance of booty. The fifth and sixth were debtors - soldiers who had lost heavily in illicit gambling. The seventh was a Bene Mo-Av who claimed a family connection on his mother's side, but turned out to be utterly mad. He was convinced that the god Enki was my patron, arguing that Enki was also known as Ea, that Ea was the equivalent of Yah amongst the Bene Bav-El, and that Yah-Natan meant "Enki has given" - implying that Yahni was his own protector and had sent him to me to be mine. Sadly he also argued, albeit with great cogency and considerable knowledge of etymology, that Enki also meant "Lord of Love", and "House on the Water"; he counselled me to move my hiding-place nearer to a river, and then to assemble an "Army of Love", which meant presumably an army without weapons but with infinite free access to nubile girls. He didn't last long.

Of the numbers who came to me in those days, there must have been at least one in every ten who was as crazy as he. Followers of weird cults, believers that the end of the world was nigh, eaters of cheese and lettuce leaves, exponents of tag conscience-wrestling and transcendental origami, people who propounded universal purification or espousal of the teachings of the prophet Zoroaster, people who sat through eternity beneath the bodhi tree or practiced synchronised self-flagellation while sitting cross-legged on a mat. The rest were simply malcontents and opportunists. Or family. Because two of my brothers came to join me there, Shammah and Chetsron, and with them came Yo-Av ben Tseru-Yah, my nephew though he was actually only two years younger than me. His elder brother Av-Yishai came too, a lesser soldier, though skilful enough, and very brave.

I had almost given up keeping the count and recording the names, when at last a real soldier appeared. Now we had the possibility of turning this rag tag and bobtail of hopeless deserters and still more hopeless idealists into a serious fighting force. Unlike Enki-man, he really had been sent by Yah-Natan, abandoning the garrison at Manachat which he had been holding for the once more reinstated Prince. In the meanwhile Yahni was secretly enlisting supporters from the ranks, and had gone to take advice from Gad, who had been elected Elder of the Guild of Prophets now that Shmu-El was too ill.

His name, like that of the priest at Nov, was Achi-Melech. He had been a commander of the Bene Chet before he married a woman of

301

the Bene Yah-Shachur and left his tribe to settle down with hers. Yah-Natan had recruited him to what he called "the cause", and he was as loyal as they came. He was one of those who breached the garrison at Geva, one of those who made the protective shield for me after the death of Gol-Yat. There was no soldier braver or more accomplished than he in all the armies of Sha'ul.

"How many are we?"

"If you count the rabble and the am ha arets, perhaps four hundred. But most are only interested in rape, and looting to pay off the debts that have driven them here."

"I shall work them till they quit or drop. If you will let me."

Let him? I would have had little use for him if he had done otherwise.

"There is little point my coming here to raise an army if all I can turn out are skittle players and pickpockets and the occasional failed gambler."

"I will need certain things."

"You have them."

"Do you not want to know what they are?"

"Only if you are unable to provide them for yourself. I have nothing except the authority of my name to give you. It may help or hinder."

"Weaponry?"

"Steal it, or make it."

"How long do I have?"

"Until yesterday. Two of my brothers and two of my nephews are here safely. I want to be able to get from here to Beit Lechem and back, bringing two aged parents and a variety of women and young children. I will need an escort capable of defending them against any attempt by the king to prevent their flight. It's a simple enough task, but it must be done by yesterday, because even Sha'ul will not procrastinate for very long."

Achi-Melech laughed.

"Sha'ul will always procrastinate for very long. And then some."

"Perhaps. But we can't take that risk. My mother is not at all well, and I have given her a promise that she will die in bed, and not as a hostage against my capture. Even if that bed is inside a cave."

But there was no need to put her to bed inside a cave, because my grandmother had already made provision for them to be well hidden

302

in Mitspeh of Mo-Av, with my great-grandmother's people. Achi-Melech went to Beit Lechem to bring them out, and as soon as it was safe we took them all across the border.

The Cave of Adullam offered as convenient a hidey-hole as was imaginable for a fleeing man. It was, too, a useful mustering-point for the malcontents of Yisra-El, and it provided a satisfactory base camp for three months training. No doubt, when the time of peace comes, its walls will furnish our scholars with years and years of fit subject for their academic studies. But once we had received Gad's warning that Sha'ul was preparing to send Av-Ner against us, it was frankly more dangerous to remain in the cave than to risk a march across Yehudah. Gad's counsel was to go still further south, into the mountains of Yehudah. At Charet there was a cutting in the woods, a shrine of his own cult, the goat-god Ba'al-Gad, where we would be given sanctuary. Achi-Melech took the men. I made my own way, going on ahead to scout the place. It was in Charet that the first of Yahni's letters reached me:

"My father sits in Giv-Yah," it read. "All day, he does nothing but sit, holding a council of war under a cypress tree. He is completely paranoid. He screams at his clerks and he screams at his house-servants: 'Are you all in league against me? Will no one have the guts to tell me about the conspiracy between my son and my son-in-law? They want to steal my throne - will no one speak? You disloyal bunch of traitors, vermin, cowards!' The way he rants, he might yet recover the good opinion of Shmu-El! Except that Shmu-El is dying."

But then a second letter, considerably less jovial than the first:

"...And in the midst of all this, my father's principal herdsman, Do'eg of the Bene Edom, turned up. What a sly, surly, gruff old man he is - the very smell on him makes your flesh creep. Sheep's blood and cattle dung and the stench of solitude. He hung about for several days, waiting for the chance to see the king alone, ostensibly about some sheep he wished to buy. But why alone, if that was all his reason? Dodi, he saw you, the vile wretch of a Bene Edom told the king that he had seen you, with Achi-Melech the priest at Nov. Prepare yourself to hear this. He summoned them to Giv-Yah. Achi-Melech and all the priests of Nov. The whole shrine. They came wearing their white robes and nothing else - no head scarves, no outer garments. Just sandals on their feet and the linen ephod. As though they knew, and were resigned to it. He lined them up in a great circle round the cypress tree, walked the line as though he were inspecting a guard of honour, hurled insults at them of the most extraordinary obscenity, then ordered his servants to cut them down. But they all refused. He summoned Av-Ner to do it, but Av-Ner refused. I thought for a moment he was going to do it himself - but the memory of Gil-Gal must have prevented him. In the end he had to order Do'eg to do it. Eighty-five throats he cut, each one of them wearing the linen ephod. Then he went back to Nov and did the same to the rest of the village - men and women, children and sucklings, oxen and asses, even the sheep. Ransacked the entire shrine, stone by stone, until you could no longer prove it had ever existed. People who saw him say Do'eg was crazy. There was a terrible glint in his eye, exactly like the one my father had that day he went to save the men of Yavesh Gil-Yad from the Bene Ammon. The madness that is induced by spilling too much blood. Nor was Do'eg feigning. There are some men who simply cannot cope with such large quantities of blood. It intoxicates them, excites their pulses beyond what is safe or sensible. Such men are dangerous - useful to a king as captains if he can control them. But eventually it becomes necessary to have them killed. Unless Do'eg did the deed himself, which is not implausible. Out of remorse. They found him hanging on a rope from one of the olive trees..."

Ah, Yahni, Yahni. If only you had seen me that afternoon in Gat, and on the road to Ekron afterwards, you would know how well I understood what you were saying. But do you not know that there is blood still worse than that which you have spilled yourself? The blood of others, spilled because of you. Eighty-five priests! And how many men and women, how many children and sucklings, how much ruination of man-made beauty? How many, Yahni? I need to know the exact number of selichot that I must say. And the oxen and the asses? Is there a special selichah for dumb beasts? Even the sheep? How many, Yahni? How many?

The grief lasts, of course, for ever. But there is the intense grief of the living moment, and it is not the same as the grief that endures beyond the time when life must go on being lived. I sat for three long days, deep in my own darkness that was deeper and darker even than the Cave of Adullam or the cutting in the wood of Charet let alone the depth and darkness of the soul of Sha'ul. Ya'aleh tachanuneyni mey erev. Prostrate on the floor of the shrine. Ve-yavo shavateyni mi boker. Neither food nor water passed my lips, except the occasional tear, licked from my cheek by my own tongue - adding salt to the wound. Ve-yeyra'eh rinuneyni ad arev. On the third day one of the soldiers brought my lyre and I strummed it randomly, plucking easy notes, familiar refrains, seeking a mood of mourning in a minor key, trying to reduce my longing for revenge from the augmented to the diminished. Until the release that is poetry, the self-therapy that is poetry, the katharsis that is poetry, began to work its healing magic and to offer me a chink of light.

And through that chink of light, the face of the king, as I remembered him that night in Gil-Gal, and on a hundred other nights.

"Why do you boast of your great wickedness? The love of god endures beyond the day. Your tongue thinks only of my downfall; like a sharp razor it carves out deception. You love evil more than good, lies more than speaking honestly. You love the words of destruction on your lying tongue. May the gods destroy you and all your house for ever..."

No, not all your house. Spare Yahni, Lord. Spare Michal. But o how those words of hate-discarded-like-a-skin felt good!

"May he throw you out of your dwelling place. May he expel you from your tent and uproot you from the land of the living. May the righteous see you, and fear you, and mock you. Behold the man who did not choose the gods for his gods, but trusted in the abundance of riches and found strength in the downfall of others..."

Was hatred ever so potently expunged as in the expression of pure hatred?

"But I am like a green olive tree in the orchard of the gods. I trusted in their love at all times. I will praise you for ever for all that you have done. I will put my trust in your name, for it is good in the eyes of the pious."

Timchey pesha le-am nosha ve-tomar salachti.

O wipe away the sin of a delivered people, and say "I have forgiven."

Avi-Atar, the son of Achi-Melech the priest, did not accompany his father to Giv-Yah to answer the summons of the king. Somehow he survived the slaughter too, with four other priests whom he had hidden. What he saw, he saw. And when he had taken the body of Do'eg of the Bene Edom down from its rope and branch, when he had buried it among the ruined corpses of the shrine of Nov, he thought what he thought, and he fled in search of me.

Avi-Atar of the golden hair. Avi-Atar who had befriended me in the nayot of Ramah. Avi-Atar who had spoken with such excitement of the hints that Shmu-El had been continuously dropping, hints that the time might soon be right to build the Temple, that the appointed time was nigh for which all Yisra-El had waited these three hundred years. No priest in Yisra-El was more opposed to Sha'ul than was Avi-Atar.

Did I really write that?

"Daoud, you put the very lives of the stars and planets in jeopardy when you move about the universe. Why did you have to come to Nov?"

Why, indeed?

"Where will you go now?"

"It's better that I don't tell you. That way Sha'ul can't force you to tell him."

But Avi-Atar had less trouble than Sha'ul in finding out. He sent one of his rescued priests to Manachat, to Yahni. It was that priest who brought the second of Yahni's letters. And Avi-Atar just a day behind.

Nor was his madness feigned. His lip trembled like a man whose nerves are damaged. His face was white as calamine. He was even more ready to kill me than Sha'ul was. He had thrown off his linen ephod and his mourning gown in preparation for the act of murder. But I made him put them on again.

"Kill me, Avi. I deserve to die. I knew Do'eg would tell Sha'ul. I am responsible for the death of your father's house. But you must kill me as a priest, not as an apostate, so there will be no sin on your head. Put on your gown, Avi, and let it be an act of divine justice, not unholy revenge. Let it be the tar, the blood-vengeance, in the manner of the Bedou."

It was pretty vacuous stuff, theologically speaking. But that was not the point. Clearly he had no serious intention of killing me. He wouldn't have known how to do it anyway, for all his long experience in sacrificing sheep and goats. In the temples, the beasts are held down firmly and the throat presented. It is practically unheard of for there to be a struggle. Whereas killing an upright man in cold blood. He would have lacked the guts, even without the moral constraints. No, he hadn't really come to kill me. He was far more terrified that Sha'ul would send after him, to kill him; lest anyone from Nov survive to tell the tale. The twin terrors were stopping up his soul, when what was needed was to let the tears flow. My words had breached the dam. Did I say "breached"?

"They say it is a great blessing to be buried on the Mountain of Our Lady of the Olives," he was stammering and stuttering as a man does who is dealing with intense sorrow. "When the Day of Judgement comes, those will be the first souls to rise again."

"This is heresy, Avi-Atar. This is the teaching of the priests of Zoroaster. There is no rising again for the dead of Yisra-El. We return to Our Lord and Lady, to Yah and Yahweh, and to the worms."

"I know, Daoud. I know. But my father lies unburied on the hill-slopes of Giv-Yah, while Do'eg of the Bene Edom has his grave upon the mount. Do you think the gods might raise the shrine again at Judgement Day?"

"I will raise it, Avi. Stay with us. Serve me as priest. When I become king, I will rebuild Nov for you and we will bury your father and his house in the proper manner."

We stood there, cuddling like children, two professional slaughterers rendered mad and grieving by a commonplace act of slaughter. We stood there, for the whole time it took the sun to go down over the Great Sea. Two exiles, two fugitives - two friends - outcast from one mutual enemy in the land of another. Yet which would prove the more dangerous - the wilderness, or Sha'ul? Only time would tell.

Parchment Eleven

Like the Cave of Adullam, Charet was all very well as a temporary hiding place, but soon enough Sha'ul was bound to track us down, and then we would be like the boar which the hounds have driven into a trap. No one could fight in those woods - but Sha'ul, at least, would not need to. Simply, he could lay siege to us, until he starved us out. And besides, we needed to keep the men in constant training, if only to prevent the mayhem that gets stewed in constant boredom.

So we came back to Adullam, and made the cave habitable. Not for everyone mind - we tented the men in the plain and used the cave for a headquarters. It was spring by this time, warm and dry and full of scents. Shepherds came from time to time, intending to use the cave to lamb their ewes, as I had done a lifetime ago. In the long hours of wondering where on earth this all might lead - and how to feed six hundred without resorting to manna or banditry - I stared at the tusks of primordial beasts, painted on the cave walls, and tried to read the hieroglyphs that Grandfather Oved alas was not there to decipher. The harmonies of the lyre resonated deep into the blackness at the hell-end of the cave. Avi-Atar taught me the accompaniment to the "Dance of the Maidens" that used to be performed in Shiloh at the feast of Yahweh before the Bene Pelet destroyed the shrine. Or we sat for hour after hour, Yo-Av and Av-Yishai and I, learning at Achi-Melech's feet the map-lore he had refined with Yah-Natan, discussing strategies for hill-battles, desert-campaigns, sieges of large towns as opposed to small, the ways to co-ordinate lance and sword, camel and chariot, resolving the problem of how to feed six hundred by resorting, inevitably, and for lack of manna, to banditry. Music and war - two of the three great arts I have spent my life engaged in. The third, the absent one, was love. Yet somehow none of us ever thought of it.

Then, as spring turned to summer, the sound of thunder as it seemed, or a minor earthquake, not five miles to the south of us, at Achziv perhaps, or Beit Le'aphrah - in the desert the merest whisper travels endlessly, and the earth rumbles like a shaken quilt. Achi-Melech took a scouting party to find out. In anticipation, we readied the men, and I put Yo-Av in command. It was, as we knew from the shouting and the dust, neither thunder nor earthquake, but an army of the Bene Pelet, dragging its siege weaponry through the scrub, descending on Ke'ilah. They were come, not to seize land, nor to threaten Sha'ul, but simply to rob the threshing-floors, just as I had suspected that day in Gat when I cut open the grain sacks and accused them openly of theft. They too had their six hundreds to feed.

"It's Sha'ul's problem, Daoud, not ours."

My brother Shammah, veteran of more wars than he cared to remember.

"Achi-Melech, you've seen how the land lies."

His habit of poking his tongue into the bowl of his lower lip, rolling it around, clucking on his gum all the while. A poor apology for thinking, which ended, invariably, in his preferring always to make the negative decision. All men have their flaws and foibles, Shlomo. Achi was amongst the best of them, but still flawed.

"I see no need, Daoud. We announce where we are, we show our strength, we lose some good men, and all for what - to fail to prevent the Bene Pelet stealing a few bags of corn. Shammah is right. Let Sha'ul fight his own battles."

Whereas Yo-Av.

"And I see every need, General. We announce where we are, we show our strength, okay we lose a few good men but there will be many more who will rally to the cause when they see how far the king's nose is out of joint. And we, not Sha'ul, will prevent the Bene Pelet stealing valuable bags of corn. Or rather..."

Not looking at me, not for a single second. Looking at Achi-Melech. And not even at Achi-Melech, but at the right he was now claiming once and for all to lead the army of Daoud.

"...Because we, not the Bene Pelet, will take home every grain of corn in Ke'ilah."

Avi-Atar turned away in disgust at that suggestion. And rightly, Shlomo, rightly. It is the duty of priests to starve to death on the moral high ground. Whereas outlaws and fugitives must forage about with rats in ditches until they find enough to eat.

"Is the grain we took from Moreshet-Gat all gone?"

"Enough for another week perhaps. Not more." Av-Yishai. Gruff. Grizzled. Grave and earnest as his father. "The priests at Ein Rimmon are opening their silos in another month, but it's a long way south to go raiding at this time of year."

"And the two dozen head of cattle we took from Yarmut?"

"Eaten."

Then it wasn't about fighting against the Bene Pelet or in support of Sha'ul at all. Each town we raided learned to fear the name of Daoud ben Yishai, and spread the net of hegemony wider. It was about establishing beyond dispute the case for anointing the heir of Pharets as the king of Yehudah. Whether now, or at the death of Sha'ul.

"The men are restless. They are already beginning to question why they are here. This will test their training as well as their resolve, and it will let Sha'ul know our horns are locked." Aye, and which side we were really on. "Sound the chatsotsra. And Yo-Av..." There was an arrogant glimmer in his eyes as he turned back to me. This would be hard, but necessary. "Achi-Melech will lead. You and I will stay with the second rank."

"But..."

I could have said: he must be given the chance to demonstrate in practice what thus far he has only taught in theory. But what came out was:

"If we meet resistance, those in the first rank will fall. I don't want you to be in that number."

He read it as conspiracy, complicity, even wilful sacrifice, as if I shared his ambition to see Achi-Melech out of the way. But it was not that. It was because he was my nephew, Shlomo. A man has responsibilities to his family, always, first and last. I could not have faced Mey-Zahav and Tseru-Yah otherwise.

The chroniclers have called it a battle, but it was no battle. Using much the same strategy that Sha'ul used at Yavesh Gil-Yad, albeit on a smaller scale, we quite simply took the place. We divided into eight groups, Achi-Melech taking the first four and having them assail Ke'ilah, making as much noise as they could, each from a different point of the compass, but all charging to the city gate. Three hundred men giving the impression of three thousand. The town sat in the bowl of a hill, and woodland started not two hundred yards across the scrub, so when the first four waves were followed by a second, who could tell how many more waves might be waiting in the woods? The Bene Pelet knew the sea, after all. Men who know the sea expect wave to follow wave, one after another, infinitely. Expect sea monsters too, no doubt - is their Dagon not depicted as a gigantic land-fish, complete with fins and scales and breathing fire like a monster of the deep? The first four waves poured through the gates and disarmed the Bene Pelet who had barely settled in from conquering it. The second flooded across the town to take possession of it, though the townspeople were already hailing us as saviours. But then a third set of waves broke against the walls, the gates that we had closed and barred to prevent the Bene Pelet from escaping. A third wave? Sha'ul, with eight thousand men, late as usual - if they ever ran a lateness competition, Shlomo, mark it that Sha'ul would miss the final - but with Av-Ner and Yah-Natan and Avi-Yam and Re'u-Ven ben Tu-Va'al and Imnah ben Raphu. All of his most senior commanders. Did he really need so large an army, so many generals, to recapture Ke'ilah from the Bene Pelet? Or was the real battle yet to start?

He must have thought he had us trapped in Ke'ilah, because a city that is closed with gates and bars is a city that cannot long withstand a siege. All around the walls, like a collection of jurassic monsters, but frozen, static, as though they had been with Lot's wife when she fled Sedom, stood the army of siege weapons that the Bene Pelet had dragged across the hills but never used, great iron dragons abandoned in the rush to take the town. From the watch-tower above the gate we observed with what excitement Av-Ner and Yah-Natan were inspecting them - the envy of Yo-Av and Achi-Melech was palpable. For this alone it had been worth the muster and the forced march. Scribes were hurriedly drawing up inventories, engineers were scratching in wax the details of the monsters' parts, so they could be taken away piecemeal and reconstructed afterwards. As we had learned iron weaponry from the Bene Pelet, so now we would learn this still more advanced craft. We! The Bene Yisra-El, I mean. At that particular moment of our lives, those of us ensconced within Ke'ilah were disconnected from the nation. We were no longer Bene Yisra-El. We had become Habiru.

All that long afternoon we watched, as the bowl of the hill filled up with soldiers' camps, tents pitched for no other strategic purpose than to ensure a level sleeping-place and a good windbreak for a camp-fire. The clattering of iron against iron occupied the silence. Whenever a siege weapon had been dismantled, another set of carts would be filled with its severed members and driven off like a plague-wagon taking off the corpses of the dead. By evening the first caravan was ready, more than two hundred carts for which Imnah ben Raphu provided the guard. By the time the moon was fully risen, the second convoy had departed under Avi-Yam. And we, the hapless watchmen, locked in the city like caged beasts, awaiting our turn to be dismembered.

When the Bene Pelet first descended on Ke'ilah, orders had been given to drive a breach in the city wall against the east, so the women and children might escape before the siege was set. In the meanwhile the men tried to hold the gate against the west. But so quickly did the city yield - the mere sight of the instruments of torture enough to induce complete and instantaneous surrender - that the breach amounted to no more than a few staved stones and a set of eyeslits barely large enough to shoot an arrow through. Under cover of darkness, I sent Av-Yishai to enlarge and to conceal the breach, though once again it set Yo-Av and Achi-Melech at odds. Whatever the one favoured, it now seemed the other would automatically contradict. At one level it was extremely useful, for it gave to every decision its full range of pros and cons. But already it was apparent that one or other of my generals would have to yield. It was hard, Shlomo. For Achi-Melech had not once offered a suggestion with which a rational man could disagree.

That night was one of the longest ever. I never left the watchtower above the city gate, unless it was to walk the rampart of the city walls. Somewhere out there was Yah-Natan, my oath-companion, my best-friend, my brother-in-law. Surely he would not let Sha'ul wipe us out? Surely there could be found some space to negotiate? I summoned Pinchas ben Rephu-El, the Elder.

"You have understood by now that Sha'ul came to fight the Bene Pelet, but will stay to fight me. If there is a battle, many of your people will be killed. I would leave, to prevent this, but I am unable. What is your will in this matter?"

So one speaks, Shlomo. After Nov, I could not have borne another massacre.

And for him, a simple choice. Or perhaps not all that simple. To fight beside me, or to fight against me from within the walls.

"I would that Daoud and the king were friends, but what is not so is not so."

Don't you just admire to the point of reverence the linguistic skills of politicians, Shlomo!

Still, it was only right to offer him a third alternative.

"Pinchas, I am minded to hand over the prisoners. Will you open the gates and provide them such escort to the king as you deem fit?"

We unlocked the gates. Two hundred of my men stood by with lance and sword in case of a sudden rush, but clearly they had not yet turned their thoughts to us at all. Pinchas could have marched the whole town out, declared his fealty to Sha'ul the Bene Yamin, left the heir of Pharets to his ruin. But just he and a dozen Elders led the captured Bene Pelet out in file, chained one to the other by the legs and escorted by a hundred men of Ke'ilah bearing arms. The rest remained with us, armed and committed. Av-Ner's men surrounded Pinchas and his troupe, and while the general took the elders to the king to parley, Re'u-Ven ben Tu-Va'al received the prisoners, and one by one he had their throats cut. It took two hours. The smell of blood, the cawing of crows, resounded from the woods to which they dragged them for unholy burial - less than the siege weapons, not even the cairn of stones one gives a criminal. By the time the slaughter was finished, Pinchas had long returned from his discussions with the king. His face was white and grave. The other elders shared his silence. The darkness hung over Ke'ilah like a shroud.

Yet when the sun came up the following morning, there outside the walls were eight thousand soldiers of the Bene Yisra-El, and there inside the walls were six hundred men of Daoud and the several thousand citizens of Ke'ilah, every last one of them prostrate on the ground, honouring the dawn with their heads wrapped in their cloaks for holiness, their arms and foreheads clasped with thongs, the priests in both camps simultaneously chanting the words which Yahweh spoke to Abou Mousa:

"Ve hayah lecha le-ot al-yadecha u-le-zicharon beyn eyneycha le-ma'an tiheyeh torat Yahweh be-pheecha. And this shall serve you as a sign on your arm, and as a reminder on your forehead, so that the Laws of Yahweh be forever in your mouth. Ki be-yad chazakah hotsi-acha Yahweh mi-Mitsrayim. Because Yahweh brought you out of Mitsrayim with a mighty hand."

With a mighty hand indeed! But not with iron swords and javelins. Not with iron siege weapons. Not by cutting the throats of prisoners. The threats of the gods are empty when contrasted with the deeds of men. But why were we so at odds? The same people, sharing the same prayers, the same gods, the same mutual enemies, yet at war with each other, as Achi-Melech and Yo-Av, as Av-Ner and Yah-Natan, were at war with each other. Petty little empire-builders, serving their own narrow ambitions, gratifying their own selfish appetites, spoiling the harmony of the whole with rivalries. As I with Sha'ul - the root of all this madness. I know. I know. Yet I was his son-in-law, for pity's sake, the husband of his younger daughter. Why were we at war?

When the prayers were done, Avi-Atar brought out the breastplate of the high priest of Nov, his father's garments, containing the Urim and the Tumim, and we cast the dice to learn the will of Yahweh. The omens were not good.

"Avi-Atar, send one of your priests to Yah-Natan. Have him tell, in front of the king, that Daoud has made plans to escape, and that he has come to reveal these plans. If he is asked why he has turned traitor, have him say it is because his father and his uncle were slaughtered at Nov, and it was the fault of Daoud who came to seek refuge there. Have him tell Yah-Natan that I intend to place my archers in the west side of the town as a decoy to protect my escape through the breach in the city wall against the east."

"What happens to the priest after your ruse proves successful? Sha'ul will kill him."

"We must hope not. We must hope that Yah-Natan will be able to protect him. We are doomed, all of us, to die here in Ke'ilah anyway."

Sha'ul moved his army to the east side of the town, to cover the proposed escape route. But what came through the breach that afternoon were only women and children, carrying water pots in hope of filling them from the stream. In the few brief moments of confusion, we threw open the city gates and fled, as we had always intended, through the west gate, protected by the men of Ke'ilah. Down through the woods, in the direction of Mareshah and Lachish, towards the Great Sea and the lands of the Bene Pelet. A great rush of men on donkey, camel, or their own two feet, a pandemonium of refugees in flight and soldiers following. Men tripped and fell, died where they lay, speared on the wrath of Sha'ul's humiliation. Men lagged behind, and lost their way, or had to make their own way now. Six hundred was reduced by fifty even before we had gone a mile. By another fifty before we skirted Mareshah and paused. But growing fewer, easier. How far would Sha'ul pursue us? To the ends of the earth in all probability. Until the last second of eternity. Before Lachish we stopped again. This was now the beginning of Bene Pelet territory. Rushing any further west meant jumping out of the cooking pot and into the fire. We had to turn back - but whither?

"It's you the king wants," Yo-Av was the only one with guts enough to say what everyone was thinking. "If we split up, at least some will get away safely."

I waited for Achi-Melech to disagree, but all he said was: "We are none of us safe, whatever we do. But splitting up will create confusion. They'll look for hoof-tracks to follow. If we give them hoof-tracks in every direction, they'll have to choose one or choose all. Either way, we're all much safer."

"We meet in Adullam in three days. Go by as wide a circuit as you can, and keep zig-zagging."

"What if Adullam isn't safe?"

"My wife is a priestess at Chevron. I will find somewhere safe, and get a message to her. If you still wish to follow me, find a way to Chevron. If not, good luck to you."

Adullam was far from safe. Av-Ner's footmen had followed our tracks back from Ke'ilah and ransacked the cave. Each group arrived to find him waiting, and had to flee again. But where to go? Further northwards was impossible. The men of Zano'ach had locked their gates against us, the men of Yarmut remembered all too well our cattle-raid. From the west Sha'ul was in our wake. To the south led back to Ke'ilah, where Yahni would not dare to help us. East then, across the mountains of Yehudah, into the wilderness of Ziph, the uninhabited yellow mountains where the air was made of salt and would-be prophets walked in search of their own still-unfamiliar spirits. Surely the king would not hunt us there. And even if he did, there were hidey-holes a-plenty - caves, burrows, dens, shelters, rocks upon high crags, the very brightness of the desert sun which blinds the seeker and makes a man invisible. At least we could be certain of one thing. Despite its name, there would be no wolves to hunt us in the wilderness of Ziph. They were still too busy, devouring the flesh of the Bene Pelet in the woods around Ke'ilah.

✡

The place that I found - at last, at last, after three weeks of living rough and wild and moving on again each morning - was on the hill of Chachilah. As dark and well-concealed a place as ever wanted man was hunted in. Shammah and Chetsron were still with me, and Av-Yishai ben Tseru-Yah, and about a dozen others. Yo-Av I had sent to Chevron, to try to get word to Michal, and to bring back provisions. He took another dozen with him, and on the way back found a dozen more. But the militia we had armed and trained was scattered now. We had no idea if they were dead, or in captivity, or hiding somewhere, or seeking us in Av-Ner's shadow through the mountains. No word of Achi-Melech, nor of Avi-Atar.

At some point in ancient history, long before Abou Raham left the flatlands of the Bene Kessed and Ephron of the Bene Chet came down from the bull-mountains of the goddess Anat, men had built a stronghold on this hilltop, dragging rocks and boulders on ropes tied to slaves or oxen. Such mud as could be scraped from the rock-floor had been mustered to construct a pair of houses and what seemed to be the ruins of a tiny shrine. Chachilah - no Habiru word that. Bene Chor, no doubt - any word you have to clear your throat to speak is invariably Bene Chor - the aboriginal inhabitants of every mountain in the region, before Abou Essav defeated them at Se'ir and transformed them into Bene Edom. The place was full of chorim of one kind or another, deep holes in the ground where vipers lived, subterranean prisons such as that in which his brothers confined Abou Yah-Suph, waterless wells, entrance-ways to the underworld so deep you found yourself looking into them at every moment, expecting the footmen of the king, or even Sha'ul himself, to emerge from his nether kingdom, chewing on a pomegranate and come to claim your soul.

Or was that simply the terrible effect of life in the desert of Yehudah - visions, nightmares, phantasies? People speak of my "wilderness years", and do not realise that this was no mere metaphor. Nights of unbearable, intense cold in which your skin seemed to freeze tight on your bones. Relative cold. That same temperature, in Beit Lechem say, in mid-summer, would have you sleeping with the mosquitoes on the roof. But compared to the massive daytime heat we now had to endure, it was a deep unpleasant cold, and you longed for day.

Until it came. Yo-Av's scant provisions were not sufficient for a week, and there was little enough living in these hills for a raiding-party to bring home. Each morning men went off to scavenge hunger out of the refuse in the yellow rocks. The shells of dead carrion, fallen from the skies already picked to bones. Stray mountain goats. Berries. A scrape of fossil, calcinated to the rock. Minuscule plants, germinated where you tripped in hungry dizziness and spilled your sweat upon the ground. Oh yes, as bad as that. In two weeks in those hills, men learned in detail the topography of their rib-cages and why hygiene and sanitation are the beginning of civilised life. Such was our plight, the birds of prey sent out reconnaissance parties daily, to report back on our readiness for eating. Buzzards, drosophila flies, vultures black and bearded. If the heat increased by even one degree, they would have to break their usual habit and be prepared to eat us cooked instead of raw. And scorpion, Shlomo, you never saw so many scorpion - black and yellow. And the owls. The owls were stupendous, and they at least were tame. Fish owls, tawny owls, short-eared owls, scops owls. And spiders. At night you woke from Lilith-dreams of spiders with the faces of Sha'ul and Av-Ner, and found them weaving their webs so close around you they could have been planning to take you prisoner and hand you over to the king. Thirst drove you crazy. Hunger reduced you to a moaning groaning whingeing apathetic lump of inhumanity that would not have felt a qualm about eating your companion if you had the strength to cut him up or he the flesh to make him worth the cannibalising. As bad as that, Shlomo, as bad as that. After all the human barbarity, here in the desert we learned our closeness to the gods. In their image, in their likeness, so they made us. Nature is far more cruel than men.

But we had survived Ke'ilah, and we would survive this.

Yo-Av's first attempt to reach Michal had failed. Sha'ul had anticipated that I would try to reach her, and warned the High Priestess to keep her close. But the second time he managed to get word to her through Timna, her maid, and soon enough men began appearing at Chachilah, familiar faces as well as unfamiliar, and more importantly - carrying provisions. Carrying weapons too, but it was the food and water we were craving.

Then Achi-Melech arrived with practically an army of his own. He had been recruiting across the whole of Yehudah, proclaiming my kingship and the rising of Yehudah against the king. Men followed him, whether because of the rewards he promised without the remotest hope of ever fulfilling them, or for knowing of the stench that emanated from the woodlands of Ke'ilah, the stench of Sha'ul restored to his madness. Without exception they spoke of it, and spat out the words' sour aftertaste. Shmu-El had dispossessed him of his spiritual authority, but left him with the realm. Now there men were ready to divest him of the temporal crown as well. Not many. Not enough. But it was a start. Daoud was no longer plain Daoud, who could be addressed by his common name, or still more affectionately as the General. Behind my back men spoke of me as Daoud ben Yishai, and it was understood that Yishai was the diminutive of Yeshi'ahu, the Anointed, and not simply my father's name. And to my face they sang "Daoud, Daoud, Melech Yehudah, chay ve kayam, chay ve kayam". It was positively humbling.

So, once again we were a camp. But camps mean noise - the braying of donkeys human as well as animal. Smells too, which travel quite as far as noise. In those high hills, on that vast lunar surface where the gods worked out the blueprint for creation, every sound and smell travelled with a freedom such as we could only envy. It brought our hunters ever closer. Eight hundred men cannot train, raid, exist, in so empty a landscape, without leaving traces everywhere. We made a clearing in the woods a hundred feet below and raised a new camp there, keeping the mountain stronghold for our main headquarters. But even so, being found was as inevitable as...

"Yahni!"

"Daoud!"

We embraced in full view of all the men, as royal princes embrace. Several started to cheer, then clapped their hands over their mouths. Now especially, silence was imperative. Yet of all the people who might have been the first to find us, this was the greatest stroke of luck we could have had.

"I have very little time. I left my hunting party to scale the peak. I must be back within the hour."

Looking around him as he spoke, at the rudimentary - the primitive - conditions. He was finding it hard not to sneer.

"We're safe here," I said. "Even if they found us, we have a complex system of advance-guards, warnings, you name it. We monitored your approach for over half a mile. If you had not been who you are, you would have been dead before you reached those rocks."

It must have sounded like schoolboys playing a game of bandits in the wood, because he said:

"You're enjoying yourself."

And clearly it pleased him to discover that this was really so. It was too. For all the hardship, yes, I was enjoying myself. Army life was drudgery and court life pampered and hypocritical. Out here I could touch the pulse and uncover layers of my self that previously I didn't even know existed. Even suffering has its attractions.

"We can't live like this for long though. We have to make a move soon."

A move - indeed! The raison d'être of this entire farrago. Aye, but what move? That was what he had come here to find out. With a gesture of his eyes, he indicated that he wanted privacy for what he had to ask. What did he expect - a royal tent, groundpegged to the rocks?

"Come," I said, somewhat louder than was really necessary, "let me show you round."

The men backed off, gave us such privacy as was feasible on that narrow, crowded hilltop. Oh, but his face was serious! So this was it. He must have spent hours upon hours rehearsing this conversation in his head. One half of a dialogue for which he had not been given the response lines.

"I wasn't born for banditry, Yahni. I am here because your father wants my life and I am not ready yet to yield it up. I can't stay here for ever. But neither can I go to the king and ask for mercy. Circumstances have made me a hero and a rebel. I have no choice but to fight. And fights need reasons."

All of this he knew. It was only the reasons that were lacking.

"The men have proclaimed me king in Yehudah."

Slow, ruminative nodding of the head. You could almost watch the mechanical processes as the brain absorbed what I was telling him.

"Then it is to be civil war?"

"I do not wish for one. But these men need a cause, and fleeing from the king is not sufficient. If it were to come to it, would you foreswear our oath?"

His face had become impassive, and yet readable. All this had occurred to him. In a sense it was what he had come here this morning to find out. Yet what could he answer?

"Yahni, we have to rise against him. Not just for the sake of power. He's destroying Yisra-El. What he did at Ke'ilah has disgusted the whole nation. And this obsessive pursuit of me. Shmu-El is dying with his legacy in tatters."

Then suddenly, like a man on a high rock above a stream who has been dared to dive, but cannot face his own cowardice, suddenly he turned aside, stepped back from me.

"I will not rise against my father."

There. It was said.

"But you swore."

"I swore to make you king in Yisra-El. And so I shall. And I shall be your Bene Yamin, your right-hand-man. But I will not rise against my father. I would not rise against any king, whether he were my own father or someone else's. And nor will you, Daoud, if you truly hold Shmu-El's vision sacred. You cannot seize the throne and demand to be anointed. If it is to be, then time and the gods will bring it."

"Shmu-El brought it years ago. He anointed me when I was twelve..."

He wasn't listening to me. He was still rehearsing the same private argument that must have been raging in his head for months.

"However mad or bad he is, he is still Shmu-El's anointed king. Even when Shmu-El rejected him, he did not take back the anointing. To reject is not the same as to overthrow. We must have patience, Dodi. Our time will come."

"Then swear again."

"There's no need."

"For the sake of these men. They are eight hundred now. Every day more men come to me, soldiers mostly, good soldiers now since Ke'ilah. They have to have something to believe in. Swear an oath with me. Before the men."

To bind him to me, before his cold feet made him freeze completely, and in going on without him, the bond that previously held us came untied.

We clambered down the sheer face of the rock and across several screes until we came into the main camp in the clearing in the woods. The men had seen us scrambling, had gathered at the edge of the clearing. Some, no doubt, feared Yah-Natan had come to persuade me to abandon all of this, and had convinced others that I would surely yield. As we emerged into the gathering, Achi-Melech raised the chant of "Daoud Melech Yehudah" in a whisper that spread through the crowd like fire through scrubland. Hands clapping. Feet stamping. You would have thought they were trying to make me change my mind.

But it was obvious that I hadn't yielded. Or that he hadn't tried. I raised my arm and silence descended. I had never really tasted power before this day.

"Farewell, Prince Yah-Natan. May the gods give you their protection."

The formal poetry of politics. Gestures large as any actor on a stage. Voice projected to the very echoes. So, again, we embraced, and the men cheered. So Yah-Natan turned to demonstrate what makes a man a prince.

"Daoud ben Yishai, fear not. The hand of my father shall not find you because of me. You shall be king over all Yisra-El when the time comes, and I shall be your right hand. My father knows this. All Yisra-El knows this. Go with the protection of the gods."

Clever. All the right words carefully spoken, and all the wrong words carefully left out - but in the gaps between the words, ah, that is where great speakers can be truly eloquent. And after he had spoken, in the very clench of our embrace:

"I must go now. The Bene Ziph are not to be trusted, Dodi. They will betray your whereabouts as soon as they are sure of them. Remember Do'eg. And Dodi..."

"Yes."

"My father may be slow-witted, but my uncle Av-Ner isn't. He sent me a present last week. Beautifully made they were too. Three blunt arrows."

Whether it was indeed the Bene Ziph who betrayed us to Sha'ul, or simply Av-Ner's slow and methodical tracking of us, I have no idea, but eventually we were discovered in our stronghold in the wood. So we had to leave the hill of Chachilah, go further south of Yeshimon. With Avi-Yam encamped at Ramat Carmel, and rumours that many of the villages around Chevron had been bought over to the king's side with threats and promises, we had no choice but to turn west again, towards Yuttah and Sochoh he-Harim and Eshtemo'a. Have you ever visited those parts, Shlomo? You should you know, when circumstances favour a gentle tiyyul, in good walking shoes, and your head wrapped in linen for protection from the sun - the breeze is deceptive; you feel it on your face and think it's cooling you, whereas in fact it rubs you raw, and leaves you burned like pitta bread. But still well worth the visit. You will never see so many hare, long-necked and pinkish-brown and with great floppy ears like Mephi-Boshet's. The eagles hunt them constantly. Many a time we paused in the march to watch a tawny eagle swoop and gather up a hare between its claws, then carry it in great sweeps across the sky, until the female came out of the treetops on the far side of the hills, likewise sweeping back and forth across the sky; then the two would meet in mid-air, transfer the prey from beak to beak, and as the female sped away to feed her nest, down came the male again to search for still more hares. And if not hares, then mice - the hills are full of dormice - or partridges. A man could do worse than spend a few months in that wilderness!

At Eshtemo'a we found a spring of tepid water, warm enough to have a pleasant bathe in - though by the time six hundred men had bathed in it, perhaps it wasn't quite so pleasant any more. We made camp, lit fires, butchered the last of the heifers we had brought with from Chachilah, then threw off our cares and slept. A foolishness, no doubt. On my part anyway. Achi-Melech had more sense. While the rest of us slept off the exhaustion of months of living hand to mouth and fear to fear, he posted sentries at every spot from which we might be seen, three-hour duties that still allowed everyone to get a good night's rest. In the twilight hour before the dawn, Achi-Melech tapped me on the shoulder, holding his finger to his mouth to warn me to stay silent. I slipped into my sandals and threw my cloak around me, covering my head in my bernous. So I followed him.

A dozen soldiers of Manachat were drinking at the spring. Yahni's men - easily recognised, for they were the only ones to wear the scarlet on their hems, to denote their status as the prince's bodyguard. Sha'ul's men wore purple, of course, and the other generals' men the turquoise that was the pure colour of the murex. These carried shortswords, but no shields, so we knew them for footmen. To take them and kill them would have been a trifle, but Achi-Melech had a better idea. We crept up close and listened. Then, when the moment seemed right, we came out to the spring - two unarmed men of Eshtemo'a, indignant and outraged as any city Elders.

"Does the Prince Yah-Natan now rule the waters of the underworld, that his spies may drink at will?"

The double-meaning was not lost on them. Yahni's men lived in perpetual fear that the prince would one day find his banishment reinstated, and themselves by consequence forced with him into exile. It had happened twice already.

"We seek the rebel Daoud, in the name of the king of Yisra-El."

"The rebel Daoud? Against what, or whom, does he rebel?"

"Against the king."

"This is the spring of Eshtemo'a of Yehudah. The city was given by Abou Yehoshua to the Bene Levi, for a temple and a sanctuary. There can be no rebels in Eshtemo'a."

"We were not sent to break the laws of the sanctuary, but to seek the whereabouts of Daoud, and to report back. As to the water, it bubbles freely from the ground, so any man may drink."

Till now I had left it to Achi-Melech to play games with them. But eventually I could no longer resist.

"Does any one of you know the meaning of Eshtemo'a?"

Blank looks, inevitably. What man in any language ever really knows the meanings of the words he speaks?

"It means 'obedience'. And yet you come looking for rebels. Go back to General Yah-Natan. Tell him you found nothing in Eshtemo'a but obedience. From the city, and from Daoud whom you slander by calling him a rebel, nothing but obedience to the king."

"Then you have seen Daoud?"

"We have seen him, yes. He came this way. Go into the woods even now and you will find six hundred of his men. But you will not find Daoud, nor Achi-Melech his general, for they are not amongst them."

"Do you know then where they are?"

"Gone, I hear, to swear obedience to the king, who wrongs them by naming them rebels."

Ah, but the looks of consternation in their faces, the sheer pleasure of the game! We took much satisfaction, Achi-Melech and I, from teasing and taunting those footmen of Yah-Natan's that night.

And in the morning, while we were preparing a hearty breakfast before returning to the march, I played my lute for the best part of two hours, and wrote the first draft of that libretto that Asaph would much later set for string quartet and choir as a michtam: the memorial song, "Does the beloved not hide himself among us?"

"O you gods, in your name deliver me and in your strength judge me. You gods, hear my prayer, listen to the words of my mouth. For strangers have come up against me, and powerful men who do not worship the gods seek my life. Behold, the gods help me. The Lord sustains my life. May he return evil unto those who make me their enemy, may he make them thirst for his truth. I will make great sacrifices to you. I will give thanks to your name, Lord, for you are good. Because you delivered me from all my troubles when my enemies saw me at the spring."

The cry of a hounded fox, singing from the snare.

✡

There must be something useful we can learn from this remorseless, relentless, ceaseless persecution of me. It lasted years. It became his obsession. It really did become a kind of fox-hunt, in which I found myself continually fleeing from lair to lair. In pursuing me, he was really still hunting for his father's lost asses, in the hope that this time he might find and keep his throne - but in all the legends of Yisra-El, Shlomo, the red-haired elder brother is always supplanted by the moon-faced younger, and there is no evading destiny. Kayin by Hevel, Yishma-El by Abou Yitschak, Essav by Abou Yah-Akov, Zerach by Pharets. Am I wrong? Am I? Or was it really just his fear of what Shmu-El called "the companion"?

To be fair to him, if I had been Sha'ul, I would have taken measures to kill me too. Only I would have succeeded, and without his scruples.

I had my chance to kill him too. Twice I could have done it. Only regicide is a terrible offense to contemplate, as I have frequently had cause to remind my enemies, as Yahni had reminded me.

But all this is a digression. The journey into She'ol does not afford digressions.

Further and further south we went, through the Kerayot of Yehudah - where we were almost betrayed again - as far as Arad and Ramot Negev and the very edges of the mountains. But Sha'ul did

324

not give up his search for us. Any further south and we would enter the desert proper, the dry scrubland of the Negev, the waterless wasteland of the Aravah where Tohu and Bohu still ruled and the Aluphim of Edom would murder us before selling our bones to Sha'ul - perhaps that was his intention. I sent Yo-Av and Av-Yishai ahead to spy on him and keep us at least one step ahead.

Compared to the complex network of look-outs and passwords that we employed, his security was negligible to the point of being almost non-existent - surprising for one so thoroughly paranoid. Being the hunter, he must have supposed he didn't need to take the same precautions as the quarry - a handful of armed guards, throwing dice around the camp-fire, was deemed sufficient. I doubt it would have been so if Av-Ner or Yah-Natan had been in charge, but this was Sha'ul travelling with his men, and frankly anything seemed to go.

One night I went right down into his camp with Av-Yishai, entirely unnoticed. Men slept without their shoes, their swords scabbarded, their dagger-belts discarded, while those still awake were too busy cavorting with camp prostitutes to notice our intrusion. Wooden poles and stone pillars guarded enough tents for a fairground on the feast of Ishtar. I stood disbelieving that this was what the Bene Yisra-El had come to, though which shocked me the more - the asherah-worship or the arrogant slovenliness - it would be hard to say. Sha'ul was fast asleep in his trench - fallen there from drunkenness, I supposed - with his spear stuck in the ground in a bolster. Av-Ner and the other generals slept on the ground beside him.

"Let me kill them all," Av-Yishai whispered in my ear. Almost too loud, though it was scarcely audible. "Sha'ul, Av-Ner, Avi-Yam, ben Tuva'al, ben Raphu. Three of his sons are over there." He pointed to a huddle outside one of the greensleeves' tents, whether in pre- or post-coital slumber. "We could take out the whole chain of command and half the royal family and get away unnoticed." He made the gesture of slitting throats. "We'll never have such a chance again."

It really would have been that easy too. But I thought of Yahni's pained entreaty and said:

"No."

"Just the king then. I cut his throat, and we vanish as invisibly as we came. They'll think one of his own soldiers did it."

The thoughts - implications, ramifications - were speeding through my brain. Av-Ner would take command, and purge the army, in theory to find the traitor-murderer, in fact to assert his own authority. Then what? Shmu-El was dying, Gad had not yet imposed his claim above Natan's. Who could stop Av-Ner having Yah-Natan arrested on some trumped-up grounds connected with his having befriended me, and installing Ish-Boshet as king, with himself in real control as Regent? Then he would move to get rid of me, and would lack the qualms and the incompetence of Sha'ul. No, it had to be none of them, or all of them, and I would not take the throne in such a manner. The gods would reject me.

"Daoud!"

"No, Av-Yishai. You cannot kill a king. We are Bene Yisra-El, not chieftains of the Bene Chet or bastard children of Mitsrayim, whose mothers are also their sisters and their wives. It is more important that we let them know we could have done so. Take his spear. I'll take his water-cruse."

We scampered through a culvert, grabbed the gear, then clambered up the hill-slope with our trophies. Achi-Melech and Chetsron were waiting for us. Now, out of the darkness, like an owl hooting, the voice of Chetsron, my brother:

"Av-Ner! Av-Ner! Are you asleep? Fetch the king a drink, Av-Ner. It's dry and dusty in that narrow trench. Fetch the king his water-cruse. He needs a drink."

The speed at which his men responded was at once surprising and impressive. Surely if Av-Ner were made king, it would not be so easy for the bandit Daoud to remain in hiding in the wilderness!

"Daoud!"

Sha'ul's voice, baying like a new-moon hound.

In this wilderness of the wolves, surely he could have managed something better!

"Daoud!"

"Why are you pursuing me like this, Sha'ul? I have done nothing to harm you. I have done nothing to offend you. Where is my wife Michal? Did I not pay you the full dowry you demanded, twice over?"

Soldiers were gathering at the foot of the hill, ready to climb up and try to seize me. But in the shadows of the camp-fire I could see Sha'ul, wrapped in a woollen blanket, and Av-Ner beside him, his arm raised to hold the soldiers back.

I held the king's spear aloft.

"I could have killed you, Sha'ul. With your own spear even. Do you not know that I have no wish to kill you, but only to serve you, anointed king of Yisra-El. I do not, Sha'ul, hold anything against you. Let this be heard by all Yisra-El. I am your true and loyal servant. Stop pursuing me."

And choosing carefully a patch of ground where it could fall safely, I hurled his spear back at him, and the four of us disappeared into the night.

But he did not stop pursuing me. Indeed, quite the contrary. The patrols were stepped up, reinforcements added, new orders given - or so my spies and those who defected to us told me - that I was to be taken alive so I could be "duly punished" for threatening the king's life. Which meant torture, I presumed.

We turned north again, trusting that some at least of the villages had remained neutral. The truth was, of course, that they feared our bandit-raids as much as they did the king's anger, and consequently welcomed both sides with equally enthusiastic expressions of support, trusting that one side would not find out about the other. So we tramped ever deeper into the wilderness of Ma'on, until we had no choice at last but to turn eastward, to come down out of the mountains and enter the scrub-desert that led towards the Aravah. More dangerous now because more open. In place of concealing woods - wide empty plains, in which the gorse bushes provided a habitat for snakes, and the vast horizon, as formidable as the heavens themselves, would reveal at miles remove even a solitary hermit wandering in his delusions. We could not easily escape from Sha'ul here. The sun was rising ever higher, even as the moon appeared to wane. I speak, Shlomo, of the physical, as well as the mythological.

Even despite the numbers who continued to defect to us, what had taken place that night in Ramot Negev - the opportunity to kill the king not taken, my declaration of fealty - had reduced our numbers to less than four hundred. Men drifted away who had thought they were fighting for a kingdom and not the mere end of exile. Men disappeared in the darkness of the night who had anticipated glory and reward but now foresaw only a hot, dry death among the rocks and scorpions. Inevitably some sought the protection of the king, offering information on our whereabouts in exchange for their own lives - a foolhardy miscalculation: the king took what they had to give, and then their lives for treachery. Nor did it matter a jot what they may have told him. The very dust our feet made advertised our presence, like the pillar of cloud that guided Abou Mousa, like the milky way that maps the network of the stars. Now, four hundred was better anyway than eight, and frankly fifty would have been better still, for after Ke'ilah we had sworn not to engage again in battle, and to men in flight the greatest dangers lie in number. You can steal food for ten without arousing suspicions, but four hundred is an army on the march. There would be nothing but manna to eat in the Aravah.

Sha'ul pursued us, with Av-Ner, one on either side of the mountain, all the way down to the Sea of Aravah. This, we had always known, would be the point of no return. To the east now - only the dead, salt sea and the Nefud, the hottest desert in the world beyond. To the south - miles and miles of salt pans and gomorrahed cities, leading ultimately to Edom. If we could find a route due north, perhaps we might find sanctuary in Mo-Av. But Sha'ul's armies had blocked every passage. Which way then? Which way? Being much quicker than they, we were able to reach the springs and waterfalls of Ein Gedi, the one and only place in all this wilderness where we might continue to evade them, and survive.

And then, precisely then, because the gods were on our side, a respite. Just when we were expecting his last assault, we learned that he had been called away. The Bene Pelet had attacked Sela ha-Machlekot, thinking to take advantage of the king's protracted absence with his armies. More fool them - a fox is never more vicious than when it thinks it has been out-cunninged. He took only such men as he thought he would require, leaving the rest to keep us pinioned in the Aravah. There were rumours of massacres, of a hundred women of the Bene Naphtali taken from a neighbouring town, murdered at the very gates of Sela to press surrender. There were rumours against Sha'ul as well, of soldiers refusing to carry out his orders, preferring to have their own throats cut rather than do the deeds of darkness he insisted on. Rumours! Once gain a reputation and it is never possible to shed it. Probably he was sitting in the shouk at Sela, smoking poppy-juice with the Elders and handing out almond-sweets to kiddies, pretending that his pursuit of me was really just a clever pretext to effect the conquest of Yehudah. But no, upon reflection, not Sha'ul. The rumours were more likely litotes than hyperbole, and he wasn't that clever. Whatever the reality, soon enough Sela ha-Machlekot deserved its name. The city held, as firm as any rock. The Bene Pelet fled.

If a man has to prepare for his own death, there can be few more stunning places in the world in which to do it than Ein Gedi. Steep coombs climbed up to rocky crags, each one ending in another spring, another waterfall. Where flowers grew, they did so in such abundance and rich colours that all the poets and all the lovers in the world could have gone on picking till eternity and never reached the end of such infinite variety. Beyond us the still greater infinitude of desert, sea, hills. The mountain goats were kidding everywhere - I helped myself with birthing one pair, both of them breached so tight it tore the mother's uterus to shreds to get them out. The water in the springs and falls was icy cold, but sweet enough to drink your fill and more than pleasant in that dry intensity of heat to swim in. We saw leopards a-plenty in the hills, but they were more wary of us than we of them. We spent long hours playing at floating on the salt water of the dead sea, belly-up like dead men, yet seemingly granted immortality. Perhaps it was an omen.

Until Sha'ul returned, with three thousand men, and the hunt resumed among the rocks of the wild goats and the hill pools and the waterfalls. We had no plan except to continue for as long as possible to elude him, and to make our getaway to Mo-Av as soon as chance allowed. And as to Sha'ul, it began to seem as though he were tiring of the chase, or as if, perhaps, he didn't really mean to capture me at all, but only to pursue me through the underworld till one of us came out the other side, the conqueror of death. For there were many opportunities, missed by misadventure, or by blunder - in truth, Sha'ul couldn't find the haystack, let alone the needle - or it could as well have been design. Yet here we were, at the Spring of the Goats, in the season of the goats, with the constellation of the goat at its zenith in the skies, in the very year of the goat. And me still not taken for the sacrifice.

And then, one night, Sha'ul went into a sheepcote to rest. We had been watching him, I and my men, for hours, far more closely than his footmen ever came near us. Deep in thought, alone save for two of his stewards who were keeping watch, he appeared to be consulting with the dark gods who inhabited his sleep at night and now were tormenting him so thoroughly he couldn't even sleep. In such moods did he require blood, or the kisses of young men, to soothe him. But there were only himself, the lilim, and a viper, diamond-browed, white as a glinting dagger, creeping through the cactuses to where he walked. How tempting, equally to call out and warn him, or to stay quiet and let events take their course. But Sha'ul was not afraid of living creatures - it was the imaginary ones that so unbalanced him. He saw the viper, crouched to face it, hissed to make it run away. Delight softened his features. In the dispatching of the snake, he had exorcised the inner daemons too. So now he could sleep. So now he turned into the sheepcote.

We waited, my men and I. He took off his woollen overcloak and laid it down for a quilt. Within minutes he was fast asleep, his arm over his eyes like a dumb chicken, and not a guard in fifty paces save those stewards whom we took captive without so much as a squeal of surprise. I made my way down the stony path to the pen, crawled in, and as he slept I cut a piece of cloth from the front of his cloak – "privily", as the annals so delicately put it - a trophy to put with the water-cruse, or to give back to him in barter for my life. Even as I did it, I was repenting of the deed. The sin of Kena'an, performed against the king of the Bene Kena'an. Perhaps I did next what I did next, out of need to expiate that sin. Perhaps. I only know that, for the second time, I could, perhaps I should, have cut his throat. He knew it too.

I crawled outside, put away my knife, gestured to the men who were awaiting me to stay quiet, but on guard. Then I called in to the cave:

"Sha'ul! My lord the king!"

He awoke with a start, reached for his dagger, found his clothes torn, understood. What a sight I must have offered, not obviously Daoud at first - a shepherd-boy prostrate on the ground before the entrance to a sheepfold. When I raised myself onto my knees, I saw only the shades of the cave upon which the sheepcote opened and whose gate it formed, the terrors and furies of the deeps and darknesses, reflected in the shadows of his face. I was, indeed, confronting the very king of the underworld, on his throne, in his eternal realm. And he was terrified.

"Why do you listen to men who hate me out of jealousy and lie to you that I wish you harm? If I had truly wanted you dead, I could have killed you right here, and no one would have known who did it. Across the whole of Yehudah men would rise and proclaim me king, first in Yehudah, then in Yisra-El. Shmu-El would support me, Gad and Natan too. Av-Ner, the other generals, do you think they wouldn't rally round the hero of Sochoh and Gat? If I wanted to be king, Sha'ul, I could be king tomorrow. But I have come to prostrate myself at your feet, and to tell you that I am your loyal servant."

All that, and how much more that the chroniclers have made up - all sorts of unnecessary symbolisms for the hard-of-understanding, such as "the moon does not wish to rule by day", and that proverb about the punishment for the wicked proceeding from the wicked, and a quite fatuous remark about dead dogs hunting for fleas - as if I would ever have referred to myself as a species of flea. The truth is, I said very little. Eyes speak more eloquently than mouths. We stared for a long time into each other's eyes, but I shall not say what memories of staring into each other's eyes were kindled. At one point he reached for my hand, and though I let him take it, I resisted his attempt to draw me into an embrace. Not that I feared his knife. It was his tears that troubled me. It was his slobbering, his self-deprecations, his pathetic whining, the desperate black darkness of his inner sufferings which he would have poured out on top of me and then inside of me if I had given him even half the chance.

"You're a better man than me, Daoud. I'm not good. I'm not righteous. You've rewarded me, where I've sought only to punish you."

It was quite sickening, to tell the truth. Such bathos! If a man had a camel or a donkey, and it bled and pussed and suppurated in that manner, he would put the poor beast out of its misery. Whereas all I could do was try not to show him my contempt.

"I loved you, Daoud."

Past tense, Sha'ul? Why suddenly the past tense. You mean this entire pursuit of me is not precisely because you still do. Go on, confess it.

"I could still love you, Daoud. But you betrayed me."

How? By marrying your daughter and befriending your son? By fighting your battles for you, at Gat, and Ke'ilah. Is this betrayal?

"Do you know how much pleasure your love gave me?"

Do you know much hatred your love engendered in me, Sha'ul.

Your sick, disgusting, perverted abomination of a so-called love for me. In me. On me. Up me. I was trembling with rage just thinking of it. I could have cut his throat so very easily.

"But you took everything from me. My son. My daughter. And my kingdom."

How can any human being allow himself to degenerate like this? How low can you rise? Are there not enough pitfalls in this world, enough traps, enough misfortunes, enough tragedies, enough disasters, that a man needs to throw himself deliberately into the mire, and wallow there with such self-pity? He was like a doormat on which somebody had inscribed: "Please walk on me. Please rub your filthy shoes all over me with utmost vigour. Please help me to fulfil my destiny."

"Daoud, I never wanted to be king - you know that, don't you?"

No, he was just being devious. Sha'ul would manipulate the very fates if such a chance befell him. And cut the throats of the gods, if it served his purposes.

"Swear me an oath, that you will not cut off my seed when I am dead, that you will not destroy my name, nor that of my father's house."

Meaning that miserable weakling Mephi-Boshet and his equally wretched younger brothers. And Merav of course. He knew well enough that I would never harm Michal or Yah-Natan. Yet what was he really thinking? That through me, through such an oath, he might yet found a dynasty after all, that Shmu-El's prophecy might be confounded? The fool! Did it not occur to him that a child fathered by me upon Michal would already prolong his dynasty and extend thereby his journey to oblivion? But then. But then. Perhaps it did occur to him. Perhaps he knew what I had long suspected. That where other women are called barren, that Our Lady's name might better be exalted when her priestesses give birth, in Michal's case it was entirely adjectival. For a moment I felt the deepest pity for him, and all my hatred vanished in its wake.

"I will swear, Sha'ul. I will swear such an oath, and you in return will swear to stop pursuing me."

So tight was he squeezing my hand, the knuckles were quite blenched and throbbing. Now he squeezed still tighter, a last gesture as it seemed of the authority he was at last reconciled to ceding to me. He pulled me so close I could smell his old man's breath and taste the memory of his kisses. I put my hand beneath his thigh - it was made of lard, not muscle - but emptily, unmoving, where once such a gesture had implied not just the swearing of an oath, but the promise of a whole night's passion. My body was stiff and trembling and trying to draw back. I swore.

"In the name of the gods of Yisra-El, I swear to maintain the House of Sha'ul ben Kish after he is gone, and to preserve his name, with the names of his ancestors, forever and forever."

"Swear by Yah, Daoud. The gods of Yisra-El are not the gods you worship; they are only the gods to whom you pay tribute when you must. Swear by Yah. She is your true mother."

The bones in my fingers were close to breaking.

"In the name of Our Lady of Sorrows and of Mercy, the Mother-Of-All-Living, the Rose of Sharon and of Yareyacho, the Queen of Heaven, and in the name of her beloved son Utu, Tammuz, Dumuzi, Yeshia-Hu, Lord of the House of the Corn of Ephratah, Adonis Adonai, and in the name of her consort Yahweh, what I have sworn unto the gods of Yisra-El, so now do I repeat my vow to her. Let Sha'ul live for ever."

He held my fingers for a long while afterwards, staring all the while into my eyes as though he were seeking evidence of mendacity. But there was none there to be found.

"Your friends," he said at last, "the ones who are hiding outside to hear us. They are our witnesses."

I nodded even as I turned and left. So Lavan and Abou Yah-Akov must have parted at Gal-Ed.

I could have killed him. Perhaps I should have killed him. But I spared him. And for a while there was peace between us.

I nearly wrote: so we were reconciled again. But it was not so. Sha'ul went home to Giv-Yah. But I and my meagre army of malcontents remained in the hills of Aravah. For if we were not yet reconciled, how much still further off the day of our reprieve?

And Shlomo, do this for me. Look after Mephi-Boshet, and keep him and Ziva from their quarrels. For the sake of my promise to Sha'ul. And in memory of Yah-Natan. Do this for me.

✡

At Aravah, in the hills of Ein Gedi, as we watched the armies of Sha'ul retreat, I wrote this psalm:

To the Chief Musician, a song to be played to the melody of "Al Tashket - Do Not Destroy Me"; a Michtam of Daoud ben Yishai, when he left Sha'ul in the sheepcote and the cave:

"Be merciful unto me, you gods, be merciful for my soul has fled to take refuge in you and in the shadow of your wing. Let me hide till my distress is passed. I will call to the god of gods, Elohim Elyon, the god who will plead my cause. He will send from heaven and deliver me. He scorns those who thirst for my blood. The gods will send their love and truth. My soul is in flames. I will lie down in the furnace. The teeth of men are like spears and arrows, their tongues as sharp as daggers. O you gods, exalt yourselves unto the heavens and let your glory be on all the Earth. They have prepared a net for my footsteps, to bow my soul down. They have dug a pit before me, but they themselves have fallen into it. My heart is ready, Lord, my heart is ready. I will write poems and I will write psalms. Awake my glory, awake psaltery and harp and I will awaken the dawn. I will praise you among the tribes, Lord, and I will sing you to the nations. For your love is as great as the heavens and your truth soars as high as the clouds. Be exalted to the heavens, o you gods, and let your glory be on all the earth."

The words of the psalms are nothing, Shlomo. Nothing - or mere libretto. The music is everything, the intensity of inwardness engendered by the act of singing, the capacity to touch your own pulse, and to feel it beating. The music, the singing, not the words. And yet, setting down that psalm, I knew I had never written better in my life.

Parchment Twelve

Shlomo, there are two subjects upon which I wish to speak most seriously, for they are matters that concern us greatly. First, burial. The priests and prophets have been disputing the matter, passionately, pedantically, bigotedly, but inconclusively, for most of the last ten years, and rather than have every one of your advisers tell you what they would like you to think I would have thought, in order to persuade you to think it in my name, there now follows a brief discourse on a subject that grows increasingly close to me with every day of sickness and disease that mercifully passes.

The Laws of Abou Mousa allow priestly burial for everyone, including suicides, criminals, adulterers and enemies - let there be no alteration to that. In the intense heat of these lands, Shlomo, burial must be on the same day, or at the very latest on the day after. No expensive shrouds, no ornamented funeral wagons, no wooden casks, no jewellery - as we came in, so let us go out. Seven days of mourning, thirty days of continuation, a full year for parents and children. These are immutable. Do not let anyone persuade you otherwise.

As to the burial itself. The Laws of Abou Mousa rightly condemn the practices of the Bene Mitsrayim. Did you witness the preparations when your father-in-law died? I was invited to attend the ceremonies for Mechen-Atep, the ambassador of Pharaoh Shishak who died during the negotiations over the desert wells. Utterly gruesome and quite barbaric - other people's customs always are. They cut his head open and took the bits out, replaced it with a sort of gummy paste. Have you ever seen a human brain? A cross between knotted sheep's wool and the oily outsides of a fish. I looked as closely as I could, but there were absolutely no working parts at all, no joints, no cartilage, nothing that you could construe as the organs for thought, or memory, or dream. Just a rather smelly mess not unlike the stomach of a goat. Those who wish to convince me that the brain is the source of intellectual activity, rather than the heart, still have a great deal of work to do.

However, the ceremony. Once the brains were glutinised (I have no proof, but I suspect that they were eventually taken away and eaten) they embalmed the body to protect it against corruption - a foolhardiness, given the lives that most men lead! First the priests consecrated the body, then wrapped it in strips of cloth, reciting various magical incantations as they did so. Then the chief priest took a vial containing no less than ten different perfumes, and smeared the body twice from head to foot, the head receiving particularly close attention. The internal organs that had been removed along with the brain were then placed on the body, the backbone immersed in holy oils which supposedly emanate from the veins of Shu and Geb. A number of precious stones were laid on the mummy, each with its own magical properties - crystal to lighten his face, carnelian to strengthen his steps. Then came the best part - I had great difficulty restraining my laughter, but I suppose all ritual is theatrical, all ceremonies a performance before a crowd, all priests and choristers actors: for some mime-plays we suspend our disbelief, for others our lack of faith; these two are not entirely the same.

A priest wearing a jackal's-head mask to represent Anpu the Conductor of Souls performed all manner of balletic hand movements and body postures and mantric mumbling-jumblings. The head was anointed again, the left hand filled with thirty-six rather disgusting substances, each representing a different form of Osher. Then still more holy oil. The toes that had been left sticking out were wrapped in linen, and after an interminably long and boring address, compounded mostly of quotations from their Tablets of the Dead and eulogies to the great man's supposed virtues, the ceremony was at last completed with the depositing of the mummy in a wooden cask painted in the most lurid greens and yellows with scenes from the mythologies of their animal-gods. You will have deduced that I am not recommending this for a new fashion amongst the Bene Yisra-El. You will have understood why the royal prince Mousa ibn Ra-Mousa was so keen to identify himself with the Habiru cause and seek an excuse for leaving Mitsrayim.

Amongst the Bene Ammon and the Bene Ashur you will find stone burials, dolmen and menhirs the size of the pillars of Gil-Gal marking every imaginable sort of barrow - long-barrows, gallery-barrows, passage-barrows, round-barrows. Amongst the Bene Gil-Yad clay ossuaries for bones gathered back from the burial grounds so that others may use the site - the ossuaries themselves reburied in cave tombs. In parts of Mo-Av they still practice that most ancient rite of inhumation that we used to bury my sister Tamar, setting the body in a shallow hole no larger than the human corpse, laying alongside it jars and ornaments, so that the deceased may not go impoverished into the next world. Next world indeed! This practice must be opposed. The burial is good - human bodies make excellent manure, and a graveyard, after a hundred years or so, may be recycled into fertile pastureland. But this growing belief in an afterlife disturbs me greatly. It is a foolishness that men have learned from that mystic Zoroaster, the Prophet of the Bene Elam as king Hu-Ram calls him - grandfather Oved studied his book the Zend-Avesta, and knew a man who travelled to the lands of the Bene Elam to worship at his feet. It is a cult that I abhor, Shlomo, because it preaches the division of all things into two, not as a natural process of bifurcation from a common root, but through opposition, distinct force combating distinct force, and thereby denies and destroys the fundamental Unity of life and man and god. On the one hand Or-Muz'd, the power of light, and on the other Ach-Riman, the power of darkness, these two competing in everything, from night and day and life and death to the hearts and minds and souls of men and women. A religion that preaches division, that encourages fragmentation, that positively embraces conflict. No, Shlomo, in Yisra-El at least it must be fought against. In Yisra-El, the Lord is One - the fragmented parts which are the universe are seeking reunification with the single body, as a man seeks a woman to recover his complete hermaphroditic self: and not the other way around. It may only seem like a matter of direction, but the direction is everything. Towards the whole, not away from it. Unity, not Fragmentation. And in the cult of Yahweh there can be no afterlife. You cannot have a Temple and an afterlife, Shlomo. You must decide.

The burying of infants in jars is a custom I fully approve, though many of the priests condemn it simply because it is a tradition of the Bene Chor. We buried your elder brother that way – Bat Sheva's first child, I mean, the one that Natan cursed. Which brings us to the controversial custom of cremation, which the Laws of Abou Mousa do not mention, presumably because in Mitsrayim it was unheard of, and in Kena'an so rare as to be almost extinct. Not any longer, it would seem, from the number of petitions against them foisted on me these past years. Gad will tell you that anything committed to the fire by a priest has a holy implication, and that you cannot make burnt offerings of human beings. But that is absurd, as it is not done in a Temple, and it is not for the purposes of eating. If the priests were not so reluctant I would authorise them straight away, for it seems to me an entirely satisfactory way of getting rid of what is no longer wanted - far more hygienic than burial too. But there are sentimentalists among us, who cannot accept the finality of death, who yearn for afterlives and even of being born again - some resurrected in the same form, some reincarnated in a different one; it all seems to depend on whether you had a happy life or not, which way you would prefer to come back again; but it is superstition either way. A body burned with fire cannot come back again – that is the unstated hidden agenda of the petitioners-against-cremation. And I say, a man dies and goes down into the earth, into She'ol, where he corrupts into food for worms, or burns in the fires that heat the centre of the planet. Life before death is what matters, not life after it. Because that is all there is. Dust to dust and ashes to ashes. What difference can it make if we burn before or after burial? - some of us spend our whole lives burning, and the fires are never quenched! Among the Bene Kessed you will find charnel houses in abundance. Among the various tribes of the Bene Yavan the funeral pyre is commonplace, as among the Bene Chet, and I have heard of tribes east of Elam where it is the custom of wives to throw themselves still living upon their husband's pyre - this I would oppose. Likewise the custom of the Bene Chem, where whole battalions are taken down into the grave with the dead: wives, children, servants, even cattle.

Now, this is what I recommend, for those who can afford it - such as royal monarchs when finally I depart this life. A low chamber cut from the rock on some steep hillside, approached by a shaft or passageway and closed with a single stone or pile of rubble. The chamber should be ranged from three to ten feet, thus providing a vault which can be used for the whole family. I have seen tombs like these - they call them sarcophagoi - in Aram and in Mo-Av, and our friend Hu-Ram has built himself a most splendid one at Tsur. But with his people too the preparation for the afterlife is now endemic. I have seen tombs filled, literally filled, with weaponry and food, with clothing, even beds, tables, stools, baskets - gameboards, can you believe it? This you must not allow. But the chambers are excellent – Sha'ul built one, as I think I wrote some months ago, for his father at Giv-Yah. The great advantage is that the tombs can be extended, even re-used - you simply build a new tomb at the side and interconnect the chambers.

It was such a tomb - the point, in truth, of all this dissertation - that I built for Shmu-El when at last we were able to fulfil his dream and establish Yiru-Sala'am between the Mount of Olives and the Hill of Ophel. Because Shmu-El died, you see - even Shmu-El! While I was being hunted through the Aravah by Sha'ul in disputation of his prophecy, he was at Ramah, being ushered into She'ol, dying, of old age and...Now here is a thought for you, my beloved Yedid-Yah. Your mother lives on a diet of berries and wheats, touches nothing, not even a carrot or a lump of cheese, in which a trace of fat or sugar might be found, drinks red wine and eats raw fish, steers clear of any activity that might be deemed "unsafe", swims twice a day in purified spring water for some purpose I have never fathomed, sits only on chairs and sleeps only on beds that have been upholstered to the exact construction of her spine - and the gods only know how many more foibles and phobias and philtres and pharmacies designed to keep her young and fit. Yet here she is dying of some cancer of the skin at sixty-two. Whereas Shmu-El.

He could have been forty, or even eighty-five - his age was an enigma, like his oracles. Repeated fasting had taken its toll upon his gut, his liver, his pancreas. Desert-wandering had dried out his kidneys, which had produced stones as hard as the blisters on his feet. The veins in his legs were varicose, and continually ulcerating so the skin was blotched and purple. His knee and hip joints were ruined. His eyes were so milky white with cataracts, the truth was he was practically blind. So swollen was his prostate gland, he rose three times each night to undergo the agony of emptying his bladder. Hail a man who lived a full and vigorous life! Hail a man of passion and achievement! Hail a man, battered by the winds of time, besieged by the salts of time, fallen like a ravaged fortress! How else should a man end his life, but unvanquished and unyielding? Lord, let me die, on top of Avi-Shag, not underneath her!

Even at that great age his authority across the land was undiminished. The king of the Bene Lachish was awaiting audience on the very day he died - a king of the Bene Pelet, come to seek advice from the Prophet of his enemy the Bene Yisra-El. But Shmu-El was too busy to see him - not too busy dying, or resting, but too busy answering a letter from a priest at Carm-El of Zvulun, who needed instruction in some confusing point of law. Not confusing to Shmu-El, it must be said, who ate a hearty breakfast containing every unhealthy food imaginable, baked or fried in olive oil, and then exegised in seven erudite and lucid strips of parchment before going to lie down, complaining of pains in his chest that were probably just indigestion, and insisting that Bat-Yah, his wife, wake him after no more than an hour because a man with the Lord's business to attend to has no time to waste on sleeping. So he lay down on his straw mat, and never woke again, except at the very final moment when some sharp pain - probably the deep-fried aubergines - first caused him to stir, then stopped his pulse. I know this because Bat-Yah came in to wake him, and realised from the silence - he always snored like a lion when he slept - that he was dead; yet still she had to close his eyes.

Remarkable woman, Bat-Yah - but then you had to be remarkable, to live with Shmu-El for fifteen years. His first wife, Devorah bat Ber-El of the Bene Re'u-Ven, managed thirty, and died of it. But she at least was the same age as him, and had two sons to raise whenever he was absent - as he mostly was. Bat-Yah was still a young woman when he married her - out of pity; do you know the story? I am sure I must have told it in these pages somewhere. How she was raped by soldiers of the Bene Pelet, and her husband, being a Cohen, a priest, was instructed that he must divorce her, because the violation rendered her impure. Cruelty exacerbating cruelty. Shmu-El's anger at this outrage was enough to shake the gods themselves. He would have rolled out earthquakes and volcanoes if he had been able, but instead he had to fall back on significant gesturing. He took the girl into his own home, and married her himself. Never slept with her, mind, whether to spare her his snores or because his prostate had unmanned him. But as an act of charity it was of the highest order.

It was Bat-Yah who washed the body and laid out the strips of cloth to wrap him in for burial. A simple grave, in the burial-grounds at Ramah - not yet the majestic tomb which, I am perfectly aware, would have reduced him to frothing indignation and sermons denouncing me across the land. But what a funeral! Nothing like it since they brought the bones of Abou Yah-Suph out of Mitsrayim and buried them at Shechem. I sent to Sha'ul for permission to attend, with messengers separately to Michal and Yah-Natan to speak on my behalf. Permission was granted - we were theoretically "reconciled" by then. I took a bodyguard anyway - the famous

340

"Thirty" on their first public outing. It seemed judicious.

The bier was carried to the burial-ground by his two sons and his two household servants - another characteristic gesture of humility and magnanimity. In both cases, for it honoured the boys he had years before disowned as much as it gave status to men who would otherwise have had to mourn alone. Igal ben Chor in particular had been with him for the best part of forty years, as scribe, secretary and general amanuensis. Should a man be disbarred from grieving for his closest friend, simply because he is born of the "wrong" tribe? Even in death, Shmu-El never ceased to issue homiletics, to dabble in politics, to mark his oracles upon the walls.

Nor was the king of Lachish alone in awaiting audience on the day he died. Word that his time was fast approaching had spread across the country weeks before, and people began to gather almost at once, rather than wait for news of the death itself, for then they would be too late for the funeral. They came from every tribe, and from lands far beyond our borders, Elders and ambassadors because they were sent, though in most cases they would have come gladly, as the paupers and the common people came, prepared if necessary to sleep beside the road for days on end, just to be able to say that they were there, just to ensure they had the chance to touch the garment of the soldier who was protecting the aides of the Elders who were escorting the families of the women who were standing by to light the candles...superstition, Shlomo, atavistic superstition. Plus a great deal of reverence and exaltation for one who was amongst the very greatest that had ever lived. They draped flowers everywhere. At the roadside especially, where the cortège was due to pass, and at the entrance to his house, and all around the burial grounds at Ramah, and on his mother's tomb at Ramatayim Tsophim, and in the ruins of Shiloh where they fasted and held special services of commemoration, not for the usual seven days, but for the full thirty days of continuation that had been given over to mourning Abou Mousa in the desert.

"El maleh rachamim shochen ba-meromim... the compassionate god who dwells on high."

Amid the wailing of mourners, both amateur and professional, I listened to the singing of the formal liturgy. A wonderful voice, a deep, rich tenor full of the most varied colours and a gravitas that would have made you weep for grieving even in a mime-play. All of our heads were bowed down to the ground, yet I could feel Yahni's eyes upon me all the while, and at last I caught his glance. With a sideways look, he directed me towards the cantor, and then I recognised, beneath the thin moustache, Yitschak ben Gershon, the young priest of Gil-Gal whose ignorance of the sagas of the gods had nearly cost me my life - it seemed like years and years ago. He had survived then. He had done well. Escaped Sha'ul's clutches with his head intact. Shmu-El had found him, Asaph had trained him - later I would appoint him as my Chief Musician - but now he had the honour I would have given my eye-teeth for, of intoning the prayers beside the grave. And what a voice! Those ululations! Those vibrati! Those oscillations, Shlomo, between major and minor keys - the key to all our music. From phrase to phrase, the song of mourning breaking into the cry of joy, and then reverting, then reviving, fourth, fifth, again and again, minor fall, major lift, like the flux and reflux of our history.

"Ana ba'al ha-rachamim zachrah lo le-tovah kol zechiyotav ve-tsidkotav be-artsot ha-chayim...We implore you, in your compassion, to remember him with favour for all the just and charitable deeds he did on earth."

So many, we might have gone on praying till eternity.

✡

Shlomo, I said before that there were two subjects upon which I wished to speak most seriously. Heed me then, closely, awhile.

I have studied, as you know well, the ancient scriptures – our own especially, but other people's too – and listened for interminable hours to the tales that are handed down from generation to generation, mostly by people who have misremembered large parts, and added what they believe to be their own improvements. I have tried to become a master of the tales in order to become a wiser king. Your own education has been my concern as well, and perhaps you are now wise enough to understand that in giving you and not your brothers so intellectual a training, it was always my intention to make you my successor. Your mother would have preferred you to be a military man, or a sporting champion, but that is not the way of Yahweh. I have tried to make you learned, Shlomo, because wisdom is the pulse of our people. To make a culture you need compost. For a human being, for a nation, for a civilisation, that compost is education. To study the tales, oral and written down. To have the capacity to argue from any point of view, using the tales as evidence. To be able to create your own texts, whether of poetry or rhetoric or mere aphorisms. And yes, for necessity, military prowess; as, for leisure, sport. A king with all these attributes could build a fine civilisation, and earn himself a kind of immortality - as you will, Shlomo, I have no doubt. You have a grasp of history, of tradition, of necessity. You see the future clearly, and can temper your romantic visions with the pragmatism of expediency. All this is good, Shlomo. Very good.

Ask yourself, each morning that you reign - what makes our people different from any other people? How shall we become a light unto the nations? That is our task, after all. That is the inheritance that Abou Mousa bequeathed to us, in the name of Yahweh, under the banner of Nechushtan, the serpent of the Great Goddess. To become Am Kadosh - a Holy People - sacred unto Yah and Yahweh, chosen by Yahweh to serve him with six hundred and thirteen laws - not just the seven laws of No'ach that bind all men. Forget my "heroic exploits"; they are as nothing - mere adventures. This is my real legacy, *to* you, but especially *through* you. Forget the game of fox-and-hounds I played with Sha'ul, and prepare yourself to make your own contribution to the literature of wisdom. Shlomo, any bullying oaf can make and hold an empire - for a while anyway - but only a great king can found a civilisation. The one takes war, the other peace. The one a fist, the other wisdom. Our covenant with Yahweh is not a builder's contract, to construct a temporary empire, which will flare up like a fire from heaven and die out like a supernova in a single generation. Our task is to build a peace and light that can endure for ever.

Now heed me further, Shlomo. The people of our dear friend Hu-Ram have developed this new skill of writing that is accessible to all men and which has allowed us at last to write down in scrolls, and in our own tongue, the Laws of Abou Mousa and the Legends of our ancestors that until now have only existed in oral form or in the picture-language of the Bene Chem. Learn it. Use it. Ensure that every adult male in Yisra-El has the capacity to write and read it; yes, and the women too; thank you Sera-Yah, for the reminder. Universal adult literacy. Now there's a goal no people ever set itself before.

But the tales are not merely literature and theology. They contain our history, our traditions, our social structure, our fiscal system, our ethical code, our priestly institutions. Yes, and poetry, fables, learned disputations. Studying these texts is not the imbibing of all wisdom - but can you suggest a better starting-point? When you have built the Temple, Shlomo, institute this as a fundamental precept for all our people - that the whole Law be read in annual cycle, week by week, so that every man shall know it intimately. Not once a year, as Yehoshua ben Nun ordained at Shechem to renew the covenant, but every week, on the Shabbat at every shrine, and on the two market days, in the gates of every city. And build more schools, Shlomo, so all our people should have the opportunity to study - not just the young, not just the priests and scribes and clerics, but all men, of all ages, for the sake and for the pleasure, until the day they die: all women too, perhaps, one day, as your stepmother Avi-Gayil would insist; though this, I suspect, you will find it more difficult, because the men in their foolhardiness will resist it, fearing that education will enable women to recognise their inequality, and then demand its rectification. But there is no true civilisation where there is no equality, of all human creatures, as fully independent and autonomous human creatures. Alongside universal adult literacy, make this your second goal - universal adult education. In the name of Shmu-El, our master.

Men may be as wicked as they may be good, and temptation is often irresistible. But until men have the capacity to know within themselves what good is, and what evil, how can they know which temptations to resist and which to enjoy? I have asked both Gad and Natan to help me with this question, but they are neither of them of Shmu-El's stature. All they can give me are rehearsed polemics, quotes from scripture, zeitgeist opinions, hand-me-downs that I could as easily find in any broadsheet; the sort that people hold because everybody else is holding them, but without taking the trouble to think them through; the answers of men who frankly do not know. "Ah, Daoud, these are mysteries of Yah and Yahweh beyond the capability of men to understand." Shtuyot! Nonsense! They may be beyond your capability to understand, but that is only because you refuse to try. Ah, Shlomo. Once we had Judges. Then we had Shmu-El, who was a Judge and a Prophet. Now we have Kings and so the Judges are no more. But where is the Prophet to succeed Shmu-El, to pronounce the oracles, to utter the prophecies? Men bear the title "Elder of the Guild of Prophets", but they are no more prophetic for bearing the name than I am a blacksmith because I once dipped my own sword in the fire. That, too, is why you must build the Temple, Shlomo, why you must compel the Bene Yisra-El to discard their other gods. To train men who can rise to the true stature, to provide a stage worthy of such an actor, to draft a mime-play of such vaulted architecture that it is strong enough to contain these fundamental questions. It is not the religion that men need, Shlomo, but the structures that can channel the divine *within themselves*.

The god of gods planted the Tree of Knowledge of Good and Evil in the Garden at Edinu, placing it alongside the Tree of Life. Why? He gave explicit orders not to eat the fruit of those two trees, knowing full well that every child becomes an adult by rebelling precisely against those things their parents most forbid them. Then why? He who was almighty and controlled all things, created the serpent and allowed it to seduce Chava our Great Mother. Why? He gave us - Mankind - dominion over all the Earth, and everything that lives upon the Earth, and a set of Laws to enable us to fulfil so heavy a responsibility. Why, if he intended to continue ruling over us himself? Why, if he was going to interfere in human history and predetermine everything? These are the questions that still trouble me, but no grandfather Oved, no Shmu-El, to give me succour. The god of gods gave us the burden of responsibility, for Earth, for good and evil, life and knowledge. Yet how can we assume that burden of responsibility if we do not, each of us and every day, go on forever plucking and re-plucking the forbidden fruit of those two trees? Find me a Prophet who can answer that, Shlomo.

Build the Temple, Shlomo, that it be a shrine to house the Law, an altar to contain the sacrifices, a palace for the god of gods, a school to teach our people, a stage for choir and orchestra and mime-play, and a beacon to the generations yet to come. A structure that can channel the divine. Praise the Lord, all you nations. Praise him, all you people. For his merciful kindness is great towards us, and the truths of the Lord endure forever. And praise the Lady too, for the male Lord cannot be One without his female counterpart. Hallelu-Yahweh. Hallelu-Yah.

345

Parchment Thirteen

Not a word, not a look, not so much as a message passed between the king and me. I had been permitted to take part in a national day of mourning, but that was all. Not even to see my wife. Now it was expected that I would depart as I had come, in dignified silence, and at speed. So it was.

We left Ramah immediately after Shmu-El's burial and turned towards the wilderness of Paran. Only a few dozen of us had gone to Ramah, but Achi-Melech had brought the rest as far as Manachat, and we all turned back towards Arad together – we had established our new headquarters among the ruins of the ancient city. The sun was furnace-hot; the desert seemed to be infested with colonies of wild goats; a wind out of the Aravah was blowing a dust-storm across our path that harbingered the coming chamsin. We rode for seven hours without pausing, till our water-gourds were drained and our hope of reaching our destination before nightfall empty. The faster we went, the more the winds obstructed us - the way you will sometimes see a bird baulked by the wind, held static by it, so it will flap its wings frenetically, simply to remain still. So it felt - increasingly as our camels tired.

By the time evening descended we had reached Ma'on. There were at least three hours riding left, but we were simply too exhausted to go further. On the outskirts of the town we stopped, intending to refresh ourselves, to bivouac for the night. Only the well was stopped. Not by rocks, not from underground. Naval the Bene Chalev of Carm-El was shearing his sheep on the banks of the wadi. He had placed several of his shepherds round the well to guard it, to make sure his sheep could be dressed if they were cut. Dirty, smelly fleeces of the Bene Chalev, riddled with blow-fly maggots! The eggs were hatching out even while the fleeces were being cut from the sheep's hides. The air was blue with them. Several sheep were being eaten away by maggots, their guts devoured even as they stood there waiting for the razor. No doubt the well-water would be skimmed with eggs as well. But it was the only well for several miles around, and the men and animals were desperate to drink. I summoned Achi-Melech.

"Take ten men and go ask the Bene Chalev for access to the well.

346

Tell him Daoud ben Yishai of the Bene Yehudah seeks his hospitality. Praise him. Praise the Bene Chalev. Recall how their forefather Chalev ben Yephunneh of the Bene Yehudah journeyed to this very well with Yehoshuah ben Nun, the heir of Abou Mousa, and drank waters far sweeter than those of Merivah. Tell him we are six hundred who request drink and rest, and our asses and our camels as well. Tell him we honour him as a sheikh who has three thousand sheep and a thousand goats and is thus a mighty man before the Lord. Tell him we are hungry, and have a long journey still to make, but that we ask only for water, not for meat or bread. Speak gently, and in the protocols of the desert."

Protocols which I confess to despising - such convoluted rhetoric, such hypocritic courtesies. Elegant though, beautifully elegant. When what I meant was: tell that little shit of a Bene Chalev that he and his blow-flied flock of shepherds had better move their red-haired arses away from the well, and go and fetch us plenty of good food into the bargain, or I and my six hundred will have to take matters into our own hands, which means moving him and his entire measly tribe, by irresistible brute force if necessary.

The question was: would Naval live up to the meaning of his name – "foolishness"?

From the way Achi-Melech came back with his tail between his legs, it was evident that he would.

"What does he say?"

"He asks who is this Daoud ben Yishai. He says that there are many servants nowadays who betray their masters, and desert them."

"Does he now? And when did he last go into battle against the Bene Pelet on behalf of the king of the Bene Ephrayim? Typical Bene Chalev. What else does he say?"

"That the original Chalev was the grandson of Pharets, the bastard that Abou Yehudah fathered on his own daughter-in-law when she was whoring at Adullam, whereas he is the descendant of Chalev ben Yephunneh, who alone of all the footmen of Abou Mousa supported Yehoshua in declaring the land of the Bene Kinnahu fit for occupation, and received the kingship of Chevron in perpetuity for his reward."

A playground bully who, like all large, hollow vessels, would make a lot of noise, and then prove empty. He was probably telling his shepherds even now, thanking the gods for his great good fortune, how Sha'ul would make him king in Chevron if he handed over the head of the pretender.

"He's bold, and risks much," I laughed. "But will he feed us?"

Achi-Melech shook his head. "No," he said. And would have stopped there, but I pressed him to tell me everything, verbatim. "He asks, Why should I take my bread, and my water, and the meat that I have prepared for my shearers, and give it away to other men, when I do not even know who they are?"

"Did you tell him we don't want his bread and meat, but only access to the well?"

"Yes."

"And?"

No answer.

"And?"

The continuing silence was making my temper rise.

"And?"

"May his children be grateful that the Chroniclers were not present to record his words."

"I see. As bad as that." It was absurd for Achi-Melech to be taking it all so personally. I put my arm across his shoulder. "Achi, get four hundred men ready. Leave the rest with Yo-Av to protect the camp. We shall go and teach the descendants of Yephunneh the Bene Chalev a lesson in respect. Let's go and shear his sheep for him."

And more to myself than intending anyone to hear, I muttered, preparing the psalm I would begin that night, but never finish:

"For what purpose should I keep anything this fellow has with him in the wilderness, since nothing will be missed of all that belongs to him. He has required of me evil where I would do only good. Now, gods, do unto me as I would to my enemies, if I leave of all that belongs to him, by the rising of the morning light, even so much as a single man, pissing against a wall."

But it never came to that.

Shlomo, it is time to speak, not of politics and war, but of women, of the great joy of self-abandonment in love, of the other joy, at once greater and lesser, of self-indulgence in the flesh. Who am I speaking of - Michal, Bat Sheva, Yehudit, Na'amah? I could easily speak of each and every one of them, borrowing from the ancient songs (I have often thought that one day it might be entertaining to gather all the ancient songs of love together, and make a kind of song of songs from them; as I have tried to do with my collection of the Psalms - a right unholy anthology that would make!)

"I am come into my garden, my sister, my spouse. I have gathered my myrrh with my spice. I have eaten my honeycomb with my honey. I have drunk my wine with my milk. Come, eat, my friends. Drink, drink abundantly, o my beloved."

The metaphors are really rather vulgar - schoolboyishly puerile, crudely obvious. One can almost imagine the teenage sniggering in the back row of the classroom - the honeycomb especially is an extremely crude figure of speech. Yes, but what language can we use, unless the purely clinical, straight from the lessons on anatomy? It is a terrible necessity, this human failing of ours, that in order to understand anything, in order to express anything, we have only the inadequacies of language, and therefore are obliged to reduce the universe to metaphors - God or Love.

"Behold thou art fair, my love. Behold thou art fair."

The use of repetition for emphasis, as Rach-El taught me all those years ago in Beit Lechem, is a part of that conviction that language is ultimately inadequate. By repeating, by making it a kind of incantation - the tribes to the east of Bav-El of the Bene Kessed have a word for it: mantra - it acquires greater power: magical, shamanistic power. Thus poetry and prayer become entwined, as love and prayer, love and poetry. A divine trinity, you might say.

And speaking of the divine:

"How fair is your love, my sister, my spouse. How much better is your love than wine, and the smell of your ointments than all spices."

Does that give it away? It is the love of Yah and Adonis, of Ishtar and Tammuz, of Eshet and Osher, of Our Lady for her Beloved Son, whom she bears, whom she marries, whom she mourns. The three graces, some men call her. The Triple Goddess, others. I had the play performed in Tsi'on, any number of times, and every company of players who came to mime and sing and dance it had their own variations on the libretto - not to mention verses added to pay homage to the king.

"Your neck is like the tower of Yedid-Yah built as for an armoury, whereon there hang a thousand bucklers, all shields of mighty men."

Fine as tribute - but can you imagine what the rest of such a woman must have been? A perfect helpmeet for the Colossus that stands across the bay at Rhodos of the Bene Yavan. Perhaps that was really their intention, for the Bene Yavan are her people.

Ah, but it was always a great favourite among the foreign embassies, particularly the female chorus scantily attired, and the veil-dancing by the Peace-Maidens Shulamit and Shlom-Tsi'on, which could tantalise a man until he was ready to sign anything you placed in front of him. That and the mime-play of the garden at Edinu, with the actor wearing his serpent mask and the protagonists in nothing but their loin cloths. They are the best of Habiru theatre.

But this is not what you want to hear. I mention women, and while you rush for your pockets, I reach for my encyclopaedia. Forgive me, Shlomo. We were hot and tired and hungry and hoping that Naval might change his mind and eat with us instead of making war with us, when all our thoughts were suddenly, magically, diverted by a vision towards the worship of the goddess.

"You have doves' eyes within your locks. Your hair is a flock of goats, that appear from Mount Gil-Yad."

I am far from certain how a woman's hair, however gorgeous, can be compared to a flock of goats. Unless the goats happen to belong to that woman's very wealthy husband.

Shlomo, there is silence, and there is silence. There is the silence of a man too frightened to give an answer. There is the silence of a man too disdainful to waste his breath in answering. There is the silence of a man who has no answer to give. There is the silence of a man who speaks and speaks for hour upon hour without pause, but who, upon analysis, turns out to have said nothing of any consequence at all. All these are, indeed, silence. And then there is the silence of a man who lies sated in the arms of a woman, or who stands, dreaming of such satiation, his sword on his thigh - literally; the crude metaphor is unintended - watching as such a woman as could silence any man appears over the brow of the hill, riding on a white donkey, wrapped in a dress of the most exquisitely coloured silks. Ah, Shlomo, a man could die, and happily, simply from the pulse-rate induced by so much beauty.

My fury at the Bene Chalev dissipated in an instant. Before such women I am rendered powerless, speechless, careless. Her eyes glowed black with kohl under hennaed eyelids. Her long, black hair flowed down her back like a Temani bride. Her figure was discernible through the curves of her gown. As the sun flickered like a guttering candle in the sky, as the wind blew her dress around her calves and ankles, occasionally the cloth would grow transparent and you could guess the shapeliness of breast and thigh and buttock underneath the silk. Ah, Shlomo, she was magnificent! Naked, of course, she would prove to be as pleasing and as disappointing as any other woman, bone and flesh garnered into the familiar shapes, all bumps and knobbles and fatty muscle and hard joints, a deceit of moles and birthmarks, a disillusion of breasts and stomach ruined by giving birth. But nakedness is never alluring in the way a woman dressed can be, and as deceits and illusions went, this one was enchanting. I had to have her. There is no other way I can describe the sensation that possessed me. I had to have her. To own her. To make her mine. To lie in her arms and expunge my need and greed and lust for her, breaking two of the commandments simultaneously in one magnificent act of shameless sin. And at the same time to surrender myself to her in the joyful abandonment of spiritual, romantic love. That is the power that women have over us. To drive us equally to love and hate. To weep on their breasts like infants and to rediscover through them the emotional completeness that a child succours from its mother - such is love. But at the same time there is a cruel enigma in a beautiful woman, an enigma that cannot be breached, and which therefore drives us to hurt them in the most intense sexual abuse. To take her from above and make her feel the power of our manhood as it thrusts inside her, a form of domination that we only require because it allows us the illusion that we are the stronger sex. And then, post-coitus, to lie sleeping on her breast again like a cradled infant, and whisper the gentlest coos of quietude and satiation in deepest penitence for any hurt we may have done.

"You have ravished my heart, my sister, my spouse. You have ravished my heart with one of your eyes, with one chain of your neck."

And because she had ravished my heart, I determined that I would ravish her. That is how it is with we poor, sad, fickle men. Six hundred of us with the same yearning - but only I who could fulfil it.

Her name was Avi-Gayil bat Yehudit of the Bene Carm-El, and she was the wife of Naval the Bene Chalev. Achi-Melech had scarcely begun to muster his four hundred and prepare his assault, when the chatsotsra sounded a second time, announcing the restraint. As she came over the brow of the hill, accompanied by a harem of beautiful handmaidens, each one of them pulling a laden donkey, camels that had been dragged from their rest knelt down again, men who had been lacing sandals or sword-belts stood and watched in sheer amazement. They were bringing a banquet to us - two hundred fresh-baked loaves of bread, two barrels of wine, five sheep dressed in rosemary and basil, five trays of corn, huge quantities of raisins, fig cakes, dates - more than enough for six hundred. So it had all been bluster after all. The playground bully had made his point, won his esteem from his cronies, had his belly-laugh - and now he could show off his generosity as well, on his own terms. Yet where was he? We looked and looked, but no Naval. Only this gorgeous woman, flanked by her handmaidens, laden down like Asherah with sweets for Marduk. And no Naval.

I stepped forward to welcome her. She was mounted on a white donkey, one beautiful creature upon another. She climbed down from its back, bowed herself to the ground, prostrated herself at my feet.

"Where is your husband, that I may thank him for this banquet?"

Even as she looked up into my face, I fell in love with her. Laugh, Shlomo, all you like. I say it again, because it is the truth. Even as she looked up into my face, I fell in love with her.

"I am responsible for this, my lord. May a woman speak in the company of these men?"

I nodded.

"Then hear me, my lord. My husband is a man who does not follow any gods. As his name is, so is he. Naval he's called, and he is very foolish. I heard your men when they went to speak with him, and I know you do not seek bloodshed."

It was, to say the least, confusing. Her manners were Bedou, yet she was town-born in Carm-El of Yehudah. The Bedou wife in her hardly dared to speak out loud in front of men, was trained, I guessed, to dog-like docility by her husband. Yet here she was, going behind her husband's back as it now appeared, perhaps even defying him. What kind of a woman was she?

"Does Naval of the Bene Chalev send us all this banquet, and not even know of it?"

She lowered her eyes. There was no need to speak the words.

"And will he then go hungry if we eat of what is his?"

"My servants have prepared enough for all of you twice over, and still food to spare. The shearers do not go short of food because of you."

"And you? Will Naval thank his wife for feeding us?"

"My husband will not know of it unless I tell him. I come, not at the behest of my husband, but of my Lord."

So this was it. She was a priestess by training, as all the daughters of the wealthy are priestesses by training, but in her case it was something she took seriously, as tribal duty and not merely the social training of a debutante. And the Bene Carm-El were clansmen of the Bene Yehudah, for all that she was married to a Bene Chalev. The next question came like an inspiration to my lips.

"There is a shrine at Carm-El..." I began. She interrupted me.

"It is only a very small shrine. A standing stone, which is believed to have been set up by Abou Raham in the hope that Emet Sarah would fall pregnant. There is a small chapel, where we light candles and recite the doxology. We are not really priestesses, but we try to keep the feast-days and to preserve the stone."

All of which confirmed my inspiration. Now it was my turn to interrupt. Her innocence was charming and beguiling, but my question pressed.

"Is there perhaps a young priest there, newly come, by name Avi-Atar ben Achi-Melech?"

She smiled. She was as desperate as I was to resort to daily language, to speak our hearts and minds, but the circumstances required formalities.

"The wisdom of Daoud is very great," she said. "He came to us six months ago, wounded as he fled from Ke'ilah. He is well now."

Healed by her own hands, and those of her women.

"He has spoken to you of me?"

"He speaks of little else. He carries the dice of Nov, and the garments of the High Priest his father. I have seen what he has seen."

"It was he who told you to bring the food?"

This undermined her courage and her generosity. I regretted saying it at once.

"It was he who wrote the blessing, and instructed me how to recite it before you ate. Come, invite your men before it stales."

353

She summoned one of her handmaidens, who proffered, of all unlikely things, a sheet of papyrus, written over in dye and quill. A woman who could read! Now I was truly astonished by her.

Where she had prostrated herself before us previously, now it was our turn. All of us went down upon our knees and faces on the dusty desert floor, our arms stretched out like divers. So she pronounced, first, the selicha, the apologia, for there were many among the men who could not easily accept the blessing of a woman:

"I pray thee, forgive the sins of this your handmaiden."

And then, as if the silence itself had granted her permission:

"May the Lord make for my lord a safe house, because my lord fights the battles of the Lord, and no evil has been found in you through all your days. Yet a man is risen to pursue you, and to seek your soul; may the soul of my lord be bound in the bundle of life with the Lord your god; and may the souls of your enemies be slung out, as out of the middle of a sling. For it shall come to pass, when the Lord shall have done to my lord all the good that he has promised, when he has appointed you to rule over all Yisra-El, that this shall be no grief to you, nor offence of heart unto my lord, either that you have shed blood without cause, or taken vengeance where there was nothing to avenge. And when the Lord shall have dealt kindly with my lord, let him also remember your handmaiden."

I liked the omens Avi-Atar had read in the Urim and Tumim. I liked his subtle forgiving my part in his father's death. I liked, best of all, such strength, such dignity, such unprecedented intelligence, in a woman whom her husband barely allowed even to be a woman. So I stood, brushed off the dust, threw down my sword in signal to the men to ungirdle theirs, and took her hands in mine.

"Blessed be the Lord, god of Yisra-El, who sent you to us this day."

It seemed for a moment as if the men would cheer. They might as well have thrown confetti too, for standing like that, locked eye to eye and heart to heart, it was truly as though we were now married.

"The advice you bring is sound and sensible," I said, relieved to be able to speak naturally again. "I never wanted to pick a fight with Naval. But we were hot and tired and very thirsty, and he has no right to deny anyone access to a well. If you had not turned up when you did – I had sworn not to leave a single man alive, not so much as a shepherd..." I didn't add the bit about them pissing against a wall.

Avi-Gayil laughed. I think it was because of Avi-Gayil that I began to cultivate a sense of humour. I loved her most especially when she was laughing.

"He has no more than forty men capable of lifting a dagger," she said. "And thirty-eight of them are too drunk even to lift another cup of wine. It would have been a bloodbath."

"You deserve much credit. But he won't thank you."

She uttered no reply, but I could tell from her expression that she hated him, hated him so much she no longer even feared him. Yet it was evident that he would break her bones, if he were still sober enough to do so. The reward for the saving of his life.

What happened next, Shlomo, many have taken as a sign, an augury of the gods. Neither you nor I, I hope, are so superstitious as to share that view, and hopefully we are both wise enough to understand that what took place is perfectly explainable in human terms. Still, one man's faith is another man's delusion, and even reason is only conjecture waiting to be disproved. But let me recount the detail.

I sent her back to Naval, with messages of thanks to Avi-Atar and hopes that we would soon be reunited. The house in Carm-El was alive with noise of drunken revelry. Naval was holding his own banquet with his shepherds and his shearers, no doubt toasting king Sha'ul and pouring vitriol upon my head as a runaway slave and a renegade-betrayer and a man too weak even to fight for access to a well. Pissed as Magog. There was neither need nor wish on her part to confront him with what she had done. Her husband hadn't even noticed. Her servants would never breathe a word of it. By morning we would be long gone and the evidence vanished under wind and sand. Quietly Avi-Gayil slipped away to bed, leaving her women to clear the debris when the feast was done at last.

He came in to her in the darkness before dawn, manly with drunkenness. Even as she slept he began to paw at her, hurting her awake. She was, after all, his chattel. As he sheared his sheep, so also his wives. He would have her do this and that, and no matter what she thought of his perversions, they were his pleasure, and he it was who ruled at Ma'on of Carm-El. When she refused, he hit her. On the face first, with the back of his hand, so the knuckles left the tiniest white indentations in her flesh. Wrapping her hair twice around his palm, he dragged her mouthwards to his cravings, and when she still refused, his knee came up to force her. But by now she was ready to fight back, and he less interested in sex than in brutality. While one fist winded her in the stomach, the other reached for his camel-whip. He had, anyway, had half a mind to try one of the other women in his household. Now the sight of Avi-Gayil might even render two of them amenable at once.

"Is this because you're drunk," she found at last the courage to risk her very life, "or because the Prince shamed you?"

So taken aback was he, he let her go.

"Shamed me? Who do you dare call Prince?"

She told him everything. Every detail. How the women had nursed Avi-Atar in secret for six months. How she had taken her bruises to the Elders on the last occasion that he beat her. The banquet, down to the very quantities of bread and raisins. The entreaty, prostrate on the ground before the Anointed Prince of Yehudah. The blessing, when he and his men had prostrated themselves before her, as before the goddess. The part of her that had resisted Avi-Atar's insistence that she take the banquet, because truly she would have preferred the bloodbath.

So she told - but he was not listening. She might as well have told the standing stone, for that was what he had become, transmogrified by disbelief. At any point of the telling, he might have stopped her with his fist. But his arms hung flaccid at his sides, invertebrate. So too his head, his jaw, his eyes, all hanging, downcast, turning to water. He could not respond to this. No wife had ever spoken to a husband in this manner, nor performed such deeds. Yet he lacked the wherewithal to kill her for it. And she was still speaking.

Now that she was embarked, there was no holding back. The entire complaint of womankind against mankind was on her lips - eleven years of all-consuming hatred, the methods she had used to stop his seed implanting, the times she had investigated poisons, the billing and cooing she had faked because it softened him in what he liked to call love-making but which was really just a...the need for crude vulgarities induced her stop. She would not demean herself by stooping to his level. She had made avowal of her truth. Now let the gods deal justly with her.

When at last the blood did resume its coursing in his veins, when the pulse resumed its beating, it boiled in him from rage and undiluted wine. So much undeserved hatred for him. So humiliating a betrayal. Perhaps it was just his age and how hard he had worked that day. Perhaps some hereditary genetic flaw and it would have happened anyway. But the blood, the pulse, were boiling over. His hands came up to his chest and his breath caught. He was trying to speak, to ask her to help him, to cry out for mercy - but the words would not come, and she would not have helped him anyway. A man who does not follow any gods has nobody to deliver mercy when the time comes. He was bereft. His head was throbbing, and now he knew it was not the wine. By the time Avi-Gayil did go out to call her women, Naval had collapsed on the bed, and would never rise from it again. His heart had broken.

For ten days Avi-Gayil, the loyal, dutiful wife, did as she had been taught to do. She stayed with him, at his bedside hour after hour, nursing him, feeding him, applying hot poultices and wet cloths, scenting the air with incense and perfume of herbs, lighting oil-lamps, keeping the flies and mosquitoes away from him. No reproach would ever come upon her head. No accusation would ever be made against her. That she was taking secret pleasure from this vigil was something nobody would ever know, nor even guess. Yet she was also deeply pained by her own contentment at his dying. However often she may have yearned for it, that still is not the same as witnessing the event, as having caused it, as recognising the cruelty in yourself that wishes for another's life to end. She had been married to him at fourteen, and he already nearing fifty. A great emptiness of life stretched out before her now. What Naval's family understood as grieving - and berated as hypocrisy - was in fact the contemplation of that emptiness, and her own terror at having to confront the void alone. She wept through every hour in which she tended him.

In the meanwhile we had continued on to Arad, oblivious to all these consequences of our passing through, and had it not been for Avi-Atar's presence at the shrine I might well have thought no more of her - she would not have been the first beautiful woman I had desired, and then been forced by circumstance to disregard. But Avi-Atar's blessing echoed with implications, and that at least could not be disregarded. I owed him too many debts.

My brother, Ram, volunteered to go on my behalf, to bring Avi-Atar to Arad. Within two days he had returned, alone, but with Avi-Atar's request for me to come to meet him, not at Carm-El, but in secret in the woods behind Ma'on. I went. He told me - almost everything - everything he knew. The version of events that was spreading like brushfire through Yehudah, changed, mythologised, with each retelling. I learned the truths only much later, from Avi-Gayil herself.

"You are held responsible for Naval's dying, Yedid-Yah." The investiture of my full name. No one had ever called me that, not since I was named at eight days old. Dodi, David, plain Daoud, any number of derogatory diminutives. To be named Yedid-Yah by Avi-Atar, High Priest in exile of Nov of Mor-Yah, was a token of esteem indeed. "You are held responsible for his dying, Yedid-Yah. It seems to be your fate, to inhabit the heavens like a supernova, and to cause other planets to die out."

Those oracular images again – he had used them before, with quite appalling accuracy.

"I did nothing wrong, Avi. The gods are my witnesses. I threatened, yes. I might have done wrong, had you not sent the woman. This talk of coercing him to feed my men is purest nonsense. We sought access to a common well. His own wickedness returned upon his head."

"Nonetheless, men blame you." There was a scar, leaf-thin, the whole length of his right forearm - the wound he had brought with him from Ke'ilah. But there were other scars, deeper, less physical. Our relationship was subtly altered. "You did nothing wrong at Nov, or at Ke'ilah. Yet death follows you, mars your best intentions. As your friend I pity you. As a priest I must ask myself why it is?"

I had never felt this cold towards a man. Something had changed in him. Some experience had modified him. This was no longer Avi-Atar the golden-haired, the enthusiast of Yahweh who I had come to love in the Nayot of Ramah. This was a man with open bruises on his heart and soul. When he spoke, you could hear his wounds ache. It upset me, but it also made me angry.

"And have you reached a conclusion yet as to why you think it is?"

And being upset himself, he too was angry.

"Yes, Daoud, I have. The gods are punishing you, for the sin of arrogance. Already you have much to expiate, and there will be more, much more. I have thrown the dice and seen the auguries. It lies in the meaning of your name. I have spoken with Gad the Prophet, and he concurs. You cannot burn and flame with life as you do, and not leave others scorched and seared. It is in the nature of fire. It gives light and life and warmth, it makes the flowers bloom and the trees blossom, it dries out care and warms the soul. But it also destroys woodland, and turns it into desert. You have much to expiate."

We train our priesthood in the art of sermonising - I suppose we shouldn't feel offended when they climb into the pulpit and deliver one.

"You say you've consulted with Gad. Have you reached a just conclusion? Or do you propose to read that also in the dice?"

That was unjustified - arrogant, indeed. So much his eyes told me. So much my head bowed. So much my memory echoed with the warnings of Shmu-El: "the gods do not require your sacrifices, only your obedience". Yes. Yes. Salachti. I will be Daoud, not Sha'ul. This will be the difference.

"What must I do?"

"Nothing that you do not wish for anyway. But you will do it, not for Daoud, but for expiation. Avi-Gayil will very soon be widowed, and she is childless. The Bene Chalev will not allow her to remain unmarried at Carm-El, nor will her own people take her home, because there are rumours that she is disgraced. There is only one future for her. Why do you smile?"

It was very hard to explain. But the word expiation had hit its mark. A man's destiny is always bound up in the destiny of others.

"Because I am the heir of Pharets, who was fathered on a childless widow when she had no alternative but the one you mean for Avi-Gayil. Perhaps I can expiate the sin of Abou Yehudah, and the sin of Daoud, in the same act. Perhaps this is part of the closing of the circle."

Even as I spoke, his coldness thawed. He heaved what was nothing less than an enormous sigh of relief.

"This is exactly what the dice described," he said.

I laughed, and put my arms around his neck.

"Avi-Atar, you are so solemn and portentous. There is nothing readable in the dice that a man can't work out with his own insights and intuitions. Come with me to Arad, and serve me as my priest again. But for goodness sake, put away your silly superstitions. I need your humanity, not your mysticism."

It was, he was right even though he didn't actually say it, a statement of the utmost arrogance. I confess my fault.

Shlomo, how do you explain a woman like Avi-Gayil bat Yehudit? She came to me, just days after they buried Naval, all that beautiful dark flesh and darker intelligence, a woman with less than nothing in the world, and already the stature of a future queen. Naval's family, for their own dignity, had held back a portion of their wrath, though it was known about the banquet throughout Yehudah, and they were shamed by her. How much greater shame though, to turn her out of doors with no possessions, and have her tell her tale in the bed of any man with an appetite and half a shekel. Yet turn her out they must, for she was a childless widow, Naval had left no brother to fulfil the Law of the Levir, no other man would marry her, and after what had taken place, there was no home for her any longer in Carm-El. So they gave her – more than Abou Raham once gave Chagar: an ass to ride, a rope with which to strap as much as she could carry on its back, a gourd of water, and, not understanding why she wanted them, directions for the journey to Arad. Five of her women followed her, on foot.

To reach Arad, she had to pass through any number of small, desert villages, caravanserai, oases. Given the speed with which her tale had spread, she might have expected to be solicited at every well, or even stoned. But she wasn't just some woman who had betrayed her husband, prostrated herself before another man, given away his goods, shamed him - caused his death. She was a daughter of the Bene Yehudah, and the widow of a Bene Chalev. Not even the most scandalous versions of the legend inferred adultery. Indeed, the opposite. Scribes of the Elders had gossiped of her complaint, and the evidence of her face gave proof to it. And then the name Daoud was mentioned in the tale. Women came out to honour her. They spoke of her as another Ya-El, the wife of Chever of the Bene Kayin, who drove a tent-peg through the head of Sis-Ra while he slept. They thought of their own lives, with their own husbands, and the times they too had tasted the bitter gall of hatred, and they hoped this new king of the Bene Yehudah when he was anointed would make their lives a little sweeter. They cheered her through the streets and named her Devorah.

More diffidently, because it was much harder for them to do - but harder still to face their wives if they didn't - increasing numbers of men joined in. In Kinah a shepherd of the Yattir clan called out her name, not Avi-Gayil bat Yehudit, but Yah-Malchat Avi-Gayil bat Yehudah, an extraordinary apotheosis into queen of Earth and Heaven all in one incongruous leap; and in the echoes men began singing "Daoud Melech Yehudah, chay ve kayam, chay ve kayam." It was like a wave of hysteria spreading across Yehudah, fuelled by ancient tribal jealousies and rivalries - with Ephrayim as much as with the Bene Chalev - or as if someone had driven an eccentric-looking bandwagon out of the desert, and by mistake it had acquired the status of a fashion, so that all the world became impelled to jump aboard. Messengers came to me with the information even while the residents of Kinah were still proclaiming it - and the Bene Ziph no doubt sending their footmen post haste to report it to Sha'ul. The messengers arrived with Avi-Gayil and her women in the van.

As she greeted me at Ma'on, so now at Arad. But where then a radiant woman had alighted from a white donkey, now a tired creature, her left eye still purple from the blow Naval had given her, dismounted from a fat, decrepit ass, and fell in exhaustion to the ground. Prostrate, if not prostrated. But she had rehearsed her speech, and she was determined she would speak it.

"Behold, let your handmaiden be a servant to wash the feet of the servant of the Lord."

Bedou customs!

I lifted her in my arms and held her. No kisses yet - though the men would have cheered us. The days of mourning for her husband were not yet done.

"We shall marry here in Arad. Avi-Atar ben Achi-Melech will officiate and my brother Ram will be my companion. It is nothing to me that you are not a virgin. You shall be my wife, and bear my son."

Formulaic words, spoken for the benefit of the gods, the stars, the dust - the men. I hadn't understood, when I first embarked upon this mad adventure, that I was becoming an actor on a stage, and that every word I spoke would require careful scripting, because someone, somewhere, was recording it for posterity, someone, somewhere, was deconstructing its ambivalences, down to the very last conceivable

361

misinterpretation. May the gods grant all public men a space of unmolested privacy. This scroll, Shlomo. This scroll.

My need for privacy though was nothing when compared to that of the women. Where do you house five women in a makeshift camp inhabited by six hundred men, most of whom have not so much as looked at any other female in weeks? Avi-Gayil was determined that the women would remain with her - with us. But the goat-skin tent in which I was sleeping would have left a taller man with his head poking out at one end and his feet the other. Avi-Gayil could fit, once we were married, because sleeping very close would not simply be a necessity of little space. But in the meanwhile? And the other five? Then Yoram ben Pagi-El brought a delegation of sixty soldiers to my door, with a linen tent dyed - though not yet dried - opaquely red with goat's blood that they had thrown together using javelins for poles and swords for pegs.

"If the women of Avi-Gayil are willing to share this tent for no more than two days, I have enough men to put up a house."

They had thought of every detail - every element of privacy a woman might require. They had even sent two men to Yattir for certain particular supplies.

Some men will do anything for a promotion, or the goodwill of their superiors. But these men wanted neither. When Daoud fell deep in love, women were permitted in the camp. But what of their amours? They wanted to prove that it was feasible to live male alongside female - and not just some tawdry trail of greensleeves servicing the camp. So that I would allow them to summon their own women. Strange what factors determine the course of history. In all my life, few ever proved more significant than this.

But how - I asked the question, and then never got around to answering it - how do you explain a woman like Avi-Gayil bat Yehudit? Beautiful, intelligent, courageous, a woman who knew her own mind. And full, to the very last, of surprises.

"Daoud" - it was the first time she had used my name – "I have brought five women with me, but I need only four. As a man may have four wives, so a woman four handmaidens. The fifth is for you."

"For me?"

A young girl quite as gorgeous as herself, if ten years younger, stepped forward, and removed her veil.

"Her name is Achi-Noam bat Yazar-El. She is fifteen. She is honoured to become the second wife of Yedid-Yah ben Yishai."

Bedou customs! The woman was full of Bedou customs, then and all her life. Nonsenses that Av-Ram brought with him from Ur of the Bene Kessed, but which Abou Mousa rightly outlawed. Sometimes she drove me crazy with her Bedou customs. And then calling me Yedid-Yah on top. Avi-Atar's influence, of course. I could not help wondering if she was in love with him as well.

"Why?"

I hadn't meant it to sound so curt.

"Because this is what Eshet Sarah did for Abou Raham with Chagar, what Eshet Le'ah did for Abou Yah-Akov with Zilpah, and Emet Rach-El with Bilhah. It is the custom."

"But you are not barren."

"Men proclaim you king of Yehudah. It is expected."

"That is not an answer. Are you then barren?"

"All women are barren, until Our Lady grants them children. Sarah and Le'ah and Rach-El were not barren either, nor Chanah the mother of the Prophet Shmu-El. It is the way amongst the priesthood of Our Lady. It is a form of words that honours and exalts the goddess."

Worst of all, Avi-Atar was standing beside her, nodding at every word she said, like some off-stage prompter who never expected the lead to remember all her lines. So utterly bewildered was I, it was only now I realised something odd that she had said.

"Avi-Gayil, you give too much honour to the lady Achi-No'am, naming her my second wife. You take too much upon yourself as well. You are not to me as Sarah, nor as Le'ah, the first wives of their husbands. Rather you are as Rach-El, whom Abou Yah-Akov loved above all other women, but took only for his second wife. If I am to be king, my queen will be Michal."

She smiled, sweetly, almost condescendingly. A buzzing of flies around my head should have forewarned me of something not entirely pleasant in the air. Ba'al-Zvuv, the Lord of the Flies, never sends his messengers without good reason.

"No, my lord. I have given you Achi-No'am as your second wife, not your third. Has my Lord not heard the news that all men in Yisra-El have heard, that Sha'ul has annulled the marriage of Daoud and Michal, on grounds of desertion, and given her to Phalti ben La'ish of Gallim as a wife?"

She was the most intelligent woman I ever knew, Shlomo - even cleverer than your mother, who is far from dull. Yet even Avi-Gayil was capable of miscalculation. This was not the wisest moment to bring me that particular piece of news.

Parchment Fourteen

Nothing ever happens for a single reason, but because a combination of causes and circumstances prevails.

We had established our base on the fringe of the Negev, as far south as we dared to flee, among the ruins of Arad - Arad Rabbah, the ancient Kena'ani city by Hormah, rather than Arad Yerachme-El which the Bene Shimon established at the time of Yehoshua ben Nun. To call it ancient is like calling yesterday's sour milk lebne. Arad had already been destroyed before most men had heard of cities. It was in Arad that the gods set up their tents, when they first met to plan Creation - and so uninhabitable did they find it, they did the whole job in seven days, and scarpered. Who could blame them? Brown dust, swirling over white pebbles, caught in the lips of black rocks. Desert snakes wandered haplessly about, bereft of hiding places, dreaming of life in Edinu before they committed the foolishness of tempting Chava. Even after the rains, nothing grew in Arad, for there was not yet a mist to go up from the ground, to water this pimple, let alone the whole face of the Earth. Dry as humour or the bones of that king who took the spies of Abou Mousa prisoner, and was ruined for his trouble. The epitome of desolation. And hot, fiery hot. Having nowhere else to go, we had fled to the innermost circle of the underworld, the place where Death went to die. All that was missing was its deity. No She'ol. And at last, though not for long, no Sha'ul either.

That was the first reason. The second was marriage to Avi-Gayil and Achi-No'am, which brought women into the camp for the first time. To accommodate them turned out not to be the problem. You could make women's quarters, private latrines, arrange for space for them to wash their bodies and their clothing unmolested; you could protect them against the men. Quite easily, in fact, for they were my women, and to touch them would have been to touch me. No one would have dared. But the effect of the women on the men was quite another story. You could have got hay fever and sneezing fits from the quantities of pheromone that wafted round and round the camp. Deprived entirely of women, men develop rituals of asceticism, which usually means the Sin of Onan, the Sin of Sha'ul, or the Sin of Abou Yehudah - less poetically: masturbation, mutual buggery, and whores. But confronted daily by these archetypes of loveliness, perpetually reminded and intoxicated, yet still denied, men's blood was liable to boil over. Yet we couldn't import whole families. We weren't there to establish a community.

While Avi-Gayil and I were marrying in Ziph, a sumptuous royal wedding was taking place at Giv-Yah too – Michal's third betrothal, and not yet twenty. Whether in anger at my marriage - though he had no reason to complain about my taking a second wife, nor a third or fourth for that matter - or in truth because kings always use their daughters to further their political ends, Sha'ul had formally annulled my marriage to Michal, and given her to Phalti ben La'ish of Gallim as a wife. The fountains of Gallim are truly splendid, the view southwards to Sala'am from the watchtower of Gallim as picturesque as any you can find, though what else Sha'ul gained from the alliance was far from clear, unless he felt the need to shore up support in his own tribe, and La'ish, if not Phalti, commanded much respect among the Bene Yamin. Either way, despite the theoretical "reconciliation" – I had been disinherited.

That was the third factor. But it was the fourth that was decisive. That same spring, Ach-Ish ben Ma'och of Gat launched a new invasion eastwards out of Pelet. No less than four armies had been assembled, reinforced by an armada out of the islands of the Great Sea. He had persuaded the desert tribes to attack at the same time - neighbours of the Bene Amalek especially, whom Sha'ul had left alone because it was only the destruction of the Bene Amalek that Shmu-El had required. The Bene Ammon too were poised atop the Heights of Gil-Yad, watching and waiting, threatening to become embroiled.

The first attack came out of the northern city of Gat, the small fortress-town on the Hadera River, backed by men of Aphek. Zvulun, Asher, Yah-Shachur and Ephrayim bore the brunt of it, with the Bene Yamin inexorably drawn in under the signet of the king. Sha'ul declared the League of Ephrayim to be once again in force, and reminded the reluctant Elders of their previous disinclinations. So Naphtali and Menasheh joined the fray, and in the south the Bene Shimon called on Re'u-Ven and Gad to arm themselves against the desert tribes. Which left only Yehudah. And Ach-Ish, though he had two armies poised to attack Yehudah - one in the north at Ekron, the other in the south at Ashkelon - as yet held back. The decision of

Yehudah would be decisive.

I wasn't at the conference of the Elders - I wasn't invited - but you didn't need to be there to know exactly what was said. And besides, it was all reported to me afterwards.

On the one hand, those like the Bene Ziph, who sided with Sha'ul in everything, and would urge Yehudah to support him, even though it would expand the scale of the war. Against them, the dithering politicians, comfortable Elders who like nothing better than to be seen to be important, to sit at the plenary table or to chair the focus sessions, to attend official junkets and to go on bunburrees to organise the twinning of town to town - but who will never make any decision of any importance, one because they might be held responsible for it, two because a decision once made no longer requires further meetings and further sub-committees, and thereby risks diminishing their self-importance. These men would urge caution, the seeking of further advice from a commission of enquiry, and then delay as long as possible, or at least until Ach-Ish forced their hand. The third group, then, who hated Sha'ul, and would not fight to keep him on the throne for a moment longer than was necessary, but who couldn't bring themselves to lend overt support to the Bene Pelet either, lest the fall of Sha'ul be the prelude to a still worse situation. These, too, procrastinated, even while skirmishes and provocations spilled across the borders daily.

So the fourth group, the smallest, the least vocal, the most unrepresented - indeed, not only uninvited but truthfully unwelcome. A group of one. Yet the voice of the Elder of the Guild of Prophets, Gad ben Shmu-El as he now styled himself, was not a voice that could be ignored, for it spoke with the moral authority of Yahweh and it carried the full weight of the Laws of Abou Mousa on its breath. Spoke? - it positively bellowed. And Gad had come, quite specifically, to remind the conclave that Sha'ul had forfeited the right to rule, that Daoud ben Yishai had been thrice anointed, was declared the rightful king of Yehudah, and had the support not only of the Guild of Prophets, but of men and women all across the tribes of Yisra-El.

"It was very noble of you, my friend. But rash, and premature."

They had hounded him out of the Tent of the Elders even before he finished speaking. He had gone there on foot, and on foot he now departed, stones hailing on his head even after he had managed to elude the first storm - of camel dung. All prophets, in my experience, are born with a powerful streak of masochism. I shall not pretend that Gad did anything but revel in his ordeal. And besides, however quixotic his heroism, in his rivalry with Natan for the spiritual leadership of Yisra-El, it did him no long-term harm at all. All of this was in my thinking when I welcomed him, desolate as the wilderness itself, into the tower of Arad.

"There was nothing noble about it, Daoud. Yehudah will be attacked by Ach-Ish soon enough. If I had said nothing, the tribe would have sided with Sha'ul, because the evil you know is still better than the one you haven't yet experienced. It is written that you will succeed him as king, but not when, nor how. A kingship must be earned, Daoud. Now half the tribe of Yehudah will come to you for simple hatred of Sha'ul."

"What exactly are you advising?"

Because I didn't like the tenor of his words. Because all men who play politics are dangerous, but especially prophets when they dabble, and not with their visions but their intellects.

"Can you live, like this, in Arad, gathering wives and children round you daily. Is it your intention to found a new desert tribe, and rebuild the ancient city, and be king here?"

Even when their intellects coincide precisely with your own.

"And while a war rages to the north, will you take neither one side nor the other? Will you sit and watch, and earn the hatred of Yisra-El?"

Even an intellect as sharp and cogent as was Gad's.

"I went to Ke'ilah, to fight Sha'ul's wars for him. A fat lot of good it did me."

And then he said, what had been in the shadows of my thoughts for weeks now, what I hadn't dared to utter, even to myself, what only a Prophet of the Lord could utter.

"You went to Ke'ilah, and you were right to do so. Your mistake was that you went to fight for Sha'ul, and not against him."

So the unspeakable was spoken. So, eventually, it would be done.

"Side with the Bene Pelet?"

"In the name of Pharets ben Yehudah. In the name of Shmu-El. It is written that you will be king in Yisra-El. Become, first, king in Yehudah. Ach-Ish will give you any title that you wish."

And the Prophet - it was almost too astonishing to think of it - the

Prophet would anoint me.

Ach-Ish's messengers left no doubt as to their king's position - the Bene Gat had no use for my friendship. And after what I had done, to him personally, and to his father, and his people - who could blame him? But an ally - that was quite another matter. A hero of the Bene Yisra-El, with six hundred trained men behind him, and a thousand more each week who might be ready to come over. What was in his thoughts? That my enemy's enemy may never be my friend, but an ally - that was quite another matter.

"What would you have me give you?"

He had received me, as his father had before, in that dreary suite of rooms, in the tower by the gatehouse which he called his palace. Undressed stone supported by cedar beams, dry-mortared. An open fire in the wall, channelled through an open chimney. No ornamentation, no gilt, no panelling, no silk, no hint of civilisation - the tombs of the Pharaohs of the Bene Chem are fuller of life and considerably more ornate. Even Sha'ul had a chest in which he kept his wax tablets. Whereas Ach-Ish could neither read nor write. The nearest I ever heard to music in that town was the yowling of a cat on heat, night after night in fact, out of alleyways that stank of refuse.

But his courtesies, however peremptory and primitive, were courtesies nonetheless.

"Let the king give me a roof over my head, a bed-chamber each for the women, and enough space for the men who follow me. I ask no more."

A world, Shlomo. A world and nothing much. Enough space. Space to dream think breathe espouse the universe and curl up in the narrow blackness of the womb alone with Yah and Yahweh. To live, until there is simply no more living left. The whole world, and nothing much. I ask no more.

Or not of Ach-Ish anyway.

"Your men are soldiers, and they are highly trained. You fought against my father, Ma'och ben Shimshon. How can I be sure you won't fight against me too? How can I be sure you haven't come deceitfully, to pretend friendship, but then to turn traitor on behalf of Sha'ul."

"Give me your oath of loyalty, and I'll swear it."

Ach-Ish laughed, darkly though, without humour in it.

"Daoud, I know you well enough. You would swear any oath that suited you, in the name of any god, with your hand beneath the thigh of Ba'al Zvuv himself, and pleasure him while you were oathing in his name. And you would turn traitor to your swearing before you even left the holy place."

Looking into my eyes, through them into my soul, even as he said these things. As though in this way to test out if his instinct was correct. He knew it was. And that I knew he knew.

"Ach-Ish, I shan't pretend that I want your friendship, any more than you want mine. If I could, I would kill you here and now, and throw every last one of your people back into the Great Sea, until the very name of the Bene Pelet was eradicated."

I would have said more, but his men were snarling. Yet sometimes the honest expression of hatred can have the same immense impact as that of love. We were drawing closer to each other, in respect if nothing else, even as he was raising his hand to stop his men from tearing me apart.

"You will fight against Sha'ul?"

"Why else have I come to Gat?"

"And kill him?"

I swallowed what could have been the pips of the fruit of the tree of knowledge of good and evil. A serpent crawled coldly down my spine.

"Yes," I said. "If it comes to it. Yes."

"And you will help me train my men?"

"Do they need training? You have four armies, better equipped and better prepared than Sha'ul's. In what could I train them?"

His steward had brought watered honey-wine and trays of almond cakes. Randomly, I took one, but then he took it back from me, literally snatched it from my hand, popped it in his mouth, devoured it. So he nodded his head, and invited me to choose again. The gesture was magnanimous, and much appreciated, though I have to say the thought of poison had never once occurred to me. I had rather assumed, in fact, that if he was going to kill me, he would find something considerably more gruesome, slow and torturous.

But the real poison that he had in mind, depended upon keeping me alive.

"Map lore."

"Never heard of it."

"They say it's General Yah-Natan's invention. His footmen come into our lands, and take back drawings of the hills and trees, but especially of the positions of gates in city walls. Why do you think they do this?"

I curled up my mouth to demonstrate genuine perplexity, honest ignorance, a sincere sharing of his desire to explain something so very strange. I said:

"We are forbidden by the Laws of Abou Mousa to make graven images. This is the only art form we are permitted. I imagine General Yah-Natan does it for the aesthetic satisfaction. He's well-known as an aesthete."

Never patronise those who suffer already from awareness of their ignorance; it will only encourage them to bullying. And yet it was so easy, so utterly irresistible.

"We would be grateful for detailed maps, of Giv-Yah especially, of the hills surrounding it, as far as Mishmash northwards, say, as far as Manachat to the south."

Grateful! No doubt he would have been grateful if I had fought the entire war on his behalf. Hah! I said:

"I have a notoriously poor memory."

"But a great need for a roof over your head, and a bed-chamber for each of your women. And I for something better than an oath. If my people are to accept Daoud, they will require proof that he is honest. We shall make a covenant, you and I, and then I will know if you are honest. Among your people, if my memory serves me correctly, the symbol of a covenant is the rite of circumcision? Then on our side, we are already sworn."

Witty man, Ach-Ish. Who would ever have suspected it?

But mutual respect, growing out of mutual hatred.

"And in return?"

"In return, Daoud, I shall place a crown upon your head, and you will be a king. I shall give you, for your city, Tsiklag. Is it sealed?"

On pig-suede, Ach-Ish. On the bladder of a milking sow. Signed and sealed, mapped and contoured, anointed with watered honey-wine. A covenant of treason.

Tsiklag! If Arad was a place of devastation, Tsiklag was a living death. No one could even tell you what the name meant, though everybody had a theory. A four-letter root - now there's something to overstretch the limited mind of man. The Bene Kena'an can barely cope with two-letter roots like Dan and Gad; the Habiru are intellectually stout enough to supplement a vowel or two, not to mention the occasional third consonant. But making words with four-letter roots is simply showing-off.

Tsiklag? There is tsakal, to bind or tie together. But no final gimmel. And besides, no people living in any town were ever less bound or tied together than the residents of Tsiklag. So discard that. Pinchas ben Dan, my seneschal as he insisted on calling himself, had a theory that it was really Yetsik Gal, which made no sense from any point of view. You had to reverse two letters to achieve it, and anyway, who on earth would name a town after the outflowing of a fountain, when there wasn't any water for a radius of twenty miles around, not dripping, not spilling, not squeezable from the morning dew, let alone outpouring from a fountain. The Tsiyim, of course, were everywhere. Bedou, nomadic shepherds, all the wandering beasts as well, the ostriches and jackals and the hoopoe birds. But if tsiyim was the prefix, who or what was kalag to complete the word? (Of course it matters, Shlomo. I was king of this Yah-forsaken town, for pity's sake. A man likes to know his etymology.) There is only one reference incidentally, in the holy texts I mean. The Scroll of Yehoshua ben Nun "binds" it, "ties it together" with Madmannah and Sansannah, of which the former means dunghill and the latter a palm branch. What should make up the third part of that trinity, do you surmise? Plenty of both, there surely were. Maybe Kalag was the first king, and I have no doubt he was as delighted to receive the honour as I was. Lord of the dunghill and the palm tree, master of the Bedou and the jackals. King of traitors anyway.

They crowned me in their temple of the sun-god Shimshon. Strange to think of Shimshon elevated to the deity, rather than being a mere tribal judge, but there he was in all his glory, sun-hero and beloved of the goddess, Yah-Chavod ha-Melech, Hera-Kles Melchat or some such Bene Cheret mispronunciation. Every year they made a new king by dressing him in the cloak and mask of the sun-god, and then tying him to a twelve-spoked wheel – a symbol of the sun's annual cycle - cutting off the seven locks of his hair, and blinding him. Symbolically, I am glad to say. The High Priestess, on behalf of the Moon Goddess - Delilah in their language is of course ha-Lailah, the Goddess of the Night, Lilit, in ours - conducted the proceedings, but sadly, unlike the Kena'ani rites, there is no ceremony of ritual copulation. Sadly, because she really was extremely beautiful, and at that time Achi-No'am was pregnant with Amnon, and Avi-Gayil was - well, being Avi-Gayil; after eleven years of sexual abuse from Naval of the Bene Chalev, her decision to give me Achi-No'am for a wife was carefully considered.

The temple was precisely the same as those the Bene Kena'an build, except that theirs are usually multi-deitied where this was the exclusive shrine of Shimshon and Delilah. It was nothing to write home about, let alone a column of a royal memoir. It was a house really, except that they had added a walled courtyard for the rituals. Their worship included bringing tribute, receiving oracles, making sacrifice and participating in covenant meals - very little different from our own, in fact. The main room, where the coronation took place, and afterwards the eucharistic sacrifices which it was part of my kingly duty to perform, was called the broadroom. You entered from one of the long sides, through an open arch. The room was in three parts: a porch, the main room with the cult niche, and then the Holy of Holies, where the ikons and teraphim and covenant stones were kept and which only the High Priest and High Priestess could ever enter, and even then only on certain days. Then there was an inner and an outer courtyard, linked by a gateway. The inner courtyard had a stone-lined basin in its centre and a gatehouse in the enclosure wall, lined with benches. There was a raised platform - hardly more than a table really - on either side of the entrance. The floor was cobbled and there were drainage channels from the altar to the basin so they could catch the blood for sprinkling on the congregation. There were also libation tables, incense altars, seals, various bronze figurines representing the god and goddess - Shimshon usually as the sun itself, or as a chariot; Delilah with her two hands stretched up towards a crescent and a disc. The roof was supported by two columns, one inventively known as Shimshon, the other as Delilah. The rear wall housed the altar, which you approached up four stone steps, eastward, towards the sunrise. It was made from unquarried stone, had four moon-horns, one in each corner, and was liberally smeared with sacrificial blood. A protective snake was engraved on the side.

To the south of the building, behind the rear wall, there was a second, an open-air altar, made of mud-brick and remade by the temple acolytes every time it rained - though it rarely did. It was as wide as four men, and still some, not much less than a tall man high. It too was surrounded by a wall and had two steps to the top. They covered the stones with soot from the sacrificial fires.

There, the royal memory functioning as it always does these days - fantastic detail of the past, but if you think I can remember what I had for breakfast then you are over-estimating my abilities. Boiled gall and roasted throat ulcers probably. Reconstituted stomach acids. Or was it regurgitated lip sores from last night's dribbled supper? I am rapidly running out of tomorrows, have virtually given up todays except for this dictation, and yesterday has already surrendered to oblivion - whereas events of forty years ago are as clear as water in the Sea of Genasseret. And anyway, you need me to record all this, because you need to know, don't you? How to build the Temple, I mean. Our tabernacle is just a desert tent, ideal for nomads and for refugees, but not much use now we have come into our kingdom. Since I am forbidden, it is you who must honour Yah and Yahweh with a proper Temple, as the Bene Pelet honour Shimshon and Delilah, the Bene Kena'an Ba'al and Anat, El and Asherah. You, Yedid-Yah, the Beloved Son. Leave out the stelae, which Abou Mousa railed against, saying they represented the divinity in stone and as such are graven images. Leave out the other figurative forms: palm trees and dunghills in particular, unless you mean to honour Tamar and Ba'al Zvuv as well. But in shape, style, architecture - look at King Hu-Ram's drawings. Isn't this how the divine couple should be housed, palatially, enmarbled like a king and queen, in Yiru-Sala'am of the Bene Yisra-El?

But while we dream of peace and building now, the environs of my kingship then were entirely warfare and destruction. Ach-Ish had launched and relaunched his invasion eastwards out of Pelet, great waves of men and chariots pouring over the hills, pressed back again and again, until the strings began to lose their tension and the instrument went out of tune. On both sides, but especially on ours - I mean, Sha'ul's. Four separate armies bearing down on you is more than any disunited people can contend with, even under the banner of the League of Ephrayim to which they were now committed in the most abject desperation. But the four armies never dwindled, despite the enormous casualties, because month by month they were reinforced from out of the islands of the Great Sea - men who came to fight for a land they had never seen, but which they believed, as we do, had been given them in covenant by the gods. Nothing yet from the desert tribes - or only skirmishes and border raids. The Bene Ammon were contenting themselves with rolling boulders down the Heights of Gil-Yad upon the villages below, rendering them uninhabitable; and elsewise simply watching and waiting, still threatening to become embroiled.

And as for me.

To seek asylum with your former enemy - one who is secretly still your present enemy, as you are his, and both dissimulatingly aware of it - you first must prove yourself a present friend. Or trustworthy ally, at the very least. That was why we gave Amnon the name we did, and asked Ach-Ish to godfather the ceremonies, to act as sandek at the ceremony of circumcision. Not that he accepted the invitation - he was fighting in the north, which gave him the ideal excuse - but it was a truly magnificent gesture of conciliation on my part. And he acknowledged it, by sending the most marvellous message of congratulation - at once his always courteous self, yet still the fief-lord speaking to his vassal. He sent, in fact, ten messengers, a minyan for the ceremony, and all of them men of Gat who had been in the market-place that day. Their herald was a short, squat, stubby, swarthy man who looked like he had been grafted on an olive tree and crossed with figs. His name in the language of the Bene Pelet was something like Ach-Nor mag Pelops, of which Ach-Nor means lipless and Pelops muddy face! No man was ever better named. And in the case of Amnon, for whose birth he came, no one worse. Trustworthy indeed. No, I shall start ranting and bring on another of my strokes.

This Ach-Nor mag Pelops - Ach-Lis, that's what it was; Ach-Lis, not Ach-Nor; Ach-Nor is their name for Kinnahu, for Kena'an - had put a plain white linen tunic and a massively embroidered, multi-coloured cloak over his military uniform, and wrapped his whole face in a crimson and white bernous, so that you couldn't quite decide if he was a priest, a Bedou, a cut-throat bandit or a silk merchant of the Bene Cheret. But when he spoke, molten brass slithered from his lips, and set hard on the air.

"My lord Daoud mag Yishai, I bring you..." I don't recall the words. He was ordered to congratulate me. He was beholden to see the child with his own eyes - and did so, by poking his nose so close to Amnon's face, the child would have bitten him if he had been born with teeth. He was commanded to remain with me as my seneschal, and to serve me as my emissary to Ach-Ish - he finished this line off with a string of royal titles for Ach-Ish that was so long he wouldn't need to travel as an emissary; he could simply tie his messages to one end of the string and let them slither to the other end. Slithering was his speciality, serpentine even when upright. Being "required" in his lord's name was the other - what a marvellous device for assuming absolute power, to claim to act in the name of another but absent power of even greater absoluteness. "Ach-Ish has instructed me." Who would ever dare to challenge him? We gave him the Habiru name of Pinchas, in tribute to his mouth of brass – pey nachash, Shlomo, the mouth of the snake; but he had no Habiru to understand that we were slighting him in the very act of seemingly honouring him. We bound him to the tribe of Dan as an honorary Bene Yisra-El. He didn't understand the irony of that either. But liked the explanation that I gave him. The false explanation of course, to conceal the irony.

"Because the tribe of Dan lived where now the Bene Pelet live, along the coast of the Shephelah. And because your founding ancestor was named Dan'au - I do hope I am pronouncing that correctly."

He was bowing his gratitude so profusely, I was mercifully saved the bother of having to think up any other sycophancies. The truth was, the man had come to spy on us for Ach-Ish, and to summon us to war, and himself caused nothing but strife among my own six hundred for the entire time he remained with us. I might have bound him to the Bene Naphtali for that - "bringer of strife and contention" as it says in the hikavtsu of Abou Yah-Akov. But Dan was far more appropriate. "Dan shall be a serpent by the way, an adder in the path, one who bites the horse's heels so that his rider shall fall backward." Ah, Shlomo, the power of words, in the mouth of one who knows how best to wield them!

✡

This was the hardest year and a half of my whole life, a time for which I know I have never been forgiven by my people, not even by the most loyal. Nor by myself, Shlomo - do you think they appreciate that? But what choice did I have?

Have you read the royal annals yet? The wars of king Daoud when he was Lord of Tsiklag. The Scroll of Yashar tells them, and the second Scroll of Shmu-El which Gad completed for the Prophet. The errors are beyond credence. First it says we attacked the Bene Geshur, and indeed we did. But these were not the Bene Geshur of Gil-Yad, your step-family...There is a breed of men, Shlomo, dour, stolid, finical, inclined to pedantry, liable to waste whole days and weeks in dialectics over the most obscure semantics, the kind of men who spend so long scrutinising the corn-blades to find a missing needle, that they fail to notice that a herd of cows has come along and devoured the haystack it was lost in. That species? Historians. It was inevitable, of course. Once the aleph-bet became known by everybody, once parchment became available to every Dan, Gad and Avi, it was inevitable that all the world's ignoramuses and every would-be scholar would take up his wax stylus and start scratching. Third-rate poets, fourth-rate archivists, tenth-rate thinkers touting their platitudes and clichés as the bee's knees of all wisdom. "He that loves instruction loves knowledge, but he who hates reproof is brutish." Put that as the epitaph on all their tombstones. Errors? The gods made fewer errors when they built the Cities of the Plain.

The writing of history is a most delicate and difficult task. You cannot simply make up the bits you are uncertain of. You cannot just guess, or make deductions by the lottery of intuition. You cannot just deny that something happened because it doesn't suit your personal agenda. A historian must check his sources, examine contradictions, look for evidence and anomalies. Take the Battle of Geshur that never was. In the Scroll of Yashar it is actually written, described in detail, totally plausible, how I took my six hundred over the Bridge of Abou Yah-Akov, over Jisr bene Yakub as it calls it, favouring the language of the Bene Ammon for a reason I am afraid I can't imagine. But sorry boys - wrong Geshur. That one was a region of Ashur, part of Gil-Yad in fact, subject to king Talmai ben Ami-Chud, whose daughter Ma'achah later mothered Av-Sala'am. Wonderful part of the world, as it happens, just north of Bashan and Argov, at the very foot of Mount Chermon - beautiful, lush countryside, deep in snow most winters. It used to be known as the Land of Giants, and once it was the kingdom of Og mag Og. When Sha'ul was king, Geshur was an autonomous region within the half-tribal boundaries of Menasheh, who were given it in the distribution of Abou Mousa. All this the historians should have known – it's in the Tablet of Deeds for pity's sake. "Ya'ir ben Menasheh took all the country of Argov as far as the coasts of the Bene Geshur and the Bene Ma'achah, and he called them after his own name, Bashan Chavot Ya'ir..." Anyway, the point is, and no half-decent scholar should have made such a mistake, it wasn't those Bene Geshur that we went to fight, but the ones mentioned in the Scroll of Yehoshua ben Nun as occupying the land of Shichor from the borders of Mitsrayim as far north as Ekron.

The next error is even worse. First the annals declare we attacked the Bene Gezer, when in fact it was the Bene Gerez. Then, again, it gets the wrong Bene Gerez, presuming we must have been at Shechem, though whether by going up Mount Eval or down Mount Gerizim it doesn't dare to speculate. I suppose the historians will defend themselves by saying that the studying of maps is the job of a geographer - but honestly, Shlomo! The Bene Pelet were at war with Sha'ul in every tribe except Yehudah, and Shechem lies deep in the northern heartland of Ephrayim. Is it seriously imaginable that...enough, my blood pressure's rising and Shavsha is threatening to summon the physicians. As it happens, the Bene Gerez of Mount Gerizim at Shechem are the same tribe, or at least a colony of the same tribe, as the one we did attack, but like the Bene Geshur, these were desert people of the southern Negev, almost into the Wilderness of Sinai...

Anyway. We attacked the Bene Geshur at the end of Wadi Shichor, and drove them east into Mitsrayim, where the Bene Goshen slaughtered them. We attacked the Bene Gerez while they were watering their camels at the Well of Chagar, south-east of Ber Sheva, and they were so utterly terrified they dropped their swords and scimitars and ran away on foot. We attacked the villages of the Bene Amalek one by one, raiding, burning, stealing cattle, never utterly destroying; until one day the order went out from Eli-Phaz ben Agag to abandon all the villages and flee; we pursued them, all the way to Mount Se'ir beyond the edges east of the Salt Sea...no, Shavsha's laughter is as bad as his scolding. I have made up, you see, the whole of this paragraph - and you didn't realise it, did you, Shlomo? As plausible as any fraudulent historian. You should have spotted the anomalies. East into Mitsrayim? Bene Goshen? Villages of the Bene Amalek? What Bene Amalek? Surely they were destroyed in their entirety by king Sha'ul? And as to Eli-Phaz ben Agag? The truth is, we did attack the Bene Geshur, and pursued them all the way to Shur, on the southern coastline of the Gaza Strip. The Bene Gerez happened as I told it, though not of course within a day's ride of Ber Sheva, nor at any Well of Chagar. I have simply followed the historian's custom of attributing everything to some place or tribe or character familiar from the legends.

And as to the Bene Amalek - another factual error of the annals I am afraid. In fourteen months of raiding through the Negev, I never even heard of Bene Amalek, let alone encountered one. We crossed every inch of southern Yehudah and all of Shimon, as far as the lands of the Bene Yerachme-El and the southern tribes of Bene Ken. Nothing of Amalek anywhere – Sha'ul had done at least that one thing properly. What we did was terrible though - on a par with Sha'ul's worst barbarities. I am not proud to speak of this. Rape, slaughter, pillage on the grand scale. Brigandage and banditry. Paid protection for the towns of the Bene Yisra-El - easily managed, because success quickly swelled our numbers, till six hundred became six thousand. The numbers of the dead I could not begin to tell you. We amalekised whole villages, dust-stormed and earthquaked substantial towns. I was accused of perpetrating massacres on the borders of Mitsrayim and I cannot say the claim is false. People said that Daoud smote the land, and I suppose I did. But it is not true that we left neither man nor woman alive. Yes, we took away the sheep, the oxen, the asses, the camels, always the swords and knives, sometimes the apparel. This was what Ach-Ish required as tribute, and he was thoroughly delighted. "He has made his people Yisra-El utterly abhor him. So shall he be my servant now for ever." So his words were reported back to me. Not that we killed or hurt a single Bene Yisra-El. It was the tag of mercenary, of traitor, the fact of psalmist turned into brutal warrior, that it would become impossible to shed. Though it was also very helpful to the building of the kingdom, when that opportunity eventually arose!

But what choice did I have? What choice, Shlomo? Sha'ul still sought my life, so I couldn't return to live in Ephrayim or Yehudah.

And with my reputation going before me, I couldn't live in exile anywhere without first proving my fidelity. Should I have gone to fight against my own people? I never did. I never attacked a village of the Bene Yisra-El. I never...Wasn't it better that I...but no, I shall not endeavour to exonerate myself. I did what I did. I have made my selichot a hundred times. Ashamti, bagadeti, gazalti, dibarti dophi. I have erred, I have betrayed, I have robbed, I have spoken slander. Sarti mi-mitzvotecha u-mi-mishpatecha ha-tovim, ve lo shava li. I have turned away from your commandments and from your good laws, and it gained me nothing. Ve atah tsadik al kol ha-ba alay, ki emet aseeta va-ani hirshati. But you are justified in all that you have made to come upon me, for you have acted truthfully where I have caused wickedness.

You will notice how ready kings are to admit and expiate their errors. Historians never do.

It wasn't all war, though. There was time to spend with Avi-Gayil and Achi-No'am, time to learn fatherhood and even friendship - with Avi-Atar and Achi-Melech, with Gad ben Shmu-El, with my brothers and nephews who, in truth, I hardly knew as men at all till now. There was time to imagine what a royal court might be, if it were not set up in haste and in the midst of war; and worse still, in Tsiklag. Adobe somehow isn't conducive - such I had already learned at Sha'ul's court in Giv-Yah. Nor were the courtiers exactly courtiers. Landholders of Yehudah, whose farms and vineyards my own men protected from the roving Bene Pelet brigands - disaffected soldiers mostly - and who had come to offer thanks in kegs of wine or garnished mutton. Elders of Yehudah, whose future support I had been purchasing incrementally, sharing out the spoils we took in Geshur and Gerez. These we might have wined, and dined, and musicked, exchanged news of the on-going wars, enjoyed the dancing of the Bedou women, discussed Law and legend - but not in the night-darkness of an adobe house, half-lit by tallow-candles, sweltering in summer and moss-damp in winter, riddled either by mosquitoes or by flies.

There was time to learn as well. The myths and legends of the Bene Pelet are not so very different from our own, if truth be told. Had grandfather Oved still being living, I would have summoned him to Tsiklag and appointed him to some sinecure such as Keeper of the King's Ceramic Jugs, or Chief Washer of the Royal Chamberpot - no, perhaps not that, but something with an honourable soubriquet attached. These kinds of patronage are in one's gift, even as the king of meagre Tsiklag. My brothers, nephews, friends, comrades-in-arms, wives, concubines, priests, counsellors, even the very townspeople I now ruled, were indifferent to a point of mental atrophy to any of these serendipitous folk-tales, but grandfather Oved would have sat up with me all night and written parchment after parchment. Did you know, for example, that Shimshon's epithet, "glory of the goddess", which is pronounced Yah-Chavod in Habiru, is rendered by the Bene Pelet as Hera-Kles, and of course you know that our friend Hu-Ram worships a god of Tsur whom he calls Hera-Kles Melchat? (Shavsha says I told you that already. Did I? Did I really?) They regard Hera as a Lion-Goddess, though she is clearly the Great Mother by another name. Shimshon's father, according to the Bene Dan, was Mano'ach of Tsarah in the hills above Wadi Sorek, and of course the story of his birth is yet again the tale of a barren woman who conceives thanks to the intervention of the gods and dedicates her child to the Temple in consideration - hail the mother moon! But the mano'ach is also a woman's period of rest after parturition, and the tsarah is the most beautiful species of hornet, huge and black and with the brightest yellow stripes you ever saw, the maker of a honey just as yellow. You get my drift, I'm sure. No? Then I shall remind you of the legend.

When Shimshon was still a young man, he fell in love with a woman from Timna of Yehudah, and visiting her one day he encountered a lion in a vineyard, and slew it with his bare hands. According to the Bene Pelet, the lion was named Nem-Yah, so it was probably a leopard not a full-fledged lion; its pelt was proof against iron, bronze and stone, and in the course of wrestling it to death, the lion bit off one of Shimshon's fingers. The next time he visited, the carcass was still there, but rather than suppurating, as a carcass ought, it had been entirely colonised by hornets, who were using its skeleton for a honeycomb. Shimshon scooped out two enormous armfuls of honey, ate some, and took the rest home for his family.

"Out of the eater came something to eat. Out of the strong came something sweet."

The priests of Tsiklag carved the riddle on the archway, at the entrance to the temple at Tsiklag. On one of the pillars someone had depicted Shimshon, rather crudely, with several of the three hundred foxes that he tied together by their tails and set as firebrands in the wheatfields. The other column showed him slaughtering randomly with the jawbone of an ass, and of course Ramat Lechi, the hill behind the town, and Ber Lechi Ro'i, the main well that served the town, were both named for that particular barbarity. According to the High Priest of Tsiklag, there are twelve such tales of Shimshon, each one placed in a different month of the calendar - which I suppose is only logical for a sun-god - each one describing the implausible overcoming of a beast of ever-increasing monstrosity. Some of the legends are really very silly though. In one - all these events took place in the lands of the Bene Cheret, from where he came - he was sent to clean out the royal stables of a king of the Bene Elim, which he achieved by diverting the course of a river. In another, he stole past the keruvim and the flaming sword which guard the way to the Tree of Immortality, and plucked another fruit from the Tree of Knowledge of Good and Evil - the way the Bene Pelet tell the story, the fruit was a golden apple, the Garden of Edinu lay on the slopes of Mount Atlas of the Bene Chet, and rather than being expelled from the garden on his belly, the serpent who tempted Chava was still there, grown to dragon-size and breathing fire from its nostrils, now the eternal guardian of the tree, which Shimshon had to slay first to reach the apple.

Fairy tales for children!

Not having grandfather Oved to study with, I had to deduce the missing parts and make the connections for myself. Some of it was easy - the name of his mother, for example, which is not given in the legend of the Bene Dan or the myth of the Bene Pelet, but which has to be Devorah, since what other name of Our Lady is associated with bees and honey? And besides, in the legends of Abou Yitschak, we know that Devorah, the "wet-nurse" of Eshet Rivka, was buried beneath the weeping oak at Alon Bachot, and anyone who has seen that burial mound will know that its viscera is scaffolded like a honeycomb and its pathways represent the uterus.

Avi-Melech ben Yeruv-Ba'al the High Priest confirmed my speculations - rather too obsequiously though, so I knew he hadn't the feintest idea what I was talking about, but wisely thought the best thing was to humour me. Sadly this has been the case throughout my life. Where knowledge of this order fascinates me, most men seem to regard my interest as being akin to those sad figures one encounters on the road between Tsi'on and Damasek, dressed in waxed goat-skins, making notches in clay tablets to record the type and number of the camel-trains that pass them by. Ha Anorachim, they call them - properly ha-Nora Achim, the Sad or Terrible Brethren...ah, Shlomo, for the sake of knowledge I would gladly have stayed in Tsiklag for another year. But not for any other reason. When the time finally came that we were able to, it was, in truth, a blessing to depart.

After the initial onslaught of the four armies, the war had raged sporadically for months, simmering and boiling like a cauldron on an open fire. Gusts of wind fanned it, then blew it cold. Dripping fat caused it to spark, then smoulder. Temporary treaties, local alliances, internecine squabbles, sons trading loyalty for power, empty threatenings - the traditional compendium of fealties and poisons that play politics with ordinary people's lives. Then the generals of the Bene Pelet gathered in Shunem, and once again made preparation for a full-scale war against the Bene Yisra-El, backed by still more armadas from the islands of the Great Sea. I knew because Ach-Ish summoned me from Tsiklag to his palace at Gat, to say that I wasn't invited to the Council, but that he expected me to fight alongside him anyway. It was to be the war to end all wars. They always are.

The Bene Pelet mustered in Aphek, and after the most enormous row in the king's tent - I wasn't present, but Pinchas ben Dan, who was, could not resist telling me every word and detail, garnished with relish - Ach-Ish sent me home. The other princes of the Bene Pelet, Gol-Yat's kinsmen amongst them, were angry that I was included in the muster, convinced that I would switch sides in the midst of battle (an interesting academic question that: would I have done? I rather suspect I would). Ach-Ish sent me away, and then went on to Shunem, where the four armies were now encamped. Where exactly the Bene Yisra-El were encamped was more a matter of divination than speculation. Troops of the Bene Menasheh were between Ta'anach and Megiddo, defending the bridges over the Kishon River and the entrance to the Valley of Yazar-El. What passed for the armies of the Bene Yah-Shachur and Bene Zvulun were somewhere on Mount Tavor, in flight no doubt, if not in hiding. The Bene Naphtali and Bene Dan had retreated to the Heights of Gil-Yad, to shore up defences against the threat posed by the Bene Ammon. So much for the bond of unity that was the League. Shambolic as all the king's ventures, fragmented into shards of jealousy and competitive sulking. Sha'ul's own battalions were the worst, because the generals had fallen into dispute over strategies and each was now doing as seemed best in his own eyes. Av-Ner was using Shiloh as a base to wrest Shechem from the Bene Menasheh. Avi-Yam was at Giv-Yah, holding the capital. Yah-Natan was somewhere in the south-west - rumours placed him in Gezer, in Beit Shemesh, in Lachish, even in Eglon. Small divisions undertaking small raids as frequently and as far apart as possible, to convey the illusion of a powerful army constantly on the move. Classic Yahni tactics that would ultimately cost him his life.

Sha'ul himself was on Mount Gilbo'a, wondering why the army wasn't answering his summons to attend him there. What do kings do when they are under attack on all fronts, when their spiritual authority has been revoked, when their generals are freewheeling, when their greatest men have switched sides, when their every plan has faltered and their every project failed - and yet, still, the nation requires them to act? I imagine Sha'ul plunged into a despair so deep, not even the ministrations of a boy, not even the most accomplished playing of the harp, could do a jot to alleviate it. What - sympathy - from me - for him? Yes, Shlomo. And why should I not feel sorry for the man? For the man, the human soul exalted in its scarlet gown. Whatever his flaws and frailties and weaknesses, however damaged in his heart and mind, no man can convince me that Sha'ul was wicked - I mean wilfully, consciously, deliberately evil. In almost every case, bad men are just ordinary men who fail, even to live up to their own low standards. You cannot damn a man for all eternity, simply because he lived the fullness of his own mediocrity, and didn't know any different. When such men are anointed kings, their mediocrity is given power. We who kneel and praise them, we who carry out their foolish orders and obey their every idiotic whim, we who demand kingship because we desire subservience, we who make the rod and bare our backs, we must bear the blame ourselves if our princes are majestic only in their second-rateness. No man is ever a victim who does not collaborate in his own victimhood, at least to some degree - that is the most fundamental law of life.

Let me repeat my question then. What do kings do when they are under attack on all fronts, when their spiritual authority has been revoked, when their generals are freewheeling, when their greatest men have switched sides, when their every plan has faltered and their every project failed - and yet, still, the nation requires them to act? Sha'ul's black mood hung like an orthographic cloud above Gilbo'a. We heard that he had called for the Urim and Tumim, but that he got no response at all save only a few augurs and bad omens. Then we heard that he had gone in disguise from Mount Gilbo'a to consult the ba'alat ov at Ayin Dor, though officially he was marshalling the Bene Menasheh at Ta'anach and Megiddo.

I try to imagine what must have been in his mind. The Tablet of the Priests is quite explicit on this subject. "Al tiphnu el ha-ovot ve-el ha-yidonim; al tevakshu le-tamah va-hem. Ani adonai eloheychem. Do not turn to those who harbour familiar spirits, nor seek advice from wizards. I am the Lord your god." It could hardly have been clearer. And he must have known how it would shock the Guild of Prophets and the Priests and even the Elders of the Tribes - unless he meant to shock them. And he had publicly proclaimed anathema against all familiar spirits, specifically abolishing wizardry and witchcraft, in the aftermath of Shmu-El's death, so his arrival at Ayin Dor must have been received with trepidation by the oracle. Was the king coming to trap her? Or was his despair by now so deep, his vision of his own impending defeat and death so certain, that he no longer saw any danger in this act, but only, perhaps, a last chance to tilt the dice of fortune in his favour? Hubble, bubble, boil out trouble – when the rational mind lets you down, go back to superstition! Did he offer her power, or money, in exchange for her oracles? Both, probably. "Conjure me up a victory over the Bene Pelet and I will give you anything you ask." Even if what she asked was the overthrow of Yah and Yahweh? Even if it meant breaking the Tablets of the Law, the Covenant of Abou Mousa, the power of the Guild of Prophets, the soul of the entire nation - just to save one man and his throne? He would have done it too. Such desperation.

Because this was the end, Shlomo, I want to imagine every detail. The village hanging on the edge of the mountain. The air, thinner and more breathless than anywhere else on Earth. The hundred deities, lurking in the trees and bushes, made manifest in every rock and stone, in rain-drops, flower-petals, beams of star-light. The permanent crash of thunder from the hollows of the hills as wind ebbed and eddied through the caverns. Crowds everywhere, the pilgrims of the Bene Kena'an come to have their fortunes told or to contract a favourable marriage. The women with their worry beads, the men with their amulets and lucky charms. Extraordinary place Ayin Dor, shrine of superstition, avatar of avatars. A town of two names, the one accepted but meaningless – "the fountain of habitation" - the other unaccepted because far too meaningful. Ayin Dor, "the eye of the generations". It was the latter of these into which Sha'ul had come to peer.

"Why have you deceived me? Why have you come in disguise, pretending you are not who you are? The oracle sees everything. You are Sha'ul the king."

He had gone down into the cave where Mot had slain the dragon Tiamat - Tehom, she is called, in the Scroll of Creation - slicing in half the body of that serpent, hatched from the cosmic egg which gave birth to the Universe. Somewhere in its deepest darkness, the descendants of Tiamat still hissed and rattled, their voices issuing through the mask and mouth of the ba'alat ov. What trepidation must have gripped Sha'ul as he approached - his wives had made him come, or so he tried to justify himself. His pagan, Kena'ani wives, daughters of Ba'al and Asherah, had bullied him into one last act of defiance of the god he truly worshipped... No, that was just an alibi, and anyway untrue. He had chosen, he, himself, the king. He wanted to know, needed to see with his own eyes. And now the blowing of the shawm, deep and resonant and lyrical, conjured up the serpent's voice. Again, and then again, four times, the final coda held until the player's breath died out. Smoke and fumes filled up the cave. Incense of poppies choked his very sinuses. Like every pilgrim, dizziness was overcoming him - hunger born of fasting, exacerbated by aromas of toadstool and haoma. His eyes were going out of focus. Something he must have drunk or eaten was now churning in his stomach - or was that too the poppies and the fasting? Nausea was inducing visions.

"What does the king come to ask?"

Soon the mockery would start again: "Is Sha'ul once more amongst the prophets?" The very thought of this inspired him. Now, at last, he knew why he had come.

"There is a man that I would speak to. A man who dwells in She'ol. Can you summon him for me?"

No face, no body, only a serpent's mask, shrouded in smoke, and the immense eye in its forehead, like those Eyes of Hor that fishermen of the Bene Chem strap to their boats, though whether good or evil remained still to be seen.

"If Sha'ul asks, from She'ol he will be answered."

Not perfect poetry, but yet, how close to perfect can you get? "Ha-im Sha'ul yish'ol, min-ha-she'ol hu yinashel." Magnificent!

"Who is this man?"

"His name is Shmu-El."

What was he thinking of? To summon up the spirit of Shmu-El! Unless, perhaps, he thought that Shmu-El would be powerless to bring down his wrath upon him from beyond the grave. Or was he hoping it would prove beyond the powers of the oracle to summon him, because Shmu-El did not believe in the afterlife, and therefore could not possibly inhabit it to be summoned back therefrom.

"What do you see?"

"A man of godlike stature rising from the earth."

"What form?"

"An old man, covered in a mantle."

"Does he speak to you?"

"Bow down. Prostrate yourself. He will speak to you himself."

It was trickery, of course. In his sanity he knew it was trickery. But there was so very little sanity remaining. And besides, men want to be deceived, men need delusions. If all answers are false and there are only questions, how can we live unless we can convince ourselves that something, something is not false? Then why not this? A witch is not evil because she worships a different manifestation of the universal pulse, she is only "evil" in the sense that her "good" contradicts the good that we have chosen to believe. So he bowed low, pressed his face into the dust. So he listened for the voice of Shmu-El, and if it was not like Shmu-El's voice at all, this was because a dead man cannot speak, except through the mouthpiece of the medium.

"Why have you disturbed my rest, summoning me from the dead like this?"

Always so angry with Sha'ul, no matter what he did.

"Shmu-El, I am in distress. The Bene Pelet make war against me. The gods have abandoned me. I have sought answers to my questions, but none have come, not in dream, nor prophecy. So I have called you, here, in the depths of the netherworld, in the darkness beyond life which appears to be my kingdom. Make me know what I must do."

But he received no more response from the dead Shmu-El than he ever had from the living one.

"If the gods have abandoned you, why do you ask me, who am nothing but the mouthpiece of the gods?"

Typical Bene Yisra-El, to answer a question with a question!

"You were my friend."

"I am your enemy."

"Shmu-El!"

"This, now, is indeed your kingdom. And soon you will return here, and remain for ever."

"Shmu-El!"

"The gods have rent the kingdom of the living from your hands, and given it to your neighbour. Daoud shall rule instead of you."

Named. For the first and only time. Not hinted at, not metaphored. Named. This was an oracle too far.

"Because you did not obey the voice of the Lord, because you did not carry out his vengeance against Amalek, so has the Lord revenged himself on you this day. Your kingdom shall be delivered up to the Bene Pelet, and tomorrow you and your sons shall be with me in She'ol."

"No!"

Desperation heaped upon desperation. It wouldn't need a battle with the Bene Pelet now to kill him. In his soul, he was already dead.

But the body does not die that easily.

"Eat, sire. Take some bread and water."

One of the priestesses of the shrine, come into him in a room he didn't recognise and which he couldn't remember entering. He must have passed out, been carried here. His mind was blank.

"No. I shall not eat."

But eventually he did. Slumped on the bed, wrapped in his mantle. His servants had killed a fatted calf and baked some pitta bread. It seemed somehow symbolic. As if he were eating his own body eucharistically.

When he set out for Yazar-El the following morning, his own shadow cast more light and heat than did his flesh.

In Tsiklag, in the meanwhile, a garrison of fifty was at the mercy of the wolves. Summoned at full force to Gat, I had left behind just sufficient to provide a guard of honour for the queen - she hated all that pomp but it was essential to her dignity, and through her my authority - and hopefully enough to hold the town should anything go awry. The walls were strong, the gate was reinforced with iron. Achi-Melech had chosen carefully, from among the best-trained and the fiercest men - in truth, he had to argue for them very hard, not because I wanted them myself so much as because Pinchas ben Dan was present, so I had to seem to want them for myself. May their memories be blessed.

The desert tribes invaded from the south, led inevitably, revengefully, by the Bene Gerez and the Bene Geshur, supported by who can say how many herdsmen, camel riders, mercenaries of Cush and Lud, descendants of Cham ben No'ach, survivors of the rebellions of Korach, Datan and Avi-Ram - only the gods had any idea that quite so many peoples still inhabited the wilderness beyond the River of Mitsrayim. Certainly Abou Mousa never encountered them, and he travelled over every inch of wilderness, at least three times. Yet there they were, scarcely armoured unless you reckoned their leathered hides and the invocation of al-Lat and Manat and al-Ahqaf were protection, tribes by the hundred and swords of every shape - curved mostly, like a bullock's horns, and sharp as gossip. You train to fight iron-clad giants, and what comes out of the desert are Bedouin on camels, wrapped in white bernous! Though any number of them were clearly mercenaries of the Bene Edom in disguise - the beards; the Bedou abhor beards. Whoever they were, they razed the town - the best thing that ever happened to the place. Nor did they pause for niceties like laying siege or parleying for surrender. Quite simply, in vast numbers, they assailed the walls, one man using another man's dead body as a ladder. Achi-Melech fell in the first attack. The gate was opened on the second - from the inside - and then they swarmed in. The cry was "Death to Daoud", plus any number of obscenities periphrated and parenthesised - only your friend Shim'i ben Gera has ever equalled them for ferocity and lewdness. Apparently I favoured guinea-fowl, in bed, not on the plate. Or so it was translated to me later - perhaps erroneously. With some phrases, the words translate, but the culture gets left behind. Strange culture, mind, that favours guinea-fowl.

But I am jesting where no jests are merited. They razed the town, house by house, until the heat of the fires caused the surface of the mud-bricks to crack. If it moved, they raped it. If it shone, they pocketed it. My wives, my child, were taken prisoner - hostages I should say, for they were treated with the utmost respect and courtesy, and ever more iniquitous statements of intent to hurt or murder them were clearly only an advancement of their bargaining position. Alive, unharmed, they were worth their weight in gold - or so much was demanded. I agreed without a second thought, requesting only time to gather up such booty. What I didn't say - but then they didn't ask - was where I intended to go to find the gold. But I am rushing ahead.

When the news reached us, we were still in Gat, a full day's ride away. By the time we had flown home, the raiders were long gone. Nothing worth mentioning remained - but then nothing worth mentioning had stood there in the first place, except perhaps the Temple of Shimshon and Lilit. The loss of life, of course, was terrible, but try as I might, I could not find a tear in me for the town. Shoddily constructed, ugly, shabby buildings had collapsed - and good riddance to them. Taverns, whorehouses, flea-markets that were, literally, temples to pagan deities, the tawdry follies of the undeserving rich, gardens in which even the yuccas and the cactuses could make no sort of life, protecting walls that hadn't, the shoddy palace of a king whose very name was "treachery" - the reality was, the desert tribes had done the citizens of Tsiklag an enormous favour. I could think of several other towns that would have benefited from a similar attack - because now there was no alternative but to build a new and better Tsiklag from the ruins. And to choose a new and better king as well.

Their disappointment in me was palpable, before we had even come through the city gates. We arrived, the vanguard of a thousand on camel-back, another three thousand following behind on foot or donkey or in carts. The messengers had been riding back and forth all day, keeping us informed, but you didn't need messengers once you came in sight of the place. Smoke hanging in the air occupied space that would otherwise have filled with carrion. Eagles, vultures, crows, ravens - the first griffon-vulture I had ever seen, and it was an awesome sight. Yes, but the loss of life was terrible. Barely three hundred were still alive, and every last forsaken one of them had gathered by the city gate, women clutching children to their breasts - dead children in several cases - men clinging on to trinkets, vestiges of what remained to them, shards of the shattered vase of life. The king had failed them. I, Daoud, anointed king of Tisklag of Yehudah, I had failed them. The gods too, but gods are impervious to human desolation. Not that it was desolation any longer. During the long hours of awaiting our arrival, that had turned to anger. Now they saw us, a black cloud on the horizon which might as well have been another tornado as a balming breeze. Should they prostate themselves, or stone me - the king, after all, is their protector, by covenant; and a man who fails in his duties to the covenant is a man for whom mere stoning is an act of clemency? Yet a king remains a king.

As we approached the gates, the crowd of keening women barred our way, and the men might indeed have stoned us, only Avi-Atar stepped between me and the devastation before which they stood. He was wearing his full priestly robes, which he had not had time to take off before we hastened out of Gat. Grimy with sand and dust, he knelt his camel and climbed down. What on earth was he doing? So intently were they watching him, they soon forgot their anger. Scrabbling among the rocks beside the road he found at last and held out in his hands two convenient slabs of stone, flat as pitta bread and twice as unpalatable.

"Do you see these stones?"

He went right up to them, the weeping, the angry, the desolate and destitute, the men and women who had lost everything - except, of course, their lives. Except, perhaps, their faith.

"Do you see what is written on them?"

Dust was written on them. Time too, scratched in what could have been graffiti. Curious hieroglyphs were marked on them, by wind and rain and no doubt by the hoofprints of the desert tribes. Nothing else that man or woman could decipher. Unless by faith.

"These are the Tablets of the Law, which Abou Mousa was given by the gods when he ascended to the summit of the sacred mountain. Look."

Pressing them right into people's faces.

"Look!"

As though there were anything to see.

"These are the commandments of Yahweh. Listen to them carefully. Do not despair. Do not give up your own life because you have seen others taken. Do not seek vengeance. Do not contemplate suicide. Do not do to others what you have witnessed them doing to you. Do not hate. Do not seek ways to gain advantage from the misfortunes of others." This one directed, quite specifically, into the stinking breath of Yerach-me-El ben Phalti, whose capacity for doing precisely that was so well-known, there must have been many who secretly regretted he had not been counted with the dead that day. "Do not turn aside from the gods, nor from the king, whom they have anointed. Do not imagine you are safe yet from the foe. Do not hesitate to begin rebuilding."

And handing me the stones, as though he were making me a present of some sacred object, he gestured to the holy congregation - what else were we? - to prostrate ourselves upon the sand.

"Baruch atah adonai, eloheynu melech ha-olam, dayan ha-emet."

Blessed are you, O Lord our god, the true judge.

Who could throw a stone now, even the most despondent, even against the forehead of the sky?

Who could throw a stone on which the priest of Nov had rewritten the Ten Commandments?

But if not a stone, why not the dice, the Urim and the Tumim? He took them now, out of the inner pocket of his scarlet ephod where he always kept them, the dice of Nov, and locked them, each into its place in the silver breastplate, for me to question. But the dice were not favourable. The amber was so cloudy with dust, it barely glowed.

"What must we do?"

My brothers, led by Yo-Av, my nephew. In the wake of Achi-Melech's death, he now and he alone was my senior commander. I looked at Avi-Atar, but he looked away. Not his duty to make practical suggestions. And I hadn't thanked him yet, for saving all our lives. I who still bore the burden of the massacres at Nov and at Ke'ilah.

"Avi-Atar will remain at Tsiklag with Shammah and Ram. I shall leave two hundred with you, to give the dead a proper burial, to defend such as are left to be defended from any who might think to return. And to begin rebuilding. Let the townspeople choose from amongst themselves who shall be king."

It might have sounded like a ploy to have them acclaim me. But I was done with Tsiklag. I had wanted to be a king, but the price of a treacherous kingship was too high to pay. This was not the crown the fates intended me to wear, and it had been wrested from me.

"I shall stay too, Daoud."

Yo-Av.

"No. I shall have need of you. We will take whatever men are left, and try to find Avi-Gayil and Achi-No'am and Amnon..."

I had barely finished half the phrase when all their faces whitened and their eyes turned downwards. The townspeople especially. So much anger in the town, so much desolation for the dead and dying, everybody had forgotten that the king still had a private grief and dread to deal with. So busy were they blaming me for what had happened to themselves, no one had bothered to think about my wives and son. Now they were ashamed.

"Sire, a man of the Bene Mitsrayim said to send you to the Brook of Besor. They will treat with you there, and set their terms. Your family are safe for seven days."

✡

We slept, briefly, and refreshed ourselves as best we could. I issued orders that only those who were willing should accompany us, but Yo-Av went among the men and press-ganged as many as were biddable. By the time we reached Besor it was obvious that most of these would hamper more than help us, so we made camp and again I issued orders that those who wished could remain here, awaiting our return.

Besor was deserted. The brook is never more than a brook at the best of times, but this was high summer and now it was completely dry. Occasional wildflowers, toe-high, struggled to find daylight between the stones. The bridge was in urgent need of repair. I set men to dig wells down through the brook, in search of drinking water, and in the meanwhile scouting parties went out north south east and west, as much to find this famous Bene Mitsri as for camel-prints and cart-trails. I suspected, to be honest, a wild goose chase - though the gods know they created everything for a purpose, even the chasing of wild geese. To find my family, that was the key. To lose one wife, as you might say, was carelessness - though I had heard that Michal was safe and well in Giv-Yah - but to lose two more wives...

And then the Bene Mitsri was discovered, sleeping in a field. He hadn't drunk or eaten for three days. We gave him what we had - fig-cake, raisins, nothing that would do his stomach much good in his condition. But it revived his tongue.

"My lord Daoud," he began that snivelling and grovelling that would go on till the end of days - of his days anyway, which were not likely to be very long.

"Just tell me what they want, and where they are."

"O majestic king, o lord of..."

O lord of brown-tongued, sycophantic, cringing, spineless toadies. I took my dagger from its sheath and pressed it to his throat.

"Where are they, and what do they want?"

"I shall take you, lord. An ounce of gold for every ounce of flesh. That was the message of the Brook of Besor."

Gerah shel zahav le chol gerah shel basar.

I laughed. Not one of us had understood the cryptic code.

He referred to them as Bene Amalek, though there must have been a dozen tribes, all of whom would have spat out such a name. But as a generic term it stood, Shlomo, and stands still. The invincible Bene Amalek – Sha'ul would not have found that half so amusing as I do. Where exactly we discovered them I cannot say, for that part of the desert is not one that we have mapped, and names are meaningless for places that are swept away in dust-storms twice each year, only to reappear, under the same name, surrounded by the same dunes, fifty miles away and six months later. Such is the desert.

We found them celebrating. Drunk. In addition to Tsiklag they had raided towns across the whole of Shimon and Yehudah - Beit-El of Yehudah, Ramot-Negev, Yatir, Aro'er, Siph-Mot, Eshtemo'a, Rachal, Charmah, Chor-Ashan, Atach, even Chevron. Alongside my own women they had taken countless dozen others, and while now they were simply forcing them to drink and dance, it was quite plain that soon enough the women would be dragged away and raped – and not for the first time either, I imagine. Several bore scars around their mouths from repeated obstinacy.

On the far side of the camp, any number of carts were standing, each one covered in a canopy of fleeces. Here, for certain, was the booty, and here, for still more certain, the ounce for ounce of gold with which I would redeem my wives. We split up into groups of eight and ten and made our ways in silence to the several carts. Each guard had one throat, and each throat required one slit. Each cart had one donkey, and each donkey would munch quietly on one handful of flowering clover plucked from some field of Shimon, however many days ago. Each fleece could carry enough booty to buy back a pound of flesh, and each pound of flesh would be repaid, an arm for an arm, a leg for a leg. So we laboured while men made carnival. And when we were done, we remembered that a carnival is a ceremony of farewell to the flesh, and we allowed them all to say goodbye, as slowly, and as solemnly, as they wished.

By the time they realised the carts had been emptied, we were long vanished back into the desert whence we came. As they began to put on clothes and arms, so we. But they were drunk, and we had never been more sober. Yo-Av had identified where Avi-Gayil and Achi-No'am and Amnon were being kept, and sent a company specifically to rescue them - Achi-No'am had been terrified, for the child even more than for herself, whereas Avi-Gayil was used to men like these, and had told the first who tried to touch her that she would bite it off if he put it where he said he would; after which they treated her like the royalty she was, and didn't dare even to enter her presence to bring her food without calling her majesty and bowing at her knees. No doubt they had heard, and doubted, the story of the death of Naval. Now they credited every word of it!

For the rest, it was each man for himself, and take as many heads off as your sword had room for notches. Mercy was not on my agenda. The entire wrath of Tsiklag, the entire razing of Yehudah, was on our sleeves, and we wore it like a bandage and a shield of honour. All that night, all the following morning, all the remainder of that day until we had tracked down the very last we could, and made an end of carnival. Four hundred who fled on camels we didn't bother to pursue. But of all the rest - none standing. As Sha'ul had done before me, so I too made holy sacrifice, and no prophet in attendance to admonish me. It wasn't pleasant, Shlomo. War never is. But necessary. Necessary.

The men waiting at Besor had heard the news before we reached them, and they hailed us like conquering heroes. How often does bad circumstance dictate good deeds? I saw that gang of cheering cowards, and in my heart I wanted to destroy them as we had destroyed the desert tribes. Yet these were my men, all I had, and who knew what the future held? We had brought more booty than even these men could share out among themselves, yet how could I distribute to the fighters while denying booty to the cowards, and not expect anarchy and murder to descend upon the camp? It needed no Gad or Avi-Atar to advise me.

"To each man who fought, and to each man who did not fight but stayed behind to hold the camp, an equal portion of the spoils, each man as much as is his due."

Saluted by the blowing of the chatsotsra, to silence the protests of the men who fought, to announce it as a statute and an ordinance of Yahweh.

And as to what is a man's due. Were there not also men who would have fought, if they had been given the opportunity, and who might yet need to be called upon to fight, in days to come? Men of Beit-El of Yehudah, of Ramot-Negev, of Yatir and Aro'er and Siph-Mot, men of Eshtemo'a, of Rachal, of Charmah and Chor-Ashan and Atach, men, even, of Chevron? I sent each one of them a cart-load, a present from the spoil of the enemies of Yahweh, to be distributed by the Elders of the towns which the desert tribes had sacked. Dare I say it showed the magnanimity, the majesty, of a true-born heir of Pharets, that it was the action of a future king?

And then came the end of all this sorry saga, in Mount Gilbo'a, and the Valley of Yazar-El. Ach-Ish had learned from his footmen exactly what discord had separated the armies of the League of Ephrayim, and wisely, instead of allowing their fragmentation to engender his, he decided to leave the Bene Yah-Shachur and Zvulun and Menasheh to their own devices, and summoned all his armies to the Kishon River, from where he marched them down the valley towards Yazar-El. Sha'ul couldn't possibly face such force alone. He sent again for Avi-Yam and Av-Ner and for Yah-Natan - but there was no reason to think they would obey him now where they had so obstinately disobeyed him previously. For two full days he waited, and not a whisper that support was coming, while the iron footsteps of the Bene Pelet thundered ever nearer. They must come, his generals, surely they must come. But in the meanwhile he gave the order to retreat out of Yazar-El towards the mountains. And the Bene Pelet followed.

They caught up with him before he ever left the valley. For a man who had never had a moment's fortune all his life - his favourite lament that, sung in the lost key of E flat minor seventh diminished, at least two octaves in the bass; even becoming king was something he now reckoned less a blessing than a curse - now, suddenly, at the most unlikely moment, fortune appeared momentarily to smile on him. Appeared, mind, and very momentary, and no more than a smile; and a smile of very serious melancholy at that. The Bene Pelet came thundering eastwards up the valley, thinking to gobble up the army of the king as easily as marsh-heron devour carp. Such was the pandemonium of Sha'ul's retreat, it patently was not strategic. This was men running, in panic, for whatever cover they could find, each for himself, to save his life. So that the sudden appearance over the northern plateau of the army of Menasheh, coinciding as it did with the equally sudden appearance from the south of Yahni's raiding parties, fooled the Bene Pelet into thinking they had been lured into a carefully contrived ambush. History repeating itself – remember Mitspeh! As they did then, so now it was their turn to turn, though the retreat sounded on the rams' horns was concerted.

Such was his stroke of luck, and if he had had the slightest jot of sense he would have seized it. With the Bene Pelet wheeling - a massive operation, akin to Lev-Yatan trying to unbeach - the opportunity was there to flee. Break up the army, head for the hills and rat-holes, and live to fight another day. But not Sha'ul. For all his many failings, no one could ever call Sha'ul a coward. He heard the cries that announced Yahni's arrival, he saw the banners of the Bene Menasheh, he heard the sounding of the retreat coming up the valley from the west - and he dared to risk everything in a final charge.

So Sha'ul engaged the Bene Pelet – not now, Shavsha; why do you have to interrupt me at this of all moments? Yes, I know the scrolls name them as Plishtim, as Bene Pleshet, or Bene Pelesht, but they were the shepherd-kings of On, the Hyksos as Hu-Ram calls them, and On was the son of Pelet; the scrolls confirm it; now will you let me tell the story? So Sha'ul engaged the Bene Pelet, and the melancholy deepened into lugube that quite erased the smile. Iron chariots versus donkeys riding donkeys. Slingers and arrowsmen who depended on a protective line of javelins, but had none. Yahni's raiders came out of every copse and thicket, descending to pick off as many as they could, but the sheer weight of numbers thwarted them. It was like picking the teeth of Tiamat which Mot had sown, each of which harvested a soldier, and each decapitated soldier bifurcated into two. There was no end of them, and Yahni's men were falling just as fast.

The Bene Menasheh, in the meanwhile, had occupied the high ground, and were firing arrows till they simply didn't possess another arrow they could fire. At some point Avi-Yam joined the fray - later Av-Ner would claim to have done so too, but no one I have ever spoken to saw pelt or fleece of him, let alone a suit of armour. The truth was, he had secured Shechem for his own ambitions, and taken his troop to Machanayim of Gil-Yad, to hold that kingdom against the Bene Ammon - a last royal refuge for Sha'ul if, or now more likely when, Ephrayim fell. His presence would have made no difference anyway.

The rams' horns of the Bene Pelet signalled ambush, and once again the army wheeled around. Open combat in such a wide valley, on such dry ground, and little by way of rock or tree except where the plain began its sloping upwards to the hills, such a contest was one the Bene Pelet could not lose. And Sha'ul must have known it. Three, four, five to one, and better armed, better disciplined - this was like iron fighting bronze, and there simply was no competition. One by one the sons of king Sha'ul were butchered. Avi-Nadav with a blow from a coulter that cleaved his head in two like a ripe grape. Melchi-Shu'ah with a double-ax. And yes, Yah-Natan, taken in hand-to-hand combat by a half-dozen Bene Pelet at the same time. He would have fought heroically, I know that, however abject the heroism, however quixotic. He would have taken as many with him as he could, and gone on fighting till the very last. Of that at least history can be certain. But his death was written. They cut him all about the body - arms, legs, torso - until he was brown and sticky with his own blood, until he could no longer stand. So, with a single stroke of the macharash, scything the way they scythe the corn, they took his head off, and spiked it on a javelin. Then the cry went up, as harsh as irony:

"Sha'ul has slain his thousands, Yah-Natan his tens of thousands, but Ach-Ish has slain Yah-Natan."

The army of Ephrayim could not have been more devastated if an earthquake had opened in the middle of the valley or a volcano erupted on their heads.

Sha'ul was wounded - shot through with arrows - and there is irony in that as well. The fulfilment of a kind of prophecy, you might well say, carved on the Stone of Ezel. We heard later that he had asked his armour bearer (theoretically myself!) to finish him off, but the boy refused. Sha'ul fell on his own sword, and then the armour-bearer followed suit. They cut off his head too, speared it like a cuttle-fish on his own javelin - the only time in his entire life when his javelin was aimed at a mark, and didn't miss. Ach-Ish took his armour to the temple of Asherah at Yazar-El, as a votive offering of thanks for the victory that day; and hung his body, with his sons beside him, on the walls of Beit She'an. All but his head. That they took in triumph back to Gat, parading it like a corn-dolly on a stick through every town along the way, a decomposing mess of blood and battered tissue into whose skull a fake crown had been driven, as though this were the mocked effigy awaiting burning, and not the authentic king. As though? The mockery was absolute. For they hung him finally in the Temple of Dagon, the very spot where the Ark of the Tabernacle had been taken more than fifty years before. And when the priests came in the following morning, it was still there, albeit stinking somewhat ranker.

It didn't stay there long though. The men of Yavesh Gil-Yad had anointed him as their sacred king after he saved them from the Bene Ammon years before, and now they claimed the right to bury him. Av-Ner, of course, was behind them, camped with his troops at Machanayim, urging them on. Ish-Ba'al was with him too, the only one of Sha'ul's sons to have survived. Av-Ner sent emissaries to the Elders of Yavesh, arguing the duty of a son to bury his father properly and to mourn him in the appropriate manner, calling on the Bene Gil-Yad to acknowledge Ish-Ba'al as Sha'ul's successor and to help him in the fulfilment of his duties. The Elders of Yavesh in their turn sent emissaries to Gat, to put the same disquisition (I choose my words advisedly, Shlomo). It was as long and turgid and complex a rigmarole as ever a foreign envoy bored a king to sleep with. Yet most profound. Yet surely irrefutable.

Ach-Ish was courteous - he was always courteous, he used it as a way of bullying - but still refused. The trophy was simply too valuable. Embalmed (and this was the substance of the disquisition), it could be kept for ever as a symbol of this greatest victory the Bene Pelet had achieved since Even-Ezer. Soon enough the head would cease to be a trophy, a mere museum-piece, and would be elevated to the status of an icon. This was crucial. Once established as an icon, the man would disappear, and the god would emerge. Sha'ul, finally, would become She'ol, the king of the underworld, emblem of evil and bringer of death. Then, one day long from now, someone would recall that his one surviving son was named Ish-Ba'al, and they would deduce from this that Sha'ul was not his father's name at all; rather She'ol was his kingdom. His name was Ba'al. But which Ba'al? Given his status as king of the underworld, Ba'al Zvuv, obviously, the Lord of the Flies. And who were the Flies that he was Lord of? Why, plainly, the Bene Yisra-El. So the process of demonisation would be complete. So, anyway, the emissaries of Av-Ner argued - though I do not imagine that Av-Ner understood a word of it himself. But where the Elders of Yavesh Gil-Yad saw no reason to disagree, the king of Gat just pointed to the iron-speared soldiers standing at his door, and courteously shook his head.

They stole the bodies that night. A cohort of Av-Ner's best led the way to Beit She'an and entered through a secret passage they had "learned about some months before" (I am quoting the annals, Shlomo, and reading it as a euphemism for paid treachery). At the same time, amongst the emissaries to Gat were several whose ambassadorial qualifications were rather less than their capacity for cutting throats and organising hasty get-aways. The head of Sha'ul was rescued, liberated, reunited with its body. Av-Ner wanted the remains brought back to Machanayim - I fancy he intended to use the funeral as the occasion to anoint Ish-Ba'al as king of Yisra-El - but the men were under oath to the Elders of Gil-Yad to return to Yavesh. And there they did what no man of Yisra-El has or ever will forgive them. They burned the bodies. Not meaning harm, but because this was the tradition of the Bene Gil-Yad - but yet they burned the bodies. They took the flesh and bones of men, and burned them as a ritual sacrifice before the gods. And then they buried the ashes, under an ash tree in Yavesh Gil-Yad. A deserved resting-place - the scene of his only real triumph - but ash, cremation, holocaust? The king of the underworld, burned with fire? Perhaps, after all, it was appropriate.

Two days after the battle, before any of this was known to us, a messenger arrived at Tsiklag where we were still busy burying our own dead. He was, or so he claimed, a survivor of the Battle of Yazar-El, wounded in the arm, and hungry. Shammah was called to question him, and brought the man to me. It was he who told me of the deaths of Yah-Natan and Sha'ul. He claimed to have killed Sha'ul himself, an act of mercy upon witnessing his wounds. He was lying - it was obvious. The man was a Bene Geshur, and he could not explain what a Bene Geshur was doing at Gilbo'a anyway, while his own people were engaged in a battle of their own, with me, south of the Brook of Besor. No, it was obvious. He was a deserter, one of those camel-riders probably whom we didn't chase, or perhaps he gained his wounds in the battle and managed to elude those who went around to finish off the dying. Somehow he had survived, and made his way northwards. He must have come upon the battle at Yazar-El when it was over, and joined the jackals and the carrion who were picking through the bones. And there, right there on the very field of battle, glistering like coloured glass, he had found the crown and bracelet, Sha'ul's emblems of office, which the Bene Pelet had somehow left behind when they cut off his head and hands. These were the most prized trophies of them all, and he had brought them to me in the hope of a reward. The fool! Had he told the truth, I might well have rewarded him - by allowing him to live. But a deserting traitorous murderer of the Bene Geshur, a coward turned thief, come to Tsiklag to gloat in its ruins? And was he not, on his own admission, a regicide, the slayer of a king? I gave him the reward his actions merited. I ordered him to be hung.

"Put on the crown, Daoud."

It felt so heavy in my hands. All that smelted gold. Sha'ul's crown, wrought in the forges of Beit Koteret, the only crown that ever king of Yisra-El had worn. And now I held it in my hands.

"Put it on, Daoud. You've earned it. There's no one else."

Nor any Prophet to anoint me.

And me, Daoud, the king of Tsiklag of the Bene Pelet.

And Sha'ul, presumably, unburied.

Something in my blood did not feel right. Some augury, some omen, cautioned me. Kings of Yisra-El do not wear crowns, and they do not have thrones. The voice of Shmu-El, warning me, reminding me. I could not put it on.

But the news, the terrible news that the Bene Geshur brought with him to Tsiklag! So many deaths, and now these deaths. I couldn't even tear my clothing, for I had already torn each piece of clothing I possessed. But ash, there was plenty of ash to pour upon our heads. And sackcloth in which to drape ourselves. I ordered seven days of fasting and lamentation, and sent Shammah to find what news he could. I have already told you what he found.

"The beauty of Yisra-El is slain upon the high places; how are the mighty fallen! Tell it not in Gat, publish it not in the streets of Ashkelon; lest the daughters of the Bene Pelet dance for joy, lest the daughters of the uncircumcised triumph. O you mountains of Gilbo'a, let there be no dew, let no rain fall on you, let the fields be void of offerings; for the shield of the mighty is vilely cast away, the shield of Sha'ul, as though he had never been anointed. From the blood of the slain, from the fat of the mighty, the bow of Yah-Natan did not bend back, and the sword of Sha'ul was not sheathed unscratched. Lovely and pleasant were Sha'ul and Yah-Natan in their lives, and in their deaths they were not divided; they were swifter than eagles, and stronger than lions. O you daughters of Yisra-El, weep over Sha'ul, who clothed you in scarlet, with other delights, who put ornaments of gold upon your gowns. How are the mighty fallen in the midst of battle! O Yah-Natan, you were slain in your own high places. I am distressed for you, my brother Yah-Natan; very pleasant have you been to me; your love for me was wonderful, surpassing that of women. How are the mighty fallen, vanquished by the weapons of war."

People have accused me of dissembling, of hyperbole, even of bathos in the writing of that psalm, of inventing a love which I did not really have for Sha'ul, simply for the purposes of rallying support among his followers. But it isn't true, Shlomo. I wrote it as a formal elegy, in the language of the formal eulogy, to teach the Bene Yehudah, as a lamentation to be published in the Scroll of Yashar. What I said of Yahni was the truth. And as to Sha'ul. It isn't possible to hate someone without a cause. Sha'ul hated me, I him – there is no use denying it. But why? What cause? This is the greatest irony and paradox of all. Frustrated love.

Av-Ner, in the meanwhile, had taken Ish-Ba'al, Sha'ul's one surviving son, to the shrine of Yehoshua ben Nun in Shechem, and called Natan to anoint him king of Yisra-El. Ish-Boshet now, no longer Ish-Ba'al. They honoured and acknowledged him in every tribe, save only Yehudah which had closed its borders in my name, and Shimon, which swore allegiance to no king of anywhere. And Bin-Yamin? What should Bin-Yamin decide, when two of its sons both claimed the throne, the one from the House of Shet, the other from the House of Tammuz, and both had been invested, if not yet anointed, by a Prophet? My throne, but sat upon by him. His crown, held but unworn by me. Clearly the time had still not come for the fulfilment of the oracle, when the kingdom would be passed to the last born of the last born, when the Beloved Son of Yah and Yahweh would embrace his kingdom. But soon. But very soon.

END OF BOOK ONE

NAMES OF PEOPLE AND PLACES IN THIS BOOK, GIVEN WITH THE COMMON ENGLISH VERSION OF THEIR NAMES

Appears in the novel as:	Commonly known as:
Abba Choshe'a	Hosea
Abdu-Chava	Abdu-Heba
Abou Mousa, Mousa ibn Ra-Mousa	Moses
Abou Raham	Abraham
Abou Yah-Akov	Jacob
Abou Yah-Suph	Joseph
Abou Yehudah	Judah
Abou Yeter	Jethro
Abou Yitschak	Isaac
Achi-Lud	Ahilud
Achi-Melech	Ahimelech
Achi-No'am	Ahinoam
Achi-Yah	Ahijah
Ach-Lis	Achilles, also Oedipus
Ach-Nor	Agenor
Acholi-Bamah	Aholibamah
Ach-Yah	Achiah
Adonai, Yahweh, YHVH	God
Adoni-Tsedek ben Melchi-Tsedek	Later Tsadok ben Achi-Tuv
Adoni-Yah	Adonijah
Aharon	Aaron
Amon-Choteph	Amenhotep
Amorim	Amorites
Arkim	Arkites
Ashur	Assyria
Avel Mecholah	Abel Meholah
Avel-Shittim	Abel Shittim
Avi-Atar	Abiathar
Avi-Gayil	Abigail
Avi-Nadav	Abinadav
Avi-Ram	Abiram
Avi-Shag	Abishag
Av-Ner	Abner

Av-Ram	Abram
Av-Sala'am	Absalom
Av-Yah	Abijah
Av-Yishai	Abishai
Ayin Dor	Endor
Aza	Gaza
Ba'al Zvuv	Beelzebub
Bar-Tsillai	Barzillai
Bat-Sheva	Bathsheba
Bat-Yah	Batya
Bav-El	Babylon in Mesopotamia
Bav-El	Byblos in Lebanon
Beit Anatot	Bethany
Beit Ashbe'a	Bethashbea
Beit-El	Bethel
Beit Lechem Ephratah	Bethlehem
Beit She'an	Beth Shean
Ben-Ayah ben Yahu-Yada	Benaiah ben Jehoiada
Bene Arvad	Arvadites
Bene Chalev	Sons/clan of Caleb
Bene Chamat	Hamathites
Bene Chem	Hamites, from Upper Egypt
Bene Cheret	Phoenicians, specifically Cretans
Bene Chet	Hittites
Bene Girgash	Girgashites
Bene Kayin	Sons/clan of Cain
Bene Kenez	Kenizzites
Bene Kessed	Chaldeans
Bene Kohat	Kohathites
Bene Levi	Levites
Bene Mitsri	From Mitsrayim (Lower Egypt)
Bene Pelet	Philistines
Bene Perez	Perizzites
Bene Shimon	Sons/clan of Simeon
Bene Sumer	Sumerians
Bene Tsemar	Zemarites
Bene Yamin	Benjamin (the tribe)
Bene Yevus	Inhabitants of Jebus
Bene Yishai	Sons/clan of Jesse
Ber Lechi Ro'i	Beer Lahai Roi

Bilam	Baalam
Bin-Yamin	Benjamin
Bli-El	Belial
Botsrah	Bazrah
Caprisin	Cyprus
Chadad-Ezer ben Rechov	Hadadezer, son of Rehob
Chagar	Hagar
Chagit	Hagith
Cham ben No'ach	Ham, the son of Noah
Chamat	Hamat
Chanah	Hannah
Chanan-Yah	Chananiah
Chanoch	Enoch
Charan	Haran
Chatsor	Hazor
Chava	Eve
Chem	Upper Egypt
Chermon	Mount Hermon
Cheshvan	Heshbon
Chetsron	Hezron
Chevron	Hebron
Chirah	Hirah
Chivim	Hivites
Chnoss	Kenossos
Chorev	Horeb
Chorim	Horites
Cush	Ethiopia
Damasek	Damascus
Dani-El	Daniel
Daoud, Yedid-Yah, Dodi	David
Datan	Dothan
Devorah	Deborah
Edinu	Eden
El-Am	Elam (Persia)
El-Chanan ben Dodo	Elchanan
Eli-Av	Eliab
El-Kanah ben Yero-Cham	Elkanah ben Jeroham
Erech	Warak or Uruk
Eshmun-Azar	Eshmunazar
Essav	Esau

Even-Ezer	Ebenezer
Gal-Ed	Galed
Galil	Galilee
Gat Shamana	Gethsemane
Genasseret	The Sea of Galilee
Gid-Yon	Gideon
Gil-Yad	Gilead
Giv-On	Gibeon
Giv-Yah	Gibeah
Gol-Yat	Goliath
Gulgolet-Yah	Golgotha
Habiru	Hebrew
Hevel	Abel
Hinnom, Gei Hinnom	Gehenna
Hodu	India
Hu-Ram	King Hiram of Tyre
Ish-Ba'al	Ishbal
Iyov	Job
Kar-Chemosh	Carchemish
Kayin	Cain
Kena'an, Kinnahu, Retenu	Canaan
Kfar Nachum	Capernaum
Kinneret	The Sea of Galilee
Kiryat-Ye'arim	Kiriath Jearim
Korach	Korah
Lavan	Laban
Levanon	Lebanon
Lev-Yatan	Leviathan
Ma'on	Maon
Mashi'ach	Messiah
Melchi-Shu'ah	Melkishua
Melchi-Tsedek	Melkizedek
Menasheh	Manasseh
Mephi-Boshet	Mephibosheth
Merivah	Meribah
Meri-Yah	Maria
Metu-Shelach	Methuselah
Mey-Zahav	Me-Zahab
Micha-El	Michael
Midyan	Midian

Mir-Yam	Miriam
Mitsrayim	Lower Egypt
Mo-Av	Moab
Mor-Yah	Moriah
Mount Chorev	Mount Horeb
Mount Nevo	Mount Nebo
Na'amah	Naomi
Natan	Nathan
Nazir/Nazirim	Nazirite
Nip-Ur	Nippur
No'ach	Noah
Nov	Nob
Otni-El	Othniel
Oved-Yah	Obadiah
Pharat	Euphrates
Pharets ben Yehudah	Perez
Phoinikim	Phoenicians
Pinchas	Pinehas
Pisgat ha-Har	Mount Pisgah
Poti-Phera	Potiphar
Rach-El	Rachel
Rechav ben Rimmon	Rahab
Re'u-Ven	Reuben
Rechav-Am ben Shlomo	Rehoboam, son of Solomon
River Yarden	Jordan
Rivka	Rebecca
Sedom	Sodom
Sepharad	Spain
Sha'ul	Saul
She'ol	The Underworld
Shephat-Yah	Shephataiah
Shet	Seth
Shimshon	Samson
Shlomo, Yedid-Yah	Solomon
Shmu-El	Samuel
Sin, Sinim	China, the Chinese
Sis-Ra	Sisera
Tavor	Mount Tabor
Tirtsah	Tirzah
Tsadok ben Achi-Tuv	Zadok

Tsaphon	Zaphon
Tseru-Yah	Zeruiah
Tsi'on	Zion
Tsidon	Sidon
Tsiklag	Ziklag
Tsilpah	Zilpah
Tsur	Tyre
Tu-Va'al	Tubal
Uruk	Warak
Ur-Yah	Uriah
Valley of Yazar-El	Jezreel valley
Yafo	Jaffa/Joppa
Yah-Achim	Joachim
Yah-Natan, Yahni	Jonathan
Yah-Nus	Janus
Yah-Shachur	Issachar
Yarav-Am ben Yedid-Yah	Jeroboam son of Solomon
Yarden	Jordan
Yareyacho	Jericho
Yashov-Yam	Jashobam
Yavan	Ionia (east Greece/west Turkey)
Yavok	Jabbok
Yechazek-El ben Re'u-Mah	Ezekiel
Yehoshua ben Nun	Joshua the son of Nun
Yehudah	Judah
Yehudit	Judith
Yephunneh ben Pispah	Jephunneh
Yerachme-El	Jerachmeel
Yeshiahu	Isaiah
Yevus	Jebus
Yiphtach	Japhet/Jephthah
Yiru-Sala'am	Jerusalem
Yishma-El	Ishmael
Yisra-El	Israel
Yitro	Jethro
Yo-Av	Joab
Yo-El	Joel
Yonah	Jonah
Zano'ach	Zanoah
Tsaretan	Zaretan

Zerach	Zerah
Ziph	Ziv
Zvulun	Zebulon

ABOUT THE AUTHOR

 David Prashker was born in London in 1955 and has lived in France, Israel, Canada and the United States, where he is currently based.

He is the author of thirty books, including contemporary and historical novels, short stories, poetry, songs, plays and scholarly works. You can follow his blogs at http://davidprashkersbookofdays.blogspot.com/ and http://davidprashkersprivatecollection.blogspot.com/ or find him at his website Davidprashker.com. For more information about his books, go to theargamanpress.com.

www.ingramcontent.com/pod-product-compliance
Lightning Source LLC
Chambersburg PA
CBHW071146250626
47159CB00001B/10